# Surrogate Evil

A LEE NEZ NOVEL

## DAVID & AIMÉE THURLO

A Tom Doherty Associates Book / New York

SURROGATE EVIL

Copyright © 2006 by David and Aimée Thurlo

This book is printed on acid-free paper.

A Forge Book
Published by Tom Doherty Associates, LLC
175 Fifth Avenue
New York, NY 10010

www.tor.com

Forge® is a registered trademark of Tom Doherty Associates, LLC.

Library of Congress Cataloging-in-Publication Data

Thurlo, David.
    Surrogate evil : a Lee Nez novel / David & Aimée Thurlo.—1st hardcover ed.
      p.   cm.
    "A Tom Doherty Associates book."
    ISBN-13: 978-0-765-31615-8
    ISBN-10: 0-765-31615-3
    1. Nez, Lee (Fictitious character)—Fiction.   2. Government investigators—
Fiction.   3. Vampires—Fiction.   4. Criminals—Fiction.   5. New Mexico—
Fiction.   I. Thurlo, Aimée.   II. Title.
    PS3570.H825S87   2006
    813'.54—dc22

                         2006006687

First Edition: December 2006

Printed in the United States of America

0  9  8  7  6  5  4  3  2  1

To the readers—always

## ACKNOWLEDGMENTS

Thanks to Rex, Joe, and Snoopy for sharing their East Mountain cabin and providing us with a setting for this adventure.

# Surrogate Evil

CHAPTER 1

For a genuine half vampire, Lee Nez's night life had been quite ordinary lately. Not that the evening shift of a New Mexico state policeman was necessarily boring. There were always DWI stops, roll-over accidents on the interstate, or calls from isolated sheriff's deputies to help break up a fight, back up the call on a robbery—or worse.

Lee took a leisurely sip of coffee, enjoying the fact that he was off-duty now and there were still six and a half hours, give or take a few minutes, of nighttime left before sunlight became an issue for him. He looked across the table of the Journey's End diner at the light-skinned Hispanic beauty who'd just shared a banana split with him—no cherries, extra almonds—and smiled.

FBI Special Agent Diane Lopez grinned back as she took the last scoop of ice cream without apology. "I've missed you, Lee. What's it been, two weeks?"

He nodded, glancing casually around the generically decorated restaurant at the half-dozen late-night diners. College kids, probably from the nearby UNM campus judging by their backpacks, were demolishing french fries and sipping Cokes while debating the merits of reinstating the military draft. By the window, an old tourist couple in Hawaiian print shirts were rehashing their adventures in Old Town and on the Tram, and making plans for tomorrow's drive and shopping trip to the Plaza in Santa Fe. It was late July and the height of the vacation season.

A solitary man in his early forties and wearing a wrinkled, western-cut suit had been on his cell phone for the past ten minutes. From his subdued tone and his frequent use of the word "love," he was talking either to his wife or girlfriend.

Lee didn't eavesdrop on purpose, it was just that his exceptional hearing, one of the benefits of being a nightwalker, put him into nearly every conversation, like it or not. It was hard to shut out information, even trivia, when his life depended on never growing complacent to those around him.

His memory was perfect, too, and he knew exactly when and where he'd seen Diane last. "Two weeks almost to the day," he said, answering her question at last. "A quick cup of coffee in Cuba the day you interviewed the witnesses to the bank robbery."

"Yeah, and that was a waste of time. The interview, not the coffee and company. But no rush tonight. We've got the rest of the evening, and I have tomorrow off. Want to come over to my place and catch up?" She asked with a slow smile.

Lee's eyebrows rose slightly. They'd taken their developing relationship slowly, both of them knowing the risks involved under the circumstances, and it had been months before they'd finally made love. Despite the eventual urgency of the first time, they'd both had the sense to take all the precautions possible.

Lee didn't know if he was sterile. Being only half vampire meant he was one of a kind. But the viruslike infection that turned humans into vampires was passed through the blood, so he couldn't rule out the possibility that it was present in semen, too. It wasn't like there was a manual on the subject, and the bottom line was that he cared too much about Diane to take any risks.

He'd been raised in the 1930s and, as a Navajo, he saw sex between a man and a woman in the same light his people did—as natural—and as necessary—as breathing. He felt no guilt for the urges, but being a nightwalker placed extraordinary responsibilities upon him. They'd talked about it, and Diane had understood. This was just one more reason he loved her.

"Let me get the check," Lee said, looking around and locating their waitress, who was standing beside the kitchen pass-through, talking to the cook.

The weary-looking bleached blonde in her late twenties, Gwen, had given them good service, and her work ethic was solid even at this late hour. Gwen had one eye on the room despite the illusion of goofing off. Lee gestured to her with a slight movement of his head, and she nodded, reaching into her apron pocket for the ticket as she crossed the room. Lee always came here when he was passing through Albuquerque, and, in his NM state police uniform, got pretty good service. Gwen even flirted from time to time, though it was just for fun. She was married with two children, and he could tell, based on their previous conversations, that she was in love with her husband.

His department uniform, technically charcoal gray with medium gray trim, and the distinctive cap with shiny bill, had not changed appreciably since he'd first put one on during the early years of World War II. The black basket-weave Sam Brown belt remained, as well, though the old Colt 45 revolver had been replaced with a Smith & Wesson 45 semi-auto.

Diane was armed, too, but her 9 mm Glock and handcuffs were at her belt, hidden by the light black leather jacket, and her gold shield was hidden in a wallet rather than pinned to a uniform pocket, like his.

"I've got it, Lee," Diane reached for her purse.

"You paid for the coffee in Cuba," Lee replied. "Besides, my paycheck is bigger than yours."

Her amber eyes twinkled, and she brushed a lock of shoulder-length brown hair aside in an attractive gesture she knew he appreciated. "You're right. Pay. I'll leave the tip," she whispered as the weary waitress stepped up beside Lee.

A minute later, Lee held the glass foyer door open and Diane stepped out onto the concrete porch of the establishment. It was still warm, perhaps eighty, but with the humidity in the low teens, the night was comfortable, aided by a gentle breeze that rustled a few leaves on the nearby trees of the residential neighborhood just to the east. Down the incline of the parking lot was a side road that connected to Lomas Boulevard a hundred feet to the north, and to the west was the interstate. The parking lot continued around behind them and the diner, ending with the U-shaped two-story structure containing forty rooms or so of the Journey's End motel.

Lee had parked his black-and-white state police unit beside Diane's unmarked Bureau car at one of the concrete barriers that basically circled the restaurant. He reached out and she took his right hand with her left, an off-duty habit he was really beginning to appreciate. "I'll follow. . . ."

Lee saw something odd going on beside one of the cars parked in front of a motel room, and stopped.

"What's wrong?" Diane whispered, letting go of his hand automatically, knowing he'd need it for his weapon.

It was almost as clear as day for Lee, with his ability to see in total darkness as if it were merely a cloudy afternoon, and he saw a tall man in a black nylon jacket standing sideways between two poplars framing the window of room 117, aiming what looked like a camera.

"Pervert or a PI?" Lee speculated aloud, then he saw another man outside the same room, crouched down low between two cars, watching the illuminated areas of the parking lot.

Lee motioned to his right. "Circle around," he whispered, taking a last look. The guy who'd been keeping watch brought out a small penlight and began working at the door lock of one of the vehicles with what was probably a lock pick. The idiot needed a slim jim, Lee thought.

They walked quietly around the opposite side of the restaurant, coming up at the rear of the building, where a big trash bin was resting beside another door. Both were illuminated by a covered bulb on the wall of the facility.

"There was somebody between the cars. Breaking into a vehicle?" Diane asked.

"Looked like it. But there was another perp past the sidewalk, against the building and standing beside the window next to the tree. He had a camera aimed through the window of room one-seventeen."

"Maybe a PI team?"

"Why break into the car? Let's grab them and see what's going on. Even if they're private cops, what they're doing is still illegal," Lee pointed out. "Don't call APD until we get a handle on this. If a cop car pulls into the lot it'll spook these guys and we might lose them."

"The perps are either brave or stupid. An obvious state police car parked just a hundred feet away?"

"Your car blocks my unit from their line of sight."

"Yeah, and your unit is low profile, no lights on the top. Probably didn't notice. Then what's the plan? I can see the guy breaking into the car, and probably get close enough to cover him. But the person in the bushes . . . he'll see us coming once we reach the sidewalk," Diane whispered.

Lee glanced up at the balcony, which gave access to the

second story, then looked to his left, where a utility pole and guy wire stood beside a high retaining wall behind the motel, which had been constructed into the hillside. "I'll get above them, nod for you to move in, then give you cover. When I drop down on the guy by the window, make your move on the other guy. Be careful. I don't see any weapons, but you never know."

"How are you going to get above them? The guy by the car can see the stairs from where he's at, Lee."

"Just keep watch and wait for my signal. Call APD if you think they might get away, but have the officers stay out of sight until you give them the all clear to come in."

"Okay."

Lee ran to his left, moving silently across the parking lot, constantly alert for a third perp or a civilian who might come out of the restaurant at the wrong time.

Reaching the braided steel guy wire that ran from the ground to the top of the pole, he jumped, grabbed the cold metal with both hands, then worked his way up the wire, hand over hand to the top. In a few seconds, he pulled himself up and stood atop the rounded utility pole, which wobbled just slightly from his six-foot, two-hundred-pound frame.

Balance wasn't a problem, he could have walked up the cable itself if it wasn't so slippery. Still, it would have been odd seeing a state police officer, cap and all, standing atop a utility pole like some show-off crow.

Lee jumped the twenty or so feet onto the nearly flat roof of the hotel, landing on the parapet in order to keep the noise down. He was light-footed, but physical laws still had to be compensated for. The stucco crumbled a little, but held. Lee stepped onto the gravel-covered roofing material, nowadays fiberglass more than the asphalt he knew as a child, and walked around the back edge in order to remain out of view from the motel parking lot.

The city was covered in a blanket of multicolored lights, and the downtown area to the west, with its multistoried buildings, was still inspiring to a Navajo who'd been raised in front of a hogan and campfire, with only a lantern or two when kerosene had been available.

It took only a minute for Lee to reach the spot above room 117, guided by the restaurant location and Diane, whom he could see standing at the corner of the trash container. When he got closer, he wondered if she could see him up in the dark against the skyline. Dark man, dark hat, dark uniform . . . he doubted she could see anything but his movement.

When he got to the parapet above the sidewalk, Lee could hear a man's voice from below.

"What the hell's going on? Put your shirt back on, and stay away from me. This some kind of sick joke?" From the tone, Lee knew it must have been coming from the room, and from the word "shirt" instead of "blouse," he assumed the one undressing was a guy, too.

He peeked over the edge, and noticed the man who'd been beside the car was now inside, reaching under the dash. The guy in the bushes was taking photographs of the bald, upset guy and the young, well-muscled man wearing just the slacks. It was a shakedown scam, apparently—relying on photos of a gay rendezvous.

Lee looked down at Diane and nodded. She nodded back, then sneaked over to the row of cars parked at concrete barriers in front of the sidewalk. Crouched low, she crept down the row until she was beside the car with the guy inside.

When she reached the end of the car, Lee stood, stepped off the edge, and landed right behind the guy with the camera.

"Shit!" the guy yelled, flinching so badly he bobbled the camera. Lee grabbed it with his left hand in midair.

"Don't move. I'm a police officer," Lee ordered softly, his eyes on the man's hands to make sure he didn't make a move for a weapon. At this range, Lee could take him out with a quick punch, if necessary.

"You're in over your head, cop. I'm with Homeland Security."

"I'm anxious to hear all about it. For now, don't move an inch unless you're looking forward to dentures."

"FBI. Show me your hands!" Diane yelled from a dozen feet away. There was a curse, then Diane yelled again. "Face down, on the ground. Put your hands behind your back."

"Okay, partner?" Diane said a few seconds later.

"Got mine," Lee replied, patting his suspect down for weapons. There was a cell phone in his jacket pocket that Lee took, but nothing else besides keys, a mint ChapStick, wallet, and a Sears Old Crafty pocketknife.

"Let's get you out on the sidewalk for a better look."

"What in the hell is going on?" Lee heard the motel guest's voice as before, and saw the thin-haired Anglo man in suit and tie staring out the door of room 117.

Just then, the room door opened farther and the shirtless guy poked his head out the door. He looked straight at Lee.

"Crap!"

The man turned to flee, nearly running into Diane, who had the guy from the car in tow, handcuffed. She showed him her pistol. "Don't do it, cutie. Face down on the sidewalk."

"All three of you," Lee added, tapping his captive on the shoulder with enough force to convey the message. As the three started to comply, Lee glanced toward the man at the window. "You alone in there?"

"Yessir, Officer. What's going on, anyway?"

"That's what we're trying to find out, sir," Lee responded. "Come outside, please."

"Yessir."

Once the three suspects were face down, Lee searched

them again for weapons and got their wallets. Diane called APD and confirmed that officers were on their way.

An hour later, Lee and Diane were alone, standing between their vehicles. Everyone at the scene had been taken to the closest APD substation for interviews and possible charges.

"Homeland Security, my ass. It sure looked to me like a little shakedown operation. If Mr. Hart was telling the truth, someone is trying to discredit him for blowing the whistle on Senator Bartolucci's hinky connections with the oil and gas industry," Diane said. "Even the local papers are putting out editorials, and up to now they've always backed Bartolucci."

"Kind of crude, though. Bartolucci seems smarter than that. Setting up a reconciliation meeting with a fired staffer, then sending in a male prostitute to get some embarrassing photos while they bugged his car. More like organized crime than politics," Lee responded.

"Politics *is* organized crime, Lee. Full of hypocrites who can't take responsibility when the finger is pointing at them for a change. Hasn't it always been like that?"

Lee nodded. "At least it's out of our hands now."

"Don't count on it. Once this gets on the news tomorrow, I bet we're both going to be getting calls from our bosses." Diane looked at her watch. "Whoops, it's tomorrow already. Let's go home."

Lee thought about it a moment, then reached out and held both of her hands. "Nothing I'd like better, but with more heat bound to come down in the morning, it would probably be better if we don't spend the night together."

"SAC Logan would never come by my apartment. His wife would kill him. I'll get called into his office—that's his way. Stay the night, Lee." Diane stood on tiptoes and gave him a soft kiss. "You weren't going to drive back to Farmington until mid-tomorrow anyway."

"Sure?"

"Very sure."

"Okay, then. You lead the way." Lee waited until she climbed into her own vehicle, then followed in his own unit as she pulled out into the street. If tonight's incident blew up into something big tomorrow when the manure hit the fan, they might not be getting much time together for a while. Even transfers were possible. He looked at the sky and the position of the moon. It was still four hours till dawn. The night was young, and for now, so were he and Diane.

CHAPTER 2

Diane got the first call, at 7:00 A.M. They were both up by then having breakfast, anticipating the inevitable, and she was on her way downtown to the Bureau office within a half hour. Lee had no idea how long she'd be downtown, and he didn't have to be back in the Four Corners for his shift until late afternoon, so he sat at the small apartment's dining table and sipped coffee. The story hadn't made the morning paper, and he didn't know if that was because of the timing or due to local and state politics. Newspapers, he noted, still played sides as much as they always had, though they all professed noble motives when their reporters and editors were on the line.

There was nothing on the radio or local television news broadcasts, either, and it didn't take long for Lee to realize that the entire thing was being hushed up. Perhaps no charges had been filed by the victim or the motel owners. Whatever the case, if the perps have walked, somebody had applied pressure, beginning at the police department.

Lee's cell phone rang. He thought it might be his Farmington district state police office supervisor, Captain Terry, when he noticed the caller ID was blocked. Instead it was Diane, calling from her office. "Hello, Officer Hawk," she said, using her business voice.

Conversations coming in, and probably going out from, the Bureau's Albuquerque field office were recorded and often monitored, and both Lee and Diane were always very careful even though their actual conversations were encrypted. They knew not to provide any information to a potential eavesdropper concerning their relationship, or even worse for their careers, a hint that he was really Lee Nez, a half vampire who looked *really* young for a man more than eighty years old.

"I need to take a rain check on lunch—my schedule has been shot to hell and I'm going to be at the office till late. Give me a call next time you're in town, okay?" Diane added.

"I understand, Agent Lopez. Till then," Lee said without emotion, then ended the connection.

There was no point in hanging around Diane's apartment any more except for the obvious need to avoid direct sunlight. Lee had already showered and anointed himself with maximum-strength sunblock to keep the wavelengths of visible light at bay, the ones that caused sunburns in normal people—and immolation for vampires.

He'd already packed up yesterday's uniform and clothes in his travel bag, a habit he'd begun decades ago when the need to move quickly became a necessity, so basically, he was ready to leave.

He glanced around the apartment, saw that everything was in order, then rinsed out his coffee mug and placed it in the dishwasher. Three minutes later, he was in his department black and white, traveling north on I-25.


Lee had an early dinner alone in his Farmington apartment, a nondescript room at a fifty-unit complex along Twentieth Street, northeast of Main Street and the old downtown. He'd been assigned to the area for months now—Navajos were a large minority population in the community and he certainly fit in—except for the nightwalker part.

He'd never seen another Navajo vampire, and all he knew of nightwalkers was from brief discussions he'd had with two medicine men, one long dead, and the other his friend, John Buck. John and Diane were the only people who knew what he was; well, besides Bridget, and he hadn't seen that cute little blonde vampire in a year now.

His extremely unique affliction didn't really require blood, like with fictional vampires, but it was certainly the most nutritious food for him. The problem was in getting a good supply of fresh blood—animal, of course—without raising eyebrows and suspicion. John Buck, now living beside Navajo land close to Albuquerque, managed to get some for him occasionally from Navajos slaughtering their livestock, sheep mostly, and some cattle and hogs, but the supply wasn't consistent, or necessary, for that matter. Like eggnog and pumpkin pie for Anglos, for him, blood was more of a seasonal treat than a year-round deal.

Lee had never tried human blood, and the thought grossed him out—like eating a relative. But fortunately, a rare chunk of sirloin would do quite nicely—along with potatoes, whole wheat rolls, apple pie, whole milk, coffee, and anything else around, even fruit and salad. Liver would have been especially good for him, probably, but he hated liver. It was always dry and pasty tasting to him, even with onions.

Looking at the three empty plates before him on the tiny round table beside his kitchen cubicle, Lee realized he was a pig. Anyone without his extremely high metabolism—a non-vampire—would have gained ten pounds just looking in his refrigerator, much less eating a nightwalker-size meal.

He'd grabbed a quick nap when he first got home, and was now ready for his shift. Bussing the kitchen, he then checked his small backup .45, returned it to his pocket, then confirmed that his commando knife was secure at his ankle. Lee adjusted his retro-thirties shiny black-billed cap, bad-ass wrap-around sunglasses, stuck his hand-held at his belt, then patted his pocket to confirm the emergency plastic bottle of sunblock.

Taking a quick three-sixty, he confirmed that everything was where it should be, then he walked out of the apartment and locked it up tight, leaving a broom straw wedged in the weather-strip to record any unauthorized entry while he was away.

Fifteen minutes later Lee parked in one of the parking slots in the gravel lot beside the rented redbrick building that contained the Farmington district state police office. The array of antennas and dishes, some of them obsolete now but nevertheless intact, gave away the purpose of the structure from several blocks away.

He'd passed the Farmington Police Department headquarters along the way and noticed a roofing crew hard at work. Part of the roof of the two-story, flat-topped structure had peeled away during a violent but relatively dry thunderstorm recently, and was hastily being resurfaced.

In New Mexico, during what locals referred to as the monsoon season, massive thunderstorms could build up in a matter of a few hours. Invariably preceded by the sudden burst of violent winds, the sky would open up for a few minutes to an hour. Or, almost as frequently, as happened last week, all they'd get was the wind, and the water would either evaporate on the way down, or flood a spot of land only a half mile away. Rain was nearly always hit and miss during monsoon season, and, around here, that often extended into September—if New Mexico was lucky that year.

Fire season was in full bloom, however, and already the helicopters and fixed wing aircraft had been used statewide in air drops of water and slurry on natural fires. He couldn't remember the last year without a big fire in the news during the summer months.

Lee checked his shades, adjusted his hat, then picked up his notebooks and handheld and exited his cruiser. He locked the door, something he'd done since joining the department for the first time in 1943, then stepped into the station lobby, out of the late-afternoon sun.

The station was small, all business, and he saw only one person behind the counter—a young, half-Navajo woman with reddish, curly hair and surprising green eyes. She was doing something with the mouse and keyboard right now, but Gail also handled dispatch responsibilities. The radio unit itself was on an adjoining table, and Gail wore a cordless headset and microphone to give her more freedom of movement.

"Hey, Officer Hunk," Gail called out with a flashy smile. "You're early. I just made fresh coffee. Wanna cup?"

"Hey, Gail. Coffee sounds good. Any calls under way?"

"Just the field work for a TA near Flora Vista. No fatalities. Officer Valdez will be tied up for another hour, probably," Gail said, then stood and walked to the small table against the wall where the coffee was brewed. She filled a foam cup with the steaming brew, then refilled her own black mug, which was decorated with the gold department emblem and diagonal white stripe.

"Careful. It's really hot," she said, handing Lee the cup and managing to touch his hand at the same time.

He smiled, always careful to be friendly but not flirt. Gail was attractive, slender with almost no hips in those long black slacks, and was juggling two boyfriends already, if his last count was still up to date. Gail didn't know about Diane, of course.

"Captain Terry said to send you in once you arrived. More than just a briefing tonight, I think."

Lee nodded, already having an idea what was coming. "Gotcha. Thanks for the coffee, Gail."

"Anytime, Lee." The girl winked, then sat back down at her chair, studying the computer monitor once again.

Lee knocked twice on the thin wooden door and heard the captain's chair creak as he sat up. "Come on in, Officer Hawk."

He went inside the sparsely furnished office, which contained a few wooden file cabinets, a big matching desk with computer screen and drawer-level keyboard, and a bookcase with various manuals. A photo of his average-looking but very pleasant wife, Marie, was on his desk, facing toward the captain. Professor Marie Terry had a Ph.D. and taught computer science at the local community college, Lee knew.

"You enlisted in a joint vice strike force without telling me, Officer Hawk?" Captain Terry said, his ruddy, round face wearing a phony scowl as he motioned Lee to a chair. The amusement in his eyes gave him away. Captain Owen Terry had risen in the department through good instincts and management skills, not his ability to play bad cop. Lee suspected that if the captain played poker, his inability to bluff made him the loser every time.

"Thought you might have gotten a call about that, Captain. I got the feeling it might just fade away once the connection with Senator Bartolucci came to light. I don't know if you took a look at my report yet, but Special Agent Lopez and I were just responding to what we observed to be illegal activity."

"I was faxed a copy of your report. Look familiar?" The captain opened one of two manila folders atop his desk and handed Lee the forms. Lee opened up his notebook, took out the copy he always made of every sheet of paperwork he did, then looked over what should have been identical pages.

Lee overlaid the sheets and held them up to the light. Except for the image of a rubber stamp that gave the source as the

Albuquerque district on the copy sent to Terry, the two papers were identical, even to the punctuation marks. Nothing had been altered.

"Know Senator Bartolucci personally, I see. Guy's a bastard, all right, but at least he didn't have the paperwork 'edited.'"

Lee nodded. "I'm supposed to keep my mouth shut about all this?"

"From the senator, to the senator's senior aide, to the state police chief, to me, and now to you. In a word, yes." Captain Terry shook his head slowly. "Friggin' politicians. Make their own rules."

Lee shrugged. He wondered if Diane had gone through a similar briefing. "What excuse did they use, national security? Let me guess—the senator's ex-employee stole a stack of official government stationery when he cleaned out his desk and might be intending to use it to send terrorist memos. The two men peeking in his window and bugging his car were protecting democracy, Mom, apple pie, and baseball from a suspected liberal."

"Your spin is pretty close to theirs. The official excuse was that the senator's staff believed Mr. Hart had made copies of the senator's classified reports and was going to make them public. The men you caught were security people being, maybe, a little overzealous in investigating that particular possibility. No charges will be filed, and the senator's office will apologize to Hart. The men involved will be warned and face whatever discipline the senator decides to provide. Probably have to stand in the corner for a half hour because they got caught and embarrassed the senator. Officially, no harm, no foul, case closed."

"And the attempt to smear Mr. Hart with the male prostitute?"

"What prostitute?"

"Right. So how does all this affect me?" And Diane, Lee thought to himself.

"Not at all, if I have anything to say about it. You know, I just love it when the state police has to suck up to the senior senator, don't you?" Terry was on a roll now, and though Lee agreed with what he was saying, he also knew that Captain Terry's butt would be on the line, too, if word got out to the press about last night. Loyalty going down the chain of command as well as up was something rare today.

"Thanks, Captain, for covering my back. Anything else?"

"I had a brief conversation with SAC Logan. He's making sure nothing detrimental ends up in Agent Lopez's file from this. She and you have made him look good more than once, and he appreciates that. We're on the same page, it looks like."

"Good."

"It's settled, I hope, but I still want you to stay below the radar for a while, Lee. Senator Bartolucci is a sneaky SOB, and he knows his office handed us a load of crap. His men were way across the line, and he's liable to be looking for a way to discredit you in case the need arises."

Lee hated the idea of anyone watching him. He lived a secret life already, and the idea of being in somebody's spotlight made him particularly uncomfortable. Anyone checking deeply into his background might stumble across the fact, eventually, that he looked amazingly similar to a Navajo cop who had mysteriously disappeared way back in 1945. Diane Lopez had been the first, so Lee knew the information was out there for anyone with the tenacity to find it.

Worst-case scenario, Lee could drop out of sight again, but it was much harder to get lost in today's world than it had been with his previous identities, and it would also cost him Diane. If Lee had to disappear, there was no way she could remain part of his life. He'd risk a lot before risking losing her.

Lee watched Captain Terry as he picked up the second folder on his desk. "How familiar are you with the East Mountain area, Lee?"

"East of Albuquerque and the Sandias? Cedar Crest, Moriarity, Chilili, Manzano. Off I-Forty north and south?"

"Well, I'm thinking of south rather than north, but that's the general area. Ever go into that area on patrol or answering a call?"

Lee thought about it a moment. "Just traffic accidents in Tijeras Canyon and near Clines Corners, farther east. During bad weather there are always accidents around Clines Corners."

"So there's no reason for anyone in that general area to recognize you if you went undercover, is that correct?"

"Far as I know. It's pretty rural out there anyway. What's the situation?"

"It's been on the back burner for a while, but all this was passed down to me this morning, for reasons that will quickly become obvious. It originated from a retired judge who had all he could take and moved out of the East Mountain area recently. He contacted the Albuquerque district and asked the department to look into a situation that's been building for several years now."

"Local corruption? Drugs?"

"A little of everything, the contact reported. There's a civilian who has everyone intimidated, apparently, especially in the mostly rural area southwest of Tijeras that runs up into the foothills of the Manzanos."

"What's the guy's name, and what's he supposed to be doing?"

"Man's name is Newton Glover. He's got a military record, with rank and years of service blacked out—classified. Served in an army intelligence unit and gets a monthly check from Uncle Sam. Seems too young to have served twenty years, but his official age is forty, so it could have happened. Supposedly Glover lives in a manufactured home on a half acre and has basically been lording over the region for a couple of years now. He's been accused of everything from stolen vehicles and property, vandalism like breaking windows, setting fires, shooting or running off livestock, dealing drugs, prostitution—a whole list."

"What about the local sheriff's department? Most of that is Bernalillo County."

"Glover's been hauled in several times, but nothing seems to stick. Evidence disappears, witnesses don't show up—like that. Our source thinks people are getting paid off or intimidated, including some of the deputies and local judges."

Lee shook his head. "So there's no way of knowing who to trust. I wish I knew why his military record is classified. Maybe he did special ops work. Is Glover violent, or just smart?"

Terry looked down at his papers. "Both, apparently." The captain read a few lines, then looked up. "He's worked over some of his neighbors, putting more than one in a hospital, but ends up getting off with a self-defense plea or having the charges dropped. Some people have disappeared, but there is no evidence of foul play, or a body. And Glover seems to know the law, using every legal trick, apparently. The source says he's become virtually untouchable."

"Chances are he's got some contacts in the community that are on his payroll in one way or the other. Racketeering is a team sport, and nobody deals with drugs or prostitution on their own. He needs products and supplies, and if he's pimping—women. I'm guessing he's not selling his own body."

"No, though our information is just heresay on some of the accusations. What we need is for someone to go in, live in the community long enough to find out what's going on, then get something that'll put him away for a long time. My superiors agree that it's vital to break Glover's hold on the community. We'd also like to nail anyone else who's dirty so they don't just pick up where he left off."

"And that's where I come in. Puts me below the radar, all right. I move into the community and try to blend in while conducting my own investigation. That about it?" Lee asked.

"On the money. But I want you to have backup, Lee. We can't count on the locals, some of them are obviously involved, and you can be pretty isolated out there a half hour or more from the main highway, and longer than that for reliable backup to arrive. I just went over the preliminary plan with the Albuquerque district officers, but it's still pretty rough so far. The idea is to pair you with a woman officer. Like you're a couple. The name that's at the top of the list is Sergeant Linda Hill. Ever met her?"

Thor, Lee thought to himself, but didn't voice it aloud. It was the tall, chunky blonde Amazon's nickname among those who'd worked with the female officer. According to what he'd also heard, she was a real hard-ass who tended to get into fights, even with fellow officers, over the slightest provocation.

Lee had shaken hands a few times and exchanged information at a crime scene, but had otherwise never interacted with the woman. Although he was concerned that Sergeant Hill might discover too much about him if they roomed together for a week or two, maybe even longer than that, Thor was also said to be tough and reliable, and that's something he could live with. With undercover work, staying alive was always a concern.

"I've met the officer, and Sergeant Hill's reputation precedes her." Lee shrugged. "Sounds like a good choice for a job like this."

Captain Terry frowned, apparently expecting a different reaction. But Lee had always been concerned with results, not gossip or department politics, and if Thor was cutting it among the good ole boy network of the state police, she had to have something going for her.

"Read the file on Glover we've begun, take a look at the preliminary plans laid out for the operation, then write out a tentative cover story and try to nail down a strategy to get next to Glover, one way or the other. If you prefer, once you're done with the paperwork here and have the chance to access any databases and records that exist on the guy, you can finish up at home. Thor . . . Sergeant Hill, that is, is taking part in a drug sweep in the Deming–Lordsburg area. I've given her captain a call, and he's going to have Hill fly up to work out the details together in my office. Plan on tomorrow morning, or a little after lunch, depending on the paperwork generated down in Deming."

Captain Terry nodded toward the open door leading into a second, even smaller office. "Use the terminal and desk in my workroom. I've already got your shift covered. I'll be around a while longer, but unless something major comes up, I'm leaving at six."

Lee worked for several hours, reading the factually sketchy report on Glover first. If the lowlife was guilty of just a few of the illegal activities he was suspected of carrying out, Glover was a real predator. It also became clear that many in the community were cowed, doing what they could to avoid contact with the man rather than going to authorities that couldn't be depended upon.

At one point, a rumor had gone through the community, even reaching the sheriff's department, that Glover had been killed. His absence for several days seemed to support that notion. But Glover had reappeared just as mysteriously, his absence never explained.

Stories spread that Glover had come back from the dead, or was invincible—a notion that Glover picked up on and fostered. Then attention shifted to his next-door neighbor, a man found dead—mutilated with a knife—in the parking lot outside an East Mountain-area bar. The crime had been brutal, but no witnesses came forward and no arrests were ever made. Glover had been questioned, along with other residents, but the case was shelved. The widow moved away shortly afterward.

Lee didn't believe in coincidences like this, but he did know, from personal experience, that there were people around who were very hard to kill. It just gave him one more reason to focus on Glover. He read the details of the undercover operation that had been developed, noting areas where more information or resources were needed, listing potential problems and solutions, and coming up with a cover story. He planned to set himself up as an ex-con jewelry maker working and selling out of his home, dealing in cash, and basically avoiding the legal niceties of business licenses, gross receipts taxes, and all the rest. Many people conducted business in a shadow economy, avoiding taxes, fees, and so on, particularly in the poorer areas of the state. He had no worries about being reported.

The appearance that he was a former criminal still breaking the law might earn him some respect, and maybe even give him an opening, when confronting Newt Glover. It was useless to plan much further ahead than that, because seat-of-the-pants operations like this had to be constantly modified and adjusted, depending on events, contacts, and relationships that developed.

Lee also knew that if Linda Hill was going to be his partner, she'd have her own skills, ideas, and suggestions to work into the overall plan. What he was doing now was creating a framework. What they ended up with depended a lot on tomorrow's meetings and Hill's input.

Lee finally decided to go to his apartment, make a list of items he'd need to establish his cover, then grab a few extra hours of sleep. Tomorrow he'd be working the day shift, normally sack time, and though he rarely got tired, after several days fatigue would eventually set in.

Once he set up a domestic situation with Linda Hill, they'd probably sleep in shifts, with him out and about mostly at night, a natural use of his special abilities. Somehow he'd have to get that notion past his partner without creating a problem or letting her think he was some nut who was allergic to sunlight.

Lee picked up his paperwork, grabbed his cap, then walked through Captain Terry's empty office into the front, where Gail was seated behind the counter, reading a paperback novel. Dispatch work was often like that, late at night on weekdays, when no calls could come through for an hour, then four or five all at once.

"Officer Hawk. We've got an Amber alert." She handed him a sheet of paper with a photo of a small boy, a name, and a description.

Lee read the paper automatically, and his eyes stopped when he noticed that the missing boy, Timothy Klein, ten years old, had failed to return home after a visit with his mother, who lived in Edgewood, just inside Santa Fe County but close to the Torrance and Bernalillo County lines—the same general East Mountain area where he was about to set up shop.

According to the brief summary, both parents, divorced and in the midst of a big legal fight over their successful joint-business interests, believed that Timothy was with the other parent, so neither noticed until the weekend had ended and the child didn't report to school. Witnesses remembered seeing a child getting into a car or van in the area where the boy was seen last, but no details were available at the moment.

"Can you believe it? Parents don't even notice their ten-year-old kid is gone for two days? He could be across the country by now. Some pervert on I-Forty probably spotted him beside the road and offered him a ride home." Gail sat back in her chair, stretched, then finally stood.

"With deputies and search teams from three counties out there looking, hopefully more information will turn up. These Amber alerts are working. Maybe we'll get lucky on this one," Lee said, looking intently at the photograph, then placing it in his notebook. Chances were the East Mountains were going to be swarming with search teams looking for Timothy Klein for the next few days. He and Sergeant Hill could move in probably without notice, and it would be a good excuse to start making contacts and asking questions.

If the kid had been kidnapped and didn't just get lost, maybe it was someone from the area who'd been stalking the boy. Kids who were taken by child molesters were usually watched and targeted rather than the victims of random activity, though the latter couldn't be ruled out. But two days was a long time for a child molester to keep their victim alive, once they were done with them. Ransom was always a possibility, especially if the parents were well off, as they appeared to be, at least financially.

Lee said good night, then walked outside to his department cruiser, thinking about the lowlife, Glover, and the missing child. These were the kind of crimes that made him want to revert to good old-fashioned vigilante justice—the kind he could mete out. He took several deep breaths. Logic and clear thinking. That's what he needed now. If Glover happened to know the boy, or either of the parents, maybe the kid had become a pawn . . . a way of gaining power or punishing someone Glover didn't like. It was a long shot, but Glover was a known problem already.

Lee actually hoped that Glover was involved, not because he was obviously ruthless and amoral, but because it would mean that there was only one sicko out there in the East Mountains communities—not two.

CHAPTER 3

His cell phone rang at 7:00 in the morning. Lee had been awake since 5:00 and was dressed, protected with sunblock, and ready to go. The caller ID was blocked, so he suspected it was from the department.

"Officer Hawk," he said curtly.

"Lee, it's me, Diane, and it's business. Can you pick me up at the airport in fifteen minutes? I'm on the way now, New Mexico Air."

"You're coming to Farmington?"

"Yeah, the Amber alert. You heard about it, right?"

"The missing boy, Timothy Klein. The Bureau was called in?"

"Not publicly. Your captain got a genius idea, apparently late last night, and gave SAC Logan a call. Logan is happy because it's going to get me out of his hair during the politically touchy days ahead. The senator who shall not be named is connected to certain bills under consideration that could give the Bureau some important funding increases."

"Here's where we're required not to bite the hand that feeds us. It figures. So that means you've been assigned to the undercover operation I'm heading into?" Lee asked.

"Yeah. I'm going to partner with you on this—unless you prefer blondes?"

There was a pause. "Read my mind," Lee said, not believing his good luck. "What's your ETA?"

"Seven forty-five."

"See you then."

Southeast of Albuquerque, in the eastern foothills beside the Manzano Mountains, Lee slowed, turning to his right off State Road 337 onto a graveled lane called Quail Run. Beside the road was one of those multiple-box postal units, a metal structure with twelve locked containers.

"The double-wide is another half mile, according to the map the Realtor gave us. West end of Quail Run, last one on the left," Diane commented.

"Lucky the Realtor was able to cut a deal with the family already scheduled to move in and get them to accept a better deal closer to the city. Of course having the request come from the local FBI office didn't hurt," Lee observed dryly.

"At least we're at the edge of the forest and it's not as flat as I expected," Diane said, noting the pines and junipers along the sloped terrain punctuated by currently dry arroyos.

"Never been off the highway here at all, but it reminds me of the foothills west of Shiprock, where I grew up. From the extra green and thicker vegetation, they get more moisture here, though," Lee added. "Lots of wild grasses for the rabbits, too."

"Dark as a well to me, this side of the Manzanos without the city lights. But at least we'll have some cover when we start roaming around at night."

Lee slowed the vehicle nearly to a crawl, then stopped as a coyote walked out into the road. The scrawny animal paused in the glare of the headlights and watched them for a moment, then strolled off nonchalantly.

"Coyote, right?" Diane asked. "Not somebody's pet?"

"I've heard that residents in this county, especially farther north, have a lot of problems with dogs attacking their livestock. Some are feral, the others just allowed to roam by owners who probably ignore their children, as well. But this was a coyote. Looked relatively well fed, for a coyote."

Lee didn't have much problem keeping to the road; it was almost perfectly straight here and since there was no traffic, he was able to check out the mostly mobile homes they passed on either side. Some were well maintained, with small permanent additions built alongside, but a few were overgrown with brush and littered with old appliances, scrap building materials and trash piles, and the frequent junker pickups or car. One of the homes had a nice-looking motorcycle parked outside, a good idea considering the distances to work from here.

Horses and a few goats were in pens. One resident had an old truck trailer with four flat tires showing that appeared to contain bales of hay. Weeds growing in a corral suggested he'd lost his animals before running out of alfalfa.

"People in this development obviously don't have that much," Diane observed offhandedly. "Having someone like Glover lord over them just makes it even worse. Made it hard for the real-estate people to get tenants to rent that close to him, too, despite lowering their rates. Word gets around."

"We'll nail the bastard. From the reports, he sounds like one sick puppy," Lee reminded.

"Sick enough to kidnap a ten-year-old boy?"

Lee shrugged. "According to the parents, they've heard about Glover, though they've never had any run-ins with him that they could remember. The disappearance may be unrelated. We can't interview them ourselves, though, not without jeopardizing our cover."

"Soldiers with Glover's supposed training are used to taking prisoners, so he'd have the skills to snatch a young boy. If he's taken up kidnapping for profit, we need to move fast and get close to the guy. I still vote for getting under his skin by making him an enemy. Befriending somebody like that will be hard on my conscience," Diane said. "And he's pretty much a loner, with reluctant allies, according to the judge's observations."

"Either way, avoid being around him alone," Lee said. "He's always hitting on women, and he likes to play rough, according to what the informant said. You're going to be giving him ideas the moment he lays eyes on you. No way anyone's going to believe you could be an FBI agent looking like that."

Diane had dyed her hair a startling shade of copper, put on pounds of makeup, and wore a halter top and tight jeans. If it wasn't for her baggy leather jacket, there'd be no place to conceal a weapon.

"Unfortunately, we need to get his attention. That's part of the piss-him-off plan. Give him a reason to tee off on us right away by showing him something he can't have. And if he's the coveting type, he'll also go for this shiny new SUV. He's got a rep for vandalizing what others seem to value most. Suppose he'll be up tonight, watching us move in?"

"I hope so. Maybe I can find a way to annoy him tonight," Lee said.

"If anyone can . . ."

"What do you mean by that, girlfriend?" Lee smiled. "I'm really an easy-going guy."

"With a devious streak and unlimited imagination. You'll find a way."

"Just be careful, Diane. You read the reports. One of his neighbors was knifed outside a bar—mutilated. My instincts tell me Glover was involved. Who knows, maybe the guy just pissed Glover off, or Glover was using him as an example to keep the locals in line. This guy is big, rough—a schoolyard bully grown up."

"I also read the rumor about him being killed, then showing up a few days later, apparently unharmed. Could he be a vampire?"

"We'll know once we see him—or don't—in sunlight. If he never takes off his shades, covers himself up, or reeks of sunblock. . . ."

Diane nodded. "Or can bend steel with his bare hands. Kinda like you. At least we'll know what to look for. But if he's a vampire we're going to have to turn him into ashes. He'd be too dangerous to put in jail."

"Vampire or not, Glover needs to be taken down now. I just hope he doesn't have anything to do with that missing child. You suppose this particular incident will put some backbone into the people around here?"

"With us around, they'll have someone to back them up for a change," Diane said. "That's our place ahead. The lit-up yard on the right must be Glover's."

They pulled up in the loaded SUV, containing suitcases with security cameras and a laptop, clothes, kitchenware, some household supplies, and Lee's silver jewelry-making tools. Using a flashlight, they climbed up the steps and Diane unlocked the door. She stepped inside with Lee for a look around.

"Smells like pine cleanser, and looks clean enough," Lee commented, reaching for the light switch on the wall and turning on the porch light, as well. The big room in front of him was a left-facing L, with the top of the L the dining area, complete with wooden table and four chairs, and the area he was in served as the living room. There was a sofa, chairs, built-in cabinets, and drawers—the usual. Double doors to his right led to a small study, and to the left, according to the Realtor, the master bedroom. The far left of the room held counters and a breakfast bar, behind the counter and cupboards was the small kitchen.

They walked across the room to check it out. The smaller-scale appliances looked to be in good shape, and the propane was supposed to be hooked up. He turned on a burner of the stove and it lit up immediately. Diane turned on the hot-water tap at the double sink. The water came out clean and steady, and warmed up quickly. She turned off the tap.

"Guess the well works," she announced. "And the hot-water heater, too. Your department did a good job setting this up with the Realtor. Now we can focus on the job without having to worry about logistics."

"Speaking of which . . . I'll start bringing in our stuff . . . dear. Or should I call you 'honey' for this operation?"

"Yuck. Do that and I'll call you Big Balls."

"Never mind. Diane it is." Lee chuckled, then stepped to the door. "Lights just went out next door," he announced.

Lee started bringing in the suitcases and boxes, every once in a while glancing over at the mobile home a hundred yards away across the gravel road. A man was moving around in the darkened room, and on his fifth trip to the SUV, Lee's superior vision viewed a small telescope on a tripod. Glover was curious.

"Glover's set up a telescope," Lee said as he came inside with two more suitcases.

Diane came around the corner from a small hall that led to the second bedroom to the right past the study. "Sure it's not some kind of directional mike?"

"Naw. He'd need to have his window open, maybe one on our side, too. Besides, I can see the gleam of the optics."

"Remind me to keep the curtains drawn and stay away from the windows."

Lee carried the suitcases into the master bedroom to the left. They'd be sleeping in the same bed, of course, to protect their cover as a couple. No wedding rings, because they were just "living together." As he set the suitcases down beside the bed, which had linens already because they were renting a furnished home, he came up with an idea.

"I've thought of a way to annoy Glover."

"What you gonna do?"

"Blind him."

Lee went back outside, started up the SUV, then drove forward out of the circular driveway until the headlights were aimed across the street and right into Glover's living room window. Lee hit the brights, and saw the man jump back from the telescope, shielding his eyes from the glare. Next, Lee turned on the spotlight beside the outside mirror, and aimed it at the telescope, too.

Leaving the engine running, he got out of the vehicle and continued to unload boxes and a large trunk, setting the stuff beside the vehicle instead of taking it all inside. He kept an eye on Glover's double-wide, and less than two minutes went by before the hulk of a man stormed out his front door carrying a wooden baseball bat in his hand.

"What the hell you doing shining your lights into my window, asshole?" he yelled, striding down a flagstone walk toward the metal gate of a four-foot-high wire fence that enclosed his front yard.

Glover up close matched the mug shot from one of the few times the man had been arrested. His blond hair was nearly marine-recruit short, and his face clean shaven and surprisingly delicate, almost feminine. His expression, however, was quite the opposite, cruel and twisted. Glover had an intimidating chest and well-tanned, bulging arms, but Lee was almost disappointed not to see a tattoo.

"You the village idiot, or the neighborhood pervert?" Lee replied coolly. "The headlights go out when the telescope gets stashed back under your bed beside the girlie magazines."

Glover began to cuss a blue streak now. He stepped out of

his yard, slamming his gate open so violently Lee was surprised it didn't fly off the hinges. Lee waited until the bat-waving bully was halfway across the road before he spoke again.

"Unless you have a baseball in your pocket, that Louisville slugger is about to vanish right up your butt, neighbor. We mind our own business, and unless you decide to do the same, you're going to be needing a nuclear enema to clear out the splinters." Lee took a step forward now, motioning casually with his fingers for Glover to keep coming.

Glover snarled, faked an overhead swing, then jabbed at Lee's chest with the end of the bat.

The move seemed right out of the second act of an episode of *Walker, Texas Ranger*. It was all slow motion to Lee, who had plenty of time to spare. He stepped inside the move, grabbed the bat halfway down the handle, then twisted it sideways.

Glover groaned, letting go before his wrist snapped, and took a step back. "What the . . . ?"

Lee snapped the bat in half over his knee like a twig, then dropped the two pieces on the ground.

Glover threw up his fists like a boxer, but Lee could see from his eyes the bully was worried now.

"Not used to having someone a head shorter about to kick your ass? I can do the same to your arm, neighbor. Or you can walk away now, put the spy glass away, and call it a night. Your call," Lee said, hearing Diane coming up from behind. She was holding something in each hand, but he wasn't ready to look away from Glover's eyes. Lee knew that if he was going to try anything else, he'd give it away there first.

"See you've introduced yourself to our neighbor, dear." Diane handed Lee a bottle of beer. She looked down at the broken bat, then laughed. "Cold one?" She offered Glover the other bottle. "I'm Diane. Nice tan, by the way. You must spend a lot of time outdoors."

Glover took the bottle, but his hand was shaking and some of the brew sloshed out. It wasn't until he took a long swig that he spoke again. "Yeah. Benefits of retirement. Name is Glover, by the way. Folks just call me Newt. Sorry I unloaded on you. . . ."

Lee smiled graciously. "Lee."

"Don't worry about the 'scope. I was thinking of selling it anyway. No offense meant, ma'am."

Diane shrugged. "You see now that we value our privacy."

"Me, too. Thanks for the beer. Good night." Glover nodded, then turned and walked back across the street.

"Where'd the beer come from?" Lee whispered, taking a deep swallow, then offering it back to her. She took a swig, then returned it. "There were three in the fridge."

"You hate beer, right?"

"Tastes like horse piss—not that I've ever had that, either. But how else am I going to play the good ole boy's gal if I don't power down a brew every once in a while?"

Lee took another swallow of the cool drink, then grabbed a box. "Hey, where did you learn to talk like that?"

"TV. And I went to UNM, remember?" Diane picked up a box, then turned and looked toward Glover's double-wide. "Those high beams were a good idea."

"Yeah. I'll turn them off as soon as he starts taking down the telescope." Lee saw Glover stepping onto his small porch.

The man turned and waved, then turned on his living room light and began to remove the telescope from the tripod.

"At least we know what he *isn't*, right, Lee?"

"Yeah. The tan. He's also way too weak and slow to be a you-know-what," Lee replied. A half vampire would have shown a lot more strength, and even if Glover had been faking his weakness, the amount of sunlight necessary for the darkened skin on Glover's arms would have killed a vampire, not bronzed him out.

Lee set the box down, reached into the driver's side, and turned off the spotlight, headlights, then the engine. He put the keys into his pocket, picked up his beer, and finished it with a long tug. Diane was already inside their new home with her load.

He turned and noticed that Glover had closed the curtains halfway and turned out the lights. Lee could see him in the dark, across the room, watching. Not wanting the man to know how well he could really see, Lee turned around, picked up the box again, and walked toward the mobile home.

CHAPTER 4

Lee found a window in the study that gave him a clear view of the front of Glover's home and remained awake the rest of the night. If Glover chose to exit out the back, circling around through the woods to avoid detection, Lee would still spot him the second he reached the SUV that was parked well within his view. He figured that Glover probably did most of his mischief, at least the more serious crimes, at night, so that was when Lee planned to keep track of him.

Arrangements had already been made for a second vehicle that Diane would use to report to work at the small neighborhood grocery store that supplied the area with basics. It was the perfect place to establish contacts. A large Wal-Mart on Albuquerque's east side, miles away through the canyon that served to divide the mountain range into the northern Sandias and the southern Manzanos, was where most of the heavy shopping took place. That place would feature in their plans, too.

Lee had spent the bulk of his nighttime hours installing small video cameras that would monitor their new home whenever they were away. The receiver was hidden in a storage drawer. Of course, nothing that would identify them as law enforcement officers would remain on the premises. They carried their personal weapons and IDs with or beside them at all times, and the laptop, though concealed, was clear of anything out of the ordinary. The silver jewelry-making tools and supplies were just for show—Lee's sometime profession.

"How'd you sleep?" Lee asked, standing up from his seat at the table as Diane stepped into the kitchen area after having crossed the living and dining areas from the master bedroom. She was still wearing the green, flowery kimono she'd decided fit her new personality, along with the pink flip-flops.

"Not bad, actually. The bed is more comfortable than I expected. Any sign of Glover?"

"He came out around six-thirty, checked out his yard, I guess to make sure we hadn't trashed it during the night, then drove off in that red pickup of his. One more thing. He searched his vehicle for bugs first. Has one of those wands that looks like a charcoal lighter."

"How CIA. I expected the Bubba response sometime after midnight, throwing a rock through the windshield of the SUV, or maybe keying the finish. I bet that apology hurt."

"Now that he sees he can't intimidate us, Glover might take his time and check us out, looking for an angle . . . or leverage. We both did what we could last night to avoid looking like undercover cops, but I doubt that'll be enough to convince him we're no direct threat. If he has the contacts we suspect he does, Glover will have one of his friends run the license plate on the SUV. Know your enemy."

"And he'll find out it's registered to me—well, Diane Garcia, anyway, from Albuquerque's west side. He still doesn't have a last name on you." Diane took a quick look out the window. "It just occurred to me. That broken bat has your fingerprints on it."

"Yeah. I picked up the pieces and brought them inside before daylight." He motioned with his head toward the small sofa. "They're in the storage compartment below the cushion. Glover came out for his newspaper around six, looked for them in the road, then tiptoed over and checked in our trash can. Now he's probably wondering what I did with the broken bat, and why."

Lee continued, "Eventually he'll find a way to get a set of *my* prints, or, when it serves us, I'll leave some for him to find. It's a good thing your people were able to get our fingerprints and bogus identities through law-enforcement databases. He'll be convinced I'm Lee Begay from Gallup, ex-military with jail time for assault and battery, disorderly conduct, resisting arrest, stuff like that."

Lee took a sip of coffee. "Glover, besides having the wand to sweep for bugs, either has some kind of alarm or his place is wired. I saw him fiddling with something just inside the door before he left. Maybe it's a keypad. We'll have to watch and see what he does when he returns. Your people are going to let us know if he has an account with area alarm companies, or has made any recorded purchases of alarm devices and other electronics, right?"

Diane nodded, looking around the kitchen counters. "Something smells good. Did you make me some breakfast?"

"While you were in the shower. French toast and hash browns in the oven, hopefully keeping warm. If not, the microwave above the stove works. I put the butter and apricot jam back in the refrigerator. And there's plenty of coffee." Lee raised his own cup.

Diane looked at her watch. "I'd better eat, then get dressed. We've got to pick up my loaner pickup at the gas station in Tijeras. I've got to be at work by nine."

"Okay. My turn for the shower. You left some hot water, I hope?"

"Maybe I did, and maybe I didn't." Diane leaned over and gave him a quick kiss. "That isn't for Glover's benefit, that's for mine."

Lee fought the urge to move to second base, knowing that any future shows of affection while in the area would have to be strictly business, the business of protecting their cover. Any other distractions could be dangerous.

He stood up slowly. Maybe a cold shower would be good for him after all.

Once Diane was at "work," Lee returned to his new home, confirmed Glover hadn't sneaked in, then began making calls on the cell phone, standing outside on the porch and keeping watch for any unusual activity in the area at the same time. If Glover had a directional mike, and happened to be at home using it, Lee's speech could have been overheard. But it was safe for the moment.

Communication was going to be through their encrypted cell phones or via their laptop. They couldn't risk leaving paperwork or a radio around that someone breaking in might find while they were away. The same was true for their vehicles, so they'd be depending on e-mails and calls to Captain Kelly or SAC Logan for updates, feedback, and information exchanges. Plans had been made for any physical evidence to be left at a drop in the Wal-Mart parking lot closest to the canyon.

From his location, uphill from the highway, Lee could see all the homes in the tiny development and any traffic coming in his direction. The forested terrain around him was uneven enough, filled with low hills and arroyos. Anyone off-road and in a vehicle would have to drive slowly and probably be making a lot of noise unless they came up one of the dirt utility access roads behind the two rows of houses. Anyone on a horse or on foot could move around more quietly, and it would be possible to use the thick vegetation and ground cover to sneak from place to place, even during daylight, until you got really close to a residence.

All this meant that Lee could go take a closer look—and listen—at Glover's house without risk of being discovered. He'd just have to keep watch and assume Glover wouldn't return on foot or horseback. Nighttime was preferable, of course, but Glover wasn't at home now, so he wanted to take advantage of the opportunity while he could.

Lee's calls didn't take long. All he did was confirm to their state police and Bureau contacts that they were in position now and had made contact. He also checked and verified that no ransom calls or demands on the missing boy had been made. Then he stepped back into the house and put on his disguise.

A change into a green-and-brown camouflage-pattern shirt and slacks, along with smooth-soled moccasins, was necessary. Then Lee added a padded "gut" consisting of towels to make it look like he was pudgy, and a thin, bow-hunter's ski mask over his head. Only his eyes would show through, and those were covered by sunglasses.

The cover-up was functional, because he couldn't risk a long exposure to sunlight even with the heavy sunblock, and also necessary until Lee determined if Glover had installed surveillance cameras. Bad guys were sometimes the most paranoid—because they knew they'd made enemies, some that might take action sooner or later.

Lee slipped out the back door of the double-wide, took a quick look down the access road to verify nobody was heading his way, then ran quickly into an arroyo he'd located earlier. Moving in a crouch, he circled and reached a point where he could examine Glover's house from the forest to the west. Most of the mobile homes, Glover's and his included, were big rectangles, and the long sides faced north and south.

From his location, Lee could see most of both front and back yards. Wire fences outlined the properties—nobody had solid walls or wooden fences. Glover had a gate in the rear large enough to accommodate a vehicle. His backyard was junky, containing a child's bike, a couple of birdbaths, a smoky-looking fifty-five-gallon drum probably used to burn rubbish, a big plastic trash container on a concrete slab, and various piles of damaged construction materials, including a big mound of dirt.

Lee recalled a police report about Glover having taken a bike away from a kid who'd been "bothering" him, then beating up the father when he'd come to retrieve his son's bike. Glover had been charged, but cleared after the beating was declared self-defense. Lee wondered if that was the bike in the report. Perhaps the birdbaths had been stolen, too, and the owners were unaware or afraid to ask for them back. They were the kind of petty crimes a bully would commit just to intimidate people. Then there was the next-door neighbor who'd been knifed to death. . . .

Using a pair of hunting binoculars, Lee checked out the building and saw no cameras at the end, though there were floodlights at the corners that probably would illuminate the entire perimeter, assuming there were two at the far end, as well.

Lee noticed movement. A camera was right above Glover's back porch, a structure resembling a couple of stacked pallets, and was sweeping a full 180 degrees. He timed a sweep, and it took only twenty seconds to scan the back. When he came back at night, Lee knew he'd have to move fast to avoid being seen. He recognized the type of camera. It was probably black and white, but with good optics and a pretty wide angle.

Lee had already been able to observe the front of Glover's house from his own windows, and hadn't seen any sign of cameras there, however, just a satellite dish for TV. If any cameras had been hidden on this side, they had very small lenses and weren't quality equipment like the one in back.

He circled back around, changed back into the clothes he'd had on earlier, including a baseball cap and different sunglasses, placed three turquoise and silver watch bracelets into his jacket pocket, then walked across the street and into Glover's yard. In case Glover returned unexpectedly, it would look like he was visiting and offering to sell the man jewelry.

After verifying that the road was still clear and he wasn't going to be interrupted, Lee crept over to the window and looked inside. The man had expensive furnishings and electronic gear, including a computer still in the original box. Lee memorized the serial number and the name of the vendor, a warehouse electronics store in Albuquerque. He'd probably be able to find out if it was a legitimate purchase or stolen easily enough. But proving Glover was a thief was lower priority—if he could put him away on bigger changes.

Beside the door, in the wall siding, were several BB-size holes. The pattern suggested a shotgun blast, but Lee knew there were fewer holes than you'd expect for a full load of buckshot. Where had the other pellets gone?

Maybe someone *had* stood up to Glover before and taken a shotgun to him. But not completing the job would have been fatal to the shooter if Glover had seen who it was. Lee decided to find out more about the neighbor, Zeke Perry, who'd been knifed outside the bar. It was possible that Glover, having survived the attack, had hidden out for a few days, then returned to even the score.

But Lee was looking for something—well, *someone*—else at the moment. The chances were remote, but Glover was a lowlife, and a boy was missing. Searching for the child was one of the first things Lee had wanted to do when he'd arrived.

No news or leads had materialized as of this morning. Since ransom requests usually came in right away, the more time passed, the less likely it was that the boy was being held for money.

Lee listened, knowing his hearing was exceptional. If the boy was inside, still alive, he might be able to hear him moving about, even if the kid was tied up and locked in a bathroom or closet. Lee moved closer. The best vantage point would be from the roof, where vents conducted heat, smells, and sounds outside.

There was nothing to climb up, but Lee didn't need a ladder. A quick jump, a grab onto the top of the porch, and he was up. Landing as softly as a cat on the fiberglass-shingled roof, Lee took a quick look down the road, then stepped over to a screened vent pipe. From the greasy scent, it most likely led down into the kitchen, probably above the stove.

Lee checked out the other vents, and despite the unpleasant odor coming from two others, he was relieved to note that it wasn't the scent of death. He could hear a slow drip, like a leaky faucet in one of the bathroom vents, and in another, coming from a hallway perhaps, the faint ticking of a clock. Nothing inside within a dozen feet of a vent was moving or breathing.

Next, Lee took a quick glance inside the windows from above. One bedroom had wooden shutters and they were closed, the other was cluttered with furniture, TVs, clothing still on hangers and thrown across a bed, three saddles and some other tack, and about everything else under the sun, including several boxes of hard liquor. Two of the boxes had labels from a local bar.

After watching the surveillance camera sweep a few times back and forth from right above it, Lee was able to look inside the windows at the back of the house without being recorded.

A window was open several inches, so Lee listened, but heard nothing. Inside were more items that might have been stolen merchandise or property placed in orderly piles, but no firearms, drugs, or missing children. When he broke in, perhaps tonight, Lee planned on checking the closets and the room corners still out of view.

The last room Lee examined from above and upside down was Glover's bedroom. The man was obviously not a compulsive neat freak. Clothes were scattered around the room, the over-size four-poster bed was unmade, and empty cans of beer were atop an oak dresser. The window was open a few inches, and he could detect body odor. The telescope Lee had seen last night, a camera attached, was on the carpet by the closet.

Taped on one of the accordion closet doors were a dozen photos of naked men and women in compromising positions. The presence of what looked like window ledges in each picture suggested Glover had used a telephoto lens or the telescope and an attached camera. Perhaps these were blackmail victims, or maybe Glover was a pervert after all. At least there were no photos of children. Lee would check out their faces when he got a closer look. Being upside down, he was having problems making out subtleties.

Inching back across the roof, Lee took another look down the road and saw dust swirling up around an advancing vehicle. Jumping off the roof, he slipped out of Glover's yard through the front gate, crossed the road in a hurry, then took out his keys and opened the door to the SUV as if he'd just come home. The truck traveling toward him, one he now recognized as being a different color than Glover's, turned off the road and parked beside the home down the street perhaps a quarter mile down. Lee relaxed, took a deep breath, then brought out his cell phone.

Diane was serving as a stock clerk at Howard's Handy Stop, one of the few remaining mom-and-pop stores in the area. Just south of the frontage road—the remnants of Old Route 66—Howard's was still a center of commerce for the old-time residents and a lot of the newer generations, as well.

The business was run by Annalese Guzman, a tall, white-haired woman in her sixties. A large, faded color photo of Anna, as everyone called her, and her late husband Howard was on the wall behind the cash register, along with a hundred or so other snapshots. It reminded Diane of her mom's living room, covered with images of every family member and neighbor who'd ever crossed their threshold.

Anna didn't know Diane was with the FBI, but understood she was an undercover officer with a local agency. Mrs. Guzman had been told that much, so Diane could land her position there quickly. Howard Guzman had been a retired cop, and Anna's son was a Denver patrolman. So far, Anna hadn't had a single non-job-related question for her, not even a "knowing" glance when she'd first come in, so Diane thought her cover was as safe as it could be. Diane had retail experience, having worked in an Old Town shop behind the counter as a teen, though it hadn't been in an "emporium" like Howard's, selling everything from milk to motor oil.

Right now, Diane was restocking canned goods, boxed meals, and checking for outdated food products still on the shelves. The kid with the wannabe beard behind the cash register, Lonnie, was just out of high school, lived down the road, and seemed to know everyone who came in the door by name. He'd already tried to flirt with her, so hopefully she'd be able to get him to tell her something about the locals later.

"Doing okay, Diane?"

She turned and noticed Anna had come up behind her with a shopping cart containing a bushel basket of apples.

Anna began to place the apples gingerly, a few at a time, on a pedestal display divided into three sections, one for apples, and the other two for pears and Texas grapefruit.

"Just fine, Anna." Diane looked up as the bell above the door jingled, announcing a customer. It was a sweaty-looking fifty-year-old man in overalls and a Purina feed cap, maybe a farmer. He was Mr. Miller, according to Lonnie, who greeted him automatically.

"Hear about the missing Klein boy?" Anna asked, looking over at Miller, then back to Diane. "Timothy."

"Search parties up and down the canyon, but no sign of him. I hear the cops think he may have been taken to Albuquerque, maybe to one of those sleazy East Central motels. My old lady thinks he probably just ran off. His parents were bouncing him from house to house like a yo-yo," Miller said. "What about you, Anna?"

"His parents have lots of money. Should be spending it on finding the child, not for lawyers in a custody battle. I've been praying that Timothy has been kidnapped for ransom instead of by some pervert. At least they'd have a better chance of getting him back. The kid's only ten years old. What's the world coming to?" she said, looking up from her work.

Diane stood, and Mr. Miller noticed her for the first time.

"Getting strange," he said, his judgment perhaps tainted by her heavy makeup, copper hair, and black, form-fitting tank top.

"I'm Diane," she announced, showing him her pearly whites. "This is my first day. My boyfriend and I live up on Quail Run."

"Know that area. Not anywhere near that lowlife Glover, I hope."

Diane looked over at Anna, who refused to make eye contact, then to Lonnie. He just shook his head.

"The big dude with the buzz cut? He's just across the street. What's with him?"

"Ma'am. You never heard it from me. But if I were you, I'd move before you find out. A young woman like you . . ." His voice trailed off, and he cleared his throat. "Lonnie, fetch me a pack of Beechnut. Make that two."

As Lonnie handed Mr. Miller the chewing tobacco, Diane turned, hoping to make eye contact with Anna. Finally her new employer looked up, checked around furtively, then whispered, "Glover is scum. He's got half the community in his pocket or peeing their pants every time he comes around. I don't know what you're investigating, and I don't really want to know, but if Newt Glover gets in your way, you'd be doing the world a favor by putting him in the ground. Not that others haven't tried. Story is that some of his neighbors took a shotgun to him one night. Glover laid low for a couple of days, but he must have nine lives. When he showed up again, he didn't have a mark on him. A few days later, it was his next-door neighbor who turned up dead. See where I'm going with this?"

The doorbell rang again and Anna looked up, fear in her eyes. Miller was leaving. Anna sighed, and Diane noticed her hands were trembling so hard she nearly dropped an apple.

"Get back to work, and be very careful what you say about Glover. No telling who you can trust." Anna glanced out of the corner of her eye toward Lonnie, who was straightening the to-bacco display.

Lee had a confirmation already on the serial number he'd run from the computer box. It matched a purchase made by a man who, according to the address on his warranty, lived just three houses east down Quail Run. He had a call in now to the county, checking to see if the resident had reported any break-ins or a burglary since the date of purchase. If so, they might have something solid on Glover, though it was not nearly enough. And if what he knew already was true, Glover would find a way to intimidate the victim before it went to court anyway.

Lee also thought of something else. If the employee at the county sheriff's office running the search was connected to Glover, the news might get back to him. Glover would then know that somebody was snooping around his place, and that might put him and Diane in the spotlight.

A part of Lee hoped that would happen. He wanted Glover

to come after him—but not Diane. He knew she was tough and could handle herself, but still. . . .

His cell phone rang. "Hello," Lee said, glad to have his thoughts structured again.

"I have some information for you, Officer Hawk," Agent Karns from the Albuquerque Bureau office said. "Someone from the Bernalillo County Sheriff's Office ran a background check on your cover vehicle. The time was oh-nine-forty-five."

"Were you able to get a location on the terminal used? A workstation?"

"Sorry. It was from a mobile unit inside a cruiser. They only log on when access to the system is required, so, like a dial-up, it can't easily be traced."

"Don't they require an access code to get into the system?"

"Our people are working on that. There's a problem, however. If we ask BCSD for the information, we'll have to explain what's going on. That could end up tipping off our target's contact."

Lee saw the problem. "I doubt that Glover used his personal cell phone, even though it's digital and difficult to monitor without special equipment. He would have wanted to speak to his source directly to avoid the chance of being recorded by someone like us, who could use special hardware to listen in. Can we get a look at the security cameras at the sheriff's offices for this morning prior to oh-nine-forty-five? If Glover is seen on their coverage, we'll know if it's someone working at one of their facilities—*if* Glover paid them a visit, that is."

"We can do that using a cover story that won't link to Glover. But there are a lot of units in the field with computer access. If the request came from one of those, we're still in the dark."

"Right, but at least we'll be able to rule out a lot of county employees. We're thinking that Glover's contact is someone assigned to this area, so I'll need a list. And see what details you

can get concerning an unsolved local homicide. The vic's name
was Zeke Perry. He lived on Quail Run."

"Understood. Give me two hours."

"Thanks." Lee ended the call, then considered trying to get
a warrant to monitor Glover's cell phone conversations. But it
was too soon for that. Maybe later, when they could come up
with something specific to be listening for. It was close to noon
now, and Diane was going to call him during her lunch break. If
she had time, she'd also be coming "home" for lunch so they
could share information and coordinate their efforts. They'd
agreed that he wouldn't call her at work today unless it was
an emergency. After that, an occasional call from a boyfriend
would only enhance her cover to customers and other employees at the store—Anna Guzman not included.

Lee was looking in the refrigerator, trying to decide what
kind of sandwiches to have for lunch, when his cell phone rang.

"Hey, it's me, sweetie," Diane said. "I'm going to get an hour
for lunch, so how about fixing us some sandwiches and meeting
me halfway? I'll give you a call when I leave, maybe in ten minutes."

"Gotcha. I've been working on some new stuff," Lee said
cryptically, not knowing if someone was standing close enough
to Diane to hear him. "I'll bring something cold in the cooler.
You want one sandwich or two?"

"One and a half? And I'll bring some chips. Love ya,
sweetie." She ended the call.

"Back at you," Lee said, closing the phone. He'd hurry with
the sandwiches and get as far north as possible, giving them
more time together. Their conversations were encrypted and no
one could listen in, but he still didn't like giving or getting sensitive information over a phone.

He climbed into the big SUV within eight minutes, the
sandwiches, two colas, and some apples in the small cooler on

the passenger-side floorboard. There had still been no sign of Glover since he left early in the morning. Since there was only one main road leading to the interstate, it was possible they'd pass each other on the way. Lee wondered if Glover would break in or carry out some mischief if he found out their house was unoccupied. The surveillance cameras in their double-wide were well hidden and motion activated now, so they'd have that covered, and the laptop was also hidden well, behind the washing machine.

Traffic was light heading north, and Lee got a good look at the Manzano Mountains to his left, and beyond that, farther north, the Sandia Mountains. The fault block range, weathered but still standing more than ten thousand feet in places, was called the Manzanos south of Tijeras Canyon, and the Sandias north of that location. I-40, of course, ran east and west through the dividing point, and was at least a half hour away on a route that at times twisted and turned through the woodland foothills.

Lee recalled the drive through the canyon back in 1945 on one of his first patrols as a New Mexico state police officer. US 66 had been mapped out by then, but the road was still narrow and dangerous at times. Its fame as the Main Street of America—Route 66—was still a decade or more away at the time, and when the weather got rough, travel through the canyon had been interesting, to say the least.

His phone rang and he answered, using his headset.

"I'm on the way, Lee, about five miles south now. I didn't get away exactly on time. Did you manage to get a good look at our new neighbor's place?" Diane asked. Her signal faded a little.

"Yeah, somewhat," he said over the static. "We might lose contact for a while because of the terrain, but try again if the connection is broken."

"Right. Hey, I just passed Glover. He's parked beside the road about a mile south of Howard's."

"You sure?" Lee hoped it was just a coincidence.

"Damned sure. I think he smiled when I checked out the vehicle. Red pickup."

"What's he doing now?"

"Don't know, I just went around a curve. I'm reaching the twisty, climbing section where the road's been cut and blasted out of the hillsides. Remember those bore holes in the rocks?"

"Think he was waiting for you?" Lee asked, then the connection was lost. The terrain was interfering again.

He waited for her to call back. She'd be negotiating the curves and hopefully had both hands on the wheel of her pickup, using her phone headset, as he was doing. The vehicle she was using was ten years old, but was supposed to be in tip-top mechanical condition, with good tires.

When the phone rang he answered immediately. "Diane?" Lee heard her voice, then it faded a little before it became clear.

". . . right behind me, being an asshole."

"He's following you, then."

"Yeah, but when I touched my brakes, he faded back about five car lengths. If he's got a stock engine in that crate, I can outrun the prick once I get out of these hills."

Lee's heart was pumping. "Think he might want to force you off the road? Don't let him try to go around you."

"I'm more worried he'll cause an accident if anyone comes around the curve when he tries to pass. He's gotten awful close already, despite the double line."

"If he's got a death wish, let him go alone."

"I hear you."

"Listen, Diane, if we get disconnected, I'll call back. Make him your priority, and don't let him run into you." Lee knew Diane was an expert behind the wheel during a crisis, but she didn't have the quickness of a vampire. And even then, a civilian in the wrong place at the wrong time could really mess up your day.

"Okay. Do we have a plan besides that?"

"How close are you to topping the mesa out of the foothills?"

"At the speed I'm going, maybe five minutes. You getting close?"

"Yeah. I remember there's a turnoff on the left onto a dirt road once you round the last curve and top out. Take it, but be watching for me in case I time my arrival too soon." For the thousandth time, Lee was grateful that his memory was almost perfect. Once he saw something, it usually stuck in his mind forever.

"I'll keep track of the mile markers. Let you know when we're close."

"Good. What's Glover doing now?"

"Getting close again. I lost speed on the hill. But he should fade as well in a few seconds."

Lee was multitasking now, his eyes on the road markers, going over the last trip this way mental image by image, passing slower traffic, and trying to decide what to do if they got Glover in a vise. Too bad killing him outright wasn't an option.

But maybe he could come awfully damned close.

CHAPTER 5

Diane, you think that Glover knows you're on the cell phone?"

"I'm not holding anything, and this amazing hair hides the earphone and mike pretty well, so I have no idea, really."

"How about if you wait until he gets close again, then fake out you're trying to make a call but can't get through?" he suggested.

"I see where you're going with this," she answered. "He may become even less cautious if he sees I'm unable to raise any help and am trying to make it home."

A few more minutes went by. Lee could hear the sound of the truck engine and Diane's breathing and an occasional muttered curse.

"Oh shit!" she finally said quite distinctly.

"What shit?"

"I was just acting out the no-signal thing, like you suggested. He must have seen it, because now he's trying to get close again. Tailgating.

"Passing mile marker twelve," she added shortly. "Nearing the top of the hill. He's right on my ass, I hope he doesn't ram me when I try to turn. If someone is coming and I have to stop . . ."

"Think positive, woman. I'm a mile away, and closing fast. I'll be there in a half minute or less."

"Wish I could see you. Damned trees."

Lee slowed, not wanting to risk a head-on with Diane if she was crossing his lane when he came upon her, turning.

A few more seconds went by. "Here we go," she shouted.

Lee heard the squeal of tires, but it was coming from outside as well as over the phone connection. His SUV dropped down from a rise. Diane was a hundred yards ahead, raising dust from the side road as her pickup tires skidded, grabbing for traction on the dirt and gravel.

Glover was sliding across the road, trying to stay with the unexpected maneuver, and looked up, seeing Lee nearly upon him.

Lee kept his cool, eased off on the gas, and steered to his left, going into the lane Glover was now leaving nearly sideways. As Lee shot past him, Glover was locked onto the steering wheel, trying to keep from rolling.

Lee hit the brakes and executed a perfect moonshiner's turn, sliding to a stop in the left-hand lane, facing the opposite direction. He watched Glover's pickup leave the shoulder, bounce a few times, then slide to a dust cloud-filled stop two hundred yards past the spot where Diane had turned off.

Flooring it, Lee raced over and pulled in front of Glover's truck, cutting him off. "Let's show him there's no way we could be cops," he said, dropping the cell phone headset on the seat.

The idiot hadn't been belted in, and was still disoriented when Lee yanked open the driver's side door.

"Picked the wrong woman to jack around with, honky," Lee yelled, deciding to play the role of a 70s pissed-off Navajo lunatic.

"Honky?" Glover mumbled, trying to fend off Lee with his hands.

Lee realized he'd been speaking right out of the stoner age and Glover had probably been in diapers at the time. He grabbed the nut by the front of his jacket and yanked him out of the cab. A cell phone fell to the ground, and Lee picked it up, confirming the provider from the logo before pulling out the battery and tossing it into the bed of Glover's truck. He flipped the phone itself a dozen feet away into some brush beside a pine tree.

Diane had stopped her own vehicle, backed up, and was now running over to join them. "Kick his ass, Lee. Kick his ass," she demanded, her clenched fists out. The less like cops they behaved the better, and now the competition was on as to who could be more freaked out and illegal, him or her.

Lee noticed a pickup stacked high with firewood coming down the highway. It slowed to a crawl as it got close. "What are *you* looking at?" Lee yelled, swinging around Glover so the driver of the old truck could see him.

The driver, a Hispanic man in his early sixties, gaped, his mouth dropped, then he sped off, raising smoke from his overworked engine.

"You're going to pay for this," Glover managed, dangling there, helpless but defiant and angry now that he realized he'd escaped injury.

"Still a tough guy, huh?" Diane yelled, a wild-eyed look in her eyes as she pointed her shiny, polished, black-and-gray–striped finger in Glover's face. "Well, *you're* going to pay for *this*." She picked up a boulder and smashed Glover's windshield. "And this, too." She kicked up with her boot and broke the headlight on the driver's side. "Following too close can lead to serious accidents, butthead."

Lee laughed, trying to sound as much like Jack Nicholson in *The Shining* as possible. Diane was doing a better job, however, and had managed to retain a very credible psycho expression without going over the top.

Suddenly she smiled and crossed her arms, pushing up her cleavage in a cheap but sexy gesture. "Sweetie. We're going to have to either beat the crap out of this gringo or set fire to him and leave it up to God." She worked a cigarette lighter out of her impossibly tight jeans pocket and held it up, thumbing a three-inch flame.

"I haven't had lunch yet, and I have to be back at work in," she looked at her flashy silver watch, "less than a half hour now. Decide for me."

"Only *you* can prevent fat-ass fires, Smokey the Newt." He turned and grinned at Diane. "Whaddya say we push his little red wagon into an arroyo and make him walk home," Lee suggested, slamming Glover into the side of the truck, pinning him there against the metal, a foot off the ground, as he pretended to consider what to do next.

"Not if I have to work up a sweat," Diane said, putting away the lighter. Then she reached inside Glover's truck and pulled out the ignition keys. She waved the keys in front of the dangling man's face, and when he reached up for them, kneed him in the groin.

He crumpled in midair, managing somehow not to scream. Then Lee dropped him to the ground. Glover went into a fetal position, sounding like he was going to puke.

"Gonna bother us again, dipshit?" Lee asked very politely.

Glover made some heaving noises, then lost his breakfast and maybe his lunch, as well.

"I'll take that as a no." Diane dropped the keys into the middle of the mess, then winked at Lee. "Let's go have lunch. All this exercise has made me hungry."

As Lee drove away north, following Diane in her pickup, he

took a last look in the rearview mirror. Glover was holding his key ring by a stick, rubbing it across the ground.

Lee and Diane were parked just off the road beneath some pine trees, sitting on the tailgate of her pickup, eating sandwiches.

"There's no way he'll think we could be cops now, Lee," Diane said. "Think he'll go home now and set fire to our stuff?"

"He'll probably want to. But Glover also knows the place is a rental, not really ours. If he decides to burn the place down, he'll want us inside at the time. My guess is that he'll hold back, maybe get some reinforcements, then try to catch us cold later on. It could be a week or two, or even later. But we've got him pissed off, that's clear. He'll want to inflict as much damage as possible."

"Like kill us?"

"Yeah, especially if that guy with the firewood lives around here and spreads the story of us manhandling him. Glover has a rep to maintain. If people start standing up to him, he loses power and influence. He can't let that happen, and it's clear that around here he's been having it all his way."

Diane finished the rest of her sandwich, then took another sip of cola before speaking. "Would he try and sic the local deputies on us? Or would he be concerned that it would tell us who's on his payroll?"

Lee shook his head. "If anyone comes after us, it'll be on the sly, Diane. At least that'll be my guess. Let's make it clear we're keeping an eye on him when he's around us, but otherwise hold off with any further contact whenever possible."

"I'll listen to the customers, ask as many questions as I dare, and try and sort out his friends from his enemies. I want to pick up any gossip, learn who's been bothering, stuff like that. But if he comes after me again, I'm not going to wait to see if he pushes." Diane reached down and patted her handgun, a small .380 she'd decided to carry in concealed mode for this assignment.

"I agree. Now let's cover what we found out on our own before you have to leave for the store."

Before they parted, Lee brought out the bullet-resistant vests they'd hidden in the SUV and they put them on. Resembling T-shirts, the vests offered some protection from gunfire—less from knife attacks—without the bulk and heat of standard-issue equipment. Diane had to button up another button on her blouse and lose some sex appeal, but she actually welcomed the idea, still being uncomfortable in the role of a "semi-slut," as she expressed it.

Lee returned home. There were no vehicles in Glover's driveway, and it didn't appear that anyone had even come up the graveled road since he'd left to meet Diane for lunch. Glover had probably taken his damaged truck to be repaired, and Lee didn't know if there were any local businesses that could immediately replace a windshield. He might have to go into Albuquerque or Moriarity, farther east.

Lee went inside, checked out the surveillance cameras, and confirmed that no one appeared to have entered the place while he was gone. There was no phone hooked up, but there was a phone book, so Lee checked and confirmed that the closest listed auto glass on-site repair place was in southeast Albuquerque along the interstate.

Looking out the window, Lee saw a vehicle coming up the road. It was a Jeep, and when it got closer he saw Glover behind the wheel. He'd obviously arranged for other transportation, and from a source much closer than Albuquerque. Judging from the amount of time that had elapsed, it was probably someone within a half hour's travel time. Lee wondered if the Jeep was a rental or a loaner from a local merchant, or perhaps a friend of Glover's.

Then again, knowing Glover, he considered the likely possibility that it belonged to someone who'd been forced to give up the vehicle. Lee decided to run the plate once he got a look at it.

The Jeep accelerated slightly, swerved to the side of the road, and struck a child's yellow-and-orange plastic tricycle with a crunch. Pieces flew everywhere. Lee thought about what psychologists called transference. Good thing there hadn't been somebody's cat crossing the road. Glover was one sick dude.

Glover was all smiles when he arrived, but he stopped in the street before pulling in. His face lost expression as he checked out his own place, maybe expecting something to be amiss. He also took a long look at Lee standing in the window, watching him. Lee nodded, without expression, to let the man know he was being watched, as well. Glover gunned the engine and pulled into his driveway.

Lee thought once again of the possibility of bugging Glover's cell phone, then considered placing a bug in his vehicle, or on Glover himself. But it was a risky proposition. There was no quicker way to warn Glover that he was being investigated than to have him discover a bug. But maybe there was another way . . . he'd discuss it with Diane when she came home that evening.

Diane arrived home at 6:00, bringing a barbecued chicken and some groceries with her. They ate while she brought him up to date. "I called SAC Logan once I left the store, and they still don't have any leads on the missing boy. Timothy's high-end bike is missing; it's what he used to ride between the two residences, apparently. The official search parties have given up, nobody got any hits with the tracking dogs, and checks with the known sex offenders in the area have still come up blank. The parents have finally stopped fighting, at least long enough to get together on the search. They're going to church groups, asking for volunteers to walk the three miles between their residences, scour the woods and any place the kid might have gone."

"Any chance that there'll be a ransom demand?"

"Nothing yet, but keep in mind it may not be a routine kidnapping. The boy's bike alone is worth a thousand or more."

"People have been killed for a lot less than that. Are they sure the kid didn't just run away? A war between parents can destroy children in the process," he said.

"Logan talked to those who'd interviewed the family, teachers, neighbors. The kid wasn't really happy about the situation, but he seemed to be coping, according to them. Of course, each parent was trying to keep him happy with bribes, entertainment . . . like that."

"Any perverts in this area?"

"None that are on the list. One businessman in Tijeras has a record with underage girls, but he's already been checked out. Has a solid alibi, apparently."

Lee nodded. "Okay, then Glover stays in our sights. Now that we've gotten him really ticked off, it's just going to be a matter of time before he strikes back. After all, he may be the one who carved up Zeke Perry. Too bad we can't get more details other than the sheriff's department report, which didn't really have much we can use. Perry's widow now lives out of state, apparently. But we'll have to be ready and catch him in the act if we intend on putting him away."

"If we could get a warrant, there's stolen merchandise in his house right now, right?" Diane asked.

"The only item I could confirm was stolen was the computer.

But Glover might be able to intimidate the rightful owner into saying he sold it to him for cash. It might even be some kind of payoff—an insurance scam. I need to get a longer look inside Glover's home."

"But without a search warrant, the evidence would be thrown out, Lee. All we'd get out of it is intelligence gathering. Is that what you're after?"

He nodded. "If we can learn anything that'll help us direct our efforts and bring him down for something big, it'll be worth it."

"Good point. Winning is the only thing that matters when it comes to putting a sleazeball like him away. Let's just make sure there are no innocents that get caught up in this, so we can live with ourselves later on."

"Agreed. There are too many innocents involved already, like your boss, who lives thirty miles away but is still afraid of him and his reach. And we'll want to target his contacts, too, especially whoever he'd got working in law enforcement against us, the same individual who found out about my 'rap' sheet."

"Okay. So if Glover leaves tonight, I'll follow him while you go over his house inch by inch."

"Actually, Diane, you should get the black bag job, not me. You know where the surveillance camera is, and you can pick locks. Once he's gone, all you have to do is make sure you leave no trace you were there. Remember the front entrance and the possibility of an alarm, though."

"Sounds doable. And it would make better use of our abilities. You can follow him in the SUV without the need for headlights—and you can overhear a conversation from a distance without special equipment."

"Wrong. My equipment *is* special," he said with a wink.

"Vampires!" she mouthed inaudibly, still careful about their most critical secret even though there was no reason to believe they'd been bugged. "Or is it just that you're a man? Every guy believes his equipment is special, you know."

"I'm not every guy," Lee asserted, then glanced for the tenth time within the hour toward the window across the living room. He'd positioned his chair so he could see the front of Glover's house and the section of driveway where the Jeep was parked.

"Our neighbor might be up to something," Lee said without inflection. "Don't make it obvious, but he's outside, poking around that Jeep."

"Like he's going somewhere?" Diane took a sip of coffee, watching out of the corner of her eyes. Like Lee, she'd learned the old cop and CIA tactic of watching but not turning your head to make surveillance more natural and less attention getting, especially from the target.

"Or trying to find a place to stash something he wants to keep out of sight. He's rumored to deal in drugs and other contraband, and won't want it sitting out in plain sight," Lee said.

Glover went back inside, and Lee checked his watch. It would be dark soon; the sun had already set.

The man came out ten minutes later wearing a leather jacket and carrying a toolbox. He had a beer bottle in his other hand, but took a big swig, finishing it off, then threw it into his trash can.

Lee thought he heard a burp, then Glover placed the toolbox onto the floorboard on the front passenger side. A minute later, the man went to the door and locked it, leaving the porch light on.

"Gotta go in a minute," Lee said, looking around the room and finding his own jacket on the small sofa. Inside the pocket, he knew, was the 9 mm Beretta he always carried off-duty. The small backup .45 was in the refrigerator, and the commando dagger was still on his ankle in the special sheath.

"Wanna take my truck?" Diane offered, bringing out the keys. "Less flashy."

"Good idea." He held up his hand and caught the key ring, then brought out his own and tossed them to her.

"Try to give me ten minutes leeway when he heads home, Lee. I'm going to need to move slow to avoid any obvious traps and such he may have set up."

"Just put the phone on vibrate and keep it close. Glover may have some skills with covert operations that we don't know about, so be aware of the obvious and the subtle when you go through his stuff."

He knew Diane had the skills, but he still wanted her to be very careful. Glover would be out to get them now, for sure, if only because he'd lost face. If he also happened to discover they were cops out to nail him, Lee had no doubt Glover would kill them the instant he got the chance.

"Lee, we never did decide about whether to place a passive bug in his home. With that wand of his, if he finds one . . ."

"Yeah. I know. We should hold off for now, but when you look around his place, see if you can find a location that would work. Just thinking ahead. If he brings women home, prostitutes or whatever, there may be some pillow talk we'd like to hear, especially if we're talking about possible druggies. It's a long shot, but . . ."

"Okay. He's getting ready to go. I'll wait ten minutes, and if I don't hear from you, I'll make a move."

Just outside, they heard Glover start the Jeep, rev the engine a few times, then back out of the driveway. He drove off in a hurry, gravel and dust raised in a rooster tail. The man had left his porch light on—a complication for Diane breaking in.

Lee moved quickly, getting his jacket and backup .45, then verifying he had his cell phone. "I'll try to beat him back. And if

I can't and he returns first, I'll wait a while so it won't be obvious I was following."

"Take the grocery bag that's still on the table. You can bring it in with you, like you made a late trip to Howard's or wherever," Diane suggested.

"Good idea," Lee said, and gave her a quick kiss. "Be careful."

"You, too." She gave him a scrunchy-nosed smile he'd learned was special, only for him, then Diane watched as he went outside and climbed into the old pickup. He set the grocery bag on the floorboard so it couldn't be seen unless a person came right up to the window.

It was nearly dark, and Lee backed out quickly, wanting the chance to look ahead and see how far down Quail Run Glover had gone. If the man decided to double back, Lee would have to put on his headlights quickly, take off on his fake errand, then wait a while before returning with the groceries.

Otherwise, Lee would move in close enough to spot Glover's Jeep, then follow him. Once on the main highway, it might get tricky and he'd have to stay sharp. Lee didn't want to cause an accident if some poor civilian got close to his unlit vehicle.

It was dark enough now so that headlights were needed by the night impaired, and all but two of the homes he passed had porch lights on and TVs glowing. A woman in a cocktail waitress's short skirt was unloading groceries, and waved as he drove slowly by. "Headlights!" he heard her yell—as if he didn't already know. He chose not to respond, of course.

Ahead, nearing the last two houses on either side of the lane, Lee could see the Jeep clearly, but there was something odd about it that didn't register for a second. Glover had left home with his lights on, but switched them off during the mile-long stretch of graveled road. The man was trying to make sure that if either he or Diane were following they wouldn't be able to see which way he'd gone.

Too bad for him. Glover pulled out to the right, south and away from the interstate nearly thirty miles away, and drove in the general direction of Mountainair, which was more than fifty miles away on this secondary highway. To the west of that community was another pass in the mountains, which had nearly petered out by then. Beyond the mountains to the west was I-25 and the Rio Grande corridor. Maybe Glover had business in Belen or Los Lunas. The area farther west was open and sparsely populated, and the largest city between them and Texas was Tucumcari, around a hundred and fifty miles east as the crow flies. Santa Rosa was about half that distance, but even smaller than Tucumcari.

Lee suspected that the man had a closer destination. Glover's strength as a bully lay in his control over a rural area where most families lived in isolation or very small developments of a dozen homes or less. In Albuquerque, the man would have just been another punk.

Before they'd gone ten miles, Glover slowed and pulled over to the side of the road, stopping to park beside several vehicles that were beside a run-down-looking place called the Buffalo Tavern. Interestingly enough, Lee recalled that it was the same bar where Glover's neighbor had been knifed.

Lee moved over to the shoulder of the highway about a hundred yards up the road from the bar and stopped, turning off the engine to listen. The faint guitar sounds of a country-and-western song drifted along the pine tree-lined road. A vehicle door slammed, then, about ten seconds later, the music got louder for a few seconds, then died away to a murmur.

It appeared that Glover had gone inside. Needing more information, Lee started up the engine again and drove by, his lights on so that anyone outside the bar wouldn't think something odd was going on. Nobody was outside, so Lee continued down the road another fifty yards and pulled over, parking off the road just enough to avoid a potential accident.

He climbed out of the pickup, shut the door as quietly as possible, then ran quickly back to the establishment, stopping behind a tree fifty feet away to watch.

The tavern was small, with only one customer entrance halfway down the side of the rectangular building—the side facing the parking lot, so it wouldn't have been smart to go inside. Glover would have spotted him immediately. Lee also knew that if he got caught snooping around outside, someone was very likely to draw a knife or fetch a gun. It was illegal to bring a firearm into a liquor-selling establishment, but that wasn't always strictly enforced in rural New Mexico, especially if you were friends with the owner. And Glover, for one, wouldn't have taken such a law seriously anyway.

Lee saw the neon signs in the windows promoting Coors, Bud, and the specialty of the house, buffalo burgers. Sissy wine drinkers either already knew this wasn't their kind of place, or would learn the bad news the moment they crossed the threshold. From the bumper stickers on the vehicles, those that still had bumpers, Lee suspected this was where the bullies, not the victims, hung out. One of the least offensive messages was DON'T LIKE MY DRIVING? DIAL 277-EAT-SHIT.

The night was quiet. Even the evening breeze sent very little information about the forest through the pines, but the guitars and wailing continued from within. Lee realized that there was an open window around the side opposite the parking lot. From the surprisingly appetizing barbecue scent wafting through the air, it was probably the kitchen window. Any eavesdropping would give him more information about the staff than the guests, probably. Still, it was worth checking out.

Lee walked back in the direction of his car, then slipped up against the rear of the building. There was a metal door about a third of the way down and a high, concrete porch that held two big, metal trash cans. A space for combustible materials had been loosely cleared away for about ten feet, but a few weeds were popping out of the ground nevertheless. Beyond that were tall pine trees. Lee decided to approach from the forest, so he worked his way in, then turned when he got to the open window, using the big roof vents to locate the kitchen.

The window was open at the top, serving as an additional vent, so Lee had two choices. He could get beneath the window and listen, in which case he probably wouldn't be able to hear much except for the music, or climb a tree and look in. Providing the angle was right, he'd be able to see some of those inside then.

The brush had been cleared away pretty well around the trees—it was a smart strategy for anyone living within a forest—and he was able to find the perfect tree. A few seconds was all it took for him to find a branch he could stand on and look through the opened window.

There were no screens on the windows, which made him wonder about bugs in the kitchen. Maybe the windows weren't open all evening. Lee angled to his right and was able to see right through the kitchen pass-through and behind the bar counter itself. Seated at the bar was Glover—a big sandwich and mug of Coors before him—and to his left a slender Indian girl who looked barely legal and had spiked, blond-frosted and black hair. She was wearing a halter top and had tattoos like bracelets on her arms, a watch, but no rings.

Glover was working on his sandwich, not talking, and the woman was sipping a cola through a straw and picking at a plate of french fries, the kind with the skins still on them.

The only other thing Lee could see was the big-haired barmaid—and the shelves just below her, which held kegs on tap and a cut-down pump-action shotgun. The downside was that somebody had turned the music up—maybe from an old-time jukebox still in service—and the chances of hearing anything less than a gunshot made eavesdropping impossible.

Lee tried to read lips, but couldn't get anything from Glover. At the moment Glover was concerned with dinner, not conversation, though he seemed to be watching the Indian gal's breasts more than anything else in the bar.

The young woman seemed amped up—edgy and nervous—and Lee began to wonder if she was supporting a habit. Perhaps she intended to score tonight in exchange for her services. Was Glover her supplier, or just a potential customer?

Hoping he wasn't going to have to watch or listen to a sex show tonight before a drug sale went down, Lee debated the best time to drop back out of the tree and get ready to relocate before his quarry took off.

He watched Glover taking a final bite of sandwich. As he was chewing, the young lady reached over and tickled the center of his palm with her finger, leaning toward him at the same time, licking her lips. Glover sat up straight. When he picked up his beer and finished it with a long, hurried swallow, Lee knew it was time to move.

Diane quickly put on a pair of black polyester slacks, long-sleeved spandex top, and black cap, tucking her hair up inside. She'd already placed her burglary tools in a fanny pack along with the small digital camera, so the final step was to put on the latex gloves.

Making certain that the phone was set on vibrate, hooked to her belt, she stepped out onto the porch with her fanny pack in place and her other gear in hand. She'd turned out the lights in the house several minutes ago, and now her eyes were accustomed to

the dark. With the city lights on the opposite side of the mountains and the only illumination coming from the yellow bug
light atop Glover's porch, the sky was surprisingly clear, the
stars twinkling in the cool of the evening. There was just a
slight breeze at the moment, but toward morning there would
be a downhill flow from the west, she suspected. Although the
silence that surrounded her would help her hear Glover's Jeep
coming up the road, hopefully Lee would tip her off long before
that.

Then she heard footsteps. Crouching low, she froze as a
slender figure in a hooded sweatshirt and sweatpants ran up the
street and stopped in front of Glover's gate. From the style of
canvas shoes and the curve of the person's hips, Diane got the
impression the person was a female. Whoever it was looked
around nervously, then opened the gate and ran up to Glover's
door.

Diane heard scraping sounds, like metal on metal, but she
couldn't see what was going on. The person was in a hurry, only
spending a half minute in front of the door before turning, putting something into her pocket, then running back out of the
yard.

"Shut the gate, dummy," Diane heard, then the woman went
back, closed Glover's gate, and raced back down the street.

Diane walked out slowly, watching the fleeing figure. A few
minutes later, the porch light of the second house down on the
south side came on for just a second, then went back out again.

"Let's see what you've done," Diane muttered to herself as
she put on her sunglasses. It was a foolhardy move in nearly any
other nighttime situation, but this was to save her night vision
and speed up the entry into Glover's house. Walking across the
road quickly and as quietly as possible, she opened the gate and
crossed to the front porch. The previous visitor had used a

sharp object to scratch GLOVER SUCKS into the painted metal door. The crude message was at least four inches high.

Quickly Diane cupped the aluminum foil cover she'd fashioned earlier over the porch light and held it in place while she pressed the attached duct tape to the building itself. A few extra strips of tape were needed to get a really good seal, but now she could be sure the foil wouldn't come loose.

The whole operation had taken about twenty seconds, and with the light hidden, nobody could see her picking the lock. She took off her sunglasses and stuck them into a pocket. It would have been a lot easier to have just broken the bulb, but her visit tonight had to go unnoticed.

Diane brought out a small flashlight with a tightly focused beam and got to work with her simple tools. She'd learned a lot about defeating locks since she'd met Lee, and she knew she'd be able to get inside quickly.

What she was doing was illegal, of course. There was no warrant and the Patriot Act sneak-and-peek provisions couldn't be applied here. But she and Lee had formulated a plan that required two things—gathering intelligence on Glover's activities so they could focus their efforts to nail him and whoever was working with him, and secondly, to convince him they couldn't possibly be undercover cops. Lee had suggested that they find a way to confront him and get him angry—basically to show him that they were equally bad, but enemies to him.

Thanks to what had happened at midday, they'd already reached their second goal. Now they needed to know more about what was going on in Glover's criminal life besides possessing possible stolen property and pissing off his neighbors.

Diane heard the click of the lock and moved it slightly so it wouldn't relatch. She swept the penlight beam around the opening, looking for any alarms. Lee hadn't seen any on his morning examination, but she was certain Glover had made some provisions inside to indicate if someone had trespassed. Maybe an interior camera that swept the doorways, or a motion detector, or something very low-tech.

Then she saw a cord, a large, round one like those attached to an appliance. Opening the door about a foot, she saw the cord went to an upright vacuum cleaner standing against the wall, out of the way but within arm's reach of the door. The vacuum was plugged in, which seemed odd. Had Glover acquired a cleanliness fetish?

The living room area carpet was a dark red, with a deep, soft pile and the pattern of the vacuum cleaner's sweep was clear even with her penlight. A quick look around the room didn't indicate any surveillance gear installed—no cameras in the corner, for instance—so Diane took a step into the room and closed the door behind her.

The only sound was the creaking of the building, contracting from daytime heat to evening cool, still, and the humming of the refrigerator in the kitchen. Like their own double-wide, Glover's had a dining room alcove on the other side of the living room, with counters and the kitchen area to the side. Beyond the kitchen was a small utility area and the back door.

Diane took a cautious step, then aimed her penlight down and noted she'd left a footprint in the carpet. Glover had gone low-tech. She'd just have to remember to vacuum up and replace the appliance in the same spot before leaving. After noting the pattern Glover had left on the carpet from his cleaning, she stepped into the room. The carpet ended in the dining room section, and down the hall to the right, so she had only one area to deal with.

Glover was no interior decorator, but there were a couple of decent-looking paintings of the Southwest, though they were impersonal enough for a credit union's decor, and Lee had correctly described the expensive furniture. The glow from a small monitor on the kitchen counter gave a decent view of the backyard, almost reaching to the fence, which was too dark to show any detail.

She moved quickly now, confirming more of the same items that Lee had reported, and took photographs with the digital camera. The flash probably wouldn't show beyond the street, certainly not all the way down the road to the next two houses in the development.

The hall closet held a couple of jackets and some kind of air purifier, unplugged, on the floor. She moved along and looked into the closets of each room, and, besides the expected clothing, found cases of expensive scotch, unopened, packaged video games, music CDs, iPods, computer software, and a high-quality scanner on a table—alone. There was undoubtedly a computer around somewhere, probably a laptop. She took photographs, close-ups to show the serial numbers on as much of the gear as possible.

When she got to the possible blackmail photographs in Glover's bedrooms, the ones with the people having sex, she took more photographs, getting as close as possible, but keeping the camera at an angle so the flash wouldn't bounce right back and mess up the image. If she hadn't been worried about the extra light, she would have turned on the lamp on the dresser to get better exposures.

If any more compromising contraband, like drugs, was around, she wasn't able to find any in the time she'd given herself, fifteen minutes. Nor did she find any weapons or a computer. She did find at least a thousand dollars in cash in the refrigerator, in the produce drawer at the bottom in one of those self-sealing bags. More money was probably hidden around the place, but she was running low on time.

Backtracking her route, she verified that nothing was out of place—at least from her visit—and the backyard monitor was clear of intruders, not counting moths around the lights. Finally back in the living room section, she took a quick look outside, verified that her cell phone was working, then turned on the vacuum and erased her footprints across the red carpet. Setting the vacuum back in its original place, she set the lock and backed outside, pulling the door shut.

The sound of a vehicle coming slowly up the graveled road alerted her to the danger. A quick grab and pull removed the cover over the light, and she wadded up the foil and tapped it into a big ball with one hand, then stuffed the flattened mass into her pocket. As she walked away, she quickly pulled off her gloves and placed them in another pocket.

The vehicle didn't stop and turn at one of the houses down the street, so she passed through the gate, shifted the fanny pack to her side, then started jogging toward the oncoming headlights, staying on the side of the road. She hadn't gone a hundred feet before the car stopped and a spotlight came on, focused on her. Stopping and faking surprise, she shielded her eyes with one hand, then noted the white, blue-striped sheriff's department vehicle. "Something wrong?"

"Good evening . . . ma'am. I noticed you came from up the street. You staying at that double-wide up on the right?"

"No, Officer. The guy who lives there is a real asshole. I wouldn't stay with him if you paid me. I live across the street. That's my boyfriend's SUV in the driveway."

She heard the deputy step out of his unit, though she couldn't see him because of the glare. Looking away from the light, she walked toward the front of the car, keeping her hands out, away from her body. No sense in getting shot because of a misinterpreted motion.

"Carrying any identification on you?" The deputy, clad in the tan uniform worn by Bernalillo County officers, was a tall

Anglo man with graying temples, glasses, and big ears. The county man looked remarkably fit for a man in his early fifties. His flashlight swept up and down her body twice, lingering on her breasts a little longer than was necessary, but understandably considering her cover identity. She'd minimized her makeup, not wanting to leave any physical evidence at Glover's, but her hot, easy-chick look, with the rebel hair and tight top, was sending signals to every man she met.

"My driver's license is in my wallet inside my fanny pack. Wanna see?"

"Yes, ma'am. Please take out your wallet slowly, then remove the license." The flashlight lingered on her hands and waist, but the deputy's free hand was lingering above the butt of his service weapon. It was an intelligent practice, considering he was alone and backup was probably a half hour or more away.

She'd been careful to put her ID, wallet, and house keys in a separate zippered pocket of the fanny pack. Showing a camera and burglary tools to a stranger or cop wasn't a smart move. She brought out her wallet. "Here you go, Deputy Harmon," she said, reading his name tag.

Deputy Harmon looked at the license, then made a quick comparison of the two images. "Changed your hair color, Miss Garcia."

"That was two colors ago. It's shorter now, too. Like it?" Diane asked, beaming a smile.

"Nothing not to like about you, Miss Garcia. You need to update your address on your operator's license, though, if you live around here now. Please remain where you are for a moment. I'll be right back."

"Okay. But can you hurry, please? I need to finish my workout before I cool down." Diane knew the deputy was going to run her cover ID and learn Diane Garcia had been arrested two

years ago for killing an abusive boyfriend . . . and been acquit-
ted. She'd picked the background herself, wanting to give
Glover something to consider when he inevitably inquired
about his troublesome neighbors.

The deputy climbed back out of his patrol vehicle and
walked toward her, his hand resting on the butt of his service
weapon and the flashlight checking her hands for a weapon.
She wondered if Deputy Harmon was Glover's stooge, and if
her neighbor would be getting the news about her background
later tonight.

"Where's your boyfriend?"

"Went to pick up some beer, maybe rent a movie. He
should be back before long."

"Mind telling me his name?"

"His name is Lee. You looking for him?"

"Lee his first name or last?"

"You looking for him?"

"I won't know that until I get his whole name, will I?"

"Guess not." Diane was enjoying being a pain in the butt. If
the deputy was honest, he was used to being jerked around. If
he was a Glover toady, he deserved much worse.

"You sure you live across the street up there?" He pointed
toward her double-wide. "It looked to me like you suddenly appeared in front of your neighbor's house. The light was off, and
then suddenly came on. Then, there you were."

Diane grinned. "Just like magic. Or maybe he has one of
those outside lights that comes on when somebody gets close. I
ran by his driveway. Hey, why don't you go check out his place?
Maybe I kicked in his door and stole his TV?" She took a step
back, opened her arms, and gave him a good look at her. Then
she chuckled.

"Okay, get stupid with me if you want. I can get a look at the
tags on your boyfriend's SUV and see just who this Lee really

is—if he exists. And maybe you should unlock your 'front door' and prove to me it's really your house."

"You trying to intimidate me, Deputy Harmon? You ran my ID through the DMV. From what you saw, I'm willing to bet you know what I do when I've had enough of somebody giving me shit."

Deputy Harmon tried to look confident when he chuckled, but his change in stance showed he'd decided she might be getting dangerous.

His hand hovered over his handgun for a second. "I can haul you in and book you as a burglary suspect, Miss Garcia. Or you can cooperate. It's up to you, ma'am."

Diane knew he was watching his language because their conversations were being recorded through the microphone and recorder most law enforcement used today to protect themselves from lawsuits and harassment. "It's getting to be a long day, Deputy Harmon. I'll go back up to my place and let myself in just to prove I really live there. You can do your job any ole way you want, I suppose. Just don't ruin my evening or piss off my boyfriend, okay? The guy across the street was spying on me with a telescope last night, and he nearly got the damned thing shoved up his butt."

"That so?" Deputy Harmon seemed impressed. He obviously had heard of Newt Glover, one way or the other.

"I'm going to jog home. Just don't run over me, okay?" Diane turned and started back up the road easily, not wanting to wait for permission, but going slowly enough to show she wasn't making a run for it, either. The last thing she wanted was to give the officer a reason to try and put her in the squad car. If she resisted, one way or the other it would blow their cover. The camera in her fanny pack had at least thirty photos of the interior of Glover's home and that would be hard to explain.

Illuminated in the headlights of the deputy's car, she made

her way up the road, sticking to the left-hand lane. When she got to the driveway, the deputy yelled. "Miss Garcia?"

Diane stopped and turned. "Yessir?"

"Please wait there a moment while I check this other residence. Then, if everything is clear, you can go on home and I'll be out of your hair for the evening."

"Go for it." Diane shook her head slowly, watching as the deputy wrote down the tag numbers and letters on the SUV behind her. He called in the information, then climbed out and walked over to Glover's front yard. Diane heard him laugh when he saw the fresh graffiti on the door. A minute later, he was back at the door of his unit. He looked inside, probably at the display of his computer screen, then turned and crossed his arms. "You and Begay are an interesting pair. Where is he right now, by the way?" Deputy Harmon, resting his hand on the butt of his weapon, aimed his flashlight toward the front porch. "Inside?"

Just then Diane felt the cell phone on her belt vibrating.

CHAPTER 6

Lee watched as Glover and the young woman—who was wearing skin-tight slacks that ended at midcalf and dressy shoes with big heels—fondled and groped their way to his pickup.

He had to decide right away whether to stay and watch in case anything went down—or in this case, up—or hurry back to Diane's pickup so he could follow in case they drove away. Instinct told him that the sex part of Glover's evening would probably take place now, in the cab of the truck right there in the parking lot. A drug sale would probably cover the cost of the entertainment.

Or maybe not. Lee didn't think Glover would be stupid enough to carry any illegal drugs on him, or even in his vehicle. If he got stopped out on the highway, the arresting officer might not be someone on his payroll. With the state on two of the big smuggling corridors, stops in New Mexico often meant searches for drugs, and if Glover was with a hooker who was high on pills or whatever. . . .

Lee decided to wait. The two climbed into the truck, both on the passenger side, and Lee could see the seat being moved back and tilted down. "Get a room" was the phrase that came to mind. Since Lee wasn't into voyeurism, he was tempted to turn his head, but that was a bad idea when surveillance was the objective.

Fortunately, everything he didn't want to see took place below window level, and other than a few annoying groans, it was a nonevent. It certainly didn't take very long. A few minutes passed, but the girl didn't leave the vehicle as he expected. Instead, she sat up normally on the passenger side and fastened her seat belt. Lee then knew he'd have to run if he planned on following when Glover drove away.

Slipping away from his vantage point behind a pine tree, Lee ran quickly back to Diane's truck. If Glover drove in his direction, he'd have to duck and hope Glover didn't notice and identify the truck as Diane's. On the bright side, the sleazeball's blood pressure might still be up and he'd be lighting a cigarette or something equally traditional and be distracted.

Lee reached the pickup and jumped inside, just as Glover's truck pulled out into the highway and accelerated back north. While Lee doubted Glover was going to take the girl to his home, she was obviously going to remain with him for a while, perhaps for a replay at a new location. He could see two heads on opposite sides of the cab as an oncoming vehicle highlighted the pickup in passing. Glover obviously wasn't into cuddling.

Lee turned on his own headlights, then pulled out onto the highway and followed just close enough to keep the vehicle in sight. Glover had no reason to think Lee had followed him, and if the man left the highway with his passenger, Lee could always pass by, kill his lights and return, then follow him down the side road.

Glover drove just at the speed limit, another smart idea. The man obviously knew that officers frequently pulled over drivers who were going well *under* the speed limit at night, experience telling them that people who'd been drinking were often very concerned about getting caught behind the wheel.

In New Mexico, a person who was convicted of DWI had to pay for the installation of a Breathalyzer device that would keep the vehicle from starting if his or her blood alcohol level was above the legal limit. Of course, since corrupt judges and officers existed, those without money or influence would get most of the new hardware, but that went without saying.

About four miles farther north, Glover rounded a curve, then pulled off the road to the right onto a narrow pair of ruts, turned off his lights, then inched forward. Lee could see an old shed beyond, just the other side of a fence.

Lee slowed, checked to make sure no other vehicles were in the vicinity, then turned off his own lights and pulled off the road quickly about two hundred yards back. Lee parked so that Glover couldn't see his vehicle without reversing his route, then ran across the road and got as close as he could, trying to find a position where he could watch. If the man drove much farther, Lee knew he might not be able to catch up, but it was a calculated risk.

Glover stopped his vehicle with the front tires about even with the faded red structure, constructed of wood planks with a corrugated-metal sloping shed roof. There were no windows on the two sides of the structure that Lee could see, but the remnants of a rail-fence corral and an ancient water trough suggested it had once held horses or other livestock. Lee was across the road, nearly opposite the turnoff. He crouched low, staying beside the tall weeds that flourished beyond the shoulders where the runoff from rains settled. As long as he stood still, there was little chance of being seen unless Glover brought out a light and started searching.

Their windows were open, and Lee could hear Glover mumble something to the young woman. Then Glover climbed out of the vehicle and turned on a powerful flashlight. Lee dropped to the ground just below the level of the roadbed as

Glover swept the light around. The beam traveled over him, wavered, then stopped right at the spot where Lee was lying.

Lee stayed still but closed his eyes, knowing they could reflect light. Thank God he wasn't wearing his cap, it would have presented a structured shape that would have been hard to miss.

Lee heard footsteps drawing closer, then Glover yelled out, "Hey! What you doing there!"

There was a rustle behind Lee, then a very distinctive *moo*.

The young woman laughed, climbing out the driver's side. "Busted by a cow, sugar? Getting paranoid in your old age."

"Quiet, Breeann. You wanna wake up the whole county?" The beam of light continued around, and Lee risked a look. Glover was still checking for unscheduled visitors. He was either planning to meet someone here, or had come to visit his stash and was making sure there wasn't a stakeout in place.

"When you gonna get my goodies? I gotta get home to my old man or he's going to come looking for me," Breeann said, her voice now revealing a nasal whine.

"I'm shaking in my boots. Just get back into the truck. I'll be back in five minutes." Glover waited until Breeann climbed back into the truck, his flashlight beam directed at her tight behind. Then he turned off the flashlight, put on a pair of brown work gloves, and ducked under between two slack wires of the fence.

Glover walked over to the shack and disappeared around the side. Lee couldn't see what went on, but Glover returned just thirty seconds later, pocketing what looked like a plastic bag as he came around the building again. He stopped by the truck, took another quick look around with a rapid sweep of the flashlight, then opened the truck door. "Here you are. Enjoy! Just remember. If you ever mention where this came from . . ."

"Yeah, yeah, don't worry. I won't tell a soul."

"I know you won't." Glover's voice was low, filled with menace.

"You can trust me, sugar. Now, how about we go back to the bar? I'm going to call it a night."

"Oh, you want a ride back? That's going to cost you." He took off his gloves and tossed them into the truck.

There was a moment's silence, then Breeann laughed. "Okay, just this once. Just don't hit any bumps or I'm liable to bite something off."

Lee smiled at the thought, then realized he'd better move fast—before Glover. He sprinted down the road, then across, reaching the truck just as he heard Glover's pickup starting. Lee jumped in, started his own truck, then backed up, spinning around and easing out onto the highway, heading back toward the bar. As soon as he completed negotiating the curve, Lee turned on his lights and raced on.

About ten seconds later, Lee saw Glover's headlights in the distance. Lee accelerated even more, then at the next road leading off the highway, slowed quickly and turned. Lee killed the lights and turned around in the narrow road, barely avoiding running into a shallow irrigation ditch.

When Glover's truck went past, Lee was crouched down out of sight. If Glover had been looking in that direction, all he would have seen in the dark was the outline of the pickup.

Lee knew where the man would be going, so he waited a full minute before starting on his trail again, taking time to put on a baseball cap and phony glasses. All Lee wanted to see now was which vehicle Breeann got into, so he drove slowly, trying to time things so he could confirm the information.

He'd memorized the tags on all the vehicles earlier, while waiting for Glover inside, and written them down a few minutes ago while waiting for the man to pass by. Lee could run all the vehicles later, but this would be quicker. Hopefully Breeann would be driving her or her "old man's" vehicle. He wanted to get her last name and do a background on her. She might become a witness, if she could be persuaded and protected.

It was pretty likely that Glover had his drug supplier drop the stuff off at the shed. Glover would want to avoid having contraband in his possession until the customer was on hand. If the drop was a regular stop, it could be staked out to identify the supplier, or worst case, the courier. Lee and Diane needed to get as much of the drug pipeline as possible to nail Glover, who in this case was merely the pusher.

Glover passed Lee heading north about a half mile from the bar, and Lee didn't see anyone else in the cab with him. With his baseball cap and glasses on, Lee believed the man wouldn't recognize him. Diane's pickup was a common, generic-looking vehicle, so he wasn't worried that Glover would remember it. Add to that the fact that he was heading in the wrong direction and he was fairly certain he'd escaped notice altogether.

Lee drove by the bar slowly, spotting Breeann just climbing into a green Ford F-150 pickup. He reached over and put a pencil check beside that vehicle on his list. Pulling over to the side in the spot he'd parked earlier, Lee brought out his cell phone. He had to warn Diane that Glover was heading home.

The number was on speed dial, but all he got was an out-of-area response. "Shit!" Lee said aloud, then checked traffic in both directions. Breeann's Ford pickup was headed north, the same direction he'd be going.

Lee whipped out onto the highway, making a U-turn, then sped north. He'd have to get closer to home and try again. Glover was probably just ten minutes away from his house by now, if that was where he was headed, and Diane needed to be home or out of sight.

Lee tried again, but got another out-of-area display. He flashed his headlights, passed Breeann going seventy in a fifty-mile zone, then hit redial.


Diane knew that it was probably Lee calling, and was quickly considering whether or not to answer. If the deputy thought it was Lee, he might decide to stay around, too. He might be curious to see who'd stood up to Glover and hadn't ended up in a hospital—or unmarked grave.

What she hadn't quite decided yet was whether Harmon had been the deputy who'd run Lee's SUV tags earlier at Glover's request. But that person would have already known about Lee Begay and not bothered to check it again. On the other hand, maybe the deputy was just being smart and covering his tracks.

Diane finally made her decision and picked up the phone. "Excuse me, Deputy, I'm getting a call."

Harmon nodded, taking a step forward.

"Hi, it's Diane," she said brightly.

"It's me," Lee said. "I think Glover is on his way home. You're clear of his house, right?"

"That's right, honey. And don't forget the beer and my pork rinds."

"You're not alone, are you?" Lee responded instantly.

"No, I said pork rinds. I hate jerky," she responded, rolling her eyes at Harmon.

"Pork rinds. You have a cop there?"

"That's right."

"Everything under control?"

"Yes. Two bags if they're fresh."

"Okay," Lee replied. "Guess I need to get some beer, then."

"Don't worry about renting a movie. It's getting late."

"I'll bring home a six-pack of Coors," Lee said. "'Bye."

"Okay. Love you, too. 'Bye." Diane hung up. "He's running late. Want to watch me open the door?" she added, glancing up the road. No headlights were visible, but the thought occurred to her that it might be a good idea to keep Deputy Harmon around until Glover returned. Their interaction might tell her which side of the law Harmon was really on.

"Was that your boyfriend on the phone? Begay?"

"Stick around and find out. He's not at all jealous, and you won't believe how much he respects the men in . . . beige." She gave him a really big smile.

"If I have the time. Meanwhile, Miss Garcia, just show me you have a key to the door." Harmon stepped up within three feet of her.

"Sure. But if I've gained a half pound tomorrow, it's all your fault." Diane brought out her keys, walked up the flagstone steps to the front door, and unlocked the handle and the deadbolt.

"Tah-dah," she said, reaching in to turn on the porch light. When she turned, she noticed headlights coming up the road. "That can't be my boyfriend. Maybe it's the asshole from across the road."

"I'd suggest you avoid Glover. He's had trouble with his neighbors, and most people around here are afraid of him now."

"How about you?" Diane watched his reaction very carefully.

His reaction was hard to read, but she noticed his eyes narrowed slightly and his fist clinch for a second. "I don't mess with him and he doesn't mess with me."

"Well, I guess you've got to leave now and go catch some *real* bad guys. Good night, Officer—or is it Deputy?—Harmon."

"Officer or deputy is fine. Good night, Miss Garcia. And if I were you, I wouldn't be running around out here in the sticks alone, especially at night. There's still some wackos out there."

Diane nodded. "I've heard already. Any news on that missing boy?"

Harmon shook his head. "No. And no witnesses have come forward. Nobody saw a thing, it turns out. The original sighting was a false alarm, unrelated. But the Klein kid's fancy bike was found in a culvert, so we know it wasn't a robbery, either. We've got our ears and eyes open." The deputy turned and walked away. "Good night, ma'am."

"You, too, Deputy."

Glover pulled up just then, honked the Jeep's horn lightly, and turned into his gravel driveway. He didn't speak, instead waving in their direction. He appeared to be in a good mood, Diane noticed, considering his experiences earlier in the day with her and Lee. It was all show, of course. Glover was a rattlesnake.

Officer Harmon nodded at Glover, his back to Diane so she couldn't have read his expression even if it had been daylight.

The deputy walked to his car, which was still running with headlights on, and backed up quickly and expertly, turning around in the process. He drove off slowly down the road toward the highway, his searchlight sweeping the margins of the road.

Diane had been keeping one eye on Glover, wondering what he'd do or say now that the deputy had left. He climbed out of the Jeep, looked at her without a word or gesture, then went through his gate and walked to his door. There was a loud curse, then he went inside.

Diane was downloading the photos from Glover's house onto their laptop computer when Lee came into the driveway. She looked up just as he tried the knob. It was locked, of course.

"I'll get it, Lee."

Pork rinds," Lee said as he set the grocery bag down on the counter and pulled out the small bag with the greasy snacks. He put the six-pack of Coors in the refrigerator. "Good clue. What'd I miss?"

Diane explained what had happened as they looked at her photos on the laptop. Neither of them recognized any of the men or women in the compromising photos, but it wasn't unexpected, because they really didn't know any people in the area yet.

"Crop the photos to capture just the faces, then send them to the Bureau and see if we can get some names and backgrounds on these people. If we get any hits, we'll have an idea who Glover may be blackmailing," Lee suggested.

"I was planning on doing that ASAP, but first let me know what went down with Glover. I got your call in time, fortunately," Diane said.

"I had some trouble getting through at first, probably a dead zone. I was close to the Buffalo Tavern—south of here."

"Isn't that the place where the guy down the street was killed, Zeke Perry?"

Lee nodded, then gave her a quick rundown of his shadowing operation, and when he got to the likely drug transfer, she smiled.

"You can find that shed again, right?"

"Of course. Wanna go check it out?" Lee responded. He wasn't sleepy, but Diane had recently yawned.

She nodded. "For all we know, he never uses the same drop twice, or maybe has a particular spot for each customer. That way, if he's ripped off he'd know who was responsible. But for sure, he's in regular contact with his supplier, who drops off the drugs and picks up the money. An arrangement like that implies a level of trust between Glover and his drug contact."

"Mutual profit and fear trump trust when it comes to the bad guys. Glover knows the guy who leaves the drugs for him. Probably another local who's being blackmailed, intimidated, or both. If he rips off Glover, Glover will come down on him hard," Lee said.

"Think it might be the property owner?" she asked. "Around here I'd think trespassers would be risking a load of buckshot, a pit bull, or worse."

"Let's take a look and get mile marker info and addresses of the closest mailboxes. A GPS position, too. There may or may not be more drugs stashed there, but if we can find where he hides the stuff, we might be able to set up a sting, or at least catch his supplier if Glover uses the place on a regular basis."

"How long do you wanna wait before we take off?"

"Let's get the photos sent, run the plate for Breeann's Ford pickup, and send the requests to Logan and my boss. We'll encrypt the data and upload it to our Internet site for storage, then see what's going on at Glover's place. Once his lights go out, we'll give it an hour, then leave quietly."

"I wonder if Glover will try to retaliate while we're gone?"

Lee reached out and placed a gentle hand on her arm. "He's going to go for us, not our stuff, Diane. He'll want to take us out permanently, and he'll do it at a time when he can cover his tracks with a solid-sounding alibi. People have seen us standing up to him, so even Glover would have a hard time explaining the murder of his neighbors. He got away with it once, maybe. A second time will require some planning, even for someone who'd supposed to be invincible."

Diane checked her pistol as she spoke. "He's going to bide his time, figure out a way to deal with us, then strike once he figures he's fooled us into believing he's learned his lesson."

"Exactly. Now all we have to do is get something on him and his contacts before he kills us," Lee said with a grim smile.

CHAPTER 7

Another hour passed. Lee learned that the green F-150 Breeann was driving was in her name, Breeann Edmonds, and that she lived in Cedar Crest in a rented home. There was no information about who she was living with, though someone in the department was checking to determine who owned the property. Eventually, the person renting it would be identified.

Breeann, originally from one of the area pueblos, had been arrested four times on Albuquerque's East Central for prostitution, and had been busted twice for possession of a controlled substance, methamphetamines. Her last job was as a stripper at an East Central bar, though she apparently no longer worked there. She was nineteen.

It was nearly 11:30 when Lee and Diane turned on the surveillance system, went out the front door, climbed quietly into the SUV, then drove away.

"Think Glover noticed?" Diane asked as they reached the main highway.

"If he was awake, he undoubtedly heard or saw us. The worse thing to do would be to make it look like we were sneaking away."

"You're right. Why don't you go north instead of south for a mile or two, then pull over and wait? If he's following us, he'll either have to stop behind us or pass us by. If he goes by, we'll see; if he pulls over, we might be able to spot him when we reverse directions."

"Yeah. We don't want him to see us checking out his drop site," Lee agreed.

Twenty minutes later, Lee and Diane walked down the narrow track near the shed where Glover had apparently picked up the drugs for Breeann. No flashlight was necessary, with Lee leading Diane by hand, and they were both wearing soleless shoes that were smooth on the bottom and left no distinguishing pattern.

Lee had owned shoes like these for decades now, and since Diane had become his frequent partner in operations, she'd acquired a pair for herself.

"That porch light over there," Diane whispered. "Was it on earlier?"

He shook his head. "No." Lee had been watching the old farmhouse since they'd first spotted it. It had been nearly blocked by the shed when he'd looked earlier, but the light was something he'd have seen because it cast shadows as far away as the shed, which was a good hundred yards closer to the highway than the house.

"So the resident had left it off. Maybe at Glover's request?"

"That would be my guess. Nobody would stash drugs and/or money in a place where they'd be easily found. And Glover didn't take more than a minute or two before he came back, so I'm assuming it wasn't hard for him to retrieve what he was after."

Diane nodded, giving his hand a squeeze. "That light will keep the owner from seeing us. Ruin his night vision."

"But not mine," Lee said. They reached the spot where

Glover had gone under the fence and he lifted up the wire, letting go of Diane's hand to climb through. Then he held the wire up for her and she followed. They walked silently up to the closest corner of the small building.

Lee crouched down low, then looked around the corner of the building toward the farmhouse. He held out his hand, but could barely make out the shadow against the wooden wall of the shed. Taking her hand, he led Diane around the corner and into a small roofed-in area enclosed on three sides that had obviously been a stall, probably for a horse, judging from the gray, crumbled remnants of road apples still scattered on the earthen floor.

"He smoothed out his footprints, I guess," Lee whispered, studying the ground.

"I'm afraid to risk a light," Diane said, looking back toward the house. She stepped back behind the doorway into the darkness. "Ow!"

Lee turned and saw that she'd bumped into a metal horse feeder mounted onto the two-by-fours of the shed's framework. Scanning the interior, he was unable to find any obvious hiding places, not even a loose board or compartment of any kind.

"Behind the feeder?" Diane whispered, realizing what she'd collided with after feeling the shape.

Lee noticed the heads of two bolts on the back surface of the feeder, and four big bolts on the outside frame of the unit, leading to the two-by-fours. The two center bolts didn't have two-by-fours behind them, so why were they there? He got down on his knees and reached up behind the feeder base from below. There was a rectangular object with a flap at the top, and when he opened the flap, by feel, he detected rolled-up paper held together with a rubber band.

"Well hidden. It's a mailbox, the kind you'd find on a porch." He brought out the roll of paper. It was cash, two hundred dollars in twenties. He held the money up close for Diane to see in the dim light from the house.

"Payment for the transaction. The supplier will be coming for the money," she said softly. "But if it's the resident over there, why hasn't he taken it already?"

"He may not be the supplier, or, equally possible, maybe he just doesn't want to risk coming out here in the dark. In the morning he can make sure nobody is hiding here, watching for whoever comes to take the payoff, like a cop staking the place out."

"He could have placed the drugs in the box anytime during the day, also keeping a wary eye out for the law," Diane said in agreement.

"Or we could make this complicated, and propose that a third party constructed this stash in secret. Maybe he sneaked in here after dark to make the drop, and plans on picking up the money sometime tonight once he thinks it's safe."

"Which means he might be on his way here now, or watching the place?" Diane looked around curiously.

"Yeah, so we'd better hightail it because we just don't know yet. I'll lead you back across the fence, then you lay low while I come back to smooth out any tracks we might have left."

Eight minutes later, the money back in the hiding place, they were in the SUV, which Lee had parked down the road in the same place he'd stopped earlier while following Glover.

"Okay, what do we do now?" Diane asked. "Set up Glover for a drug bust?"

"We could, but I vote we keep learning from the man, tracking his activities. He's got allies around here doing some serious bad stuff on his behalf, and even if we manage to put him and his drug supplier away, the others will still be out there. Putting away Glover and his drug contact won't be enough, not in my eyes."

"Agreed."

Lee didn't need sleep as long as he was eating well and regularly, so while Diane went to bed almost immediately upon their return, he wrote and e-mailed an updated report on their activities—glossing over some of the specifics, like roughing up Glover, smashing his pickup, and breaking into his home. The report, and a daily log of their investigation, would be kept at an Internet address Lee or Diane could access. At the same time they'd be keeping the laptop clear of any information that could give them away in case the device was stolen or compromised.

Lastly, he prepared the flyer he planned to distribute tomorrow, something to leave in doors and in business windows, to let the community know that a Navajo silversmith was now selling silver and turquoise jewelry at bargain prices. He'd already had a tech in the state police department design a Web site for him, and it would be accessible to anyone in the rural area with a computer and dial-up. Their address was also posted, as were hours when visitors could drop by to look at his collection.

That cover would allow him to keep his own hours and interact with the community. He'd prepared a sample box that he'd be taking with him from now on to justify his travels.

Next, Lee called the state police watch commander in his area for news on the missing child. The Amber alert had been canceled because they no longer had solid information that a kidnapping had indeed taken place. All known reports of children getting into vehicles had been checked out and cleared. All they had was that the boy failed to return home, and that his bike was recovered. That was it.

Glover didn't appear to have the boy, at least not at his home or at any place he'd been known to visit today, so if the sleazeball was involved, he was covering his tracks well. All the local agencies were still questioning known sex offenders in the area, but no real leads had surfaced.

It was nearly 1:00 in the morning by now. Just before turning in, Lee decided to take one last look outside. He went through the kitchen and small utility area and slipped out the back door, then circled around the other end of the building, coming around the corner.

Across the street, Glover's lights were out and there was no movement in the yard. A cottontail sat between the fence and the road, munching on some ground-hugging plants. The gray-and-white creature raised its head and watched Lee for a moment with big, black eyes, then went back to eating.

All the driveways were half circles in this small development, their closest point near the front doors, and Glover had parked the Jeep directly in front of his door. From where Lee was standing, he could see the license plate. He'd run the letters and numbers and see what he could learn about the owner. Glover had acquired a vehicle within an hour, which meant he had connections, a lot of cash on hand, or had located a very trusting local repair shop owner.

Lee glanced across the front of their own yard, noted that the SUV and pickup appeared undisturbed, then reversed his course and reentered the building from the back, locking the door behind him.

A quick check revealed that the Jeep was registered to a businessman who owned several properties across Bernalillo County, including a gas station at Tijeras and a cabin near Chilili. A quick background on the businessman, named Brian Sully, showed that he was fifty-two years old, long divorced with no children, and had been arrested once for solicitation. He had bailed himself out, later paying a small fine.

Lee thought about Breeann Edmonds, nineteen, and decided there was a chance she knew Brian Sully, one way or the other. He and Diane had to learn more about both of these people. Good or bad, young or old, they were both associating with Newton Glover.

The next morning Diane crossed through the living room over to the kitchen. She was fully dressed for work in a designer knockoff version of green camouflage pants, a military web belt, and a lavender knit top beneath some kind of fashion-trendy, short jacket.

Lee almost did a double take. "It looks like you're going duck hunting at the mall," he said, waving a hand toward a plate on her side of the table. It was covered with another dish to keep the pancakes, eggs, and bacon warm.

"I'm supposed to look like I'm going through my second teenhood. And this outfit gives me a place to keep my backup weapon and still wear the vest," Diane said, patting the jacket pocket as she crossed the thin carpeting to the dining table. "I wish these extra pockets were for real, though."

She sat immediately. "Thanks for fixing breakfast. I could smell the bacon all the way from the shower. But this thousand-square-foot house is still huge compared to my apartment."

"Yeah, I've never had a home this big. The stove is well designed, and I'm used to cooking with gas, so I thought an old-fashioned greasy breakfast was just the thing."

Diane sniffed, looked around, then stood. "Coffee?"

"Eat. I'll get it." Lee's chair was close to the opening into the kitchen area, between counters, and he could reach the coffee pot without standing. "Toast?"

Seeing her nod, he added, "One or two slices?"

She held up two fingers because her mouth was full.

Lee poured Diane a tall mug of coffee, black, then walked over to the little toaster oven, where a package of French bread was sitting. He sliced two thick pieces and placed them in the toaster oven.

"Where did you go after I went to bed? I heard you leave. . . ."

Lee told her what he'd done and learned about Breeann and the businessman, Brian Sully. Glover had managed to get the Jeep at a moment's notice, so he either paid a lot of money or had some influence with Sully.

"Sully was arrested for solicitation?" Diane asked. "Was it with a woman?"

Lee shook his head. "Don't know, though my assumption was that Sully was trying to pick up a female, and got caught in a sting or whatever. APD made the arrest—someone from the vice squad. You're wondering if the prostitute was really young, or maybe male?"

"Yeah. I think we should follow up on this—interview the arresting officer and get the details. Meanwhile, I can check with Anna and see if she knows anything about Sully. His gas station is just down the road from Howard's, according to the addresses."

"Like gossip about his relationships with women, how closely he watches little boys, stuff like that? Good idea."

"How about you have someone interview the vice squad cop who has the details? Or maybe you can track him down yourself, if he's available." Diane looked up as the toaster oven sounded.

Lee reached back and handed the toast over as she brought up her plate. "I'll make the call as soon as you leave, then let you know if I have to go into Albuquerque. You going to come home for lunch again?"

"Depends on what I can get in gossip from Anna. I'll let you know about eleven-thirty. I can always grab something at the store, then go down to Sully's gas station and top off the tank. You know, look around, ask innocent questions. . . ."

"Flirt with the mechanic, see if Sully's there and checks you out. Ask about Glover's Jeep, too, and see if his pickup is in the shop."

"Yeah. Sounds like a plan," Diane said with a nod.

She looked across the table at Lee, who was finishing his coffee. "How long do you think it'll take before Glover makes a move against us?"

"If he's as devious as our initial informant suggests, it might be a week or more. My guess is he's going to be ignoring us for a while, hoping we'll think he's been scared off. But don't go outside without the vest. He could be a back shooter," Lee said. "And remember that a vest is still vulnerable to a knife attack."

Diane nodded absently as she looked across the room toward the street. "On the way to Howard's, I'm going to call Logan and see if he can get the Bureau to dig as deep as possible into Newton Glover's background. You still have that broken bat?"

"Excellent idea," he said, nodding in reply to her question. "If I end up going to Albuquerque for an interview, I'll leave it at the drop. Your people can lift Glover's prints and run them through federal and defense department databases. All we got from county records is a verification that the guy really is Newton Glover, but for all we really know about him, he could be anything from a retired postal clerk to an NSA analyst. Just to make sure we get things rolling, I'll package it up. Then, in case I don't make it into the city, I can leave it at Howard's. I noticed a pickup box for FedEx out front."

"Works for me," Diane said. Then she stood and started to clean up the breakfast dishes.

"Just put them in the sink. I'll get the dishwasher started after you leave."

The table and counters were clear in seconds, then Diane walked over to the bedroom and adjusted her jacket and collar, standing in front of the mirror attached to the back of the door. "I look just like one of those mannequins in the Gap window display at the mall."

"But much more animated—and shorter."

"The heels on these shoes had to be low. I may have to run after a perp, you know."

"Or run from one. Be careful. Working at Howard's is like working at a convenience store. There's a lot more guys out there besides Glover who may want to poke a gun in your cute little face."

"I'm *not* cute. This is my 'sassy and sexy' look. Designed to get men talking."

"I know it's just been one day at work so far, but how have the women customers reacted to you?"

"Lots of hard-looking women live around here, and they don't seem to care as long as I'm not making a move on *their* man. If I did, they'd probably jump me in the parking lot. As far as the older ones go, I think they're taking their lead from Anna, and she's accepted me."

"She might end up being a good source all by herself, Diane. She and her late husband bought that store fifteen years ago, didn't they?"

"Yeah, but I'm still moving slowly with her. She knows I'm a cop, but not why we're here. That would make her too vulnerable. I don't want her to become a threat to Glover or those working for him."

"Bet the widow of a retired cop is as tough as nails."

"You're probably right. But she's afraid of Glover, I can tell. It'll be nice taking him out of the community." Diane looked at her watch. "But one thing at a time. I've got to leave now."

"I'll walk you to your pickup like a good boyfriend," Lee said.

"You better."

A minute later, Diane climbed into the pickup, rolled down

the window, and gave him a quick kiss. "This isn't just for show. I've missed not working with you, Lee!"

"Me, too. Be careful, and let me know or leave word where you'll be."

"Back at ya." Diane started the engine, and he stepped away as she drove forward around the half-circle drive and out into the road. There was still no sign of life across the street.

"Later, babe," Diane yelled, driving off down the street.

He avoided looking over at Glover's house as he returned to the front porch. As he opened the door, he turned and glanced through Glover's front window.

Glover was standing well back in the room, in the darkness and out of view of any normal human. The man was aiming a pistol equipped with a laser sight in his direction. Lee felt a spot of warmth in the center of his forehead, and knew instantly where the red dot was.

CHAPTER 8

**R**esisting the instincts that screamed *dive*, Lee turned and stepped inside as calmly as he could muster, expecting at any second to feel the sensation of a bullet striking his head. Blood, brains, and bone fragments would explode onto the porch, front door, and wall into a crime scene investigator's nightmare. But there was no shot.

He made it safely inside, stopped, and caught his breath. His pistol was out now, so he raced along the wall on his left, ducked into their bedroom, and ran over to the window. Angling his body to avoid presenting a target, he looked over at Glover's house.

The man was still at the back of his living room, now aiming in other directions, waiting a few seconds to get a sight picture, and maybe dry-firing. It was just practice for Glover, not a real hit attempt.

Lee sat down on the edge of the bed and put his pistol away. It was possible he could have taken the bullet and healed back within a half hour or less. Since it wouldn't have been a shot to the heart, his brain might not have shut down completely. But it would have been close, even for a vampire—half vampire—like him.

Lee walked into the bathroom and looked in the mirror. He smiled, remembering the common lore about vampires not having reflections. The knowledge most people had about his kind was filled with misconceptions. As he studied his face, Lee saw a slight discoloration in the center of his forehead—an additional tanned area that was barely noticeable. It hadn't burned, at least, and he automatically reached into the shelf and brought out his sunblock for a quick touch-up. He'd known that certain wavelengths of light, those found in direct sunlight and light-bulbs with a natural spectrum, could injure or fry a vampire. But until now, he hadn't known that a laser beam—or more to the point, the wavelength used on laser sights—could have the same result on vampire flesh, even through a window. It was a lesson he would remember.

A half hour later, Lee managed to speak with the APD patrol officer who'd arrested Sully, a young-sounding woman named Andrea Moore who was now working with the gang unit. "Andy" was on duty, making some community visits, and reluctantly agreed to let him catch up to her later while she finished her rounds.

Around 9:00 A.M. Lee arrived in Albuquerque. He turned right off Central, drove a half block north, then entered the parking lot containing an east Albuquerque Wal-Mart. He cruised slowly across the lot, following cars stalking good parking spots up front. The drop site was an old blue Chevy van, always parked directly in line with a security camera in one of the sections designated for employees, farthest from the entrances. Every day it would be moved a row or several slots to avoid attracting attention from Wal-Mart employees. The store manager had been told about the drop, but was under instructions to keep her mouth shut.

Lee managed to get behind two vehicles jockeying to pounce on a handicapped-only slot, and with a big pickup behind him, he couldn't move forward or back. Meanwhile, the customer about to vacate the spot—an elderly woman probably close to his chronological age—was still loading her groceries in the trunk of her ancient-model Cadillac.

He couldn't get out to help the woman without leaving his own vehicle in traffic, so, like everyone else, he just had to wait. Finally, painfully slowly, the Cadillac pulled out. The closest car was too close, and was forced to back up, but the driver in the third car, who also wanted the slot, refused to give ground.

Lee, hot and impatient, was seriously considering getting out and shooting somebody when the Wal-Mart security guy came around in his ridiculous-looking golf cart/truckette. He flashed his yellow lights, then climbed out and waved everyone back. The man looked nearly as old as the lady in the Cadillac.

Lee was finally able to make a right turn, go to the next lane, then pull into a slot at the end, several spaces down from the drop van, recognizing the vehicle tags and various Wiccan bumper stickers on the rear door. One read BE WITCHED.

The vehicle had alarms, but Lee had the gadget to disable them and unlock the driver's door. He climbed inside with the bag containing the baseball bat parts, signed his name, adding the date and time, then picked up the paper sack supposedly containing photos of East Mountain-area government and departmental employees, plus those of any high-profile businesspeople in the area. There was also supposed to be a copy of the paperwork concerning the Zeke Perry homicide.

Glancing at his watch, Lee realized he had only fifteen minutes to make it all the way across town to the north valley. "Andy" was going to be talking to a middle school faculty about gang activity in their area, and he was supposed to meet her there so they could speak as soon as she finished.

Lee returned to his unmarked SUV and punched out Officer Moore's number. He got her voicemail, and left the message

that he was across the city and would need at least twenty minutes to arrive. If she couldn't wait for him, perhaps he could
meet with her at her next stop.

Lee got on I-40 again, then took the Santa Fe exit and entered I-25 North. Farther down, there was an exit that would
take him west, just one street north of the school where Moore
was speaking. He was five minutes away when Lee got a call. It
was Officer Moore.

"Officer Hawk. I'm taking Seven at Two Bits, which is just
south of Five-twenty-eight. It's two lights up, then an eighth-
mile south from the intersection with Corrales Road. Meet me
in ten?"

"Gotcha. What's close to Two Bits?"

He heard a groan. "You'll pass Hooters on your left. Oh, and
there's a big bookstore just past the turn," Officer Moore added.

"I know where you mean. Two Bits has the barbecue sandwiches and the big fries."

"That's it. See you there." Moore ended the call.

Five minutes later, Lee crossed the Rio Grande, and not
long after that drove into a slot in front of the liquor store beside
Two Bits. He could see the APD unit several cars farther east,
but it was empty. Officer Moore had gone inside, apparently,
but he figured her dark blue uniform wouldn't be hard to spot.

It wasn't. Once inside, he saw the young woman across the
dining area sitting at a table beside the wall. Like most law enforcement people he knew she chose to sit with her back to a
wall and her eyes to the door. Seeing him, she nodded.

Despite having managed to keep his image out of the papers
and off TV, his photo was on file. A year ago, he'd also worked
with Diane on a case that had involved the APD. A murder had
taken place in full view of virtually the whole nation, including
the visiting U.S. president. Police officers normally had long
memories and that wasn't a case anyone would be likely to

forget. These days most APD officers had heard of Lee, and quite a few had seen him on the job. Long-term exposure for a man whose appearance never changed could end up becoming a problem. He was already thinking of ways of making himself look older, maybe adding a little gray to his hair, if he stuck with the department much longer. Maybe he could push it another ten years if he transferred around a lot.

Lee took the room in at a glance. The establishment had just opened for the day, and tables with customers planning an early lunch held businessmen, upscale tradesmen, and a few retirees with good teeth and knowledge of the extraordinary barbecue sauce served here. One could also hoist a beer or two, something the Subway down the road couldn't provide. He didn't see any ladies alone except for the policewoman and the waitresses.

Satisfied there was no obvious threat, Lee walked over to Officer Moore's table. She must have been over twenty-one, with short, strawberry-blond hair and pale blue eyes. Andrea Moore's slender arms suggested she was a little gal, but it was hard to know for sure because the outline of her bullet-resistant vest was apparent beneath her blue uniform shirt. Officer Moore looked like a teenager except for her eyes, which were hard despite their attractive color.

"Officer Hawk, I've heard of you," the woman officer said in a low monotone, standing to shake his hand. Her grip was firm, dry, and confident, but she'd obviously not learned that, traditionally, Navajos didn't shake hands with strangers. Or maybe she suspected Lee wasn't a traditional Navajo, being a cop.

"If it was complimentary, feel free to believe all of it," Lee responded with the hint of a smile. He'd learned long ago to walk on eggshells around female cops. They were often quick to suspect ulterior motives from male officers, admittedly with reason, and got defensive easily. Truth be told, keeping it cool and professional suited him fine, too. After many decades of living alone—personally and emotionally—he'd lost the ability to feel completely comfortable around women.

Diane was one of only two women he'd ever let into his life. He'd married the first, and lost her to Navajo wolves—skinwalkers—due to his own lapse in judgment. Lessons like that stayed with a man.

"Coffee?" Officer Moore offered, raising her hand and waving to a waitress who'd caught her eye.

"Yeah. You having an early lunch, Officer Moore?" He noticed a menu resting on the table by her right arm, opened.

"Got to do it now while I have the chance, Officer Hawk."

"Think I'll join you. A working lunch? I'm hoping to glean some old details from your days in vice."

"Shoulda stayed in vice, wearing those tight jeans and tube tops, trolling for johns. I traded a group of horny sickos for carloads of young, hard-core shitheads who'd just as soon shoot you as look at you. And every look is mad dogging to them. Punks. And that's just the girls."

Moore was harsh, but she was telling it like it was today, even in small New Mexico towns like Los Lunas and Española. Lee remembered neighborhood gangs back in the fifties, when knives, clubs, chains, and fists were the weapons of choice, and a car less than fifteen years old was a luxury. Nowadays, even the wannabes were packing serious heat and racing around in brand-new cars. And, with cell phones, bad guy backup was just a speed dial away.

He nodded just as the waitress came up.

"Would you like a menu, sir?" The young woman was definitely not a Hooters girl with her high collar, conservative white blouse, and loose-fitting black slacks. She gave him that big-tip smile as she poured Lee a cup of coffee and topped off the female officer's mug.

Lee looked over at Officer Moore, who offered him a look at her menu. He waved it off. "I'll have a beef barbecue sandwich, large fries, and coffee. Then a second sandwich packaged to go."

Officer Moore added, "Me, too, but only one sandwich. And I'd like extra sauce for the fries."

"I can do that, Officer," the waitress said, then hurried away.

"I've eaten at their place over in the northeast heights, and the one south of the university. Didn't know they had a third location," Lee said, looking around the establishment.

"This one's still pretty new," Officer Moore said, then her voice lowered, taking on a husky tone. "You wanted to know what I remember about a bust I made a few years ago. A scumbag businessman—Brian Sully?"

Right down to business. Lee liked that in a cop. "He's the one. I know it has been a while. . . ."

"I looked it up to refresh my memory, but it wasn't really necessary. Another female officer was working with me. We were both posing as hookers near one of those run-down East Central motels. She's built like a brick shithouse, so every time the perps hit on her first. Even in my tightest jeans and tube tops I'm pretty much straight up and down. My self-esteem was going down the toilet. But this guy Sully just couldn't wait to get his hands on *me*. Never gave Monica a second glance."

"This officer, Monica. She's tall?"

"Yeah. We looked like Nicole and Tom out there."

Lee would have said Mutt and Jeff, but Andrea wouldn't have had a clue. "No offense, but you're small and look like a ninth grader. Maybe Sully was into jailbait."

"Could be. You can imagine the kind of crap I went through at the academy. My instructors and most of the guys in my class thought I was either gay, androgynous, or still going through puberty. Once I was in the field, though, the department took advantage of my lack of obvious attributes. I was assigned to vice to lure in the pedophiles."

That was the kind of insight Lee was looking for. In the dark, with a boyish figure, maybe Sully had thought he was picking up a young man. Lee thought about the missing boy. . . .

"A light just went on behind those dark eyes, Officer Hawk. Care to enlighten me?"

"Call me Lee. And, yes, it makes me even more interested in Brian Sully. You know about the latest Amber alert."

"That ten-year-old from the East Mountains? Timothy Klein? Don't tell me Brian Sully lives out there. Any question of him being a pedophile?"

"He's not on the list, but that might just mean he's never been caught. Sully's got several businesses, including a gas station in Tijeras, and property farther south, according to what I've managed to learn. He's a contact of someone we're investigating right now—undercover. My partner and I will check into any possible connection Sully might have had, or is having now, with a minor."

"Good. If it's him, nail the bastard. I won't blow your cover by talking this up at the substation. But if you need some backup in APD jurisdiction, give me a call, will you? Kids are screwed up enough already without perverts messing with their lives."

Lee handed her his card with his cell number on the back. "If you think of anything else, give me a call. I'm just Lee. And don't identify yourself except as Andrea, okay."

"Andy. They call me Andy. Now, here comes lunch."

Andrea gave him a smile, a real one, and he was relieved to see that despite her frankness she hadn't become completely hardened by the job. Working vice, then the youth gang unit, could burn out anyone in record time. Or maybe she'd just become a great game player, living her work.

The waitress set down the big toasted sandwiches, piled high with shredded roast beef and tangy barbecue sauce. The fries, which were thickly sliced and unpeeled, complemented the meal. No salad needed or wanted here.

Lee asked for the bill, used to paying immediately, not knowing when he might have to leave. He watched Officer Moore for a reaction. Some women, particularly in their profession, took an offer to pay for the meal as a power or sexist issue, or a debt to be repaid later. He'd heard an officer once describe the courtesies he'd grown up with, like men paying for meals and opening doors for women, as benevolent sexism.

Her expression was benign, a reaction he suspected was only temporary. When the waitress had left, Officer Moore finally spoke. "You paid for my lunch—because . . . ?"

"Because you gave me the information I needed without having to go though the bureaucracy—an unofficial courtesy I respect. It was not payment for something a professional should have given freely, nor did it have anything to do with the fact that you're a lady, although I was raised to respect values some might call old-fashioned these days."

"Either you're every woman's dream, or a heavy-duty bullshitter, Officer Hawk."

"Something to ponder while we're having lunch, Officer Moore." Lee shrugged, then began to eat.

They both finished their meals quickly, from habit, and Lee was taking his second-to-the-last sip of coffee when Officer Moore got a call on her handheld. From what Lee could hear there was someone at a west side high school who'd just been arrested by campus security, and she was being sent to the scene.

"Gotta go, Lee. Next time, I'll at least buy the coffee." She pulled out two dollars and placed it on the table.

"Deal, Andy. Be smart out there."

Officer Moore stood, as did Lee, and she smiled as she grabbed her cap off the seat cushion. "'Bye."

She was gone in seconds. Lee took a final sip of coffee, stood, and picked up the foam container containing the sandwich he'd bought for Diane, then left the Two Bits lounge for his SUV.

He was back on I-25 in ten minutes, heading for the Big I, where he'd exit for I-40 east. Lee picked up the phone, thinking of calling Diane, then decided to wait. She was supposed to call him, so if he hurried he could probably catch her at Howard's in the canyon. They could get Cokes at the store and discuss the morning while she ate her sandwich.

He was already in the canyon, Manzanos on the right, Sandias rising above him to the left, when Diane called.

Diane had been working the cash register today, with Lonnie supposedly training her. Anna had updated the old cash register since Howard died, and the computer software and hardware were very familiar to Diane. It was virtually identical to a system she and Lee had used while working on the jewelry-smuggling case last year.

There had been no problems at all, but Lonnie continued to hover, watching her breasts and ass more than the transactions, and it was starting to get annoying. She'd tried a few scowls, but he just didn't seem to get the message.

A pen rolled off the counter, and she bent down to pick it up. Glancing over, she saw Lonnie looking down her blouse. "You look at me one more time like that and I'll crush your nuts with my bare hands."

Lonnie turned pale. "Oh—sorry, Diane. I wasn't staring. I was just wondering if I should pick that up for you."

"How? You're on the other side of the counter. Just keep

your eyes to yourself unless you want to be staring up your ass with them."

Out of the corner of her eyes, Diane could see Anna, restocking the candy rack, trying to keep a straight face and pretending not to hear.

"Umm, I apologize for making you think I was checking you out. Really. I don't want any trouble."

"Good. You give me a reason and you're going to be singing soprano." Diane was having a hard time keeping a straight face herself. Lonnie had withered up like a prune and was definitely out of his league.

"Um, you've got the register handled, so I'm going to clear out the storeroom." Lonnie left in a hurry.

Diane was starting to straighten out the display containing the lottery scratchers when Anna came over. "You really reamed him out good. Reminds me of my late husband Howard and some of the punks who came in here trying to make trouble. You ever work for the prison system?"

"Worse. I attended public school all the way to graduation," Diane responded. "I really didn't know how to destroy a boy completely, however, until I was in the eighth grade."

Anna laughed, then grew serious. "You mentioned wanting to take a little break and look over the Trident gas station down the street," Anna said, lowering her voice and looking around to make sure neither of the two customers over in the dairy section could hear.

"Yeah. How about now? Fifteen minutes tops?" Diane asked.

"Take your time, but hurry back," Anna said.

Diane chuckled. "You must have kept Howard in stitches," she said, taking off her store apron and setting it beneath the counter.

Anna nodded. "Made life a little easier, considering what we'd been through when he was on the force. You got a man, Diane?"

"I think so. Or he's got me. Maybe both. We're moving slow. Two years now."

"Better decide, girl. You won't live forever."

"Yeah. That could be part of the problem," Diane said, her voice fading slightly. It was something she'd thought about often since meeting up with Lee.

She managed to turn the expression into a smile, and Anna's puzzled gaze suggested she was still two sentences behind in the conversation. "Be back by ten-twenty, boss." Diane walked out the front door before Anna could come up with a response.

The Trident station, with a mechanic on duty according to the sign, was only a quarter mile down the road, facing the frontage road and old Route 66. I-40, higher up and just north on a higher-elevation roadbed, carried hundreds of cars past every hour, and the gas prices, Diane noted, were only a few cents more than the best in the city. The pumps were self-service with an attendant inside, and the garage had two bays. Looking at the center block and sheet metal structure as she pulled up, she judged that except for the newer signs and the fancier pumps, this station could have been here fifty or more years ago.

Diane drove up beneath the shaded pump island. The gas inlet was on the right-hand side of the vehicle, which gave her a clear view of the interior of the garage. She'd had a brief look the other day when Lee had dropped her off.

Glover's red truck was in the bay closest to the office and cash register. A new windshield had already been installed, and a mechanic in a red uniform shirt and jeans was bent over the engine compartment. Judging from the boxed items and tools on the little cart beside him, he was doing a tune-up.

"Be right with you," the blond-haired man she remembered as Mike said without looking.

Role playing was necessary when undercover, but Diane

still had problems looking at herself in the mirror after saying and doing some of the things required of her.

"I'm not in a hurry," she replied, releasing her seat belt, then leaning out the driver's window slightly. The key here was to use the sexiest tone she could manage. With the "come and get me" makeup, it was using all her assets to best advantage.

The "voice" got results. The slender, fair-haired mechanic turned his head around so fast he'd probably be needing a chiropractor. His arm came around a second later and he knocked the spark plug wrench off the fender. It clanged to the concrete, bouncing twice noisily before coming to rest.

"I got it, Earl," Mike replied eagerly, beating the chubby guy behind the inside counter to the punch. Mike had already decided his service to her was more important than the tool on the ground, apparently.

"Hey, girl. I remember you from yesterday. Fill her up?" Mike was smooth, at least in his own imagination, and she barely kept her smile from turning into a laugh.

"You got it . . . Mike," she said, opening the door and climbing out of the cab. Mike stood there a second to watch, then ran around to pump the gas.

"Key?" she offered, holding up the set.

"Key? Oh, right, for the gas cap." Mike came back around, taking the key, his face turning red as he made eye contact. Mike had to be eighteen, tops, and was probably still living at home.

Still, Diane conceded, he was a potential informant. She'd need to find out everything he knew about Brian Sully and, hopefully, Newt Glover. She stepped closer to Glover's truck.

"That looks like my neighbor's truck," she said loudly enough for Earl to hear. He was standing in the doorway watching her anyway.

"You live near Newt Glover?" Earl said, stepping out to talk.

A customer, likely a tourist judging from the out-of-state plates, came up behind the man, waving a credit card.

"Hey, Earl. You've got a customer. Turn around," Mike yelled from across the other side of the pickup.

"Oh, right." Earl turned to help the man with the credit card. They both went inside, but Mike came out around the vehicle to join her.

"Check the oil?"

"No, it's fine. This Glover guy, the one who owns the pickup. He some kind of nut or something?" She said it loudly, and Earl, inside, turned to look.

"Oh no," Mike said, equally loudly. "He jokes around a lot, but he'd a good ole boy. I like him." Then he turned to make sure Earl had heard.

The pump handle clicked, indicating the tank was full, and Mike went back to the handle, completing the operation and locking her gas cap back on. Then he came back around, stepping up within arm's reach to hand her the keys. "He's an asshole, a real troublemaker," Mike whispered. "Stay away from him. But you didn't hear it from me. Got it?"

Diane nodded. "Thanks, Mike. I got it." She reached for some money in her pocket and had to struggle a bit because her pants were too tight. Mike didn't seem to mind waiting, and when she brought out a twenty, he waved her toward Earl. "You have to pay inside, ma'am."

She nodded. "I'd better let you get back to that pickup."

"Yeah," Earl said from his vantage point in the doorway. "Or Glover's gonna kick your ass."

"And your ass, and Sully's, and everyone else's all the way to Moriarity," Mike added, walking back over to the pickup. He reached for a tool, then suddenly remembered it was still on the ground. "Stay away from Glover, I mean it," he whispered as he bent down to retrieve the wrench.

She nodded again. "Who's Sully?" she asked, loud enough for Earl to hear. He was coming out with her receipt.

"Mr. Brian Sully owns the station, a tire store in Albuquerque, and some apartments," Earl said. "He's our boss."

"Then why should he worry about Glover pushing him around? Glover lives in a tiny house out in the sticks and drives a five-year-old pickup," Diane said, putting her hands on her hips and shaking her head with an attitude.

"Mr. Glover has a lot more money than he's showing, don't let that little double-wide of his fool you. He runs half the—"

"Keep it down, Earl," Mike said, looking around to see if they were still alone. "We're the lowest peckers in the pecking order around here. Remember what happened to Sully the other day? His Jeep?"

"The same Jeep I saw this morning in Glover's driveway?" Diane pressed.

Mike nodded. "You tell her, Earl."

"What if it comes back at us?"

"I'm not going to be talking to Glover. He's pissed at me and my boyfriend anyway. We're the ones who broke his windshield," Diane said.

"Glover said it was a flock of ducks coming up from a marsh beside the road," Mike said, looking at Earl, who nodded.

The two gas station employees took a step away from her, as if she'd suddenly become radioactive.

"So what's with the Jeep, guys. Our secret?"

Mike looked at Earl, who shook his head. There was a pause, then the cable rang and they all looked over at the same time. A woman in a small sedan had just pulled up at the gas pumps. "I got it," Earl said, eager to leave the conversation.

Mike nodded, gesturing her over beside the pickup. "Glover came in, pissed as hell, and demanded to borrow Sully's Jeep. Sully offered him my beat-up piece of crap over there instead,"

Mike said, indicating his ancient pickup. "But Glover grabbed
Sully by the . . . zipper, called him a pervert, and told Sully that
he owed him a lot more than the keys to the Jeep. Sully nearly
fainted, then gave him the Jeep."

They spoke a little longer, Diane getting as much information as she could. Finally she ended her conversation with him
on a pleasant note and headed back. She had a lot to follow up
on now. Glover was turning out just as expected, and Brian
Sully was definitely worth investigating further.

She'd pass the information on to Lee ASAP, and they'd decide what to do next. It was a long shot, but if Sully had anything to do with the missing boy, he'd become their next
priority. Plans would change and Glover would have to wait his
turn.

CHAPTER 9

W e need to shift our focus to Sully," Diane said as soon as Lee pulled out of Howard's parking lot. They were in the SUV, heading toward a picnic area just south of Tijeras.

"I agree. Sounds like we've both made progress this morning," Lee replied, keeping his eyes on the road.

"What's that wonderful smell. Barbecue?" She saw the foam container. "Two Bits. Good choice. Where's yours?"

Lee took a sip of the Coke she'd given him when she climbed inside. "Ate mine already. Part of my story."

"Okay. You talk, I'll eat. Been around food all morning, never took a bite." Diane unfolded a napkin on her lap, then reached inside for a piece of sandwich. The serving was cut into quarters, the bread was so big, and she had to be careful, keeping the container on the towel, to avoid dripping sauce on her lap.

While Diane ate, Lee drove and explained what had happened this morning. She asked questions between bites, and by the time he pulled off the road beside a concrete picnic table, his story was done and her sandwich was finished.

Instead of getting out, they sat in the vehicle, parked in the shade beneath a tall pine with the windows down, appreciating the scents of the forest as Diane told him about her visit to the Trident station.

"I'll get everything anyone has on Brian Sully, and try and track him down. Did you get any idea on where he might be at the moment?"

"From Mike, at the station, I gather that Sully stops by the station randomly, any time of day or night. I also know he's got a home on private property somewhere near the turnoff to the Fourth of July campground. There was a photo at the station that Anna saw once and she described it for me."

"And he also has apartments in Albuquerque, right? The Northeast Heights."

"Right. But Mike said that he overheard Sully tell someone that he's been staying at the cabin for the past month."

"Why the switch in residence?"

"If Mike knew, he didn't tell me. But he did notice that Sully's been buying a lot of camera equipment, lights and such. He saw the packages and boxes in Sully's other car, a white Camry, while he was gassing up the vehicle."

Lee thought about it a minute. "There are two main specialty camera dealers in Albuquerque that I know about. I'll give them a call for more information. Then I'll start looking for a link between Sully, the missing boy, relocating to a remote residence, and that camera gear. . . ."

"You're thinking kiddie porn? New Mexico has always had weak laws in that area. You might want to check and see if there's anything in the records linking Sully to something like that," she said.

"I'll do it. And unless something happens between now and then to lead us in a new direction, I think we're going to want to pay Sully a visit tonight," he answered.

"Every second is important when it comes to a kidnapping, Lee. Get some officers to check out Sully's properties."

"You're right. And I'll have them keep him under covert surveillance if they happen to locate the guy. If Sully does have Timothy Klein, and the boy's still alive, Sully may panic and try to get rid of the evidence. The thought of getting caught spurs a lot of perverts into killing their captives," he said.

"I'm with you. We'll want to tread carefully and softly, though in haste. And if Sully has to be taken down, it'll be best if it isn't one of us. Any locals on the scene, even deputies, can't be trusted not to give us up to Glover. I want to get the boy back *and* still get Glover, if at all possible."

"Okay, then. I'll drive you back to Howard's, and find out what I can about Brian Sully without tipping anyone off."

"If something comes up and you need some backup, Anna knows I'll have to blow off work at the store," she said.

Lee started the SUV, checked for traffic, then pulled back out onto the highway. "One more thing I forgot to tell you. I can confirm that Glover is armed with a laser sight-equipped handgun." He told her about becoming the target for Glover's dry-firing activity earlier.

"That's bad news. You think he knows you saw him with the pistol? That could change his timetable for retaliation."

"I doubt it. He doesn't know I can see in the dark, and into shadows during daytime. And he's much more likely to set me, or you, up cold, out on some isolated stretch of road where there are no witnesses to the hit."

"Anyplace but at home, right? Like after you drop me off? Be careful, Lee. Making yourself a target, even with your capabilities, is still a very dangerous strategy."

"I'm equally worried about you, Diane."

"As much as the thought makes me want to barf, I think Glover would want to get close, put his hands on me first—before killing me. He's a sadist."

"And apparently a good strategist. He's seen now that we're

not pushovers, so he's going to try and come up with a plan, not just straightforward and direct. He may try to use one of us to get to the other," he said.

"I can't see in the dark, or jump onto roofs, or tip over cars like you, but if the bastard gets close to me again, I'll blow his head off or poke out his eyes. He's a human, not a . . ."

They didn't even like to use the word "vampire," knowing how easily bugs could be planted in cars, and how electronics could pick up conversations hundreds of yards away. They were passing the ranger station in Tijeras now, and Howard's was just a quarter mile away.

"Keep in mind that anyone we talk to around here could be an informant for Glover—Mike and Earl included," Lee said. "I wish you could carry a second, backup pistol."

"If I did, it would pretty much give away the fact that I'm in law enforcement. The little three-eighty and the pocketknife will have to do until I lose this hottie disguise."

"Let's find you a denim jacket with inside pockets."

"Great for up at the house and at nights, but in the store, all I have to hide behind is the apron." She paused, then added, "I can get a pair of those parachute pants with all kinds of actual pockets. Why didn't I think of that before?"

"I remember the days when there were army-navy stores all over the place. Give me the size and details. I'll get our contacts in the city to find a pair and send them to the house, next-day delivery, or maybe drive them up to the store, if they can get them there before you leave."

"Thanks."

Lee drove up into the parking lot. There were four cars in the close slots, so he turned to find another space.

"Just let me out here. Anna has her hands full, it looks like. I'll see you this evening, earlier if necessary."

Lee gave her hand a squeeze. "Be careful."

"You, too, Lee. 'Bye." She climbed out of the SUV, having to use the narrow excuse for a running board. Diane was short, barely five-five, though her punkish hairstyle added another four inches, perhaps.

She waved, then walked quickly to the entrance. Lee waited a second until she was inside, then turned around and drove back onto the highway again. He'd already blown off the idea of pretending to be a silversmith, at least for now. There was real business to attend to. He put the headset on his cell phone so he'd have both arms free, and reached down and felt the 9 mm Beretta in his jacket pocket. Beside it was a small plastic bottle of sunblock, equally important to him on a bright afternoon.

Glover's loaner Jeep wasn't parked at his place on Quail Run, and it appeared he wasn't at home. Lee checked their own video surveillance system, noted that nobody had been inside while he was gone, then reset it. Then his cell phone rang. It was Captain Terry.

"Leo, we've been getting excellent cooperation from local departments and the feds, and plainclothes officers have been sent to all of Brian Sully's properties. At your suggestion, they're using the cover of a fugitive search. But nobody has admitted seeing Sully today. We have a Code Five out on him—locate and place him under surveillance, but do not approach or apprehend. The only address we haven't sent a team to is that residential cabin in the East Manzanos up by Fourth of July Canyon. The watch commander for the sheriff's department has a couple of deputies on the way right now, but we haven't heard in from them yet."

"They using the same cover story?"

"Not quite. They're really looking for the missing Klein boy, but are being asked to check a list of other homes in the area, as well. They don't know Sully is the specific target, or that we may have a reason to put him on the suspect list. But they're under

orders to report which residences are vacant when they stop by—
per visit—and Sully's first on their list. It he's at home, I'll get a
call via the sheriff's dispatcher, and I'll relay the word to you."

"Good. Wherever he turns up, I want to hear about it
ASAP," Lee said.

"Planning on putting him under surveillance?"

"Yes, and maybe more." Lee smiled to himself as soon as he
spoke. He now had plans for Officer Andrea Moore.

Fifteen minutes later, after getting a call, Lee was on the road
heading south, essentially paralleling the mountain range to his
right. The popular hiking and camping area called Fourth of
July Canyon—probably because of the brilliant fall colors from
aspens and scrub oaks, as well as pine—was about halfway
down the Manzano range.

There were dirt and graveled roads leading off, usually pretty
straight and perpendicular to the highway where it was flat
enough to construct such a route. Invariably these roads led to
one or more private residences for people with the resources and
personalities needed to live in an area only now beginning any serious development. The older homes were the modern equiva-
lent of homesteaders, though they more often were retirees or
employees at large or small businesses than serious farmers or
ranchers. There was livestock out here, of course, but more often
it consisted of chickens, goats or sheep, or maybe a horse or two.

The street signs were usually there, but sometimes hand
lettered on graying wood instead of enamel on metal. Lee spotted the dusty road that led to Sully's house from a distance.
Monarch Lane began in an area resembling a prairie—nothing
but short grass and gentle slopes—but farther to the west the
foothills popped up quickly, and the first junipers and piñons
were visible from the highway. Beyond that the forest began.

He turned in, slowly, looking at the tire tracks. The last two vehicles out had gone north—the deputies—so Sully was probably still at home. About fifty feet down the road was a wide spot with a single mailbox and a newspaper tube, and as Lee passed it by, he could see where the postal carrier always turned his vehicle around. He stopped, looking far ahead, trying to see if any vehicles were coming his way from Sully's cabin, located a few miles west, if his information was correct.

He'd passed the two sheriff's department units coming north just three minutes ago and, after that, he'd watched oncoming traffic. Sully was driving a white Toyota Camry, but the only vehicles Lee had encountered were a forest service pickup in the opposite lane, and a big UNM SUV headed south, full of what appeared to be college kids. It figured, since there was an observatory on Capilla Peak, southwest of his location.

According to State Police Captain Kelly, the deputies had found Sully at the cabin, chopping wood, but there was no sign of any child there. They'd called it in as ordered, then proceeded to their next stop.

Lee drove closer, ever aware of the need to make sure he didn't expose his vehicle to Sully if the man drove by. Lee found a gully that would hide the SUV from the road, then topped off his sunblock and left the vehicle on foot.

The forest here was thin, in transition from grasses to taller plants, and the trees were naturally smaller and farther apart. Ahead, as the elevation increased, Lee could see that they were closer and taller. Moving from the shade of one tree quickly to the shadow of another, Lee stopped when he heard a thump. When he heard another, he recognized the sound of an axe striking wood. If Sully was guilty of taking the boy, he'd kept his cool and continued his work.

The forest was all around him now as Lee got close enough to see, so he decided to wait in a deeply shaded spot. When the entire area became enveloped in deep shadows, close to sunset, then it would be time for his next move.

Lee met Diane at the highway beside Sully's mailbox at 7:30. The sun was west and behind the mountains, and everything was shaded now. He'd lived in the eastern foothills of a mountain range a lifetime ago. He'd been married to his Annie back then and had trusted her with his secret. He could remember every detail of those special late afternoons they'd spent outside together, sharing nature at a time when she could see clearly and move around freely with him.

"Hey, Lee. Tell me about this plan of yours," Diane said, bringing him back to the present as she pulled up beside him and spoke from her open window.

"While I'm doing that, let's get your truck out of sight in case Sully decides to leave home before his visitor shows up." He walked around and climbed into the passenger side. "Just go up the road, slowly, and I'll show you where to turn off."

"I'm not the visitor?" Diane drove slowly west up the dirt road, keeping an eye out for potholes. This was a private road and it hadn't been graded since the last thunderstorm or two, obviously.

"No. Turns out Officer Moore—Andrea's her first name— busted Sully on that solicitation charge, and she remembers that case well enough to want to check this guy out further concerning the missing boy.

"Turn here. The ground is solid enough. Just follow my tracks," Lee continued and pointed as they arrived at the spot where she'd be leaving the road.

"Better take over. It's too dark for me to see that well, and I don't want to turn on the headlights."

"Wanna climb over me?" Lee slid closer, then scrunched back in the seat.

"Yeah, but I'll go around instead," she said, then chuckled as she climbed out the driver's side. Lee moved over to take the wheel, and Diane climbed in where he'd been sitting before.

"One can hope," Lee mumbled. "Ready?"

She nodded, so he drove down into the arroyo in low gear, moving about fifty feet, then climbed out into a grove of pines and parked beside the SUV.

"Nice hidey-hole. Can't see the road, and can't see this alleged cabin. Where is it from here?" Diane asked.

Lee pointed. "That direction, about a quarter mile. I don't think he could have heard the pickup. The wind is blowing from the west, down slope. I could hear him chopping wood all the way from here earlier today."

"Lee, you could hear a piñon jay on the western slopes."

"Not quite. But he *is* listening to a radio talk show right now."

"Idiot. I can't hear a thing."

They both climbed quietly out of the truck, then Diane followed him through the forest, uphill, for nearly five minutes. He stopped, motioned to the grassy slope, then sat down. She joined him, breathing heavily. She hadn't gone climbing at this altitude for a long time, apparently, though she was in good physical shape.

"Hear it now?" he whispered, gesturing with his thumb to the left.

She sat there a moment, tuning out the chirps, rustles, and hops of birds fluttering around in the branches above them, and the sound of rustling leaves. Then she heard a voice, faintly. Diane nodded.

"We'll move up close enough to see the cabin and his white Toyota, then hide out and watch for Officer Moore. If she manages to get him agitated or nervous, he may make a move to check on the boy—if he actually has him—when she leaves. She's a hard-ass cop. If anyone can rattle him, she can."

"Got to meet her. Sounds like my aunt Linda."

"She's not a cop, is she?"

"Worse than that. She's my godmother."

"I'm not sure I want to meet Aunt Linda."

"Smart cop. You still planning on checking out the place even if he doesn't take Officer Moore's bait?"

"Got to. We need to know if the Klein boy is hidden somewhere around here. My worst fear is that Timothy might already be dead and buried. If Sully takes off, it may just mean that he's decided to run for his life."

"We'll stick to the plan then, unless he does something unexpected," she said with a nod. "Is Officer Moore going to be safe going in there alone?"

"I checked up on her. She's a capable officer and her experience with youth gangs has placed her in tough company. Andy knows not to turn her back on anyone, and she's going in with full uniform and vest."

"Andy? And you two only had one date."

"Lunch. Business. Professional. Nearly as tough as you. Maybe it's the uniform and the short 'do she has. I think she respects what she's heard about me—and you—in the news."

"Because we've been kicking vampire and shapeshifter ass?"

He smiled, shaking his head. *Nobody* was more fun to be around than Diane Lopez. "Shall we?"

Lee stood and held out his hand. She reached over and grabbed it and let him pull her up. Diane held his hand with a tight grip as he led her through the twilight toward Sully's place.

They finally settled in behind a fallen tree, with a clear view of Brian Sully's cabin. It was actually a metal, pitched-roof cottage with blue-stained wooden siding and an enclosed front porch occupying one end of the rectangular structure. The house was built into the hillside on a stone foundation, and was off the ground enough on the porch end to require six wooden steps. No storage building was visible, but there was a small pump house where a well provided water. Lee had heard it start up earlier a few times. Though a stone fireplace was built in at the end opposite the porch, a propane tank provided reliable gas for a stove.

There didn't appear to be any electrical lines leading to the home, so, although the lights could be gas-powered, any electricity inside was probably coming from a generator, perhaps in a basement.

"Cozy," Diane whispered.

Lee felt the vibration of his cell phone and opened up the receiver. He read the text message: "set2go."

He entered "k," sent the message, and waited. A similar response came back: "k."

"Officer Moore is coming up the road," Lee confirmed.

Diane nodded, then reached into her jacket and brought out a pair of binoculars. "For the night-vision impaired."

Five minutes passed, then a small, imported SUV came into view, pulling up beside Sully's Toyota. As Lee and Diane watched from cover, they saw Sully looking outside from beside a curtain in the front room. There was a low murmur, then a bright floodlight came on, illuminating the grounds and the two vehicles.

"Bingo. The generator," Diane said softly.

Officer Moore, in her dark blue Albuquerque Police Department uniform, kept the engine running for a moment and examined the grounds and edge of the house with a floodlight beside her side mirror, then turned off the light and vehicle engine.

She stepped out of the vehicle just as Brian Sully crossed his screened-in porch and walked halfway down the front steps.

"What's going on, Officer?"

"You Brian K. Sully?"

"That depends. Who are you, and what are you doing here?"

"I'm Officer Moore of the Albuquerque Police Department. Remember me, Sully?" She took off her cap.

"Should I?"

"I used to work vice. Tight jeans, halter top, short hair, figure like a boy. You offered to pay me for a blow job one night."

"Oh. *That* Officer Moore. That unfortunate incident was my first and only experience with the seedy side of life. I showed up in court and paid my fine. Check my records. What are you doing here, anyway? Isn't this one mountain range beyond your jurisdiction, Officer?"

"I'm doing some off-duty checks for other agencies, Mr. Sully. There's a ten-year-old child missing somewhere in the East Mountain area. Timothy Klein. He may have been kidnapped."

"I heard. Of course, maybe he just got lost out there somewhere while hiking. Either way, I have a business in the canyon, and me and my employees have been keeping our eyes open."

"What do *you* believe happened?"

"Who knows? The parents are divorced, aren't they, and the papers said they're in the middle of a court battle over control of their business. Maybe one of them is hiding the kid from the other. Revenge—leverage. Couples get pretty ugly when they break up."

"Maybe, but that's not my concern. My job is to rule out the perverts who abuse children. So I'm following up on anyone I've arrested in the past who showed an unhealthy interest in young boys and girls."

"Hey, I knew you were a woman. Old enough, too. You just happened to catch my eye. Don't blame me. It was entrapment. I remember you looked hot that night."

"Yeah, right. I looked thirteen, that's what got your attention. The other cops said I looked like a *boy* in drag."

"Now you're trying to make me say things that just aren't true. If you don't leave, I'm going to file harassment charges. Wait until my lawyer hears about this. You have a tape recorder on? You're on private property without a warrant, you know, and you have no authority here."

"Would I call you a perverted asshole in a fruity beach boy shirt if I was recording, Sully? You're just pissing in your pants, afraid of getting caught. I bet that little boy is locked up in your basement right now. God, I wish I *had* a search warrant. I'd have your ass in jail by nine P.M."

"Screw the warrant. Go ahead, search everything, top to bottom. Dig up the forest, too. Then get the hell off my property and go do some real police work instead of harassing innocent citizens minding their own business."

"Now you've pushed your luck, Sully. I'm calling your bluff. I'm going to search this dump from top to bottom right now. Here's a frigging release. Sign it if you've got any balls left dangling."

Officer Moore reached into her uniform shirt pocket and brought out a piece of paper and a pen. "I'm assuming you *can* read, you prick." She aimed her flashlight on the paper, and after a minute, Sully read and signed it. He was so mad, Lee could see his hand shaking. Then he tossed it at her.

"Here you are, bitch. And don't try to plant any phony evidence. I'm going to be right beside you."

"Damned right you'll be right beside me. And keep your little boy-grabbing hands where I can see them. You make a move on me and it'll take a tow truck to pull my boot outta your ass."

"I wish she was wearing a wire. I'm not catching everything," Diane whispered. "She seems a little over the top. Think Sully is going to catch on?"

Lee shook his head. "Moore's with the gang unit, and there's nothing more dramatic than teenagers on the edge. Results are what count, and she's getting exactly the kind of reaction we want."

Sully waved the female officer, a foot shorter than him and probably forty pounds lighter, toward the front door.

"You first, Sully," Moore ordered. Sully suggested something about Officer Moore's sexual preferences, but he stepped inside the screened porch, followed by the officer. They continued on into the house, and were only partially visible through the windows.

"Now we wait," Diane said.

Lee hated to be out of contact with Officer Moore when she could be the subject of an attack—if Sully was a kidnapper—but he couldn't risk coming up closer to the house and being seen from the inside. The ground had been cleared out to a distance of about a hundred feet in every direction—a good fire prevention strategy—so there was no cover, especially with the generator-powered outside lights.

An uneventful twenty minutes went by—apparently Officer Moore was checking everywhere, not just in a place where a four-and-a-half-foot boy could be hidden in one piece—then Sully led the way as they came back out onto the porch. Sully watched while Moore aimed her flashlight all around the enclosure, which held only an outdoor café-size metal table and two chairs, then the two came outside.

They walked all the way around the outside of the building, Officer Moore directing her flashlight along the ground, searching for openings in the foundation and the roof, as well. When the two appeared again, after checking the sides out of view of Lee and Diane, Sully spoke.

"Told you I haven't got a damn thing to do with that missing kid. You come back here again, you'd better have the sheriff *and* a legal warrant. Then you can waste his time, too, and piss everybody off."

"Thank you for your cooperation, Mr. Sully, but don't think you're off the hook. Not until I get every piece of property you own checked out. You don't think I know about your Albuquerque apartments? Hell, I may even check out your station in Tijeras."

"Knock yourself out. I'm going inside." The man turned and stepped back onto his porch. He'd just shut the screen door behind him when Officer Moore, who'd been looking around the yard, suddenly whistled.

It was so loud, Diane flinched, and so did Lee.

"Hey, dickhead. One more spot. Pop the trunk on your Camry so I can have a look."

"I should make you get another warrant," Sully said, but he came back outside. Removing the key chain from his pocket, he thumbed the remote. There was a tone, and the trunk popped open a few inches.

"Okay. Now stand still." Moore walked over, lifted the truck up with the rim of her flashlight, then directed the light inside. She stepped closer and took a closer look.

"Full-size spare. Good thinking. Flares and chains, too. Bet you need them in winter sometimes, getting to the highway from here. Have a pleasant evening, Mr. Sully." She walked to her vehicle, climbed inside, then started the engine and drove off quickly, spraying gravel.

Sully waited until the dust had drifted away, then walked over and closed the trunk on the Camry. Next, he inspected his car windows, perhaps concerned that they had been struck by flying gravel. He mumbled some obscenities that Lee couldn't hear, then flipped a finger in the direction of the retreating taillights. "Bite me!" Sully yelled at the top of his lungs.

Sully started laughing, and his amusement continued all the way into the house. A minute later, the outside floodlights were turned off.

"Now what?" Diane whispered to Lee.

"The night is young. If he has the Klein boy hidden somewhere he might just want to go check on him."

"But not if he thinks he's being watched or set up. He may come back out now with a light and search the surrounding forest for spies. Us."

"Good point. Let's get back to the vehicles. You stay there and get in contact with Officer Moore on the cell phone. I gave you the number, right?"

"Yeah. You going to come back here and play cat and mouse?"

"Sully doesn't come across as the Navy SEAL type, and besides, I have the advantage at the moment."

"More than one. So let's get moving before he grabs a shotgun and a lantern." Diane stood up, grabbed his hand, then tripped over a branch.

"Oops." Lee kept her from falling by pulling her against him and held her close for a second to steady her. "Let me lead the way, okay?"

It took only about five minutes to reach the vehicles. Lee picked an easy route, and because it was so dark, only other vampires or men with flashlights could pose a threat to them now. They encountered neither.

Diane was already calling Andrea Moore when Lee started back to Sully's. He ran uphill, treading lightly and uninhibited by the need to conceal his half-vampire speed and agility. None of that Hollywood vampire turning-into-a-bat fiction was really possible, though shape-shifters capable of turning into wolves or wildcats were as real as vampires. Lee knew that firsthand. Until he'd met Diane Lopez, his only goal in life had been to hunt down and kill the Navajo skinwalkers who preyed upon innocent Navajos, like Annie, his schoolteacher wife.

He hadn't seen, or sensed, a shape-shifter in human, wolf,

or mountain lion form for more than a year now, but the last pack he'd done battle with along the Rio Grande Valley had nearly killed both Diane and him.

In less than a minute Lee was back in position, watching Sully's house for activity. He was farther back now, not needing to be as close so Diane could hear and see, as well. If Sully did come out again, Lee wanted to have enough room to move fast and avoid the beam of a light.

Five minutes later, the generator came back on, and a moment later, the floodlights. Sully came out, wearing a hooded sweatshirt, baseball cap, and carrying a handgun and powerful flashlight. He stepped off the porch, directed the light slowly around the area, sweeping the darkness of the surrounding forest and searching for movement. A rabbit froze as the beam passed her by, then took off into the brush as soon as the light moved on.

Lee ducked behind a tree well before the light reached him and waited. Satisfied, apparently, Sully checked to make certain nobody was beside the house, then he checked the car, even getting down on the ground and looking beneath. Maybe he was searching for a tracking device.

Sully went back inside, turned off the generator, then came out. He locked the inside and outside doors, then climbed into the Camry, placing the pistol under his seat. Then he drove slowly away.

Lee was on the phone immediately. "Lay low, Diane. Sully just left in his car. I'll be coming down the hill as soon as I hang up."

"Thanks for the warning," Diane said. "I can see his headlights in the distance."

Lee ran quickly, already knowing the route to take. When he reached Diane, she was standing beside her pickup, looking in his direction.

"It's me," Lee said, coming close enough so she could see him clearly even under the starlight.

"I heard you, barely. Thanks for giving me a heads-up. It gives me the creeps sometime when I turn around and see you standing there."

Lee moved toward his SUV. "Must be the Indian in me. We know how to move silently."

"It's not just the Indian," she commented. "You lead, I'll follow. Headlights are okay, right?"

"Yeah. As soon as we get rolling, I'll call you."

Lee didn't need the headlights, of course, but once he got within Sully's sight, Diane's lights would illuminate him anyway, so he'd be using them. But right now, he had to get close enough to see whether Sully went north or south at the highway. He started up the vehicle, drove quickly out of the arroyo, then raced east down the gravel road.

When he topped the last hill before the mile-long, straight stretch to the highway, Lee could see Sully pulling out, headed north. He got on the phone immediately and relayed the information to Diane. She acknowledged, and he noticed her headlights in his rearview mirror.

Lee turned on his own lights now and raced to the turnoff. Three minutes later he had Sully's car in view again, so he let off on the gas and slowed to fifty-five. Sully was going the speed limit on this stretch, so he had to pace him.

Lee plugged his cell phone into the headset so he could drive easily now and still talk to Diane.

"Think he's going to one of his properties in Albuquerque, maybe to check on the boy?" Diane asked.

"Could be. He checked all around his place to see if anyone else was lurking around before he left. He wanted to make sure he wasn't being followed."

"But he knows there's a vehicle behind him now, right?"

"I'm far back enough so he can't make me, but, yes, he's got to know he's not the only one on this road."

"If he turns, then break off. I can take the chase up from there," said Diane.

"Agreed," Lee said. "Why don't you call the Bureau and see if there's anything they can add to Sully's background? His financial situation and so on. Also, ask if they'll compare his photo to any unsolved child predator reports in other communities—those that have a sketch or description that might fit."

"I can do that. Hanging up now."

Lee continued to follow Sully for another ten minutes, then watched as the man pulled off the road to the right and came to a stop.

Diane was available, and he got her right away. "He pulled off the east side of the road and stopped. I've got to pass him. I'll go on by, then pull off myself. If he comes by me again, I'll let you know. Wait for him to start up again, and don't let him get behind you."

"Gotcha, Lee. I see your taillights, so I'm going to pull over now. Watch him from your side, if you can."

"Okay." Lee quickly put on a baseball cap, backward like the current teen style, then turned up his collar and found a radio station playing obnoxious rap. He slowed a bit, rolled down his window, slumped slightly in his seat, then cruised by Sully's parked car. He watched the car as long as he could with his eyes, but didn't turn his head.

As soon as Lee got to the next curve, he pulled over, turned off his lights, then climbed out of the SUV quietly and looked back down the road. Sully was sitting there, alone in his car. Five minutes went by, then Sully pulled out onto the road again, turning on his lights.

Lee waited, then, as Sully's lights began to reach his location, turned away, hunched over, and pretended to be throwing up just in front of the SUV.

Sully was no good Samaritan; as a matter of fact he speeded up as he passed Lee doing his act.

Once Sully was down the road a few hundred yards, Lee jumped back into the SUV. Diane was coming up from behind now and he let her pass. "I've got him now," he heard her say as he picked up his headset. "What were you doing, answering nature's call?"

"Naw, pretending to be a hurling rapper."

"Sorry I asked."

"Thought that might keep him from looking too closely."

"Would have worked for me."

They continued to follow Sully's car, Diane now leading, until finally Diane spoke again. "He just turned left, up Quail Run. I'm going on past him without making the turn, then pull over like you did before. If he's trying to ditch me, this'll make him think it worked."

"He knows Glover, maybe that's where he's headed," Lee responded.

"I'd like to know what they're going to be talking about. You think he's going to ask Glover to check up on Officer Moore? Try and find out what's going on?"

Lee thought about it a moment, then decided to turn and follow Sully. If Sully stopped at one of the other homes on Quail Run, he'd see, and if the suspect went all the way to Glover's, Lee would still have a reason for being across the street. He lived there.

"I'm going home. Not as likely to arouse any suspicions doing that, and maybe I can eavesdrop on Sully if he's really headed for Glover's."

"Okay. I'll hang around by the highway for a while and stay

in touch. Both of us shouldn't return at the same time. That'll look strange," Diane said.

Lee drove up Quail Run several car lengths behind Sully, who was going just over the posted speed of 15 mph. Lee could tell he was being watched via the man's rearview mirrors, but if his presence was making Sully paranoid at the moment, too bad. Sully slowed to a crawl, then pulled in behind the Jeep in Glover's driveway.

Sully stayed in his car, and Lee could see Glover looking out his living room window at the white Camry as he drove up, pulled into his and Diane's driveway, then stopped and climbed out.

Lee walked up to the front door of the house and fiddled with his keys, watching Sully's car. Glover had moved out of view.

Lee opened the door, went inside, turned on the living room lamp, then walked into the kitchen area, disappearing from view of the front living room window. He continued into the utility room just beyond, ran quickly out the back door and circled, inching his way up to the west side of the house, crouched low. Once he reached the corner of the building, Lee stopped. From here he could finally see what was going on in front of Glover's place.

Sully opened the driver's side door and Glover came out, hurrying to the car.

"What the hell you doing here, Sully? Don't tell me your moron mechanics screwed up my pickup. It was supposed to be delivered this afternoon."

"No, no. That's not it," Sully said, climbing out of the vehicle. He turned and looked toward Lee's front porch. "I got a visitor tonight and I need to talk to you about it."

"Let's go inside. The guy across the street is a trouble-maker."

Sully's laugh was nervous. "Not for long, I'll bet. You'll take care of him."

Glover slapped Sully on the head, likely a throwback to his high school bully days. "Shut up, asshole. Just get inside."

Lee reached down to his pocket and switched his cell phone to vibrate as he watched the two men climb up the small porch and go inside Glover's house. Glover took another look outside, toward their front window, then turned on his porch light.

Lee sprinted across the road, leaped the low fence around Glover's yard, then inched up to the corner of the house. He considered keeping flush against the wall and hoping he could find a window to listen at, then decided he'd be in full view once either man came back outside.

Wishing for a second he could shape-shift into a jaguar, like a skinwalker, Lee settled on his vampire-enhanced athletic ability. Jumping flat-footed, he grasped the edge of the roof, then did a slow, careful pull-up, easing onto the fiberglass shingles and lying flat. He then stood and quietly walked, step by step, until he was above the living room window. Flattening once again, Lee lowered his head over the edge and noted that the window was open about four inches.

"Stand still. If you're wired or somebody attached a bug to your clothing, this scanner will pick it up."

"Where the hell did you learn all this James Bond crap, anyway? Never mind, I don't want to know," Sully said.

"You're not as stupid as you look. You're clean."

"Then talk to me, Glover. What's going on?"

"They don't know shit, Sully, how could they? If that cop had anything you'd be handcuffed in the back of her car and there would be a crime scene van in your front yard. She's just grasping at straws, trying to break a big case and get promoted to sergeant or whatever."

"Maybe. But I don't believe in coincidences. Do you?"

"Remind me to scan your car before you leave. Last thing we need is for you to be seen with me. You didn't leave anything at your house that would lead to me or suggest I had the merchandise, did you?"

"No, no, everything was pristine or I wouldn't have allowed the search. I'm keeping the deal. No money, no merchandise."

"You screw around with me, you're dead, Sully. Until I get the rest of the cash, you get nothing. I put my life on the line to get this for you, and I'm not taking any chances."

Lee thought his heart stopped for a moment as he heard the words. Though the term used had been "merchandise," it sounded to him like Glover was implying that he had kidnapped the boy and was *selling* him to Sully. And if the Klein boy was the merchandise, where was he being kept?

CHAPTER 10

Lee felt his phone vibrating, but wasn't exactly in a position to answer it. He needed to continue listening to Sully and Glover in order to get a lead to the "merchandise."

"Things are getting too hot now, Newt. Life in prison isn't on my career path. Everything has to be put on hold."

"Probably a good idea. But that doesn't mean you can hold off on my money. This was all your idea," Glover answered. "You placed the order months ago, and a few days ago I had the opportunity to grab the merchandise. Don't screw with me unless you want your entire world to go up in smoke. Or worse."

At least two minutes went by before Sully spoke again. "I'm supposed to get a check deposited tomorrow, then I'll start withdrawing cash. When you get the next five thousand, then I can see . . . what I'm paying for, right?"

"Yeah. It's your funeral if something goes south and you end up being identified later on. But you try anything, like going to the cops now—*boom*," Glover said.

"Everything's as promised, right?"

"Fit as a fiddle. Just get the money. And don't come by my house again, ever. We meet at the gas station only. Got it?"

There was a moment of silence, then Lee realized that Sully must have nodded, because the front door opened. Lee thought about getting up and crossing the roof, hiding behind the peak, but knew it would make a lot of noise if he moved fast. He had to flatten and hope Sully or Glover wouldn't look up.

Just then, lights illuminated the street outside. A vehicle was coming up the road.

It was Diane, Lee noted, relaxing a bit. She wouldn't give him away.

Diane pulled up into their driveway just as Sully walked into view, heading for his car. The man turned his head away, trying to keep Diane from seeing his face, then climbed into the Camry.

Glover came out with the scanner in his hand, saw Diane was there, and turned around and went back inside.

There was nothing Sully could do to prevent Diane from seeing his license plate, but still, Sully drove away quickly. By then, Diane was at the front door, holding a Wal-Mart grocery bag Lee knew to be a prop. Probably it was her jacket inside, not food. She opened the door and went into the living/dining room, then around the corner into the kitchen area.

Lee moved very slowly to the corner of the roof, listening after every step, then eased down off the roof, crouching low beside the building. His cell phone vibrated again. He brought out the device and looked at the display. The first message reported that Diane was coming home. The current message said she saw him on the roof.

Lee nodded to himself, looking across into the window, where Diane was barely visible over by the kitchen, her cell phone in hand.

He sent her the text message: "Lt me no wn I cn mv."

There was a quick response: "k."

Lee waited for about ten minutes, and finally Glover's porch light went out. Another three minutes went by, and Lee felt the vibration of a call. The text message was simple: "go."

Lee made no sound as he walked to the fence, stepped over,

then walked across the road into the shadows of his house. Once he was out of sight of Glover's, he ran around to the back door. Diane was waiting.

"Got some news," she said, then noted his expression as he stepped inside.

"Me, too. I think Glover took the Klein kid."

Diane just stared at him for a moment. "No shit?"

"He and Sully were careful not to give specifics, even after Glover scanned for bugs. But yeah, that's my guess."

"That fits with some of the news I have, but yours first. Coffee?" Diane moved over to the coffee maker and began to fill it without waiting for an answer.

Five minutes later, they were sitting at the dining room table, munching on sweet rolls and sipping hot java. Lee had just brought her up to date.

"It sounds like you've nailed it, Lee. I've heard and seen a lot of sick things since I joined the Bureau, but to refer to this little boy as 'merchandise' adds a new low. I still find it hard to believe a pedophile would pay someone to steal a kid for him. These kind of people are usually loners. Having anyone else know what they're doing, well . . . they just don't do that."

"I was thinking about that, too. Sully doesn't have a record for any under-age sexual activity, though he could have just been lucky so far. Or maybe it's just business, and he doesn't really plan on harming the boy—at least physically. Remember all that camera gear he was supposedly collecting?"

"It wasn't at the house we visited tonight. I talked with Officer Moore on the phone while you were roof-dropping, and she gave me the skinny on what she found in his home. There was no porno of any kind, just a few R-rated DVDs, no kiddie photos or indication that a child had been there, well, except for a Halloween mask. He had a pistol in a locked box and no contraband at all. The place was clean, and there were no hiding places she could find in the time she had. He didn't have a computer, either, so she couldn't check it out. He was arrogant the entire search, recommending places for her to look. Sully sure made it look like he's clean."

"Andrea Moore is used to reading people who are lying or keeping secrets. A mask would allow Sully to be around the boy without showing his face, if he planned on letting him go later on. Did she ask him about it?"

"Yeah. He said it was a gag gift from the crew at his tire dealership a year or two ago. So he kept it. He threw it away while she was watching."

"Believable. He wouldn't get any trick-or-treaters at the house, and Halloween is still months away. What did her gut tell her about Sully?"

"Andrea said that beneath his act of indignation she thought he was really pretty nervous and hiding something. Any eye contact he made was whenever he was busy playing his role. When she caught him off guard, he usually looked away. And he was sweating the whole time."

"That fits with what I overheard. But there's more, right?"

Diane nodded. "And it fits with Sully having to raise some cash for something big. Before I met with Andrea, I got a call from SAC Logan. Sully sold two of his properties within the last year, one of them at a considerable loss and the other within the past month. That must be where the cash is coming from."

"We might be able to lean on Sully if he knows something about the kidnapping. Sweat him out," Lee suggested.

"He'd just point his finger at Glover and ask for protection. All Glover would need to do, unless we could somehow produce the boy, is claim that Sully is lying and where's the proof? Without any, we'd be stuck. Glover would stay away from where he's hiding Timothy Klein, knowing we'd be watching, and the child would be in even greater danger. Besides, we really don't know for sure they're talking about a kidnapping. It could be stolen property, drugs, you name it."

"'Fit as a fiddle' implies something that is alive," he pointed out.

"Or a Mercedes convertible in excellent condition."

"Either way, Glover is the key, but we're going to have to handle him carefully. There's another place he owns, visits, or controls, apparently. The place with the 'merchandise.' Hasn't Logan been able to get any more details on the guy?" he asked.

"Some, and here's where the kidnapping angle comes in," Diane began. "Glover has twenty years of military service. The last five of that was spent as part of a military unit trained to snatch enemy soldiers and bring them in for interrogation. He never made it to sergeant in all that time, but he received extensive training and has combat experience and service ribbons. Glover gets a pension, but his records indicate the army was glad to get rid of him, and jumped at the chance for a medical discharge for some minor injury. He'd been disciplined a half-dozen times over the years. You won't be surprised to learn Glover has a problem with authority."

"Everything seems to fit. Is it possible Glover owns, or is renting or leasing, other property we just don't know about?" Lee asked. "In a different name?"

"Maybe someone he's been pushing around is letting him use a place? If that's the case, there wouldn't be any paperwork because everything would be under the owner's name. If it's Sully, then he might know a possible location for the merchandise."

"Can we get a list from the retired judge that put us onto Glover that'll give us some hints on where to check? Even gossip the judge overheard would be a place to start," Lee said.

"I wish we had more options regarding listening devices. Bugging Glover or Sully's vehicles or residences would be risky, though. Glover knows he's living on the edge, and he's going to continue those sweeps. If we plant a bug and he spots it, he won't go anywhere near something that can get him arrested."

"He'd probably leave the device in place, clam up, lay low, and be on his guard for a tail," Lee agreed. "We *could* install a bug we can turn on and off by remote, but if the sweeper he has is an upgrade of one of those old Scan-Lock receivers, it'll zero in once we activate it, even for a moment or two. It's too big a risk."

"Especially because at the moment he doesn't know who we are, or that we're this close to nailing him for something. If he spots any of the high-tech gadgets I can get from the Bureau, we'll really blow our cover. To get that extra intelligence it might be better to use a low-tech solution. We need to put a full-time tail on Sully and Glover, someone with the skills to avoid detection. Together we can cover Glover. But we need someone to follow Sully. He's paranoid by now, obviously, but he doesn't have the countersurveillance training Glover has picked up. With Glover using bug-detection gear, we have to be very careful when using anything high-tech unless it's completely out of his league, like NSA- or CIA-level hardware."

"Let's do some quick checking, and see if we can borrow Officer Moore and some APD officers to cover Sully in their jurisdiction. Most of his properties are in Albuquerque. The trick is, what about in the East Mountains? The sheriff's department deputies working this side of the county are still suspect," Lee pointed out.

"We still need somebody who knows the area. How about someone in *your* department? If not a current patrol officer, then maybe a state cop who's worked the area before?" Diane asked.

"Well, this assignment originated with the state police, so let me see if Captain Kelly can get someone for us."

An hour later, Lee and Diane had used their contacts to get the cooperation of the Albuquerque police chief. A state police officer, Felix Rodriguez, currently working out of the Albuquerque district, would begin tailing Sully in the morning. Officer Moore would try and determine his location, checking first at the cabin, then keep him in sight until State Patrolman Rodriguez took over.

With their strategy in place, Lee and Diane went over their intel, checking out the people in the East Mountain area who may have been corrupted or mistreated by Glover. That list included current county law enforcement personnel working the East Mountain division.

"Here's Deputy Harmon," Diane pointed out. "He's hauled in Glover twice on criminal complaints, but the charges were dropped both times when the complainants or witnesses recanted. One witness who recanted lives right down the street, a Martin C. Weiner. I remember seeing the name on a mailbox."

"We can't trust Deputy Harmon yet, that's for sure," Lee agreed. "How about we go over this information one more time before we send it to our secure website, then you get some sleep? You look beat."

Diane yawned. "Good idea. I'm going to have to talk to Anna first thing and work out a new schedule. If I drop the job completely and just hang out, Glover might get suspicious with neither of us employed."

"Suppose you can get fired?"

"Yeah. But is Glover going to wonder where our money is coming from then?"

"Let him think we're into something illegal. He doesn't have a job, after all."

"Yeah, and he already knows you have a criminal record. But that said, I'd still like to hang on to the job a bit longer. Maybe I can get more information about Glover—like where he may have property. Stuff that is off the records. The official hunt for Timothy Klein is at a standstill right now, but we may be on the trail to finding him—if Glover snatched him for Sully's entertainment."

"You have a point. So we'll play it day by day, depending on how tricky it gets to keep track of Glover. Let's go through these files one more time."

Diane yawned again, then scooted her chair over closer so she could see the screen images on the laptop a little better. "Ready."


C rap. I've got a flat, Lee," Diane said, coming back up onto the porch. The sun was just creeping over the horizon and she was ready to leave for her cover job at the store in Tijeras.

Lee came out, having already put on his sunblock and long sleeves after the shower. He adjusted the bill on his cap, sunglasses on, and looked toward Glover's house. The Jeep was in the driveway and there was no sign of anyone moving around inside. Lee had watched the house until around 4:00 A.M. then grabbed two hours of sleep, knowing that if their neighbor drove away, the engine noise would awaken him. "Glover?"

Diane shrugged. "There's a screw in the tread. It's all scratched up, but that's what I'd expect on this graveled road. I suppose he could have come over and done the deed during the night. But why not just stick a knife in the sidewall?"

"He could have sneaked over while I was grabbing a few z's

just before dawn, but he'd have probably done more than just mess up one tire. And it would be clearly deliberate, so we'd know it was him. We can change it in ten. You've got the time, right?"

She looked at her watch. "Barely."

They moved quickly, Diane getting out the jack and Lee the spare. Once the flat tire was off the ground, Lee used the lug wrench and quickly took off the flat and replaced it with the full-size spare. They were both experienced at this task, and the job was done in close to seven minutes.

Lee placed the spare in the bed of the truck and the jack on the floorboards. "We'll stow it properly later. The first break you get at the store, you might want to take this to Sully's garage to be fixed. You'll want a spare coming home."

"Okay. Gotta go now. I'll call with anything I learn, and you do the same. Good luck today," Diane said, giving him a quick peck on the lips. "And remember to keep plenty of sunblock at hand."

"Always." He put his arms around her, holding her close for a moment. "Good to see you're wearing your vest," he whispered gently.

"You aren't. Put it on before you come outside again. Our next-door neighbor is the biggest threat to you, sunlight not included."

"Yes, ma'am." Lee stepped back and released her.

" 'Bye." Diane gave him that wrinkly nose smile, then climbed into the truck and drove down the dusty road.

Lee looked over toward Glover's house. There was still no sign of activity, so Lee went back inside.

A short time later, Lee's cell phone rang. It was Diane.

"Lee, this just isn't my day. Just had a blow out. It was the spare. I've pulled over three or four miles down the road. Between mile markers, I think."

"You okay?"

"Yeah. There was a pop and a few scary moments, but the tire stayed on the rim. Fortunately I was just coming out of a curve and going pretty slow."

"Want me to come and get you? It'll mean leaving Glover alone for a while."

"Up to you. I can always call the station in Tijeras. But that'll take a half hour or so, at least, even if they send someone right away."

"I'll take you and the original tire into Tijeras. Once it's fixed, we can arrange for someone to pick up the truck and drop it off at Howard's." Lee was already turning on the video monitoring so that their place would be covered while he was gone.

"How about I call Officer Rodriguez and have him relocate to the main highway? If Glover goes south past Sully's turnoff, Felix can pick him up, and if north, Glover will have to pass by us. There's just the one highway."

"Sounds like a good idea unless Glover is really familiar with the off-road trails. I'm on my way. I'll be there in a few minutes." Lee was walking down the steps of the porch now, adjusting his cap for maximum coverage. Early in the day, the sun could penetrate areas usually covered later on, and he'd always been forced to put sunblock around his hairline.

He was wearing long sleeves and plenty of sunblock so he tossed his jacket on the seat beside him as he climbed into the SUV. Besides, the ballistic vest under his shirt was hot. Two minutes later, he reached the main highway and turned left. Diane said she was only a few miles down the road, on the right, and there were no Jeeps in his rearview mirror. Maybe Glover was sleeping in, not even leaving his home unless it was absolutely necessary.

Lee opened all the vents, enjoying the fresh mountain air as he drove down the narrow highway, still getting complete harmful wavelength light protection from the window glass. Picking up speed until the SUV reached sixty, he could see an old pickup ahead. Probably somebody going to work, but otherwise there didn't seem to be much traffic. Anyone working in the city had left a half hour or more ago.

Along this stretch the forest came right up to the road and Lee breathed in the scent of pine needles and a faint undertone of wildflowers. Fall was still over two months away, and they should be gone by then. Too bad. The leaves on the aspens would be turning to gold, and the scrub oaks to a deep red. Here he was reminded of the tall trees in the Chuska Mountains of the Navajo Nation, along the Arizona border. It seemed wetter here, but after growing up in the Four Corners, any forest was welcome to a child of the desert.

A van was now visible in the rearview mirror, one he thought he remembered being parked beside one of the houses in his neighborhood. Probably someone else pushing the envelope getting to work.

As he entered a tight, right-hand uphill curve, Lee slowed, seeing Diane's vehicle ahead. She was waving on the driver in the old pickup, who'd obviously slowed and offered help.

Lee looked ahead for the best place to pull over and realized that Diane had taken the only viable spot to her right. The best alternative was a wide section right across from her at the far end of the curve on the left side of the road. He'd park there and go across to get the salvageable tire and Diane. It was better than trying to double-park on a nearly blind curve.

Signaling, Lee quickly pulled off across the oncoming lane onto the wide spot of shoulder, then stopped.

He climbed out, then turned around to see how far back the oncoming van was, intending on crossing as soon as it passed. Suddenly he felt a pinpoint of heat on the back of his neck.

Lee spun around. Glover was standing just within the forest, trying to keep the laser sight of his .45 on him.

Glover fired, and Lee, still in motion, felt something slam into his arm. There was searing pain beneath his arm and another explosion, and Lee dropped to the ground.

"Lee!" Diane screamed somewhere in the distance.

CHAPTER 11

Glover turned around, hiding his face by putting his back to the highway and the van cruising by. Lee took advantage of the diversion and rolled beneath the SUV, giving him both shade and cover. Diane fired from across the road, and from the sound in the brush, Glover had decided to haul ass.

Diane came running up, her pistol in hand. "Lee. Where are you hit?"

He tried to focus on her face, but the image was fading in and out, and he felt a bubbling at his lips. Warm, like blood. "Chest—lungs. Bullet missed vest," he managed. "Glover set us up."

As Lee's vision faded to yellow, red, then purple, he heard Diane somewhere off in the distance. "Stay with me, Lee."

Lee found himself drifting, like a leaf across a pond. It was painful at first, especially in the lungs, like he'd been running five miles in the snow, but soon the ache went away. Now it was a comfortable feeling—warm and enveloping, warmth flowing around him instead of the coldness of a mountain stream. His arm hurt for a while, but that faded even faster.

Soon he could hear a voice, and felt a hand wrapped around his own.

"Lee? You back?"

It was Diane. He opened his eyes and saw her bending over him. Either she'd suddenly acquired allergies, or she'd shed a tear or two, but that didn't keep her from giving him that special nose-crinkle grin.

"One of these days, Lee, you're going to drive me nuts. When I saw that one of the bullets had gone under your arm . . . your heart's on that side. I thought . . ."

Lee was feeling better now, stronger. He looked over at his arm, the one that had been struck with the first bullet, and raised it up. "Nuts, I understand. But see, I'm okay. Lucky I reacted when I felt the sight on my neck."

"Didn't want to lose you." She squeezed his hand, then gave him a kiss on the forehead before standing up.

Lee sat up. "I'd give you a hug, but I'm probably a mess." His sleeve was covered in damp blood, which would steam away once the shirt came into contact with sunlight. "I must have a quart of blood beneath the vest." He looked around, not seeing any vehicles in either direction, then stood for a second before sinking back to his knees. "Oops. Better stay low and in the shade. Glover?"

"I missed him, but at least my shot drove him away. I went after him, but he'd already reached an old gray-primer Ford pickup he'd parked a hundred yards back on a side road. Never got a second shot off."

"We can find the pickup. He probably stole it from our own neighborhood after sneaking out his back door. Is that guy in the van long gone? I don't want him to see me like this. Lots of blood, no wounds."

"Dude was oblivious, missed everything. Coffee in one hand, cell phone in the other. He never even looked in your direction. I'll get your jacket and something to wipe up the blood. I recovered his shell casings, but we won't be able to use any fingerprints, I guess," Diane added.

"Wait a sec. How long was I unconscious?"

"Ten, fifteen minutes. Something like that."

"You call for backup?"

"No. Once I saw you were healing, I realized we had some serious choices to make concerning Glover."

"Yeah. So we need to get moving. How about that jacket and cleanup stuff?" Lee took off his shirt and protective vest, then tossed them over to a sunny spot on the gravel shoulder. The blood flared up with a bright flame, but he knew the fabric would only be warm, like out of the dryer, not burned. It was some quirk of vampire blood—it oxidized, but with very little heat.

Diane returned quickly from across the highway with a small blanket, some prepackaged hand wipes, and a first-aid kit. While he wiped off the blood around the healed-over bullet wound in his side just beneath his arm, and on his lips where he'd coughed up frothy blood, Diane brought his jacket out of the SUV where Lee had left it.

"Both bullets passed right through me. And the exit wounds weren't any bigger than the entry points." He lifted up his bullet-resistant vest. "And look at the right side of the vest behind the arm hole."

She held up the heavy protective material. They weren't wearing ceramic plates or metal, but the fabric would stop most pistol bullets. There was a hole about the diameter of a pencil in the back just behind the right arm opening. "Went right through, barely shredding the fiber. Glover was using armor-piercing ammo."

"He's ready to shoot it out with anyone, then. And maybe he's wearing a vest, as well. If he does have contacts in law enforcement, he may have gotten a vest and AP ammunition from them. A vest would explain why the shotgun attack from his neighbor that we heard about failed to put him down permanently."

"Right now we could arrest Glover for assault and attempted murder of a law enforcement officer," Diane commented, watching Lee rubbing on sunblock. "Only one problem."

"I can't prove I was shot, or that he even fired a shot, and this vest would be hard to explain. Unless we could get the pistol and recover a slug, his lawyer could get him off. All we'd have is our own testimony. And we'd have to lie about some of it. We need to nail the bastard on something else."

"He's smart, though. Flattened my tire, then took off on foot out his back door so you wouldn't see him. Sneaked down the street and probably stole one of the neighbor's vehicles. I think I remember that gray truck at one of the homes close to the highway."

"He had this spot already picked out, and believed I'd come and pick you up. Shot out your left rear tire as you slowed to take the curve. Knew you'd probably pull over there," Lee pointed across the highway, "and I'd stop here."

"We can't just pretend nothing happened. He saw you get shot and go down. If I don't call the sheriff and the EMTs, he's going to know about it and suspect something."

"What? If he thought I was really a cop or an innocent civilian, of course you'd go to the police. But if we . . . you, had something to hide, you just might try and get me to a doc on your own and not report it. My cover identity shows I have a record."

"But he knows I know he was the shooter. So I'm a threat. And if you managed to survive, you'd be coming after him. So what now, Lee?"

"We don't want to draw the public's attention, only Glover's. Reporting the incident would work against us. If this gets out, the local TV stations might send a camera crew. One photo on the air and somebody is bound to recognize you or me as law enforcement. Let's keep Glover wondering whether he's really gotten away with it or not." Lee straightened his cap, which he'd somehow managed to keep on, then stood and put on his shirt and vest again.

"Okay, but what do you want to do with the pickup? We don't want the county to haul it away."

"I'll drop you off at work, then track down Glover. You tell Anna that you had two flats, so I had to give you a ride. Call somebody at Sully's station and try to get Mike and Earl to go out, put on a spare, and bring it in to the station. Basically, you pretend that everything is okay, except for the two flats. Anything you need from the pickup?"

"No. Let me lock it up, though. And I'll leave a note on the windshield with the number of the store and my cover name. So the cops won't take it to impound."

"Good. Okay, I'm ready." Lee jumped into the SUV, checked for traffic, and finding none, maneuvered across the road and picked up Diane, who'd already crossed the road on her errand.

As they were nearing Tijeras, he added, "You might want to remind Anna that you're carrying a weapon. And keep your eyes open in case Glover decides to make a move on you."

She nodded. "He may just do that since I'm a witness."

"My guess is that he believes I went down hard. I'm already looking forward to the moment when he sees me again."

"He'll probably assume you were wearing a vest that somehow stopped an armor-piercing bullet, but that's going to convince him that you're in law enforcement. Why don't you put a bandage on your arm? Then he'll come to the conclusion that one of the rounds must have gone wide, but he still managed to score a hit."

A few minutes later, he dropped her off at work. She'd called ahead, telling Anna she was running late, so there weren't any problems.

As Lee headed back south, anxious to check on their neighborhood and see if Glover had returned, he thought about the shooting. He'd been careless and lucky at the same time. If he hadn't reacted to the intensity of the laser light on his skin, a neck shot with a .45 might have decapitated or disabled him enough to prevent his vampire biology from healing him. But also, by turning, he'd inadvertently exposed the vulnerable arm opening in the vest, allowing a bullet to penetrate his chest cavity. A heart shot would have almost certainly been fatal. No pump, no way for the healing properties of his vampire blood to do their remarkable work.

Mouthing a Navajo prayer of thanksgiving, he continued on, watching every approaching vehicle. Glover was out there somewhere, perhaps in hiding, or equally as likely already at home, thinking he was untouchable.

For a moment, Lee considered just finding and killing the man and ending his hold over the community once and for all. But that would have broken the link between Glover and his contacts. For now, Lee knew he'd have to let things play out at their own speed.

As Lee got closer to the turnoff down Quail Run, he realized that it might be good to hide the SUV—for now. In spite of the daylight, once he topped off his sunblock, he could move quickly from shadow to shadow through the forest and get close enough to enter their home through the back door. If Glover was back, he wanted to make sure the man didn't see him return. Lee planned to remain inside the house until dark. After that, he'd be free to move around, the advantage all his again.

A half hour later, Lee opened the back door of the small home he and Diane now occupied and stepped inside. Staying low, Beretta out and ready, he searched the entire house for any signs of entry. He took a look across the street through a small opening in the bedroom curtain and saw no signs of Glover next door. The Jeep was still in the driveway.

Going to the hidden control box, Lee turned off the surveillance cameras and rewound the CD. A quick review of the morning's recording through the review feature revealed a potential problem. For some reason, the system had stopped recording, having shut down from a power failure about twenty minutes ago. Checking the power supply, Lee discovered one of the batteries had slipped, losing contact. He put it back in position and checked everything, verifying that the problem had been corrected. Then he scanned the recording. Nothing showed up except the change in shadows as the sun rose in the sky.

Still, he was worried about the missing twenty-minute segment at the end. An intruder could have come in, found the system and shut it down, then gone through their belongs, planting bugs, bombs, and doing almost any form of mischief. Fortunately, there was no evidence of who he and Diane really were around the house, and even the surveillance equipment was a commercial product with no law-enforcement identifiers.

Lee stepped out back, brought out his phone, and called Diane. She answered within fifteen seconds.

"Hi, it's me. I'm home," he said. "The surveillance system shut down about twenty minutes before I got here. I'm calling from outside in case the place is bugged. I'll check and make sure we're still clean. Any news?"

"Hey, sweetie. I went ahead and called Mike at the Trident gas station, and arranged for someone to pick up my truck and bring it to Howard's," Diane reported.

Being called "sweetie" told Lee that someone was close enough to hear her side of the conversation, so he'd have to ask the questions and dig for information. "I understand. I decided to hide the SUV close to home and go the final distance on foot through the forest. I'm keeping an eye out for Glover. I'll check with our help and see what Sully's status is, and basically get up to date."

"That's good. I'm going to take a short lunch today to make up for coming in late, so don't come over. I should be home at the regular time, but if I have any problems with the truck, I'll let you know."

"Be careful, Diane, and call once you leave the store."

"Okay. Love you, too," Diane ended the call.

Lee went to the sink, checked below the trash bag, and brought out the laptop. It required a password to get beyond the initial screen, and a special check beyond that point would report any attempts to access the device. It hadn't been tampered with.

After spending several minutes searching for bugs, Lee decided that none had been placed inside their home. Glover was technically very savvy, and obviously monitored people without them knowing, but it seemed unlikely he'd bother to bug a home, especially just after he had reason to believe he'd just killed or maimed someone who lived there. Glover had already proved he dealt with his enemies through direct confrontation.

Lee took another, careful look around back, checking the lock for signs of being picked. If anyone had come in that way, they'd left no evidence or tracks, or else rubbed them out expertly. He wasn't going to check the front, because if Glover was home, he'd be seen. They'd have to check Diane's pickup for bugs later.

Then Lee called Captain Kelly, who'd been sent to the Albuquerque district office to serve as his immediate state police contact. "I need any information or reports of a Ford pickup, year and make unknown, gray-primer color, reported missing in the East Mountains within the past twenty-four hours."

The wait was less than thirty seconds. "A 1995 Ford F-one-fifty matching that description was reported stolen this morning from a Quail Run address. Your street, Officer Hawk."

"We know who stole it—Glover—and why, but for now I'm going to be sitting on the information. Give me a call if the vehicle is located, will you?" Lee asked.

Next, a quick check by Captain Kelly revealed that Brian Sully had gone to his tire dealership office in Albuquerque briefly, picked up some papers, then had gone to a mortgage company and bank. He was still in the city, at a restaurant, under surveillance.

With his own secrets to keep, Lee held off asking for anyone to watch for Newt Glover. He gave Captain Kelly the address of the property Glover was using as a drug drop-off and his boss already had someone checking on the owners. The information would be e-mailed to him ASAP.

It was noon now, and Lee was getting hungry, especially from all the energy reserves his body had consumed repairing the damaged tissue. A quart of fresh calves' blood would have hit the spot, but Lee had to settle for two lasagna TV dinners, a German chocolate cake also from the freezer, a big can of mixed nuts, and a half gallon of milk. He moved around the place cautiously, keeping the curtains drawn to avoid being seen from the outside. With Glover's location unknown, Lee had to be careful. If the man got a bead on his head, a third pistol shot might do the job. Lee was certain that once Glover discovered he'd failed to kill him, he'd try even harder the next time—and Diane would be part of the package.

The thought of Diane being in Glover's crosshairs—or laser sight—made Lee want to cover her back immediately. But she'd known the danger all along as well as he had, and Diane Lopez was better at her job than anyone else he'd ever known, his equal in every way. She was the only normal person to have ever uncovered his true identity and condition. He knew he could trust her abilities and instincts. After all, *she'd* been the one who'd avoided getting shot.

CHAPTER 12

A call came though around 2:00 in the afternoon. The stolen gray pickup had been located, parked beside a house in Tijeras less than a quarter mile from Sully's gas station. Lee got on the phone to Diane immediately.

"Glover came through your area, probably picking up another vehicle at the Trident or catching a ride back home."

"Suppose he knows where I'm working?" she asked softly. "The mechanic and attendant at the station certainly know."

"Would they have volunteered the information to Glover?"

"Only in passing, unless he asked specifically," she said. "That doesn't seem likely, though. Why would he let them know he was focused on me just before killing you? It would point any investigation right at him."

"Yeah. Glover wouldn't want anyone, even his lackeys, to connect him to a murder with any kind of traceable evidence. Not unless he's already got them directly involved. Hmmm. I don't want you to get paranoid, but . . ."

"Too late for that. I've already decided that nobody around here can be trusted, except for Anna."

"And we're sure about her?"

"My instincts tell me she's a hard-ass on the inside, not just the outside. She stuck with her late husband, a cop, for thirty-plus years. She wouldn't rat me out."

"Okay. Your call. On the original matter, you think you can find out what kind of transportation Glover's latched onto? We'll both need to know what to look out for—you, especially, coming home alone tonight."

"I'll be walking over to the Trident, that is, unless one of the guys brings it over here early. They said it'll be ready on time and they seem to be competing for my attention."

"Duh. You're a hottie in your punkish rebel look."

"Yeah, and I'm getting too old for this shit. Everyone who comes into the store has to flirt. Anna noticed and she advised me not to take any crap. She's not at all concerned about driving away a customer with a congenial 'fuck off' if they get personal."

"She said that? My kind of gal. Got to meet her."

"Okay, sweetie. Thank's for checking in. I'll be home at the regular time." Diane's tone signaled that she was no longer free to speak, and she ended the call.

Lee had a big, late lunch, then loaded up with sunblock, grabbed his binoculars, and slipped out the back door, taking as much care as possible so nobody would see him leave. Of the two houses down the street, only one of them had a vehicle in front of it, a minivan. Lee assumed that meant a mother at home with children, but maybe that was his generation speaking—a time when stay-at-home mothers had been the rule instead of the exception. Today, most mothers worked, and when a baby was born it wasn't long before the infant was with a mother or mother-in-law, sitter, or at a daycare center.

He leaped the four-foot fence with little effort and hurried into the forest. Circling around out of view, in case Glover was at home, he found a concealed, shady spot uphill where he could watch Glover's front and back doors, his own house, and the street leading down to the highway. With the binoculars, he could even spot traffic down there.

Not knowing what route Glover had taken earlier when sneaking out, Lee also made sure he was in a position where the man couldn't sneak up on him, or stumble across him accidentally. Munching on an apple, Lee kept watch, his cell phone set on vibrate.

Sometime after 3:00, a recent-model pickup came up the street. From the beginning, Lee could see it was the newspaper deliveryman—for obvious reasons. The driver stuffed the rolled-up Albuquerque *Tribunes* into small plastic boxes mounted on metal or wooden posts, like a mall carrier. Four residents subscribed, and maybe Glover, as well. He had a receptacle attached to a fence post beside the gate.

Lee felt a vibration on his belt and reached for the cell phone slowly, careful not to allow an abrupt movement to give away his location to the delivery person, who was now approaching Glover's house.

He watched the carrier get out of the vehicle, walk around, and carefully insert the newspaper in the tube. Either the *Tribune* carrier gave great service to everyone, or he'd learned about Glover the hard way.

Glancing down, Lee noticed that the call was coming from Captain Kelly. "Yes," Lee answered softly.

"Officer Hawk. You need to know that someone in the sheriff's department just ran your fingerprints. Any idea where that may have come from?"

"Give me a moment." Lee was backtracking in his mind, trying to figure where his fingerprints had been left and why they'd been run, when Glover came out of his house and strolled up the walk. Whistling some sixties tune like he had no cares in the world, the man stopped at the gate, grabbed his newspaper, then stopped and looked around.

Lee froze, knowing that he was in the shadows, behind several branches, and unless he moved it was unlikely the man would see him. Glover's glance was cursory at best, going through the motions rather than actually searching, and he immediately walked back inside, still whistling that tune.

Lee continued. "Perhaps someone lifted a fingerprint from my SUV last night, or our pickup. There's an outside chance it was lifted from inside the house while I was away."

This would explain the missing twenty minutes on the video camera system. Glover could have come in through the front, found the system, erased the segment showing him coming in, then rewound it back to the moment before and dislodged the battery. He lifted a fingerprint, probably several, and had the larger prints run by his sheriff's department inside man.

"Wherever it was found, it's a good thing we inserted your cover background into the system," Captain Kelly responded.

Diane's prints were linked to her cover identity, as well, a good precaution they'd decided upon after learning that Glover had contacts in law enforcement.

"I'll call back," Lee said, then hung up. He waited, checking the shadows to make sure no major leakage of direct sunlight was touching his face or hands, then moved farther into the forest, watching and listening for any sign of his neighbor.

Still laying low and out of view from across the road, Lee called Diane. He got right to the point. "Glover must have caught a ride home. He's also had my fingerprints run. My best guess is that he snooped around inside our house this morning before I got back."

"Hang on a second, sweetie," she said. Fifteen seconds later, she spoke again. "Didn't the video system pick him up on camera?"

"I think he may have come in the front, found the system, then erased the section that showed him."

"When I get back, I can run a check on the software and see if it was erased or just stopped on its own," she said. "And there's no way that kind of tampering can be hidden without destroying the disk and/or deleting files. And that would be obvious, too."

"Good. I'll look over your shoulder and learn."

"Any idea how you're going to return, Lee?"

"Yeah. I'll sneak out of here just before you're due back, pick up the SUV from its hiding place, then drive home very publicly, bandage on my arm and loaded for bear."

"I'll be ready, too. We still don't know how Glover is going to react when he sees you again."

Lee smiled. "Surprised, I think. It should take his ego down a peg. Check his sights."

"Well, we've goaded him into taking action once already, hopefully next time, we'll be able to take him down in a way that won't jeopardize . . . you know."

"I just hope we can do this without somebody else getting hurt. Give me a call just before you leave and I'll run down and pick up the SUV. Once I have it, I'll call you back and we can coordinate our return."

The conversation ended, Lee went back inside via the back door and looked around very carefully, wishing he had Glover's bug detector.

Later, Diane might be able to tell him exactly when Glover accessed their system, and from there, know the maximum amount of time he'd had to erase his image and snoop around the house. Nothing anywhere seemed out of place, so the man showed some really good black bag skills. He'd obviously tried to cover any sign of his presence, and was hoping they'd buy the battery issue as a reason the cameras stopped recording.

An hour passed, and Lee saw Glover, wearing a cap, wrap-around sunglasses, and a bulky jacket, come out onto the front porch shaking a can of spray paint. He locked the door, then quickly painted a small section of the door with a closely matched color. After tossing the aerosol can into the trash, Glover walked over to the Jeep and climbed in.

Cursing the fact that he had no vehicle, Lee watched through the binoculars as Glover drove down to the highway. Then he pulled over beside the mailboxes and parked. When Glover didn't get out to check his mail, Lee decided that maybe something else was going on.

Lee stepped out back and climbed up onto the roof, giving himself a good view of the highway from this elevation. He watched Glover's Jeep for around six minutes, then a sheriff's white, blue-striped department car pulled up beside him. Lee tried to read the number of the vehicle, located on the roof pillars behind the rear passenger's side window, but it was just too far away to make out. Glover and the deputy were obviously talking, perhaps exchanging information. Hoping to get close enough to learn which officer was in the white-and-blue Ford, Lee jumped off the roof and began running parallel to Quail Run behind the property lines of his neighbors and downhill toward the highway. It was at least a mile away, but if he managed to cut the distance in half, maybe the ten-power binoculars and his own exceptional vision would be enough to get a plate or vehicle number.

Passing through the trees, Lee had to make certain none of the residents saw him. He was moving quickly, and that, along with his suspicious presence, might result in a call to the sheriff's office. The deputy down by the highway would be the one to respond, and . . . Lee thought about it for a second longer. If the deputy did answer the call, it was possible he'd be able to get a look at him, or her, and see who Glover was meeting.

He slowed to a human pace and glanced around for someone in their backyard or kitchen window whose attention he might draw, but, just his luck, no one was looking out. The second house was occupied, judging from all the kid toys in the yard and the noise inside, but no one came to the window.

Lee stopped, three houses down, and checked to see where Glover was now. "Damn," he muttered. His neighbor was now driving back up the lane, and the deputy was heading down the highway, north, too far away to identify even with the binoculars.

Lee glanced ahead and saw an attractive woman wearing what looked to be a cocktail waitress's uniform—short black skirt, mesh stockings, and white, frilly blouse—walking to her car from the Weiner house. That was the name on the mailbox at the end of the lane that corresponded to the address.

Glover must have seen her, too, because he stopped the Jeep right in front of the house. Lee crouched low behind a small juniper and waited. The man was looking in his general direction and Lee didn't want to be seen—at least not yet.

"Hey, sexy. Need a ride? My bedroom is just up the street," Glover yelled out the window.

The woman stopped and looked back at her front door, but didn't speak. Lee got the idea she was wondering which direction to go, away from the crude comments or toward her car, which, unfortunately, meant going in Glover's general direction.

The sleazeball, meanwhile, turned off the Jeep's engine and stepped out into the street. "Your bed will do, though. Or the kitchen table?"

"Don't come into my yard, Mr. Glover," the woman finally replied, her voice shaky. "I'll call the sheriff." She fumbled in her purse for a cell phone, then took it out and held it up so he could see.

Lee stood and began to move toward the Weiner house, using the building to screen himself from view. He'd have to do something if Glover tried to force himself on her.

Lee could hear Glover laughing. "The sheriff's going to have to find his own piece of ass. All you've been getting is a little Weiner, lady. Time for a beef stick."

Lee reached the back of the Weiner house, grateful that they didn't have a dog to give him away. He'd already decided that if Glover forced her back into the house, he'd be there to throw him out . . . preferably through a window. Glancing at the cheap lock on the back door, he estimated he could pick it in fifteen seconds or less.

Inching around to the corner of the house, Lee stopped and listened. He heard a car door slam, then an engine revving up—a car engine, not the one in the Jeep. Tires spun on gravel, slid, and raced off down the road. Mrs. Weiner had toughed it out and made it to her car.

Glover laughed. "I'll come by later, honey," he muttered, a hint of menace in his voice. A vehicle door slammed, the Jeep engine started, then Glover drove off. Lee stepped over far enough to verify that he was heading home, not after the woman.

Relieved that the woman had managed to drive away and he hadn't been forced into a premature confrontation with Glover, Lee relaxed and checked his watch. It was too early for Diane to call, so he returned home, unseen.

Two hours and forty-five minutes later, she called, letting Lee know she was now heading home, and he took a minute to tell her about the incident with Mrs. Weiner. Diane wasn't surprised.

Still wondering what Glover had been up to earlier with the deputy, Lee skirted the neighborhood completely this time and jogged east to the highway. He had his arm ready to slip into an improvised sling—not willing to bare his skin even to show a bandage. Vampires, even half vampires like himself, ran a risk exposing that much skin, even with maximum-strength sunblock applied.

The SUV, only three miles away, had been screened around

the outside by old bales of moldy hay Lee had quickly restacked, and it took just a few minutes to move the alfalfa from the front end. Lee slipped inside the vehicle, trying to ignore the waves of heat that had been trapped inside since nothing had covered the hood or top. The second thing that caught his attention was the heavy scent of a substance he immediately recognized—pot.

Getting back out of the vehicle, Lee looked beneath the driver's seat. Someone had planted several sealed bags of marijuana there. One had swelled up so much from the heat inside the car that it burst at the seal, which explained the characteristic scent.

Lee put on gloves and removed the bags, then took them over to an old, rotting horse manure pile and emptied each bag. Taking a large stick, he scattered all the pot around until it more or less blended in. Knowing the grass was now unretrievable, he took the bags over to a clear spot on the ground and melted them into a small blob with a couple of matches. Whoever had planted them, probably this morning while Lee had been asleep, wouldn't have left their prints.

He drove a half mile away from the hiding spot, then pulled over and got out his cell phone. Lee got Diane immediately. "Somebody, probably Glover, tried to set me up in another way, it looks like." He explained about finding the pot beneath the seat.

"You don't think he found the SUV and put the stuff under the seat *after* shooting you?"

"No. The vehicle was too well hidden. Besides, the bales I used to hide the SUV were falling apart. He couldn't have unstacked them, put in the pot, then restacked the bales without me seeing all the extra debris. The way I figure it, he put the stuff under the seat at the same time he ruined your tire, right in our driveway before dawn."

"Wouldn't you have smelled the pot earlier? You've got the scent ability of a bloodhound."

"No, it was sealed up at the time, and I'm not *that* good. But the heat that built up while the car was in the sun all day swelled up the air inside the plastic bags and cooked the batch just a little. Hell, you could get high from the smell alone."

"Glover must have intended on having your murder explained away as the result of a drug operation gone bad. Cops would find your body, maybe mine, too, and then discover pot in the SUV you'd been driving. No need to ask about trouble with your neighbors, then. Even with Glover's rep, the evidence would suggest somebody else was responsible."

"It could have worked," she admitted. "But where did Glover get the weed? Dealing pot, even by the kilo, seems too penny-ante for him. Unless it was from the same source that provided the coke or whatever he supplied to Breeann."

"A deputy could have found the stash in a raid and given it to him days ago. The same deputy he met with earlier today, probably. Cops get the best dope—ever hear that?"

"If some of the cops around here *are* corrupt, and we're operating under that assumption, it makes sense. Now we need to find out which deputies have access to their evidence rooms, and have taken part in pot busts within the past few months.

"I'll pass this on to SAC Logan, and you can do the same with Captain Kelly. I'm within five minutes of the turnoff now, Lee. I'm going to hang up, then keep both eyes open for trouble. No telling what's going to happen when Glover sees me come into the driveway, alone."

"Worst-case scenario, shoot him. Don't hold back, either, if it comes to that. A double tap in the face just in case he's wearing a vest."

"At least he's no friggin' vampire."

Lee laughed. "I'm in position to watch you pass by. I'll come up the lane five minutes after you pass the mailboxes. By then, Glover's heart is going to be pumping overtime."

There was a moment's pause, then Diane spoke. "You know, he's really got me pissed off. Sexist asshole."

"Just stay your normal cool, collected self without giving him a target."

"Yeah. See you soon, I hope." Diane hung up before he could reply. Lee turned the SUV around, backing farther off the road, but remaining close enough so he could see her pass. Maybe he'd follow just four minutes behind, or three and a half. A minute could be a lifetime if you were driving into an ambush.

Lee ran the air-conditioning and fans on full, with all the windows down except the driver's door glass, hoping to vent out as much of the pot scent as possible. Even with the actual contraband removed, it still had an odor he could detect, though it *was* fading.

Once he started up Quail Run, Lee slipped his left hand into the sling—constructed from the first-aid kit materials—and drove with his right. His Beretta was in his waistband, in sight for anyone looking closely—like Glover. It served as a warning. If the man made a suspicious move, it would be his last.

Checking his watch, Lee saw that Diane had passed by only three minutes earlier. The dust on the road was still drifting and she might still be outside in the driveway or walking up the steps of the porch. That would require her to put her back to Glover for a moment. He'd be watching her, that's for sure. Resisting the impulse to speed up, Lee kept the fifteen-mile-an-hour speed limit, unrolling his window and turning off the air conditioner so he could listen. If he heard a shot, he was driving right through Glover's yard and into his living room to take the man out.

Then Lee remembered that they hadn't checked for a bug in Diane's car. Glover might know they were coming—and everything else. He speeded up.

Diane's pickup was there, right in front of their door. Good thinking! She'd used the vehicle to screen herself when she got out of the vehicle. Nobody was in sight, not in their yard, and not at Glover's. When he was close enough for the angle to be right, Lee slowed, looking into Glover's living room window.

The sleazeball was beside the curtain, blocked mostly by the wall, gazing intently at their house, keeping an eye out for Diane, who was, hopefully, also watching Glover, as well, her pistol ready. This end of the street was an armed camp, Lee thought for a second.

Then Glover saw the SUV. He stepped back, probably certain he was hidden now, and watched. The street was in shadows, due to the mountains just west that made for an early sunset, so there was no glare keeping Glover from seeing exactly who was behind the wheel.

Lee pulled up right behind the pickup and stopped. The vehicle would provide him cover and concealment, and also probably cause Glover's blood pressure to rise. The lowlife had no idea what Lee would do next, so he undoubtedly had a weapon at hand.

Left arm in the sling, Lee got out of the SUV and stood so that his torso was protected by the engine compartment, then he looked over at Glover's house and gave it the generic finger. It was petty and juvenile, something only a punk would do, but it fit his new identity. Gestures like that still felt odd, though. He hadn't flipped anyone off in seventy years.

Stepping onto the porch, Lee let his jacket come open enough for Glover to see his pistol tucked into his waistband, then opened the door and slipped inside. "Honey, I'm home," Lee said loudly, bringing out his pistol.

CHAPTER 13

He had a pistol in his hand when I stepped out of the pickup, but he set it back down on a bookshelf. I can't see him now. What's he doing?" Diane asked.

Lee stepped back into the room, making sure he was in shadows and not outlined by anything behind him, and took a long look. Glover had stepped back in the room, as well, away from the window, and Lee could only see half his face. "He's just watching, trying to see what *we're* doing. I don't think he's going to be walking around close to the windows for a while."

"Think he's got a low-light or infrared scope? He might wait until dark and take another shot at you."

"Or you. It's safer to assume there's going to be danger here twenty-four/seven from now on. He'll want to get us before we make a move on him. And because he had a background check done on my fingerprints and 'knows' I'm definitely not a cop, and we didn't report his ambush, he sees we're not going to play by the rules."

Diane poked her head out from the small study at the far end. "He'll be wondering what illegal things *we're* up to. We should sleep in shifts from now on. You want to keep watch while I brew some fresh coffee and get some dinner started, Lee?"

Lee gave her a thumbs-up with his "injured" hand. "I'm just going to wear this sling in front of Glover. It should make him think he's at least slowed me down a little."

Forty minutes later, having eaten dinner and cleaned up, Lee and Diane brought out the CD and the recording system to check if portions of it had been erased.

"If you know where to look in the software, the system will give you the time of starts and stops. It automatically logs in when and where portions of the captured images are erased or edited." Diane had connected their video equipment to the laptop and was able to look at the files on a bigger screen than before.

"We used media that could be overwritten to save a few dollars. But there are CDs that cannot be erased, correct?"

"Right. But these were definitely erased. Then one of the batteries was pulled loose to cut the power. The time of the power loss is recorded." Diane pointed to the number on the screen.

Lee looked at the screen. "The timing is right. He had about a half hour to erase what he wanted, loosen the battery to kill the system, search the place, then get out before I showed up."

"Think he was wearing gloves?"

"Probably not. Why bother? He must think we're up to something illegal ourselves, putting in a surveillance system like this. Or maybe he's assuming we're covering ourselves in case there's a break-in. My silver jewelry, materials, and tools are worth something."

Diane shrugged. "He's probably more curious than ever, us not reporting the shooting. My guess is he'll jump to the conclusion that we didn't want the cops involved because we're doing something illegal."

"Speaking of illegal, there are two sheriff's department cars coming up the street—no headlights. Think they're about to bust Glover?" Lee offered with skepticism in his tone.

"Only if Mrs. Weiner reported the harassment incident, and I doubt she'd risk the retaliation from Glover. Hopefully she told her husband, and they'll be more careful going outside when that sleazeball is around. My guess is that they've come to see *us*. Now that Glover sees you've survived the murder attempt, he's probably hoping we'll get busted for dealing pot. You sure you got it all?"

Lee nodded. "Even aired out the SUV quite a bit. Unless they've got a dog, they shouldn't even pick up a whiff."

"Well, let's be normal, I guess. We'd better put our weapons in the nightstand." They both walked into the bedroom and placed their pistols and ammunition into the nightstands on each side of the bed.

They returned to the living room. Hearing vehicles stopping outside, Diane hit the remote and turned on the TV. "Let's see what happens. And watch the deputies."

"If they go for the SUV and check under the seat, that'll let us know at least one of them is in cahoots with Glover," Lee said.

"'Cahoots'? That word is straight out of an old movie," Diane said with a grin.

"Hey, what can I tell you? Those *old* movies were new to me. I particularly loved westerns and cowboys like Roy Rogers. Only chance to see someone playing an Indian."

"I remember Roy. And Trigger. Their lunch boxes go for big bucks on eBay," Diane said, then laughed.

Lee tried not to react as a deputy walked past the curtained window, most likely going around to cover the back door. The officer was in the dark and believed he couldn't be seen.

There was a firm knock on the door. "Deputy sheriff, Mr. Begay. Can I speak with you a moment?"

Lee nodded, pointing to the remote. Diane put the TV on mute. "Whaddya want?" he yelled.

"Just talk, Mr. Begay. Come on. Open the door."

Lee smiled, then walked across the room. The deputy was standing to one side, not visible through the small window, with his hand on the butt of his handgun, but Lee could see his distorted figure through the little viewer.

Lee opened the door less than six inches. "I'm here, what's going on, Deputy? Somebody kill that asshole across the road and you want us to sign the thank-you card?"

Deputy Harmon, who'd been there the other day talking to Diane, cleared his throat and looked a bit awkward for a second. "Umm, your girlfriend here, too? Maybe you both could come outside for a moment. I've got some questions. Apparently there's been some trouble in the neighborhood."

"It's that deputy, the one who escorted you home the other night, babe. Wanna go outside with me for a moment?" Lee grinned at Harmon. "Diane told me all about you, Deputy. Protecting the neighborhood and all."

Diane came to the door. "Okay, I'm here, sweetie. Whatever the deputy wants, we're cooperating. Right?"

Harmon stood back as they walked down the steps, and Lee heard the other deputy's footsteps as he came around the corner of the house behind them.

Diane turned at the sound. "You didn't walk through my garden, did you?" she asked the second officer.

The young officer looked back with his flashlight for a second. The ground was bare. "Very funny, Miss Garcia."

"Hey, your fame precedes you, Diane," Lee joked, noting the officer had known her name, though she hadn't given it to him yet. Seeing Glover standing on his own front porch, watching the action from a distance, he added, playing innocent, "How'd you know our names?"

"It's our job. That your vehicle, Mr. Begay?" Officer Harmon pointed to the SUV.

"Yup. Even got the pink slip. Well, I did last time I looked. We just moved here a few days ago and it's probably still in a box."

"You sure, Mr. Begay? We had a report of a stolen vehicle matching this make and model."

This line of questions ruled out the incident with Mrs. Weiner as the reason for their visit. The real reason the deputies were there was connected to the pot Glover or whoever had planted in the SUV—the setup. "I thought you said there was trouble in the neighborhood. Don't tell me someone down the street owns an identical SUV," Lee said, adjusting the sling on his supposedly wounded arm.

Deputy Harmon walked over to the SUV and aimed his flashlight inside, while the second deputy kept his eyes on Lee's hands. "Got the registration inside the vehicle?"

Lee reached for his pocket and saw both officers move their hands toward the butts of their handguns. "Whoa. Lighten up. Just getting my keys. Only got one hand available tonight."

Diane laughed. "I'm the only one around here who watches for a bulge in my old man's pockets, guys."

Lee brought out the keys with two fingers, then tossed them to Harmon. He grabbed for them with one hand, but they bounced off his knuckles and fell to the ground.

"Nice catch," Lee said dryly.

The officer picked up the keys, then opened the SUV driver's door, watching Lee out of the corner of his eyes. Harmon was getting a little annoyed, and Lee could also see his hand shaking slightly, either in fear or anticipation.

Both Lee and Diane knew enough to stand perfectly still and keep their hands in view. "It's in the glove box," Lee said.

"Watch these jokers," Deputy Harmon said, leaning across

the interior, then realizing he'd have to sit inside to reach the box. He opened it up, brought out the various papers, then found the insurance card and registration.

Lee watched as the deputy looked them over carefully. They were real and authentic, the best the state police could forge.

Then Harmon looked under the front seats, shining his light. He climbed back out, then searched the backseat and the floorboards. Lastly, he aimed the flashlight into the rear section. The storage area was empty except for the spare tire compartment.

Lee had noticed, out of the corner of his eye, that Glover had come over to the middle of the street and was watching closely now. The second deputy had glanced at Glover briefly and nodded, but continued to keep his eyes on Diane and Lee.

"Can't find what you're looking for?" Lee asked Deputy Harmon, then looked over at Glover and smiled.

Harmon looked at Glover, then at Diane. "Mind if we look inside your house, ma'am?"

"Think we hid the stolen SUV in the den? I'd like to see *that* on a warrant," she said, then chuckled.

"We about done here, Deputies? My wounded arm is starting to ache from the cold," Lee said.

"Wounded? What happened to your arm, Mr. Begay?" Deputy Harmon asked, now curious again.

"My neighbor took a couple of shots at me this morning with his forty-five. Just a scratch, though. He's a really piss-poor shot, even with a laser sight. Want to be a good citizen and confess, Glover?"

Glover obviously hadn't expected this and his face turned red. Yet, in the weak light out there in the street, Lee suspected he was the only one in a position to know that particular detail. Glover's expression had remained neutral almost, a credit to his self-control.

He finally forced a laugh, but it was short-lived, and neither deputy joined in, though the younger one sneaked a look at Glover, gauging his response.

"You're a real comedian, Mr. Begay," Deputy Harmon responded, shaking his head. "Let's go, partner." He nodded to the other deputy and gestured toward the cars. The young officer took another look at Glover, then stepped toward his unit.

"Aren't you forgetting something, Deputy?" Diane asked.

"What?" Deputy Harmon stopped, as did the other officer, who was beside his vehicle now.

"Our registration and proof of insurance." She pointed to his hand.

"Right. Okay." He gave the papers to Diane, then turned and walked to his open car door. "Stay out of trouble, you two," he said, indicating Lee and Diane, then got inside and started the engine and turned on his headlights.

Glover was walking away now, but still watching them out of the corner of his eye. Lee waited while Diane put the papers back in the glove compartment and locked the doors, then they both went back up the porch steps. Glover was staring at them from the front door when they stepped back inside.

They immediately retrieved their weapons. "So which deputy do you think is on the take? They both seemed concerned with Glover's reaction to what was going down," Diane pointed out.

"I'd put my money on the older guy, Deputy Harmon. Glover would want the people with seniority. They make the decisions. The young deputy . . . he might still have some integrity left."

"I agree. He was watching Glover's reaction when you said who shot you. And he sneaked a look just after that. Too bad he's under Harmon's thumb," she said.

"Let's see what the Bureau can dredge up about Deputy Harmon's record, personal life, background, money situation, and like that," Lee said.

"I'll make some calls. You going to watch for visitors?"

Lee nodded. "Glover moved quickly last time we pissed him off. I'm thinking he's going to do the same again, only next time, he'll choose a different weapon."

"Like?"

"Trying to burn us out, blow up our propane, force us off the highway, or drop coconuts on our head."

"Coconuts?"

"Hey, I read in the newspaper a few months ago that more people die from coconuts falling on their heads than from shark attacks."

"No freshwater sharks around here. So we worry about coconuts. Got it." She started to laugh now, and he joined in.

After a few moments, Lee remembered a problem they'd have to deal with if they intended on tracking Glover. He'd sneaked out the back either last night or early this morning, with serious consequences to them. They'd have to find a way to keep watch on the rear of his home so he couldn't pull the same thing again.

"We need a motion detector or something that'll warn us when Glover goes out his back door," Lee said. "It'll have to be small, pretty much undetectable, and capable of sending us a signal whenever he tries to sneak away. The weapons labs and Sandia Corporation probably have some, and maybe the old nuclear weapons facility. Think you can get one for us so we won't have to hide out in the woods twenty-four hours a day or bring in more help?"

"I think so. I've seen some disguised to look like rocks. The various national labs here in New Mexico use them along remote fence lines to catch anyone trying to climb over or snoop. Area Fifty-one out in Nevada probably has hundreds of them. Let me call Logan. We can probably borrow one or two."

"In the meantime, I'll disguise one of our remote mikes—a

sound-activated one—then plant it beside his back gate. He's not going to climb the fence, he'd just walk out. We couldn't see him from here and he knows it," Lee said.

"What about his surveillance camera? You could be spotted."

"It angles down. My guess is that it only covers the area close to the house and, at night, it can only see what's within the range of the floodlights. Along the fence line things will be nearly dark. I can attach the mike to the underneath of a small pine branch, then put it into position close enough so it'll switch on and send his footsteps or the clank of metal to our receiver when he opens and closes the gate."

"Okay. He probably doesn't even view the camera images unless he thinks something has gone down, like you or me sneaking around back. See the footprints, view the video, right?"

Lee nodded. "I'll get one of the devices ready, then put it into place ASAP."

They both went to work on their tasks, and fifteen minutes later Lee joined Diane in the study. "I'm going to pay a little visit to Glover's backyard. I'll take the phone, but won't be talking, probably. Text message me."

"Okay. Logan is having one of our agents pick up a remote monitor from a lab for us. It's sensitive enough to pick up cat footsteps within fifty feet."

"You're kidding."

"Maybe, but that's what the tech at the DOD said, which is where Logan dug one up. They're reconfiguring the alarm. We'll be able to pick it up on our cell phones if Glover or a stray cat sets it off. That'll eliminate the need for a classified monitoring center that would take a delivery truck and gather way too much attention."

"Cool. I'll be out, sneaking around."

"Be careful. If he happens to have a low-light scope, he might be watching for us."

"I'll see him first. My eyes are much better than any of those night-vision devices. Unless, of course, his is attached to a rifle."

"That's why I said be careful, smart-ass."

"Hey, you're really taking your cover identity to heart, woman. You've got *attitude*."

"Hell, Lee, we both have attitude. Why shouldn't we? Think of all we've been through the past two years."

"I see your point." He put on his black cap, backward, adjusted his leather gloves, also black, then checked the Beretta in the holster at his waist. "Cell phone in my pocket, and listening device tied to a branch out on the back steps. See you in a while."

"If I notice Glover coming outside, I'll send you a buzz." She said, then looked down at the laptop screen, where the summaries of the officers who watched Sully today had been posted.

Lee left the room silently and stepped out back, passing through the tiny utility room. He locked the door behind him, then walked quickly, straight to the tree line. Once inside the forest, he circled around, grateful again that they were at the end of the street—and the small development—and he had cover to the west instead of another cleared area with houses on each side and in front.

From his vantage point he could see down the street, the front and one end of his and Diane's house, and the rear of Glover's place. He could also see the left-rear fender of Glover's Jeep.

The camera mounted on Glover's roof moved slowly. Diane had seen the monitor inside, so they had an idea about how far

out from the structure it retained its effectiveness. At night, even with the 150-watt floodlights, the camera probably had an effective range of fifty feet, not even to Glover's fence, in a half circle.

Lee saw lights on in Glover's kitchen and bedroom, but no sign of Glover. He crouched, picked a path through the brush and past three trees, then moved slowly forward. Fifteen feet from the fence, he froze beside some rabbit brush and watched the sweeping camera, timing the motion. The gate wasn't centered along the property line, so the area, a third of the way from the eastern corner of the fence, was out of frame slightly longer than if the gate had been centered.

The camera covered an arc of slightly less than 180 degrees in ten seconds, give or take a second, then swept back after a two-second pause. After watching the motion for a few minutes, and assured that the cycle never varied, Lee made the final adjustment on the bug, hidden at the bottom of the branch, and stood. When the camera reached the seven-second point, the gate would be out of view. He'd have five or six seconds to run out, place the branch close to the gate, then drop back out of range. He'd worn moccasins, which left no tread or heel marks, so the tracks he left would be minimal. He could go back and erase them, if necessary, once the bug was in place.

Lee stood, watching the sweep of the camera and counting down, when the light in the bedroom went out. He waited a beat, remaining behind cover. If Glover was going to bed, he reasoned, wouldn't he turn off the kitchen light first?

Then the kitchen light went out. Lee remained in place, thinking that maybe Glover had just forgotten the light in the kitchen. But it was too dangerous to be impulsive around someone who'd tried to kill him earlier in the day, so he held his position. A few more minutes, then he'd go.

If Lee hadn't been a vampire, he would never have seen the back door opening. But evening was like a cloudy afternoon to a

nightwalker, and Lee dropped behind cover as Glover stepped outside onto his small back porch, gym bag in one hand, flashlight in the other.

Glover locked the door, then walked straight toward the gate—and Lee, who was just beyond.

CHAPTER 14

Τhe man wasn't using his flashlight, concerned, perhaps, that the beam could be seen by someone watching from a distance. "Shit!" he said, stubbing his foot on a stone and stumbling slightly.

Reaching the gate, Glover turned on the light for a moment to find the padlock, opened it with a brass key, then went through, locking the device behind him. The man was standing so close Lee could smell his BO, and, if Glover decided to look around, he'd probably spot him. But Glover didn't hesitate. He walked right down the fence line toward the east, his eyes on the street he was paralleling.

Once Glover was a hundred feet away, Lee brought out his cell phone and punched the number that would dial Diane. "Glover's leaving on foot," Lee whispered. "Heading east. Can you get to the SUV and stand by if I need a ride?"

"Gotcha. What if he's just going for a walk or a window peep with a camera at the Weiner house? Remember those photos in his bedroom?"

"Or he's got other plans after being rejected earlier, especially if the husband is gone. Glover's carrying a small gym bag and a flashlight." Lee looked down the fence line. Glover was fifty yards away, striding quickly. "Gotta go." Lee placed the listening device he'd brought by Glover's gate, making sure he wasn't seen by the camera, then took off.

If Glover tried to harm the woman, he'd have to find a way of protecting her without risking their investigation, or the safety of Timothy Klein, assuming Glover was involved in that. At least in the dark, Lee might have a chance to avoid identifying himself to the man.

Moving into the forest just enough to avoid being seen if Glover decided to look back to the west, Lee moved in the man's direction. All he had to do was keep him in sight and not make any noise.

Just as Lee had feared, Glover stopped at the back gate of the fourth house down—the Weiner house. It was an older-looking double-wide with a clutter of junk in the backyard, including two derelict vehicles and a clothesline with one of the poles leaning halfway to the ground. A burned-out fifty-five-gallon drum and scorched ground around it showed how the Weiners dealt with trash and weeds.

Lee stopped, fifty yards away, watching. Glover stood there only about ten seconds before the back porch light came on and a skinny, shirtless man in jeans and engineer boots came outside.

"Turn off the fucking light, dipshit," Glover said with a growl.

The man slipped back inside and turned off the light before coming back out again. He walked across the yard. "Sorry, Mr. Glover."

"So, where's the Harley, Weenie?"

"Out front. You're not going to be long, are you? I need it for work tomorrow. Rhonda has the car."

"You tell your old lady that I can either ride her or the Harley. What's it going to be?"

Lee saw the man's fists clinch, but was too far away to read his expression. "Stay away from my wife, Glover. Here's the key to the bike." The man reached into his pocket.

"Bring it here, Weenie." Glover aimed the flashlight in the man's eyes.

Weiner took a look behind him. Mrs. Weiner was standing just inside the doorway, holding what looked like a shotgun. The darkness kept Glover from seeing her there. The Weiners were afraid of their neighbor, obviously, but they weren't stupid.

Mr. Weiner walked over to the fence and opened the gate, handing the key reluctantly to Glover. "Here. Just leave it in the driveway when you get back."

Glover brushed past Weiner and walked toward the back porch. Mrs. Weiner took a step back, the barrel of the shotgun pointing in his direction.

Glover must have finally spotted her. "Maybe next time," he teased, then pivoted ninety degrees and proceeded to his left, disappearing around the side of the building.

Lee called Diane as he watched Weiner go back inside. "Meet me beside the mailboxes in a couple of minutes. I'll have to see what direction Glover goes when he reaches the highway. He's gotten himself a loaner Harley from the Weiners."

"Okay."

"You'll probably hear the Harley once you get outside. Just make sure he doesn't spot you. 'Bye." Lee ended the call, then started running east through the edge of the tree line. Once Glover got on the bike, he'd probably reach the road within a half minute. Lee had to be there to meet Diane. Losing Glover now could be a disaster if he was going to meet one of his criminal sidekicks. Or a kidnapper of a young boy?

Picking up speed, Lee sprinted out of the trees and ran along the clear-cut zone between the forest and the east-west fence line. Glover would only see him by luck in the dark, and he had to be in position to catch Diane.

Though he knew from the sound alone, Lee also saw Glover roaring off to the north when he reached the highway. Turning back, he stepped out into the road and waved just as Diane turned on her headlights. The SUV slid to a stop about ten feet away.

Lee jumped into the passenger side. "North. Go north." He buckled his seat belt clumsily in the moving vehicle, not used to being a passenger and hooking up on the left side.

"What's he up to, Lee? It's nearly ten P.M." Diane said.

Lee looked over at her, noting that she was wearing a ball-cap like him now, and dressed in a nonslutty pullover sweater and relaxed-fit jeans.

He told her what he'd seen and heard.

"Glover's got the whole neighborhood under his thumb. Where I grew up, in Albuquerque's North Valley, if anyone had said something like that to a husband, he'd get shot," Diane said.

"I'm sure Martin Weiner had that in the back of his mind. At least he had the good sense to have his wife cover him like that. But Glover probably had his own pistol in his belt or the gym bag. The Weiners could have gotten themselves killed. They're not professionals when it comes to violence, like Glover," Lee said.

"One thing is for sure. The more we hear and learn about the man, it's a wonder he's still alive," Diane added, her eyes on the road. "See the Harley anywhere ahead?"

Lee didn't need the headlights, but the road was lined with trees, hills, and curves, so the man on the cycle could be a half mile away and they'd never know except from the sound of the noisy bike. "Roll down your window. If he takes a side road, maybe we'll hear it before we see him."

"Yeah. Harleys have that distinctive rumble."

Finally they reached a straight stretch of highway alongside an alfalfa field, and Lee spotted Glover about a quarter mile farther north, going the speed limit. "There he is."

"Yeah, I see the taillight—barely."

They continued on a little farther, then went into another series of turns as the road passed through a section with several east-west canyons. "I've lost sight again," Lee said. "Better slow down and listen. There are several secondary roads around here, if I recall."

"With a memory like yours, it's more than just recalling, Lee. How many?"

"Five, by the time we get out of these canyons. Two on the west, three on the east. The next one coming up is to the west."

"Show-off."

Lee smiled, though, in the dark, nobody could see except another vampire.

Going downhill, Diane let off on the gas. Lee could hear a rumble to their left. "I think he took the west side road. Slow down a little more."

They came around the corner and Lee looked to his right. No Harley was ahead on the highway.

"Dust. A little dust at the turnoff. You're right," Diane announced. She pulled off onto the narrow road and turned off the headlights. Wide at the highway, just ahead the dirt path turned into two ruts winding up the north side of a narrow canyon. A misspelled, hand-lettered sign on the fence said PRIVITE DRIVE, but there was no gate, just a battered mailbox with self-stick numbers.

"I can hear the bike. We follow?" she asked.

"Yeah, but let's switch places. I won't need the headlights."

Diane opened the door. "I'm way ahead of you."

By the time she was back inside, Lee was at the wheel. He put the SUV into gear, then drove down the road slowly, listening to the fading roar of the motorcycle, which was still unseen.

Picking up the pace, Lee tried to stay close, but five minutes later there was an intersection. The road continued on toward a home, clearly visible to him ahead. There was a closed gate, and no Harley. Glover would have still been visible if he'd gone that way.

"Hear anything to the left or right?" she asked.

He turned off the engine. After a moment, both of them heard a faint rumble to the right.

"Gotcha." Lee turned on the engine, turned right, then headed on up the road, which was better here.

"This owner must have more money, or connections with the county. Notice the gravel? This road was graded recently," she commented. "And wet down to settle the dust."

"Probably another route back to the highway, too. Only problem is, this road is noisier, and forget about spotting tracks." Lee speeded up, but couldn't see the Harley anywhere ahead.

They came to another intersection. Lee turned off the engine and they listened. After a while he shook his head in disgust. "I think we lost him."

"Okay. But I don't think he knew we were following. So he has to be around here somewhere," she pointed out. "Let's drive around and see if we can find the Harley parked beside a house."

Lee nodded, then started up the engine. Leaving the lights on, they continued toward the west. The road circled around a big loop through the forest, with signs indicating future home sites and the name of the developer, FAC Hideaway Homes. But they failed to locate the Harley, and there were no structures where it could have been hidden. Eventually they returned to the same intersection where the road divided.

"Let's go back to the east. I think that area is already being developed," Diane said.

They drove down the graveled road, and within a few minutes reached an area similar to the last one, except this graveled street contained several completed homes, others under various stages of construction, and a model home with signs. From the porch and accent lights, the paved driveways, and the vehicles parked beside the homes, it was clear people were already living there. They found a street sign, Mockingbird Lane, which led east, probably to the highway.

"There's a motorcycle in that driveway," Diane pointed out as they passed a ranch-style home with two stories and dormer windows.

"Wrong color," Lee said. "This one is green. The one Glover took was blue."

"Too subtle for me to tell. You sure?"

Lee nodded. "I'm sure. Let's retrace our route and take one of the other roads."

An hour later, after reaching dead ends or single dwellings with no motorcycles, they finally reached the main highway again. At the stop sign, Lee spotted an oncoming headlight. "Crap. You know who that is?"

The motorcycle passed by, heading south, and Diane cursed, as well. "Glover. Where the hell has he been?"

"Well, we know it was somewhere north. Maybe in the new development. We missed him, somehow." He pulled onto the highway, following the motorcycle from a safe distance.

"He's probably heading home now. Let's make sure, but don't drive up to our place right after him. He'll get suspicious."

"We'll give him fifteen minutes. Meanwhile, I've got a Wal-Mart grocery bag under the seat. We'll fake a trip into east Albuquerque."

When Glover turned down their street fifteen minutes later, they continued on for a short distance, then stopped by the highway. "We'll give him enough time to drop off the Harley and walk home. Twenty minutes, okay?" Lee asked.

Later, they drove up the lane to their house, noting the motorcycle parked in the Weiner driveway. The lights at Glover's were out, and they returned to their own door without incident.

"I set the surveillance system, Lee, but I doubt he had time to come over here," Diane said as they entered the living room. Lee had gone in first, not needing to turn on the lights first before checking for an intruder.

"Okay, you check the recorder, I'll make sure he hasn't planted a bomb or listening device," Lee said.

"I wish I could say you're just kidding, but with this guy, anything is possible."

"Ain't that the truth?"

Diane checked the system and it had recorded the entire time. Nobody had entered the building, which ruled out the possibility of a recently planted bomb or bug.

They returned to the dining room table, moving their seating positions so they couldn't present a visual target from Glover's place, then discussed the evening's events.

Diane brought up a database that had recent maps and photos of the East Mountain area between their location and I-40, and the development area was there, barely. "Only three houses were completed at this time, a year ago, though several more were under construction," she pointed out, zooming into the display for a closer look.

"There's another structure, farther back, on a small road that ties into the development," Lee said. "Zoom back out again."

Diane nodded. "We still don't know where Glover went, and when you add all the houses there now, including that model home, we're talking about twenty or more structures. We'll have to check them all out, and even then, we might not learn anything helpful. What if Glover went to visit some woman, or just a business contact?"

"Why sneak away from us at night to do it, then? Maybe he's got Timothy Klein locked up in some basement and needed to check on him."

"I'd thought of that, which means we'll need the names and occupations of everyone in that area," Diane responded. "That could lead us to people who might be under Glover's influence, connections that have kept him out of trouble while he's been doing his dirty work around here. Or giving him a place to hide the boy."

"Yeah. But let's get help. How about we ask Logan to assign someone from the Bureau to get names and backgrounds, and a state policeman or two to do a house-to-house for signs of the missing child," Lee said. "If they pick up any vibes, they can pass the information along to us."

"I'll talk to Logan, you set it up with your people," Diane said, reaching for her cell phone.

"One more thing, Diane. Let's get all we can on the company doing the developing, FAC Hideaway Homes. Even if this has nothing to do with the Klein boy, Glover might be sticking his finger into some very large pies."

Hours later, Lee was still working on the laptop. Diane had gone to bed to catch some sleep. Taking a sip of freshly brewed piñon-blend coffee, Lee heard the familiar beep notifying him that he'd just received an e-mail.

The sender was a tech he knew at the state police office in Santa Fe. Lee read the message, committed it to memory, then forwarded the text to the Internet Web site that only he and Diane could access before deleting it from the laptop.

The message had contained information on the developer, FAC Hideaway Homes, and the identities of the four partners hiked Lee's interest. He checked various websites, looking for more information on the individuals, and was quickly able to connect one of the partners to Glover. When Diane woke up, he'd give her an update.

She was awake at 6:30 and still in the shower when Lee noticed Glover coming out his front door. Lee walked to the bathroom and knocked.

"Come on in," she called out.

"Glover's gone outside. I may have to follow him. If I do, I'll call."

"Okay. Thanks. I'll be out in a few minutes."

Lee crossed the bedroom and entered the living room/dining room again. Glover was getting into the Jeep, his bug-scanning wand still in his hand. The guy was careful, Lee had to admit.

Putting on his jacket and cap, Lee watched as Glover started up the Jeep and backed out of the driveway. Patting his pockets to confirm the presence of his cell phone, pistol, and sunblock, Lee walked to the door.

He had to hurry, driving down the lane, to make sure he knew which direction Glover would be going, and was surprised to see the man heading south this time. The sun was nearly up and traffic was heavier than usual, with so many people heading to work. It made it easier to follow Glover, hiding among the other vehicles.

Wondering if the trip had anything to do with Sully, who lived in this direction, Lee attached his headpiece and called Andrea Moore. He didn't know whether she was actually the officer currently watching Sully, but if not she'd know who'd taken her place. He'd left the coverage arrangements to her and the others, not wanting to micromanage as long as they did the job.

The officer in place turned out to be Felix Rodriguez. Lee dialed his number after thanking Officer Moore. "Felix. This is Lee, and I'm heading south on Three thirty-seven, following our main subject. He's driving a green Jeep. Anything going on at your location?"

"Maybe. My subject just entered Three thirty-seven, heading your direction in the white Camry. He's about a mile north of his turnoff, and I'm in traffic, about a quarter mile back."

"Give yourself enough room to pull over and hold position if he stops anywhere. Glover may be planning on a meet, though I doubt it would be right beside the highway."

"Understood. I'll keep in touch. We should meet up in ten minutes or so, depending on traffic. So if it's going to happen, it'll happen soon."

Lee confirmed, then ended the connection. Looking ahead, he saw Glover's brake lights go on, then he slowed, made a quick one-eighty in the road, and pulled off the road beside the north-bound lane.

Lee stopped, pulling off onto the shoulder, wondering if Glover had spotted the tail, and was waiting for him to pass by. His eyes on Glover's Jeep, Lee dialed Felix. "Hey, bro. Glover stopped and took a position on the eastern shoulder, facing north. I've stopped and pulled off to observe."

"It all depends on Sully now. I'll be watching for the Jeep, and see what my rabbit does." Rodriguez hung up.

Lee had great vision, but Glover was over a quarter mile away, so he reached into the glove compartment for the small monocular. Glover had climbed out of the Jeep and was getting the jack and lug wrench from the vehicle. None of the tires were flat, so, to Lee, it was obviously a ruse. He hit redial.

"Felix. Glover is faking a flat tire. Expect Sully to come along and 'help' him. I'm going to try and get closer to watch. Stick with the plan and I'll keep you up to date."

Felix confirmed, so Lee ended the call. Noting that Glover was busy jacking up the Jeep, he took advantage of the distraction and pulled his SUV farther off the road, between two pine trees. Slipping out, Lee crossed the highway, jumped the fence easily, then moved south through the forest, putting on tight leather gloves. His hands were vulnerable to sunlight because he'd been handling things, wearing off the sunblock, and he had no idea how long he'd have to be outside. If Sully stopped, Lee wanted to watch and listen, and that meant he might not be able to choose a shady spot.

Judging the distance as he ran, Lee was about fifty yards away from Glover's Jeep when he felt the phone in his pocket vibrate. He stopped and opened the unit. "Sully is stopping. So am I," Felix said. "Want me to keep the line open?"

"No. Text message me," he whispered. "I'm too close to talk." Lee ended the call and crept forward as quickly as he could and still remain quiet. Vehicles had been roaring by every minute or so on the road to his right, and each time his ability to hear was drowned out.

Finally, seeing the Jeep just ahead, Lee crouched low behind a tree. Any closer, and he'd be spotted for certain. A car door slammed.

"Good idea, faking a flat tire."

"I'm a genius, Sully. Got the money?" Glover asked.

"Ten thousand, total. Five now and five more when you get me the girl. She looks young, doesn't she?" Sully answered.

"Hell, she could pass for twelve, thirteen."

"But she's legal, right?" Sully insisted.

"Of course. I always ask to see some ID before I screw a hooker."

"Good idea. Keeps you from getting busted," Sully answered.

"God, you've naïve, Sully. Now quit jacking around and give me the money."

"Here."

Lee couldn't see the actual transaction, the Jeep was in the way, but it sounded like a paper bag was being crinkled.

"It's all there."

Several more seconds went by. "You're a thousand short, Sully."

"What? No way."

Glover laughed. "Just messing with your mind. So do I get a copy of your upcoming production?"

"You want one? They're going to go at five hundred a pop."

"Maybe I'll wait until it comes out on rental." Glover laughed. "Now get out of here. I'll send you a call on your throwaway number when I pick up your leading lady."

"Tonight, I hope?" Sully asked.

"We have a regular appointment. You'll be thanking me later. She's *your* kind of girl."

"I hope so. I'm going now," Sully said.

There was the sound of footsteps, a door slamming, then Sully made a three-point turn and headed south.

"What a pre-vert," Glover cracked. Lee started to back away, hearing the sound of the jack being lowered. Since Glover was going to be packing up things, Lee wanted to be back at his own vehicle in time to follow again.

As he ran back through the trees, Lee checked his cell phone. No calls, no text messages. Diane was really keeping her cool. If it had been her following Glover, he'd have checked in by now.

By the time Glover passed by, Lee had already turned his SUV around and was waiting. He ducked, not wanting the man to see him if he happened to glance in that direction, then pulled out onto the highway after a furniture delivery truck passed. Delivery charges this far from Albuquerque must be a bitch, Lee thought absently as he confirmed Glover's Jeep about a quarter mile ahead.

Punching out Diane's number, he filled her in on what had just transpired.

"I'm ready to roll, Lee. Think he's coming home, or about to do some more business?"

"If he's going to pick up a hooker, I'd think he'd do that later in the day, toward the afternoon or evening hours. That kind of business doesn't even begin until men start dropping into the taverns for lunch."

"I'm no expert on that, but you're probably right. Maybe he's just going to pick up some breakfast."

"He certainly can afford a decent meal with the cash he's apparently got on hand. I'll let you know if he heads your way."

Lee continued to follow, keeping his distance. Traffic was heavier now than before, and he'd sometimes lose the visual around a curve, but Glover seemed to be in no hurry. By the time they reached Quail Run, two faster-moving vehicles had already passed him.

Seeing Glover continue north, Lee punched out Diane's cell number. "Come on and join me. If we end up going into Albuquerque, I'm going to need some backup."

"You've got the lead," Diane pointed out. "If he takes I-Forty exit west, let me know and I can get us some unmarked support from Logan and APD. Officer Moore seems like she's on the ball, and Glover hasn't seen her yet."

"Agreed," Lee said. "You should be able to make up some ground and get close by the time we reach the canyon, but once we're on the interstate, Glover will make better time. You'll have to fly to catch up then, and that would draw too much attention from APD."

"Glover doesn't want to get pulled over, Lee. Not with all that unexplained cash in the Jeep with him, and no allies that we know about on the city police force," Diane pointed out.

Lee continued to follow, worried about Glover's comment concerning Sully's "kind of girl." Was the man referring to a boy instead, maybe Timothy Klein? And was Glover on the way to retrieve him? Or was this more of a pimping operation for a young hooker? Either way, they couldn't afford to let Glover give them the slip.

Lee was relieved when Glover took the interstate toward Albuquerque, as expected. He'd just relayed the information to Diane, who was only a few miles behind them, when he got another call from Felix Rodriguez, the state cop shadowing Sully.

"Lee, thought you'd want to know. Sully's at one of those rental storage places in Ponderosa, just west of the Elks' lodge. He's taking some stuff out of a storage unit."

Lee thought about it a second. "Camera cases, tripods, lights, maybe?"

"That's what it looks like. I was wondering. Like stuff from a portrait studio. Think it's stolen?"

"Nope. But keep a close eye on Sully, even if you have to call in reinforcements. I think he's about to go into the porno movie business, and if he is, we've got to find where he's taking the gear. Whatever you do, don't tip him off. One of his 'actors' might just be Timothy Klein—the missing ten-year-old."

"Damn. Hope you're right. Want me to keep you up to date?"

"Definitely." Lee ended the call. He knew already that Sully had plans to film the hooker Glover was going to track down for him. Hopefully, Sully wasn't just kinky and planning to film his own action, or worse, coming up with a short film for the next Raindance Festival.

CHAPTER 15

Glover stopped at a pancake house in Albuquerque's Northeast Heights, and Lee kept watch. Diane picked up the more sophisticated motion detector and some additional camera gear they'd requested be left for them at the Wal-Mart drop, then went to another close-by fast-food place for breakfast burritos.

When Diane returned, she parked the pickup behind the pancake place and joined Lee in his SUV, which was in a position to watch the entrance and their quarry's Jeep.

While they were eating, they discussed their strategy. "I've arranged for Officer Moore to join up with us this afternoon, earlier if necessary, and APD has an unmarked unit on standby at two of their substations. All it'll take is one call," Diane said, then she took a sip of coffee from the foam cup.

Lee glanced over at her as he finished his second green chile breakfast burrito. Diane was smart, tough, and good looking, as well. She'd left the house with her hair still wet, but the way it had dried, kind of wild and stringy, merely reinforced her cover identity as an attractive wildcat who definitely marched to the beat of her own drummer.

"I'm hoping he'll want to put his money somewhere safe and maybe lead us to a stash," Lee said. "Someone with his background and living on the edge like he does, probably has money, weapons, supplies, and whatever hidden in a couple of places."

Diane nodded. "In case he has to split in a hurry. You've got yours, too, Lee."

Lee had told her about one of his caches. There were actually three of them, and a couple of vehicles in two New Mexico locations, and one in Holbrook, Arizona. He would have told her about the rest, too, but she hadn't wanted to know. As she pointed out, she already knew the ways skilled interrogators could get information, even from sources determined to resist. She just didn't want to be in possession of information that could cost him his life if he were ever discovered and had to try and disappear.

Lee trusted Diane completely, of course. He'd never met such a strong-willed person in his life. She already knew the biggest secret he could ever have. But he humored her. People who cared about each other did that.

Glover had a leisurely breakfast and they were beginning to wonder if he'd somehow slipped out without notice, when he strolled out the entrance, toothpick in his mouth. Diane slipped out of the SUV. "Here we go," she whispered, then walked briskly toward her pickup, picking her way around vehicles in the parking lot so Glover wouldn't spot her.

Lee, with his baseball cap on, dark sunglasses, and sun visor down, knew he was barely discernable, even if Glover decided to look in his direction. When they'd begun this assignment, Lee and Diane had provided themselves with various details—different hats, jackets, and so forth—to subtly alter their identities, and now was the time to confuse Glover, if possible.

While Glover had been inside the pancake house, Lee had added a quick dealer plate to the front of the vehicle, to try and make the generic silver-gray SUV appear a little different to

Glover, and stuck a magnetic business sign for a local building contractor on the door panel. The sign had been well hidden, out of sight beneath the spare tire, and there was no indication that Glover had seen it the other day when he planted the bags of marijuana.

Diane had also stuck a magnetic license plate for Arizona on her pickup while picking up breakfast, and added a rosary to hang from the rearview mirror. A subtle touch, but still it altered the look. She was also wearing a cap and sunglasses, and had just put her hair into a ponytail.

Glover looked around casually, and Lee froze, knowing that movement attracted attention. If Glover even noticed that the SUV was occupied from this distance, he showed no reaction. Walking over to a newspaper box, Glover put in some quarters and pulled out today's edition of the Albuquerque *Journal*. The man checked his watch, then walked slowly back to his Jeep, reading the paper.

Lee felt the vibration of his cell phone and opened it up. It was Diane.

"He's just killing time, you think? I saw him check his watch from my new position," she said. "I'm out of your view on the other side of the IHOP."

Lee had sneaked a look at his own watch. "It's almost nine. Maybe he's waiting for a bank to open."

"He wouldn't put the money into an account. But maybe a safety deposit box?"

"Perhaps, but not all of it. Banks keep short hours, and require a transaction or sign in," Lee pointed out. "Then there are all the cameras. Too complicated and public for a guy like Glover."

"So we wait."

Nearly fifteen minutes went by, then Glover drove out of the parking lot and headed west down Central. At Louisiana, he turned north. Traffic was heavy, but moving well, and Lee had no problem keeping the Jeep in sight. Diane was somewhere behind him, following Lee. If she lost track of him, or Lee needed her to take the lead, a quick cell phone call was all they'd need. Lee had placed his headset on so he could keep both hands on the wheel for any quick maneuvers, and knew Diane had probably done the same. She'd been the one who'd gotten him used to the practice, actually.

When Glover turned left, stopping in front of a gate leading into a long storage unit complex, Lee knew what the man had in mind. "Diane. Glover's pulled into a storage place on the west side of the street. Go to the right just before the facility and stop where you can watch the entrance gate. I'll move in for a closer look, and if this is a decoy or evasive maneuver, we won't both be out of position and unable to follow."

"Clear."

Lee continued to the next street down from the storage units, turned left, and parked at the curb beside a mini-mall containing small business offices and a cleaners. He left the SUV quickly and walked south down the sidewalk. Glover, who'd halted to sign in with the security guard at the gate, was just driving in.

Lee stopped. If he kept walking toward the gate, the security guard would see him and perhaps approach. The problem was he couldn't get into the storage area without being seen, not in broad daylight, because it would take a careful climb up a very high fence, and a scramble over three strands of barbed wire that extended outward at an angle.

Glover was now out of sight, but his target wouldn't be able to leave without his vehicle and alerting the security guard, who also had to sign people out of the storage areas. Lee decided to circle the block on foot, finally, just to make certain the storage facility only had one way in and out.

Five minutes later, out of options, Lee waited for Glover. Whatever the man was leaving behind or picking up from the storage unit would remain a mystery at least for the moment. Later, when Glover was gone, he'd find the means to check the storage unit, if necessary.

Lee strolled by the gate quickly, walking north on the sidewalk, and glanced casually down the road that divided the facility into two long rows of large garagelike units facing inward. Glover's vehicle was parked beside the open door of a unit. Wondering if Glover had a backup vehicle inside, he noticed in passing that the Jeep was blocking the open space. He couldn't bring out a second vehicle, not with the Jeep there, so Glover was probably not switching vehicles.

While walking around the block, Lee noted where Diane had parked and now called her on his cell. "He's still inside. The front's the only way in and out without cutting a hole in the fence or leaping the thing. And that would be a trick, even after climbing onto the roof."

"I can see the left fender of the Jeep from my position. You think I should walk across the street for a better angle?"

"Naw. Anything sneaky is going to take place out of sight of the security guy and the video cameras they have aiming down the rows. Glover is going to be careful. Remember how he searches his vehicle every morning for bugs?"

"Okay. We'll just wait. Again."

A full fifteen minutes went by before Diane called Lee. "The Jeep is turning around. Looks like he's about to leave." Several seconds went by, then Diane added, "He's signing out now, and he's got on a pair of sunglasses and a hat. Different shirt, as well, and a leather jacket."

"Taking on a disguise, huh? Good eyes."

"Thank the ten-power binoculars." There was a brief pause, then Diane spoke again. "He's heading south down Louisiana."

"Good. That'll make it easier for me to get out in traffic," Lee said. "Stay on the line, and get ready to slip in behind me."

Glover returned to Central Avenue, then turned right, west, and continued down the wide street, formerly part of Route 66. Lee recalled all the hotels and motels that had formerly lined this street, and how, over time, most had become unprofitable, run-down, and eventually the hangouts of drug dealers, prostitutes, and other lowlives. A lot of violence had taken place along this road, and more and more of the hotels were being taken over by the city and condemned. The aging structures eventually ended up at the landfills.

Prostitution was alive and well in this area, especially at night around the numerous bars, so Lee began to suspect that might have been what had drawn Glover here. "Naw," Lee said out loud. It was just too early, not even 10:00 in the morning.

"You say something?"

"Sorry. Forgot I was still on the line. I was thinking that Glover might already be looking for this woman—the hooker. Then it struck me how early it still was."

"Central was always a hot spot for just about every vice you can imagine. Most of that is farther downtown these days, but I think we're still in the right location," Diane said.

"Maybe we should check with an APD cop, someone who's worked vice and is relatively current on the subject."

"Your Officer Moore. Good idea, Lee. She probably knows all the pickup spots."

Though she wasn't supposed to be available until afternoon, they were able to schedule a quick meet with Officer Moore at a coffee shop after Glover stopped at a Jeep dealership, then went into a waiting room while the vehicle was being serviced.

Another officer was watching the shop and would contact them once Glover got ready to leave.

Lee and Diane had just sat down at a rear booth when Andrea came in. She was wearing sunglasses and took them off to look around the room. She was dressed in a sleeveless knit top, jeans, and a short, shaggy hair style that was infinitely practical. Andy looked more like a high school student than an experienced cop. The small leather purse she carried and her metallic gray lipstick just added to that image.

"That her?" Diane whispered. "She looks so young and . . ."

"Naïve? Wait till she opens her mouth," Lee said, then waved enough to catch her attention.

"Hi guys," Officer Moore called back cheerfully, playing the role of civilian to the other patrons who'd noticed her.

Lee looked at Diane, then rolled his eyes. "Forgot. We're not cops at the moment. That was probably just for show."

Andrea walked over casually and both Lee and Diane scooted around. She eased in beside Diane, who, like Lee, had removed her cap. "Wish you'd been on my team when I was working the street, girl. You'd have attracted all the johns and all I would have had to do was Mirandize them and slap on the cuffs."

Diane held out her hand. "I'm Diane Lopez. Shall I take that as a compliment?"

"Nothing but. Call me Andy, Diane. You guys order yet? The cinnamon rolls in this joint are to die for." Andrea sat her purse on the cushion beside her, then winked at Lee. "Good to see you again. Think we're going to nail—" She stopped speaking as the waiter came up, holding laminated menus.

"Here for lunch, folks?" the young man with curly red hair asked, beaming a smile that flashed briefly on Lee, but then switched back and forth between the women.

Lee waited a few seconds, then decided to buy some time for the ladies to think it over. "For me, just coffee and one of those highly recommended cinnamon rolls."

"Mocha, cappuccino, latte, frappuccino, espresso?"

"Just coffee. The kind your grandfather would drink—with cream."

"I'll have to check . . . just kidding. We call it 'cowboy coffee' here, sir. Tall, white mug—thick and black. Best in the city," the waiter said with a chuckle.

"Espresso for me, and a cinnamon roll, too, I guess," Diane added.

"Yeah, me, too, what she's having. Screw the diet," Andrea said.

"Whatever diet you ladies are on is definitely working," the waiter said. "I'll be right back with your order."

Fifteen minutes later, after agreeing on their tactics, they finished up their brunch. Lee and Diane would continue to track Glover's movements, taking turns at the lead so he would be less likely to notice a particular vehicle. Andrea was going to arrange for backup cars, so they could switch in the afternoon if necessary. She was also going to get a GPS for them, a small unit they could place on Glover's Jeep the next time the opportunity arose. He'd already checked the Jeep for bugs earlier and, if his routine held, wouldn't be doing it again today. They'd have to remove the unit later, of course.

Officer Moore was sliding out of the booth when the cell phone hooked to her jeans began to buzz. She brought the phone to her ear, then nodded at Lee and Diane. "He's at the counter now, and the mechanic just drove the Jeep out of the stall."

They'd paid when their orders arrived, so Diane and Lee had no reason to wait around. "Stay in touch," Diane said, nodding to Andrea.

Lee looked at Officer Moore's chest and saw her tense up. "Better add a vest, Andrea. Before tonight."

"Oh, right. Thought for a moment you were doing some comparison shopping."

Diane shook her head. "I should have made the suggestion myself. Glover's a shooter."

Officer Moore looked back at Lee. "Something happen I don't know about?"

"Trust us on this, Andy." Lee looked her in the eyes. If Glover was still carrying the .45 and the AP rounds, the vest wouldn't be of much use. But he might have switched to a smaller, easily concealed pistol with regular sights for around town.

Andrea held his gaze, then nodded.

"Gotta go, Lee," Diane said, moving toward the door.

He followed, putting on his cap and sunglasses before stepping outside. The Jeep dealer was only a half block down the street. They could tell Glover hadn't left yet because the Jeep was still outside the stall, beside the garage's office.

"Take the lead," Lee called out to Diane, who'd already reached the SUV. He headed toward the pickup—his ride for the next few hours.

Glover stopped a few miles farther west on Central at a local gun shop. Lee had been into that store on several occasions, mainly for extra ammunition for his various weapons, and knew that the proprietor was ex-military and had a good reputation. Unless Glover had already made an earlier purchase and had a background check completed, he couldn't be picking up a firearm.

Ammunition, however, was available just by submitting an ID, though at this place, he knew AP ammo wouldn't be sold to a non-officer. Lee's best guess was that Glover was here to get some conventional rounds for his .45 or whatever he had in his current armory. Diane would be able to get SAC Logan to confirm that later.

Glover was inside for an hour, longer than expected, so Diane, who was closest, reported immediately when he came out. "Glover's carrying a small bag, so we can rule out rifle and shotgun. From the way he's using two hands, it's relatively heavy. Several boxes of ammo, maybe."

"He's expecting another encounter with us, so that would be my guess."

The rest of the day was spent tracking Glover all over the city. He had lunch at a downtown Fourth Street café, roamed around the city shopping, and now was on his second hour at a sports bar. Lee would have been bored stiff if it hadn't been so important to stay alert. Glover had already proven himself to be dangerously unpredictable.

As Lee sat there in the dark, across the street from the sports bar—a hot spot for prostitution according to Andy—his cell phone buzzed. It was Diane, who was in the bar's parking lot, also watching.

"Lee, I just got a report from Officer Rodriguez. This afternoon Sully took the camera gear to his house and hauled it all inside. Rodriguez got a look through binoculars, and said that Sully seemed to be messing with the lights and a camera, reading manuals, stuff like that. Getting to know the equipment."

"The bastard is anticipating his directing career. I've got mixed feelings about the missing kid. One part of me is hoping to find young Klein tonight, and the other is praying that Klein's elsewhere, safe and far away from sickos like Glover or Sully."

"Yeah, Lee. But I'd rather find him tonight under these bad circumstances than discover his body three months from now in a shallow grave."

"Yeah. It just really pisses me off."

"Well, at least you got a chance to place that GPS on the Jeep. It'll help us track Glover when he delivers the hooker to Sully."

"And we can turn it on and off by remote, which means that if Glover just does a signal search without a visual, he won't find it at all." Lee stretched and yawned. He'd had lunch from the car seat, picked up when Glover had gone into a clothing store, and the truck still smelled like french fries. It was 7:00 P.M. now, and he was getting hungry again.

"Lee. One of those new-model VW Bugs just pulled up. Yellow, with a really young-looking female driver. Suppose this is the hooker Glover is pimping for Sully?"

"I see the car. Andy said this was a common pickup spot for prostitutes. Let's see if her outfit gives us any clues."

The young woman, dressed in sprayed-on pale blue satin pants and a short-length jeans jacket, walked into the sports bar's side entrance.

Lee's phone indicated another caller. He put Diane on hold.

"Glover's got a visitor. This must be the girl," Officer Moore said in a whisper. She'd been inside, across the room from Glover, for an hour now. "She came right over, recognized him immediately. God, she's young looking. If she's legal now, she probably didn't start out that way."

"This has got to be the girl he's getting for Sully. Give us a heads-up when they start to leave," he answered.

Lee switched back to Diane, then noted two men standing by her car door. They must have approached while he was watching the hooker.

He could hear her voice over the open line. "Fuck off, assholes. My boyfriend is inside, and if you're still hanging around when he comes out, he'll kick your balls up into your kidneys."

Shit! Lee knew Diane was tough, but if one of those losers decided to get rough she'd have to fight, and that was bound to create a lot of noise and attention. If Glover saw and recognized her . . .

Lee stepped down out of the pickup, stuck the phone in his pocket, and jogged across the street, moving in from the back of Diane's SUV and, at the same time, remaining some distance from the sports bar. They'd have to depend on Andy for a few moments until they could get rid of the troublemakers.

Diane wouldn't get out, but she was also remaining quiet. Under normal circumstances, screaming and yelling helped a woman in trouble, but she also knew the consequences a ruckus would have for them. She'd scooted across the seat from the driver's window, and when one of the thugs reached for the door handle, she kicked. Lee, coming up from the back, heard a curse and the guy jumped back, holding his hand. The other man, standing beside him but out of reach of Diane, laughed.

"Walk away, guys," Lee said, loud enough to be heard by just the troublemakers. He sneaked a glance at the bar and nobody was outside, not yet.

The man who'd laughed glanced over and saw Lee less than twenty feet away. He reached into his pocket and pulled out a knife. "You the fucking boyfriend?"

Diane, who'd lost their attention when Lee arrived, whipped open the door, slamming the idiot with the knife. The blade flew out of his hand and clattered across the pavement. "Let's take these dorks out fast, Lee," she said, jumping out.

Lee was already moving. He grabbed dork number one, the guy with the injured wrist, by the collar and belt, then threw him over the hood of the SUV. The guy hit hard, like someone sliding face-first into third base. Unfortunately for him it was asphalt, not loose dirt.

Diane met the remaining guy—without the knife now—as

he was rushing in, catching him in the groin with her heel. The force knocked her backward, but unlike her opponent, she kept her balance. The disabled man groaned, then fell to his knees and rolled over, gasping for breath.

Lee took a step forward, noting out of the corner of his eye that the man he'd just bounced across the pavement was crawling away. "You guys want some more action?"

The attacker Diane had kicked, his face pale and his hands hovering around his groin in a defensive gesture, shook his head and mumbled.

"Let's just shoot them and get it over with," Diane said, bringing out her pistol.

"Okay. Why not?" Lee agreed, showing his pistol but not removing it from his belt.

Groin forgotten, the injured man struggled to his feet and tried to raise his hands. "No, no. Don't shoot. We'll go."

"Put your hands down, asshole. Then pick up your buddy and get lost. I haven't shot anyone all day now, and I'm getting real jumpy," Diane said, shaking her pistol slightly.

The man never looked back. Staggering over to his friend, he helped him up, then the two dragged themselves over to a bright red Mustang.

Diane and Lee watched as the car raced to the far end of the parking lot, then, tires squealing, pulled out into the street and roared away.

"Damn. Now what?" Lee reached for his phone, realizing it was vibrating, and remembered cutting Andy off.

"Where the hell you guys been? Glover just left," Officer Moore whispered harshly through the receiver. "And now the girl is getting into her yellow Bug."

Lee turned around to look and so did Diane. Glover's Jeep was pulling out of the parking lot and the Volkswagen was moving in that direction.

"I'm on Glover," Diane said, jumping into the SUV.

"No. Take the girl, Diane. I've got the GPS, remember? I'll find Glover," he said. Then he jogged away toward his pickup, remembering Andy was still on the line. "I'll ask Diane to get in touch, Andy. You can help her track the girl. Glover is still the priority target for me, and I have the GPS to help me out."

"Understood, Lee," Andy said. "I'm on my way to my unit now."

Lee reached the curb, saw an opening in traffic, and raced across to his pickup. Once he was heading in the direction Glover had gone, east, Lee realized that Diane was ahead of him. That meant that the hooker must have been going in Glover's direction, as well. Maybe she was following him to the meet with Sully.

A quick call to Diane confirmed his suspicions. She'd heard from Officer Rodriguez, who'd reported that Sully had placed his camera gear in his own vehicle and was now heading north from his mountain home.

Hanging up, Lee increased his speed. Within ten minutes he'd passed Diane and located the yellow VW, which stood out clearly. Even a nonvampire would have had a hard time losing that car at night.

Confirming with the GPS display on the seat beside him that Glover was enroute to I-40, Lee realized that he should avoid passing the Bug as long as the girl continued to follow Glover. No sense in pointing out that he was following Glover, too.

The caravan of five vehicles—only the first two close to each other—entered the interstate, then continued east into Tijeras Canyon. As expected, Glover turned south onto Highway 337, and the VW followed. Traffic was much lighter here, so Lee made a decision and called Diane.

"I'm going to stick with Glover, but if he and the girl end up at the same location with Sully, we can't all hang around. Have you heard anything new on Sully?"

"Rodriguez said that Sully had stopped off the road just across from that FAC development. He's just waiting there, apparently."

"Glover is less than five minutes away from that location, if my timing is anywhere near right. If he stops for Sully and we all pass by, Glover is bound to at least notice you and me," Lee pointed out.

"You stop before the FAC road, Lee, and I'll pass on by and pull off farther south. I'll ask Andrea to continue and cover the back road into the development, the one we took the other night when we lost the motorcycle. We'll have every exit covered."

"So what about Rodriguez?" Lee asked.

"He should continue to watch Sully, don't you think? We know he's going to be hooking up with the girl, and that might lead us to the kidnapped boy . . . hopefully," Diane said.

"Good. I'll contact Rodriguez."

Lee couldn't keep a continual eye on Glover because of the forest and the twisting highway, but most of the time at least he had the VW in sight. When it slowed and pulled off the highway to the left, Lee killed his lights and moved off to the right side of the road.

He could see the big billboard advertising the FAC housing development, and, across the highway, the three suspect cars they'd been following for the past half hour.

Diane passed by, not slowing down or showing any interest at all in the vehicles.

Taking out his binoculars, Lee watched as the girl stepped out of the yellow car and strolled over to Sully's car window. Less than a minute passed before the girl walked back to her car. Sully then got out and walked over to Glover's Jeep.

Officer Moore drove by just then. Lee watched as Glover handed Sully a small boxlike object, then Sully walked back to his car. Immediately Glover turned out onto the highway, heading in the same direction as Diane and Andy. That left Sully and the girl.

Lee picked up the phone and quickly called Officer Rodriguez. "Felix, change of plans. Glover is coming your way. Follow, but keep enough distance between you to avoid getting made. My guess is that he's going home. His part in this should be done for the night. I'll take Sully."

Lee then quickly punched the number to reach Diane. "New plan. I'll follow Sully—Rodriguez is going to take Glover. As soon as Glover passes you, come back north. If the girl doesn't go with Sully, let her go. Just have Andrea stand by and continue to watch the roads in case Sully tries some fancy footwork. You and I should concentrate on Sully and the girl. My guess is that they're going to meet at one of the houses in the development. We can't afford to lose them, so be aware that they could disappear in a heartbeat if they end up ducking into one of those double garages."

"I get you. Glover hooked them up and, if Sully liked what he saw, he and the girl are going someplace around here to do their thing. But tonight, with luck, it'll be much more than that," Diane responded. "Okay, gotta call Andy." She hung up.

Lee watched as Sully started his car and drove across the highway into the housing development. If the VW followed . . .

CHAPTER 16

**I**t did, and Lee notified Diane as he pulled out onto the high-way. Fifteen seconds later, he made the turn into the develop-ment's main road. Ahead he could see the VW as the vehicle came out of a low spot in the road. The girl was following Sully, who was just ahead.

They continued past several homes, some occupied and others at various stages of construction. Lee had seen all of them the night before. Tonight he'd probably learn where Glover had been last night.

The road formed a big flat ellipse, like a paper clip, and at the far curve was the model home. That's where Sully pulled in. Either he'd been given a remote, or somebody was inside and had seen him drive up, because the double garage door opened immediately. Lee, who'd been driving without headlights since he'd entered the housing development, came to a stop several lots away beside a sign that read FOR SALE.

The VW Bug came onto the concrete pad of the driveway and stopped. Lee could see Sully now, outside his own vehicle, and he motioned for the girl to park inside, as well. There was a slight hesitation, then the VW pulled up beside Sully's Camry. The garage door closed.

"We're here," Lee announced to Diane over the phone link. "Model home at the far end. Try to come in with your lights out, then pull up behind the pickup. If anyone wonders what we're doing here, like a resident or security guard, we can be a couple shopping for a home site after work."

"I'll have Andrea come up via the back route, then find a place out of sight of the model home to stand by. If we need to make a move, we can use backup."

Lee acknowledged the plan, then hung up. A single light had gone on inside the model home. He decided to wait outside the vehicle for Diane.

She arrived two minutes later, moving slowly with her lights out so she wouldn't run off the road. There were no streetlights yet in this area, and except for a few porch and low-wattage yard lamps, the stars and moon provided the only illumination.

Diane climbed out of the SUV. She'd kept the dome light off, so no one except a vampire could have recognized her until she stepped into point-blank range. The forest was still in transition here, mostly junipers and piñon pines, but the vegetation managed to turn the entire area dark and quiet, since it absorbed sound quite well. The click of her door closing couldn't have been heard a hundred feet away.

"Time to do a little window peeping and eavesdropping, huh?" she said in a low voice. "But if Timothy Klein is in there, we're going in, Glover or not, right?"

Lee nodded. "We still might be able to link him to whatever is going on in there. After all, he undoubtedly gave Sully access to this model home."

"Which suggests what we already suspected, that Glover has some kind of tie, and maybe leverage, too, over the developers."

"With one of them, at least, or maybe an employee who has the keys to this office. We still need more background on this project. That'll give us a possible link. Now let's go snooping."

"What about a security guard? I haven't seen one yet, but with the model home and all the sites still under construction . . ."

"Didn't consider that. Maybe Andrea can keep a lookout and tie him up for a while, if necessary," Lee said. "Not literally, of course."

"She may have seen plenty of that while working vice," she joked. "I'll give her a quick call."

Two minutes later, Diane put her phone away. "She's already on it. They have a roving patrol, probably a service that does regular checks. A security vehicle came into the development at the east end, and she's going to intercept them and ask for directions. When they come this way, she'll have already given us some lead time."

They hurried, hoping to avoid the guards altogether. There were no sidewalks, and the undeveloped lots still contained their original vegetation, plus standard real-estate signs. Lee and Diane moved through the edge of the tree line. The model home was bordered on three sides by field fencing held up by posts nearly railroad tie size, but the front was open to the street.

They circled around the right side of the structure, checking for interior lights in a back room. If Sully was going to actually film something, he'd need light, and even the blinds weren't light tight.

The back of the house retained its mostly natural landscape, had a deck, a flagstone walk to a flower garden, and a few taller pine trees scattered about. At the opposite back corner of the house, they detected an interior light. Lee noted that the light was coming from windows with closed shutters—half shutters, open at the top. You'd have to be eight feet tall or on a ladder to see in.

He turned around and eyed the back porch.

"You going for a climb?" she whispered.

"Yeah. If I'm quiet, I can see from the roof without them knowing. The window might be open a crack, too, so maybe you can hear something. Or you could climb that tree and look right in."

He pointed to a twenty-foot-high ponderosa pine in the center of the yard.

"Too far away, and I'm a terrible tree climber. I'll check the window up close."

Lee nodded, then walked over to the deck and found a spot where the rain gutters didn't extend. Jumping up, he grabbed the edge of the roof and pulled himself slowly and gently onto the terra-cotta tile. The building itself appeared to be less than two years old, so he was hoping none of the tiles were loose. If they were, he'd make one hell of a racket.

Moments later he was able to lower himself to his belly and inch toward the window with the light. He couldn't see Diane, which meant she was close to the wall, but now Lee could hear a voice. The window was open at least four inches. That meant Diane would be able to hear from below, too.

Sully was making an awkward, mostly one-sided conversation with the young woman. He mentioned lighting, camera positions, depth of field, sound levels, and other terms Lee recognized, but nothing about sex, boys, or porno.

Judging from the light shining out onto the yard that he was right above the window, Lee inched downward, headfirst, intending on looking inside like he had at Glover's a few days earlier.

"You want me to strip for the camera, Brian? Or I can just get naked and . . . whatever. You wanna film having sex with me, right?" The hooker certainly sounded young. If Sully went for children, she was about as close as he could get to legal, assuming, of course, that the woman wasn't fifteen or younger. Diane had already run the plate while on the way here, and the vehicle was registered to a fifty-five-year-old woman. The girl's madam? Lee hoped it wasn't her mother, though situations like that weren't uncommon.

"I want you to be the naïve, innocent, little girl, Katie. So while I'm getting everything set up, you need to change into these clothes."

Lee had taken his cap off and now he could look over the edge. He scooted a little farther, making sure none of the clay shingles would slip or break off, and then took a look. Sully was attaching a camera to a tripod and there were two big lights on stands in front of a children's-size bed. The decor in the room, even upside down, indicated to Lee that this was a decorator's idea of a children's room. From the pinks and pastels, the stereotype side of his brain said a girl's room. It figured.

"I was expecting a cheerleader's outfit, but hey, this is like what I wore in sixth grade," Katie said. "Oh, *now* I get it."

Lee stretched out as far as he could, trying to see if there was anyone else in the room, like Timothy Klein. If he was around he'd have to be under the bed or pushed against an outside corner. The closet was open enough to reveal it was empty. Sully had clamped some kind of light on the door, aimed up to give some indirect lighting, he supposed.

After about ten minutes, Lee realized that Sully was more interested in filming someone posing as a child doing . . . well, things he suspected perverts liked to watch. Lee didn't watch for long, except to confirm that Katie was being instructed to pretend she was a youngster involved in self-discovery, and when Katie was encouraged to vocalize her phony excitement, Lee was tempted not to listen, either. But he remained there for a half hour more, hoping to hear anything that would tell him more about Sully, Glover, and the possibility that they knew something about Timothy Klein.

Finally, Sully announced they were done.

Katie sounded surprised. "That's it? You don't want to do it with me? Or me do you? Price is still the same, you know."

"No, everything's fine, child, and here's your money. Are you going to be available tomorrow night? Same time, here? Next time I want you to play around and have sex with someone *I* bring. I'll film you two."

"Another porno film?" Seeing him nod, she added. "Okay, but here's the deal. Girls, okay. Men, duh. But no sickos who are into pain. You try anything like that, my boyfriend is going to cut off your balls."

"Relax, Katie. You'll be in control the whole time. You'll be the older one. And if you decide something isn't for you, just say so. You'll still get half your fee."

"Plus twenty more for gas. Or thirty."

"Twenty-five for gas."

The bargaining annoyed Lee, more so because he hadn't heard or seen any direct evidence that Sully knew about the missing boy. The only mystery was the identity of the "someone else," the one who was younger than Katie that Sully was planning on bringing tomorrow. Hopefully, if their suspicions were right, they'd be there to rescue Timothy Klein.

Lee looked down and saw that Katie was putting her clothes back on and Sully was watching. "Change your mind?" she teased, cocking her head.

"No, no. Just thinking about how exciting tomorrow is going to be. I'd better get this gear put away. The salespeople are going to be here at eight A.M. and I still have to straighten things up. Here's my cell number. Call by seven P.M. only if you can't make it. I have to pick up the other . . . actor, so I'll need to know."

"Whatever. Well, I'm out of here," Katie said, and he heard footsteps fade away on the hardwood floor.

Lee began to move away now, picking his way carefully

across the hard, uneven surface, which was a little dusty. If it had rained recently, the roof would be hell, but fortunately the clay, fiberglass, or whatever was dry. He'd want to discuss strategy with Diane and decide what to do about Katie.

Suddenly, as he heard the garage door open, then the sound of the VW leaving, an idea came to him and he grabbed his cell phone. He text messaged Diane and she answered immediately. After ending the call, he worked his way to the deck and lowered himself down beside Diane, who was crouched low, keeping watch for Sully.

The garage door sounded again, and from the thud, he knew it was coming back down. No second engine noise told him that Sully was still inside the house, or at least his car was. Lee looked over and noted the bedroom light was still on.

"That was a good idea you had, Lee. Andrea is going to tail Katie home, then stake her out. We'll have to decide how to handle tomorrow, and if we want her around when we bust Sully—if he brings the boy." She whispered very softly, knowing Lee could also read her lips. "And, by the way, I got a text message from Rodriguez. Glover went straight home."

He grabbed her hand. "Good. Now let's haul ass while Sully is busy loading his gear and restoring the model home."

They moved quickly, Diane trusting his eyes and letting him lead her around the house. Once they were out front, the few remaining lights still on at the houses down the street made it a lot easier for her. They picked up the pace, and in two minutes were inside their vehicles.

Following his lead, Diane drove away, lights off, until they were nearing the first occupied house. He turned on his headlights then, and she trailed behind a little farther, then turned on her own.

He'd put on his cell phone mike just a few seconds before she called. "Sully? Do we follow him?"

"I think he's going home when he's done here. We'll have Felix pick him up when he passes Quail Run, and we'll cover Glover again."

"Okay. And we need to follow up our queries about this FAC company and find out whether it's Glover or Sully who has the connections that gave him access tonight."

"Now that I think about it, the object I saw Glover hand Sully out at the highway was probably the garage remote. So that suggests Glover's the one who has juice with FAC," Lee said.

"No surprise, Lee. Let's see what dirt Logan and your people have dug up on the developers—or the real-estate agents who operate from the model home."

"Hopefully it'll give us more to hang on Glover. We need someone to be able to stand up in court and testify against the man—several people, really. Sully might do, if we can protect him from Glover. Especially if he ends up as a party to kidnapping and hopes to cop a plea."

"That's something that's bugging me, Lee," Diane replied. "We'd hoped to find Timothy Klein tonight. Are we way off track, or do you think Glover's really going to deliver him tomorrow for Sully's kiddie porn production?"

"Maybe we've been looking in the wrong direction, Diane. We wanted to believe that we're really on to something and that the Klein boy is still alive and relatively safe, and that skewed our perspective. This could turn out to be a dead end."

"Waiting's always the hardest part, Lee. If I thought we'd get answers, I'd be perfectly willing to grab Glover and start shooting off body parts until he decided to talk."

"Yeah, but neither one of us has slid down to his level yet, and, besides, the guy is a black bag professional. He'd die before giving himself up. Then we'd have squat, and our own futures would be in the outhouse."

They decided to wait until they got home to make any more

plans, so the call ended. Lee drove on, spotting rabbits by the highway and, once, a deer off in a small orchard. Diane had passed him, going home first. Lee followed, intending on stopping by the mailboxes at the end of the lane and waiting for fifteen minutes or more before going that last mile.

Out of habit, Lee checked the mail, even though it was unlikely that his or Diane's cover identities would get mail. Inside were several fliers for businesses and car dealers in Moriarity and Tijeras, one of those "Have you seen this kid?" notices, and a letter, hand addressed to Lee Begay. Inside was a color photo of Diane, standing on the porch, keys in hand. In red, crosshairs had been drawn, centered on her head. Judging from what she was wearing, the photograph had been taken their first morning at the place.

"Screw waiting. I'm going now," Lee said, half aloud. He stepped back to the pickup, then drove up the lane, his lights off.

When Lee arrived, everything seemed normal enough. Glover's living room light was on and there was a glow from the area where his large-screen TV was located. There was light coming from their own front room, and as he pulled up behind the SUV, he caught a glimpse of Diane beside the curtain.

He had one eye on Glover's place as he walked to the door. They had a rule to keep the doors locked, always, so he had his key ready. A moment later, he stepped inside, locking the deadbolt behind him.

Diane held up one hand for him to wait. Her other hand held her cell phone to her ear. From the look on her face, he knew something was going on, but she was listening, not talking. She brought out her pen, then started walking around the room, looking for something. Lee brought out the small notebook he carried in his shirt pocket and held it up, revealing a blank page. She nodded and took it from his hand.

Setting the notebook down on the dining table, she wrote a quick sentence. *They've called off the search for Timothy Klein.*

"Dead?" he couldn't help but mouth.

She shook her head and wrote some more: *They're waiting for some new leads. The manpower is needed elsewhere. God forgive me for saying this, but I hope Glover <u>does</u> have Timothy Klein.*

Lee grabbed the pen: *I understand. At least that'll mean we've got a chance to find him.*

CHAPTER 17

Diane hung up the phone a minute later. Lee had occupied his time starting a pot of coffee. "What else?" he asked as soon as she sat down the phone.

"Not much. All the leads have evaporated, and all the ground within miles has been covered. At least the parents are together again. They've pooled their resources and have hired a tracker with bloodhounds."

"Didn't the search teams do that already? I thought they'd lost the trail beside the highway, above where the bike was found," Lee said.

"The dogs are going to be taken to some of Timothy's favorite places, in case he's hiding out, angry with his parents for fighting over him, and money."

"Divorce is rough on kids. They'll try anything to get their parents back together, Diane."

"Well, that's already happened, at least for now. But we have to find a way to get to Glover, Lee. What's going on with him and Sully? Why would he pay Glover thousands of dollars, apparently, for pimping legal-age young people who look younger? He's *got* to have the kid."

"Well, that's the likely explanation, of course, unless it's all coincidental and Glover intends on providing Sully with somebody else's boy, someone we don't know about, or . . ."

"Or Glover is using the disappearance as an opportunity to scam Sully, making him think that he has young Klein. As long as the boy is still missing, Glover can make excuses and stall, milking Sully for money as long as he can," Diane pointed out. "But if Glover is forced to offer a much older male—not the Klein boy or, heaven forbid, another minor—we're not the only ones in for a big disappointment. How's Sully going to react, paying for something he could have obtained for a hundred dollars or so?"

"Nailing Glover as a pimp—which is something we'd have difficulty proving with neither of us even in the room—puts us back to zero. Besides, Diane, we want to nail Glover for something that'll put him away for a long, long time. Kidnapping would have worked, but arresting Glover for conning a child molester out of ten thousand dollars? Hell, most of the parents in the community would be on *his* side. The DA wouldn't even consider pressing charges."

"At least Sully might be vulnerable, *if* Katie's under age, or we can tie him to someone who is. I still wonder what's really going to happen tomorrow? Is Glover going to offer another excuse, then deliver someone new, maybe another young prostitute, or continue to string Sully along? Or does he really have Timothy Klein for sale?"

"We need to be there, either way," Lee added. "I'm just concerned, now that the search has officially ended, that we're going to lose some of our backup and nailing Glover is going to get tougher."

"Without more evidence against Glover, all we have is his implied connection to the child out there somewhere. But if we can confirm Katie's status as a minor by getting her real age, that'll help. Let me make a call to Officer Moore. I sent her a query, so maybe they've got something for us already."

A few minutes later, Diane hung up. "Katie is still fifteen, so we can bring molestation charges against Sully, at least, if we're willing to blow our covers. We'd have trouble getting much on Glover, though. Katie lives with her stepmother, the owner of the VW. That lady has several arrests and convictions for prostitution, which explains a lot. And she'll have to answer for this, as well."

"Let's go forward with our plans, then." Lee proceeded to install their additional video camera, working without further comment.

Diane respected his silence. She'd learned it was one of his Navajo traits, valuing silence and contemplation before speaking or taking action. In law enforcement, especially when out in the field, time was usually in short supply, but tonight, having to wait for Glover and Sully to go the next step, they had the opportunity to weigh every option.

Diane went over and poured herself a cup of coffee, offered Lee one, then brought out some peanut butter and jelly and made them both a simple sandwich. He took his with a nod. Halfway through the cup, the sandwich now history, Lee looked up.

"We can still turn this over to local vice units and have them bust Katie's stepmother, Sully, and whoever Glover provides—if anyone—and keep ourselves out of it. Katie will end up with social services unless they can find a relative to take her in, someone safe. Andrea can take the point, and even with corrupt county deputies involved they should be able to make it stick."

"But nailing Glover for pandering just isn't enough," Diane said, reinforcing their earlier conclusions, "and we just don't have enough evidence to put him in jail for the other crimes he's probably committed, at least not for long. An arrest would also alert him to the fact that he's being watched. We'd get zip, or so little that it wouldn't be worth it."

Lee glanced across the room, coffee cup in hand. "If Glover has the boy, we're in a good position to take him down and recover the child. But if it's someone else, somebody of legal age, this line of our investigation is going to end. And Sully will be all we have."

"Follow that line of thought, Lee. Suppose Glover shows up with someone else. Sully has already paid out a hunk of money for human contraband. And unless Glover provides someone that makes Sully happy . . ."

Diane shrugged at her own hypothesis, then continued. "Can he stand up to Glover? Sully is weak, a child molester or close to it, who hopes to make a ton of money selling kiddie porn on CDs. Glover is the kind of man who protects himself from indirect attack. He's going to have insurance, particularly if Sully tries to implicate him for kidnapping. For all we know, there's a hidden camera or recorder in that model home— something Glover intended to use to shut Sully up if there was any problem. From the photos we saw in Glover's apartment, taking pictures is a favorite blackmail strategy of his."

Lee's eyes lit up. "You may be on to something, Diane. Glover seems like the kind of animal that would love catching someone in their own game. It would also explain why Glover went over there last night on the motorcycle—ahead of Sully's movie-making visit—and what he was carrying in the gym bag. He could have placed a small camera—for example, like the ones we have on our surveillance system—in the bedroom Sully was going to use. He could have had it on a timer, set to record at the time Sully had booked the girl, and bingo, instant blackmail, and protection in case Sully tried to turn him in."

"Glover still at home?"

Lee glanced out. "Yeah, I think so. The little bug I left there before hasn't gone off, so he didn't leave by the back gate, and his Jeep's still there. He's in no rush. There may be enough recording media in his camera setup to cover tomorrow night, as well, so there would be no reason to pick it up after Sully left tonight."

"I'm not sleepy, Lee. Wanna go break into a model home?"

"You've got yourself a date."

It took them a half hour to install the extra surveillance camera Diane had brought with her, then Lee sneaked around to Glover's backyard and replaced the low-tech bug with the motion detector—disguised as a rock—that the DOD had loaned them.

Later, well after midnight, Lee and Diane reached the rear of the model home property after a jog through the woods via an old fire road. The pickup, less conspicuous than the SUV, was parked behind some trees a few hundred yards away.

The fence was only four feet high, and Diane climbed over at one of the posts, feeling her way. Lee jumped it flat-footed. "Show-off," she whispered.

He took her by the hand . . . the moon had already set in the west and it was even darker now than before, especially with no lights on in the house. "Good. The window's still open a crack," he said as they walked across the backyard.

He lifted her up, holding her there by the waist as she took off the screen. Diane slid the window open, then, with a leg up from Lee, climbed inside. He jumped up, grabbed the windowsill, and pulled himself over and into the room.

"What if there's a motion detector in the hall?" Diane said, aiming her small but powerful flashlight around the room.

"Then I guess we're screwed. But I don't recall seeing any alarm keypads and there aren't any prowler lights outside or we would have set them off earlier. If Glover did set up a camera to record Sully's directorial debut, then we should be able to find the hidden lens—probably in a duct or grille. If we don't find it, then there's no reason to venture any farther."

"Check the GPS monitor and verify where Glover's Jeep is, Lee. We've been having trouble predicting what he's going to do next."

"Yeah. That's what makes him so dangerous." Lee brought the small display, about the size of an iPod, out of his pocket and touched a button. A small outline of a map section appeared. "Crap, Diane. You psychic?"

"He left home?"

"Yeah. He hasn't gone far yet, but he's definitely driving north, in our general direction."

"How long have we got?"

"It took us fifteen minutes to get to where we left the truck. He's going a faster route part of the way, but farther by a few miles unless he takes a route we don't know about. I think we've got fifteen until he reaches the sign at the highway, five more or less to reach here. If that's where he's headed, that is," Lee added.

She started to search the wall opposite the bed, looking behind the mirror above the child-size dresser first. "Then we really need to work fast, don't we?"

"Better put on the gloves. Our fingerprints might end up in Glover's hands, and we know he has someone on the county's force in his pocket. I'll search everywhere above eye level," Lee said, looking up toward a heating/cooling vent in the ceiling. Putting on the latex gloves he'd had in his pocket, Lee moved one of two chairs in the room, stood on it, and gazed up at the vent. A close examination revealed dust on the metal vent frame, and no smudges or rubbed-off areas. He brought out his own penlight and checked behind the metal louvers. "This vent is clean."

Moving the chair, he then ruled out the light fixture.

"Same with the mirror."

They continued to search for several more minutes, without success. Diane checked the GPS monitor. "Glover's halfway here, I think."

"We still have time. Did you check the bookcase?"

"My next target," she answered, moving in close and looking for gaps or anything transparent that might be concealing the lens of a camera.

"Hello. Lee, I think I found it. Just under the third shelf." She aimed the light at a small, dark circle in the wall in the gap where the long wooden bookshelf, resting on decorative wrought-iron brackets, didn't quite touch the wall.

"Yeah. When the lights are on, that spot would be in shadow." He stepped over and removed the six hardcover editions of the old Nancy Drew books just above the hole. Hidden behind the volumes was a cutout piece of Sheetrock about the size of a paperback book, held back in place with masking tape where it had been removed earlier. Lee pulled off the tape along the top and sides, then pulled the piece out.

In the opening was a small video camera with a fiber-optic cable. The lens at the end was aimed through the hole Diane had discovered. A digital readout displayed the current time, and a green light indicated the unit was receiving power, though not, apparently, capturing images at the moment if Lee read the display properly.

The camera was fastened in place with duct tape and thumbtacks. Lee cut the tape with his pocketknife and began removing the tacks. "How much time?"

"He's almost at the turnoff, I estimate, but the developer's road doesn't show up on the GPS overlay. If he turns, the dot will move west on its own."

"Just a few more minutes. I don't want to drop the camera where it'll break and be hell getting back out." Lee worked at a stubborn tack with the tip of his knife blade, not wanting to break off the knife point.

"Can you pop out the CD? At least we'll have that—and Glover won't."

Lee looked at the device. "I'd thought I'd seen every type of electronic device, even back to the early radar sets. But this is a new model, apparently. Can you figure out what button to push? I can't read the labels without pulling the unit."

Diane aimed the flashlight at the camera. "I've seen this one. It's a new, state-of-the-art machine. The Bureau uses a slightly older version to monitor offices and the waiting areas in our own facilities. Push the button right there, but hold your hand under the panel when it swings out. Those suckers can pop out sometimes." She adjusted the flashlight to project a fine beam and pointed at the button.

Lee did as she requested and the small, gold DVD disc fell right into the palm of his hand. "Gotcha. How we doing on Glover?"

"He's gotta be at the turnoff now. We're going to have trouble getting out unseen unless we leave pretty soon."

Lee grabbed the camera and yanked. It came loose easily, undamaged, with some of the duct tape still attached. "We have time to put things back like they were?"

Diane looked at the display, then held it up so Lee could see it, too. "What do you think?"

Lee pushed a button, zooming out on the display to show a larger area. "It looks like he's at the turnoff, all right, maybe even past it. The coordinates don't mean jack without knowing the reference points for the road leading into this development."

"Zoom in on the GPS. We can at least find out what direction it's moving."

Lee did as she asked. "It's moving west—no, more northwest. Now north. There aren't any curves like that on the road coming here, are they?"

"He's passed the turnoff, Lee. Remember the big curve about a mile north? Glover's passed us by. We've got time."

Lee sighed. "We needed a break. But maybe this will cost

us, too. Wonder where he's going? I wish we had somebody on him now. My bad."

"One thing at a time. Let's restore this place so at least Sully won't know we were here, then split."

Lee put the camera in a plastic bag and the DVD in another smaller one, then inserted the DVD between the pages of the notebook in his shirt pocket for further protection. Diane carried the camera in her jacket pocket.

In four minutes they had the small piece of Sheetrock taped back in place behind the Nancy Drew books, the small pieces of debris from the floor picked up, and the chairs and furniture back where they'd been before. Lee opened the bedroom door, looked down the hall, and saw there were no alarms. He let Diane out the back door, relocked the deadbolt, returned to the bedroom, and climbed out the window. Once the window was closed the same amount as before, they reattached the screen. Diane went over to the fence and climbed across. Lee followed, smoothing out their tracks as well as he could.

The entire process of leaving the house and brushing out the tracks took about five more minutes, but finally they were on their way back to the pickup.

"We're safe here, Lee. Check on Glover, if you don't mind."

Lee brought out the GPS monitor and activated the display, then held it between them so they could both see.

"Glover's in Tijeras. That address, isn't it about where the Trident gas station is? Sully's business?" Diane asked.

"Exactly. But what's he doing there? If he'd have wanted to see Sully, he'd have gone south to Sully's mountain home, right?"

"We're forgetting one thing, Lee. All we know for sure is where the Jeep is—not Glover."

Lee nodded. Instinctively taking a quick look around, he heard a faint rustle in the trees. His hand slipped down toward his pistol just as Diane turned on her flashlight.

A pair of eyes gleamed from the brush, then Lee chuckled.

"It's a deer, Lee," Diane whispered. "I've never seen one this close except at the zoo."

They watched as the big doe stared back at them, slowly chewing whatever she'd just taken into her mouth. Quietly they climbed into the pickup. Lee, driving, kept the lights off and let the truck roll back down the narrow track as far as possible before starting the engine. When he looked back a last time in the mirror, the doe was still watching.

"You think Glover decided to have something done to the Jeep, or do you think maybe he finally went to pick up his truck? The damage we did to it must have been fixed by now," Diane commented.

"Your guess is as good as mine. Check the blip on the monitor once in a while. I'll drive, but keep your eyes open for a sneak attack. If Glover found the bug, he could be playing games. Hell, he could be right behind us now."

"Except that you can see in the dark and you'd notice, right?"

"You bet. Look, for all we know, he's home, watching Jay or Dave on TV, and one of those guys at the station just returned his pickup and drove the Jeep back to Tijeras."

"What would you do if you'd just tried to kill your next-door neighbor, failed, and knew he knew it was you?" she asked.

"I'd assume my own life was in danger, *real* danger. I'd be looking over my shoulder, expecting a retaliatory strike. In Glover's case, he's probably not getting much sleep right now. He's either going to try again soon, or is just hoping to stay alive long enough to raise one last chunk of change before disappearing."

"He already knows we're dangerous and don't want any connection to the police ourselves," she answered. "Your identity says you've got a criminal record. My guess is he probably assumes we're doing something illegal right now."

"Considering the fact that this little trip isn't going into our reports, he's exactly right. But yes, I get your point. Obviously we're a danger to him, and him to us. We should expect him to try to shoot, bomb, or burn us out at any time, day or night . . . as long as he can't be identified as the culprit," Lee said.

They were less than a quarter mile from the highway when Lee noticed a squiggly mark atop a sandy mound several yards off the road. "Whoa!" He stopped the truck.

"What? You see something?" Diane asked, looking off the side of the road. She unbuckled her seat belt and turned around on the cushion.

"Looks like a motorcycle track. Let me take a look," Lee said, turning off the engine and stepping out of the pickup. He walked over to the side of the road, where a grader's blade had formed a little ridge along the edge the last time the county maintenance crew had worked on the road.

The sand-and-gravel ridge had been reshaped in the spot where the bike had driven over it, but a few feet beyond, out of sight from the driver's position, motorcycle tracks were fresh and clear. They continued up to the spot where the bike had fish-tailed a bit in the sand, then continued up a narrow canyon as far as he could see.

Diane came up with a flashlight and examined the area. "Good eyes. Looks like somebody erased the marks where they left the road so you wouldn't notice their exit trail. But farther away, they didn't see the need or have the time to wipe out the tire tracks. If we'd passed by slowly in daylight, we might have had a better chance to find them."

Lee nodded. "If I'd have been looking ahead instead of to the side, I'd have still missed it. These tracks have the right pattern, so this must be where we lost Glover the other night when he had the Harley. He pulled off the road, reconstructed the little ridge to hide the obvious, then continued over the sandy spot and up that little canyon." Lee pointed.

Diane aimed her flashlight in the direction. "We can't take the truck in there, we'll get stuck, high center, or get hemmed in by the vegetation. Now we walk?"

Three minutes later, their pickup off the road and locked, Lee and Diane began to follow the motorcycle tracks uphill. The ground was rocky in places, but Lee had no trouble following the motorcycle tracks at all, despite the blackness of the night. The stars were countless in number, twinkling brightly to the east and overhead. The mountain was another enormous shadow ahead of them, west.

Diane kept close to Lee, depending on him instead of the flashlight, which would indicate their presence. They'd decided not to use a light in case Glover had gone to the home of an ally. He stopped abruptly and she bumped into him.

"There's a small block building about a hundred yards up, against the hillside," Lee whispered. "It's well hidden by the pines, though."

"I can make out a squarish shape. No lights, though. Isn't there a barrier or something in the way. Vines or something?"

"One of those big security fences, with the strands of barbed wire, or maybe razor wire, at the top. The fence must be twenty feet high," Lee added. "A sign on the fence says it's a federal facility."

"We saw some official maps of this area, supposedly up-to-date within the last month or two. I don't remember this site being listed, if my sense of direction is working," Diane replied. "Let me make a call to SAC Logan." She brought out her cell phone, and, fortunately, was able to get a signal.

A few minutes later, she had the answer. "We're on private land owned by FAC developers. This is listed as a storage shed, according to what my boss could learn from the coordinates I gave him. There aren't any government buildings within miles of here, according to him."

Lee reached out and took her hand. "Then somebody is trying to ward off trespassers with a bit of a con. That doesn't make it necessarily illegal, just suspicious. I'll get us closer and we can check it out. There has to be a gate somewhere."

"Just follow Glover's motorcycle tracks."

"Exactly."

Three minutes later, they were standing beside the tall, heavy-gauge chain-link fence, peering at what looked more like a concrete blockhouse or bunker than a residence. The building was very low, barely a story high. It had no visible windows, a metal roof, and a recessed entryway with a single door. Ten feet away, attached to the fence, was an official-looking sign that read FEDERAL FACILITY. NO TRESPASSING.

"So where's the gate, Lee?" Diane whispered. "Glover parked the Harley under the tree back there."

Lee was searching the ground for tracks, but was not finding any. "We'll walk the fence line until we find a gate or signs of any hidden entrance. I can climb the fence, but you would have trouble."

She felt the mesh of the fence, then looked up. "Yeah, the weave of the wire is too small to get a foothold, and I can't see pulling myself up this thing and down the other side by my fingertips, even if I could make it over the barbed wire sticking out at the top."

"And your climbing gear is in your other purse, right?"

"Along with my cutting torch and bolt cutters. Let's keep looking. Gotta be a way inside for us non-you-know-whats," Diane whispered.

Several minutes later, after walking the entire perimeter of the square enclosure, they found themselves back where they'd started. If there was a hidden entrance on the ground or within a thicket, they hadn't found it, and they'd looked.

"If Glover actually got inside that fence, he certainly did a good job of hiding any tracks getting there," Lee said, frustrated. "He has very good skills, obviously, when he's working at avoiding detection. And the more careful he is, the more curious I get about what he's hiding."

Diane reached over and touched Lee's arm. "You really think you can scale the fence? We've got to know why he came here. This would be a perfect place to hold a kidnap victim. Hard to find, off the maps with no road leading in, and nearly impossible for vandals to penetrate."

"Yeah, and no obvious way into the building except through a solid-looking door. Looks like heavy-gauge steel from here," Lee said, his eyes on the recessed entryway. He kicked at the ground. "Just as hard packed here as everywhere else we checked. I could go and get a shovel, but it looks like this fence goes down into the ground a ways. I can dig like a gopher, but still . . ." He looked up one more time at the top of the fence. "I'll use my jacket to cover the barbs, I guess."

"Be careful. Once you're over, I'll try and find what route Glover took driving out of here. It wasn't the way he came in," Diane pointed out, "or we would have seen the second set of tracks. It should be safe using my flashlight, as long as I keep it aimed low."

"Okay. Call me if anything goes down, like you spot Glover coming our way," Lee said. "And you don't have to stick around to watch me climb. It shouldn't take long for me to reach the top, and once I'm up there, I'll swing up and over the barbed wire."

"You won't break your neck, legs, or something?"

"Nah. I'm kinda light on my feet," he said, then smiled.

"I've noticed. Still, I'd like to stick around a moment and see this," Diane said.

"Just keep your distance in case I miss or something."

She took a step back. "Don't tease me like that. Okay?"

He saw her expression and felt a little guilty. "Don't worry so much." Lee put on his leather gloves, having no need to wear them at night, but keeping them in a pocket in case something happened and he couldn't get inside or beneath shade by dawn. Sunblock tended to rub off his hands when he was active.

Next, Lee removed his leather jacket and draped it over one shoulder. He checked to make sure his pistol was secure, then took five steps back and picked a spot to shoot for. Taking a deep breath, he sprinted forward and leaped. Arms and fingers extended, he reached for the steel top rail just below the first strand of barbed wire, nineteen or so feet up. The move was awkward, because he had to keep his head tilted back.

"Gotcha." His face was so close to the bottom strand of barbed wire that angled out at a forty-five-degree angle—the reason for arching his neck back—it was out of focus. His lead had been as vertical as possible to keep him from bouncing off the mesh, so when his chest hit the wire, he'd barely made a sound, if that mattered. He'd been more worried about the impact anyway.

"Whoa!" Diane muttered from somewhere below. "Be careful," she whispered, then Lee heard her walk off.

Once Lee was certain of his grip, he rocked back and forth a little, testing the sway of the fence. The structure had been constructed solidly, with upright poles every ten feet and tight mesh. The thing barely moved at all.

Concentrating on his next move, Lee let go with his right hand, slipped the jacket off his shoulder, and began the process of draping it over the barbed wire with one hand. Angled out from brackets attached to the uprights, the fence was designed to keep people with less-than-professional climbing and acrobatic skills from getting over. At least the builder hadn't used razor or concertina wire.

The barbs were dulled and rusted out a bit, so they didn't snag too much, though Lee knew it was going to lower the resale value of his favorite jacket considerably. Maybe he could write it off on his expense vouchers.

He'd scaled fences like this one before, though not one quite this high, so Lee knew his tactics would work. At the end of World War II, when he'd gone after the German vampire who'd turned him, circumstances had required him to enter and exit facilities surrounded by protective walls and high fences like these.

Now came the tricky part, turning around and grabbing the bottom strand of barbed wire, placing his back to the fence. Throwing out his right arm and pivoting at the shoulder, he reached up and gripped the leather-covered wire. His left hand got nothing but air, however, and he swayed to the right, dangling from one hand.

Lee went with the motion, then kicked back to the left, bringing his free hand up again. This time he got a solid grip. Once his body was still again, both hands secure, Lee pulled himself up, raising his legs up and kicking backward, doing a backward flip over the fence just high enough to clear the wires.

Releasing both hands, his body did a three-sixty in the air. He arched over the top wire, barely, and his thighs and knees bounced into the inside of the fence this time. Lee grabbed the mesh with his fingertips, held position for a second, then slid rapidly to the ground, braking just enough to make what was essentially a controlled fall. He was inside the enclosure now, safely to earth.

He turned around, examining the rectangular block structure, which was pretty much centered within the fenced-in
square. His jacket was still up there atop the wire, but he'd get
it later, on the way out. It would be much easier going up and
over from this side since no backward flip was required.

As he walked toward the recessed entrance, Lee realized
that the small building was even lower than he'd noticed before, probably only ten feet high, not including the metal roof.
The structure had either been built for short people, or had
foundations several feet deep. It reminded him of the entrance
to a bunker or underground garage—or a disguised fallout shelter from the Cold War era.

The entrance was a low tunnel, also of cinder block, and
his head almost touched the ceiling. There were no fixtures for
lights, only a metal door set in a metal frame. There was a grab
handle and a strong brass lock of a type he recognized. The
place had been designed to keep intruders at bay, and a burglar
would need a drill, sledgehammer and heavy tools, torch, or explosives to get beyond this door.

Unless, of course, you knew how to pick the lock and Lee
had that skill. A vampire unable to get in out of the sun quickly
was vulnerable, so any nightwalkers who hadn't learned how
to pick even the finest of locks could quickly make an ash of
themselves. The ability to break into buildings was almost as
important as sunblock, and sometimes even vampire strength
wasn't enough to defeat a well-constructed entrance.

Lee's pocketknife was more than a bladed tool. With the
lock picks it contained, he was able to unlock the door. As he
did, he heard a faint click, but it was a familiar sound, the right
one.

He didn't open the door, not yet. Another quick look around
the mechanism and jamb was necessary—in case there was an

alarm. The fine New Mexico dust that covered everything, all the time, showed no smudge marks whatsoever, fortunately. So either Glover hadn't come in this way, or they were on a wild-goose chase. Lee banked on the alternate entrance theory. It made sense.

Then, his sharp hearing attuned, he heard someone breathing. Lee pulled on the handle, opened the door a few more inches, and saw another fence. He stepped into a small, cool, unlit room, letting the door close behind him as he studied the interior. The fence was actually a large, welded-steel hardware cloth cage welded to a steel frame and bolted to the concrete floor. Crowded inside the four-foot-high, ten-foot-square structure was a cot, a plastic chair like those used on patios, some kind of portable toilet, and a cardboard box with packaged food, water, and other supplies. There was a bulky shape on the cot beneath a blanket. Lee's heart almost stopped.

"Timothy? Timothy Klein?" Lee asked gently.

The blanket moved, and Lee saw a face he recognized from photos. It was the boy!

"Who are you?"

"I'm a police officer—a friend. I've come to get you out of here and take you to your parents," Lee said, relieved and happy to see the boy alive and apparently unhurt.

"I can't see you. My flashlight batteries ran out and he didn't leave me any new ones. Turn on the lantern. Please?" Timothy said, his voice shaky as he sat up on the cot and swung his legs around. He had a small flashlight in his hand.

Lee noticed a battery-powered lantern in the corner of the room. It was the only object in the room outside the cage. He walked over and turned it on, bathing the space in a pale, yellow light. Timothy stood, blanket wrapped around him loosely. His pale blue eyes were blinking from the sudden glare.

"Are you injured in any way?" Lee asked, his earlier relief giving way to anger as he thought of the kidnapper and the ordeal the boy had already endured.

"No, I'm okay," he answered. "I was worried you might be wearing a mask. The big man who brought me here always has one on, except when he pretends to be a woman. How did *you* see me in the dark?"

Lee ignored the question. "Was there more than one man? And how did you find out he wasn't really a woman?"

"I only saw one person at a time, and the voice was about the same. When I first saw him, down off the highway, he had on sunglasses, makeup, lipstick and stuff, black gloves, and a long wig, kinda gray and black. He also had on a long green dress with flowers on it, like old ladies wear. He was pretending to look for a lost puppy in that culvert, but when I got off my bike to help, he grabbed me. He taped up my hands and feet and my mouth, so I couldn't yell for help. Then he put a pillow cover over my head and put me in the back of his van. After that, he was wearing a Halloween mask and regular guy clothes. You know, jeans, long-sleeved shirt, boots. And his voice was different, not soft anymore, but still the same person. Can we go now? He said he'd hurt my mom and dad if I ran away or told anyone about him." Timothy set the blanket on the cot. He was wearing dirty jeans of his own and a sweatshirt, but was barefoot.

"Why don't you put on your shoes and socks while I open this cage?" Lee looked at the big padlock, brought out his pocketknife, then went to work.

"The man took them. But I can still walk. Do you have keys to all the locks?" Timothy stepped over to where Lee was working, curious despite the situation.

"Don't need one." Just then the lock came open. Lee could

see tears forming in the boy's eyes as he removed the lock and opened the framed, steel-mesh door.

Timothy hesitated, not really trusting Lee, apparently.

"Grab the blanket and anything else you want to take with you, Timothy." Lee checked out the big entry door on the opposite side of the room, then did another quick survey of the room. There were old-looking charts and diagrams attached to the walls. Age had caused them to come loose in places. They had information on edible plants, first aid, and survival tips. From their content, Lee realized one of his guesses had been right. This place had been constructed as a fallout shelter, probably back in the fifties or early sixties. There was a small vent in the floor, which let in fresh air, but it was too small for anything larger than a cat to crawl through.

"Timothy. Did the man use that door?" Lee pointed, realizing from the size of the interior that there must be another ground-level room.

"Yes, but he locked it on the other side, I think. And people call me Tim. Except for my mom when she yells at me." He managed a weak grin. Then he stepped out of the cage, holding the blanket wrapped around his shoulders. It was really cool in here, Lee realized.

"The man who kidnapped you. Would you know him if you saw him again?"

"Maybe, if he had on lipstick and stuff. But except for the time when he had on the wig and makeup, he was wearing a mask that covered his whole head. It was some cartoon guy he called Tricky Dick. I didn't look at him too closely when he was wearing a dress. Guess I should have, huh?"

"When did he come here last?"

"Yesterday, maybe. Or two days ago. I've gotten hungry five times since then. That's the only way I can tell time without my watch. He took it when he took my shoes and socks," Timothy replied. "But let's go, okay, before he comes back?"

"I can protect you, Tim." Lee showed the boy he was carrying a pistol. "But we're leaving, so don't worry." Lee walked over to the door and checked the lock. It was the same type as the one on the other door.

Tim joined him. "Can you open this one, too?"

"Sure. Get the lamp for me, okay? Just don't touch it anywhere except at the handle."

"The man had gloves on. Remember?"

"Maybe he forgot to wear gloves when he handled it earlier."

Tim carried the light over by the bail, holding it carefully, away from his body. "Or when he put in the batteries."

"Now you're thinking." Lee could see that Tim was starting to calm down a little, looking a little less like a deer in the headlights than before. Also, helping out would give him something to do, and later, he might not remember that the Indian state policeman could see in the dark.

Lee had the door open in thirty seconds. Tim handed him the lantern, then, together, they walked into the next room. It was smaller and had a trapdoor in the floor, covered by a thick, steel door with massive hinges. There was a big hasp, but no padlock. After all, Glover had to be able to get in.

"How did you get in here before, Tim? Did you have to climb up some stairs?" Lee asked.

"A ladder. I almost fell because it was really dark and I was scared." Tim stepped forward. "We have to lift up this door and climb down into the tunnel. It's narrow and smells like dirt," Tim said.

Lee raised the trapdoor and found a metal ladder leading down into a narrow passage. "I'll go first, but you stay right behind me, okay, Tim?"

"Okay. I just want to get out of here, Officer. . . ?"

"Officer Hawk, Tim." Lee turned and shook the boy's hand, then climbed quickly down the ladder. The floor was safe for the boy to walk on barefoot, but once they got outside, Lee would have to carry him if they needed to make any speed. As Tim followed, Lee led them along the block-lined tunnel, which was less than five feet high, forcing him to stoop. The space smelled funky and was very dusty toward the far end, but the area was dry and solid looking, and there were no major spiderwebs, something Diane would have noticed and commented on immediately.

After about fifty feet, they came to the end of the tunnel— a blank wall and another ladder. Above was a skillfully constructed and expertly fitted trapdoor, complete with copper weather stripping. There was a set of sturdy hinges, and two large deadbolts welded onto the door that would fit into the strong metal frame when latched. But the locking mechanism was intended to keep someone out, not in. Lee pushed on the door. It was heavy, probably weighing fifty pounds or more, and dust cascaded down around the edges as it opened.

Lee climbed up the ladder and out onto a small hill he remembered passing before. The top of the door was the color of the ground, sculpted with a fake, undulating layer of rock to disguise its size and shape. Brush growing around the spot had also helped conceal the location, and the handle for lifting was a rock anchored in place. In addition, Glover had covered the outline around the edges with dirt, obviously, or he or Diane might have seen it earlier.

The fence to the compound was ten feet away, beyond two trees, and the building another fifteen or so feet farther. He heard movement and saw Tim coming up the ladder, excitement growing in his eyes.

Lee reached down with a hand.

"I'm okay, Officer Hawk," Tim said. "I just want to go home."

"It won't be long now," Lee said, then reached for his cell phone. Wherever Diane was, she had to hear the good news. If things went smoothly, Tim Klein would be with his parents within the hour.

Two hours later, Lee and Diane were driving south again. They'd scored a sweet victory today. Lee would always remember handing Tim Klein over to his parents, then seeing the family driving off in a black SUV to a safe house, where they'd remain in protective custody.

Unfortunately, Tim didn't think he could recognize the person who'd kidnapped him. The boy thought he might be able to recognize the voice, but the man had only spoken two or three times, and the first time he'd disguised his voice to sound like a woman's.

One of the Bureau techs had been assigned the task of altering a photo of Glover, adding makeup and putting him in drag, but that wouldn't be enough to stand up in court, Lee knew, even if Tim identified him as the man.

Stolen vans were moved up on the hot sheet, and a forensics team was on the way to make a quick search of the fallout shelter. They'd have to walk up a trail Diane had found on the north side of the compound that led down to a road connected to the development. The crime team would be looking for any trace evidence that might lead to a suspect.

The officers and techs would be required to pull out before dawn, covering their tracks under the direction of people Lee and Diane trusted. Then the site would be placed under surveillance and inquiries would be made concerning the legal owners of the property, and who might have been given permission to use it. If anyone but Glover showed up at the old fallout shelter to check on Tim Klein, they'd be apprehended.

Since Glover was still the most likely suspect, they wanted to handle him according to plan. Solid physical evidence was needed, and unless the forensics people came up with Glover's fingerprints or DNA at the place where the boy had been held, there was no reason to launch a preemptive strike. Lee and Diane were banking on catching Glover in the act of committing a crime, but keeping an eye on him was vital if they were going to succeed.

There was no way of predicting what Glover would do once he found out Tim Klein had vanished and he'd lost his "merchandise." The only thing they knew for sure was that Glover was going to be more dangerous now than ever before.

Around 3:00 A.M. they arrived at Quail Run and Lee drove slowly up the road toward their house. "The Jeep's still in Tijeras?"

Diane checked. "Yes, and I don't see any rubble or glowing embers ahead, so he didn't try to burn us out—yet."

"His red pickup is repaired and in his driveway. That explains the location of the Jeep. We were worried about nothing . . . or maybe Glover is playing again."

"Assuming he knew about the tracking device we stuck on the Jeep. And why should he have cared to check it again, knowing his pickup was coming back? *That's* what he's going to examine for bugs from now on."

Lee pulled up behind the SUV, parked in their own driveway. The lights were off at Glover's home. Although he was invisible to mortal eyes, Lee could see him standing in the dark, watching them. "We're in the spotlight. Guess Glover *isn't* getting much rest."

"Neither are we. But we can't be complacent. We need to check for booby traps, unscrewed gas connections, bugs, and other little goodies. We've been gone a long time, and he's full of surprises," Diane said.

"Right. We already know what kind of guy he really is. Remind me to check on the motion detector, too, in case he went out the back way." They climbed out of the pickup, moved around to the driver's side of the SUV so they'd be blocked somewhat by the vehicle, and Lee took a look at the tires, then the door lock of the utility vehicle.

"No sign the lock was picked, but he could have used a slim jim or some other method to get inside the vehicle. We check the ignition and look underneath before driving it again, okay?"

Diane nodded, then walked up onto the porch, not really turning her back completely. Lee followed.

He quickly examined the door for signs of forced entry. As he put the key in the deadbolt, he noticed a faint scratch on the mechanism.

"Good skills, picking the lock, Glover. But you left a mark," Lee whispered, "and you gave yourself away a second time because you had to leave the deadbolt unlocked when you left." Lee then checked the knob. It had been relocked by Glover when he left, so Lee had to use a key. "Glover's good enough to pick a good-quality deadbolt, and smart enough to have locked the doorknob mechanism when he left to play with our minds and confuse the issue."

"Yeah, so we wouldn't worry, thinking that, after all, the door *was* locked when we came back." Diane brought out her flashlight and looked for trip wires or electrical contacts along the door and trim. "No bomb triggers evident. But they could be inside."

"Don't hit the light switch until I look around. We don't want to set off an incendiary device. With fires so lethal in these types of homes . . ."

"I'll use the flashlight. Take it slow, Lee."

Lee looked around carefully before taking more than the first two steps. Nothing seemed out of place, so he moved farther into the room. Through a gap in the drapes, Lee could see Glover standing there, watching. The man wasn't using any special viewer, so he couldn't really see them at all in the dark, so what was he expecting, or was he just nervous, waiting for something to happen?

Diane got down on her knees, sweeping the likely areas for a bomb or other booby trap, and searching for trip wires using the flashlight. It was a good idea, Lee concluded, because Glover couldn't determine her location without seeing the flashlight beam.

"You moved the video recorder, Lee. Think he found it?"

"Probably, if he took the time. For a while, though, he'd have been distracted by the guy who brought his pickup back. I'll check our little warning system." Lee had left a paper match on the floor below the wall duct where he'd relocated the recording unit, thinking that Glover might think it had fallen out and needed to be put back into place somewhere. Or he might have been tempted to pick it up, but then conclude it was a trick and set it back down.

Lee had placed the match in a particular position, trying to psych out the intruder, and could now tell that it had been moved. If Glover had been thinking at the right level, all he would have had to do was leave it alone. A burglar, who usually trashed a place, wouldn't have noticed or cared about putting things back because he was there for the loot. Game theory among black bag specialists was tricky.

"He found it?"

"Yeah. Let's hope he didn't find the second unit."

Diane directed the light at the base of the big floor lamp in the corner. The lamp didn't work . . . the power cord supplied a small infrared video camera in the base they'd installed earlier that evening. The camera had a wide-angle lens that covered nearly the entire room and was activated by a motion sensor. It was a special bonus they'd picked up earlier from the Bureau techs along with the "stone" motion detector.

Lee and Diane, working together, lifted up the lamp and removed the camera. "It's been running since we came in, so we'll have to go back to the beginning and see what else we've got, if anything," Diane announced, examining the camera.

They sat together on the floor in the dark and reviewed the video on the tiny LCD display. "It's Glover, and he's moving real carefully. Afraid we've set a trap for him?" Diane suggested.

The man had a small penlight, but the beam wasn't enough to impair the effectiveness of their camera. They watched as he came through the front door, searched the living room side of the multipurpose space, first pulling out the drawer where the recording system had been before, then quickly using the small light to find where Lee had relocated it in the heating duct.

Glover was wearing a jacket with big pockets. He brought out a Leatherman-type tool, selected a screwdriver, then unfastened the duct. Removing the camera, he took out the CD and replaced it with another one from his pocket. Then he put the system back into the duct, positioned the camera, and replaced the vent cover.

Glover looked down and noticed the paper match, picked it up, and held it up to the duct. "Trying to figure where it fell from," Lee said. Glover cursed, then sat it back on the carpet.

He moved outside again, returning in a few seconds carrying a gym bag, the same one he'd carried the other night. Then he disappeared around the counter into the kitchen, out of view from the camera. There was the sound of metal or glass, the closing of doors and the clanking of tools, and five minutes later Glover came back into view. The man took a quick look around, then left out the front door, setting the knob to lock when it closed behind him. A few minutes later, the camera, no longer registering motion, shut off. It came back on, showing Lee and Diane entering the front door.

Diane switched it off. "What did he do in the kitchen, or utility room? It sounded like he was opening and closing things and fiddling with tools."

"Opening and closing cupboards? No big deal there. But beyond are the hot water heater and the furnace."

"The furnace is shut off for the season, right?"

"Yeah, and no off-season pilot light because it uses one of those electronic deals. We can rule out the stove because it's electric. Same with the refrigerator."

"So what was he messing with? The electrical panel? The hot water heater?"

"I'll go check. You should go outside, find some cover, and wait until I'm sure it's safe. Glover may have set a booby trap and there's no reason to endanger both of us."

"Four eyes are better than two. If it turns out I can't be of any help, then I'll leave. Not before then."

"We're not turning on the lights yet and you can't see in the dark."

"Wake up! I've got my flashlight," Diane argued. "But you can lead the way, macho man, because you have both hands free."

Lee in front, they crossed the living room area and stepped through the opening between counters into the narrow kitchen area. Everything looked undisturbed. "I smell something burning."

"Yeah. And maybe something else, like cleaning fluid or kerosene. But I can't see any flames or smoke."

"Turn out the flashlight for a moment."

They waited for a while, looking from a distance toward the small utility area, and finally Lee spoke. "It might be a candle. See that flicker of light on the chrome trim of the washer?"

"Yeah. It's coming from some place out of our field of view, though. And what is that line over by the back door?"

"Yeah, it comes and goes." Lee took a step forward and stared. "Maybe a string or wire? Use the flashlight if it helps."

Diane aimed the beam, focusing it to a fine point again. "It's like fishing line, Lee. And look, it's tied to a screw eye in the wall on the other side of the door. It's a trip wire."

CHAPTER 18

Lee stepped closer, leaning around the corner without actually stepping into the room. "Take a look, but step lightly."

Diane came up beside him and aimed the flashlight over beside the door. A small, lit, votive-type candle was on the floor beside the gym bag and a large can of shortening, which appeared to be the brand they used. It had obviously been taken from their cupboard. Atop the container was an unopened can of soup. Balanced gingerly atop the soup can was a sealed mason jar half-filled with an amber liquid. The bottle had the other end of the fishing line duct taped around it.

"If we'd have come in the back and bumped the line, the bottle would have fallen to the floor and broken beside the candle. There must be kerosene or other flammable in the bottle."

"There's something in the gym bag, too."

"Can you blow out the candle, Lee? I'm smelling fumes."

Lee reached over and tapped the flame with his finger. It went out. Next, he picked up the jar, holding it tight while he pulled off the tape and fishing line.

"I'm going to check out the bag." Diane used her flashlight and opened the zipper a few inches. "There's something loose in the bottom. Black, like . . ."

"Gunpowder. I smell it now," Lee said. "Better zip it back up again. We should get the bag and that bottle outside."

Lee, holding the bottle, opened the door with his free hand and stepped outside. He paused, making sure Glover hadn't circled around while they were inside and was now in an ambush position, then walked over to the far corner of the fence and opened the bottle top. "Camp stove fuel?" he muttered, then set it down.

Diane came out with the gym bag, and, with Lee watching, opened the bag completely. The bottom was filled several inches deep with black gunpowder, the kind used in earlier-era weapons and fireworks. "It looks like a commercial product. We can have this traced back and identified—to some degree. And if Glover bought it legally, there will be a record. We know he was in a gun shop recently."

Lee nodded. "At least we know why he's watching the house so closely. The initial fire would have set off the black powder and we could have been killed, or at least badly burned. He was counting on us coming in the back door, or maybe going out back later with the lights out, not spotting the trip wire or candle before it was too late."

"Maybe we can take advantage of our luck. I've got an expensive idea, Lee. This house is insured, right?"

"Ah, I thought about that, too. But if we blow this place up and hide, making Glover think we're dead, what's going to happen when they don't find any bodies? Glover will discover we're not really dead, with his connections, and then he'll lie low, maybe even disappearing and never going back to the fallout shelter and further incriminating himself. There's bound to be an investigation no matter what. The county has a fire marshal, and if anyone discovers gunpowder residue, questions will be asked, especially about our next-door neighbor. He's hated and feared, but somebody is likely to make an anonymous call hoping he'll get nailed."

"Yeah, well then, I guess I'll have to keep wearing tacky clothes a little longer. We don't want Glover to put his dirty little plans on hold just for us," Diane said, "and I sure want to nail him for kidnapping. But we should have the bag checked for prints and the gunpowder traced."

"I'll put the gunpowder back inside for now, in a sealed container. You want me to pour out the liquid?"

She shook her head. "No sense in contaminating the soil. I think I saw a fuel container around here somewhere, left over by a previous tenant. There's only about a quart there. We can get rid of it later."

Before long, they were back inside, turning on a light in the kitchen so they could have a snack. Glover had obviously deduced they'd seen and dealt with his bomb. At least he was no longer looking out the window.

Lee checked and found that Glover hadn't tried to slip away out the back. The motion detector was still in place and operating normally, unless he'd somehow avoided passing within range of the device, which, according to Diane, was sensitive out to fifty yards. For that, Glover would have had to leave via the front.

He turned to Diane, who was eating a toasted cheese sandwich. "Glover has to have a stash at his place we haven't found yet where he keeps his weapons and deadly toys—and the keys to the fallout shelter and the mask he wore around Tim Klein. There's probably another hiding place he can access without signing in as he would with a safety deposit box, a place he uses to hide his blackmail material—photos, whatever."

"We didn't have the time to do a really careful search, Lee. But my guess is that the blackmail material probably isn't at his home. If it was, it could be lost in a fire set by a desperate victim. Same with his vehicles, which could be stolen. The stash has to be in a protected spot, a structure, hole, or cave not linked to him, that he can access any time, day or night—like the place he kept the boy. As for the gunpowder, instead of buying it from the gun shop, maybe he's gotten it from visitors we haven't known about who came in the front, maybe one of those deputies? A lot of them are into recreational shooting, muzzle loaders and such. Even paying with cash, buying a lot of gunpowder legally requires some record keeping by the proprietor."

"So let's look for the hiding places. I'm going to do a search, using the laptop, and see if I can find any structures in the area within a decent walking distance of here that we haven't seen or don't know about. Maybe a place with a cellar that is safe enough from burglars, vandals, or curious kids."

"Or another Cold War fallout shelter." Diane yawned. "And now that I'm not worried about the boy anymore, maybe I'll be able to get some sleep. I don't have your stamina." She looked at her watch. "You might want to check in with whoever's still got Sully, and whatever else we can get on that Katie girl. Wake me up if I sleep past six."

Lee worked for a while, wandered to the refrigerator, then gazed wistfully inside, wishing he had some calves' blood to sip. Blood wasn't required by real vampires, but it was especially nutritious, which probably brought on some of the fictional stories that persisted. Those vampire bats, which actually fed on the blood of living animals, didn't help the notion, either.

Lee settled on a Coke, and logged onto the websites of the morning Albuquerque newspaper and the three major local TV stations. All still carried discouraging news about the abandoned search for the missing boy, but it was no longer their lead story.

His and Diane's recovery of the victim was going to be kept

secret and the parents had agreed to remain in protective custody, hiding from the press, media, and even their own relatives. SAC Logan had made the arrangements himself. The cover story was that the family had gone into seclusion—true enough. Cooperation was vital now if they were going to catch the kidnapper—presumably Glover.

Lee called the cell phone number of the person who was supposed to be watching Sully. The man, a retired APD detective named Bill Sullivan, answered with a sleepy voice.

"This is Officer Hawk. Good morning. What's the latest on our subject?"

"Officer Hawk. Good to talk to anyone. It's been quiet out here, except for about a half hour ago."

"Except? What happened, Bill?"

"Thought he was leaving, but all Sully did was drive down to his mailbox and pick up his newspaper."

"But he went back home, right?"

"That's correct. Otherwise, I'd have been calling *you*," Bill added.

"Okay. Just let Agent Lopez or me know the minute Sully leaves again. Good job, and hang in there. Your relief will be bringing breakfast, I hope."

Lee sat down to work on a plan to finally snare Glover. With the recovery of Tim Klein no longer an issue, Lee suspected that their additional manpower support was going to dry up pretty soon, especially with two officers assigned to guard the Kleins twenty-four/seven. With no physical evidence yet that he was the kidnapper, they would have to fall back, for the moment, to establishing charges of extortion. To find out whom Glover had corrupted, therefore, they had to find a way to make Glover reveal where he was keeping his blackmail material.

Lee opened up the laptop, accessed the secure Internet site containing their case files, then realized he'd just stumbled on the answer. He now had a good idea where Glover was keeping his stuff. He couldn't recall seeing a set-up computer at Glover's house, but he'd seen a scanner, and that implied the presence of a computer. Maybe, like them, the man had a laptop hidden on the property. That was all Glover would need to digitize extortion material and hide it electronically.

I agree that Glover *might* have uploaded all the blackmail material he has onto a private website—like we've done with our reports and materials for this investigation—but how do we get to it?" Diane asked.

"Though the Bureau hasn't managed to get a closer look at Glover's background, it may include training and experience with computers. If I'm right, that's going to make things tougher. We already know he's fond of using photographs to gain leverage. The Bureau has managed to identify most of the people in those sex photos you discovered taped to Glover's closet door. None of the individuals are married to the other person in the photo. The guy with the two young women, for example, is the chief at the closest fire station," Lee noted.

"The blackmail photos are what keeps them from turning on him," she answered. "So again, how do we get to the originals and the rest of the images we *haven't* seen yet?"

"If we get a chance to examine his computer—probably a high-end laptop—we could have a tech search his software and see which sites he's accessed. Or maybe we can find out how he pays for the service that provides the site."

"Most providers require a credit card, cash transfer, or check. If we can find that trail, there are ways to cut off his access—like changing the passwords. If he can't use the blackmail material, his hold over his victims is lost."

"Not necessarily. As long as they believe he *can* blackmail them, Glover's still in charge. We need to find his stash, then get somebody to stand up to him and force Glover to prove he can still ruin them—in other words, drive Glover to the material. Glover must also have hard copies somewhere, probably on CDs. They would be a lot easier to store and hide than stacks of photos, tapes, and such."

"We take them away and Glover's empty-handed," Diane added with a nod. "So what we have to do is block his access to his Internet storage area, force him into a position to put up or shut up, then nail him with the hard copies."

"I'm assuming Glover has wireless, so let's make some calls and see what we get. There are only a few services available in this area. Can the Bureau get that info?"

"Yeah. There are several protocols already in place. The local office has eavesdropped on wireless activity in Albuquerque during some high-level DOD and DOE investigations. If the provider won't cooperate, we have equipment that allows us to get around protection systems and even record passwords and keystrokes."

"Can you make the necessary calls?"

Diane nodded. "And you'll want to start priming the pump with Sully, the guy we know for sure is linked to Glover. I suppose you want to use what we have on him already."

"I also want to get some help following Glover while we still have the attention of the right agencies. We're going to have to take some trips."

Glover was still at home, taking an occasional peek through his curtains, when two big, hard-driven pickups pulled up outside, diesel engines rattling. Lee had heard them coming almost from the highway.

Stepping out onto the front porch, Lee nodded and yelled.

"Hey, bro. Glad you could make it. Park over there." He pointed to the curved, west end of the street, knowing that otherwise the pickups would screen out the view of Glover's house, something he wanted to avoid.

Lee nodded in greeting as four men, two of them approaching the average college linebacker in size and physical stature, exited the two vehicles. All were wearing hunter's vests or jackets bulging with obvious ammo boxes, jeans, and work boots and carrying hunting rifles or shotguns. Two of the men were carrying belt holders with large, lockback folding knives. To most New Mexicans, it was a group of good ole boys about to go hunting.

Lee pointed directly toward Glover, who was standing beside the window, almost out of view, and the men nodded or otherwise indicated they saw the man. The two biggest guys stood there, holding their weapons loosely in their arms, while the others carried fiberglass gun cases into the house. Diane opened the door each time and greeted the men warmly, as if they were old friends.

Soon, all but one of the men were in the living room. The fourth was outside, standing between the trucks, his rifle across the hood of the rear vehicle within easy reach, watching Glover's property.

"Think we got his attention?" The speaker was nearly bald, his hair shaved close, and he had no neck atop shoulders as wide as the doorway. "I'm Sergeant Allen, ma'am. Call me Jack. Officer Hawk knows me from the Las Cruces district." Jack nodded to Lee, who was helping the other two men unpack their electronic gear from the gun cases. "Gonzales is the officer keeping an eye on our target."

Diane shook his hand, which dwarfed her own fingers. "Glad to meet you, Jack. Glover's a bully, but I think you fellows got his heart thumping when you pulled up. Glad to have more state policemen on hand to help us nail this guy. Glover's a treacherous bastard."

"I understand he gained entry last night and positioned a crude bomb, Agent Lopez," another man, smaller than Jack Allen by a hundred pounds, said as he brought a large laptop computer out of a case.

"This is Richie Brock, Lee, one of the Bureau's technical experts. He and Hal," Diane nodded toward the man unpacking a small antennalike device, "will be tapping into Glover's cell phone calls and computer activities. Right, guys?"

Richie, who was clearing space on the dining table for the laptop, nodded. "We've already identified his local provider and account and all the necessary warrants have been issued to get full cooperation from the phone company and his cell phone carrier. Even if he tries to route his communications through a supposedly secure network or cloned phone, we'll pick it up from here. Everything he sends or receives on a computer will be mirrored and saved to the hard drive, or relayed to us by his ISP carrier if he uses the laptop from another location."

"And while these boys are busy peeking in his electronic closet, Gonzo and I will handle the rough stuff," Jack said, then grinned. Beneath that leather jacket was a knit sweater like the one worn by commandos and below that the faint outline of a bulletproof vest. Lee knew Jack from a couple of incidents where shootings had taken place, and the man had been fearless *and* competent, a good combination when backup was required.

"You want us to place a GPS on the pickup?" Hal asked. The young man, a field agent with the Bureau before switching to technical work for the FBI, had experience with computer fraud and crimes committed via the Internet. Diane had told Lee about him earlier. With Hal on the job, no firewall or computer security was good enough. The NSA had actually recruited him first, but Hal had chosen the Bureau.

"Glover sweeps for bugs every morning before he drives away. An old habit from his days doing black bag work for the army overseas, I guess," Lee pointed out.

"Ah, but I've got a state-of-the-art unit here that'll evade any sensor he could get his hands on. It'll pick up a sweep and automatically shut itself down," Richie said.

"He also does a quick visual. What if he sees the unit? We don't want him to guess who we are and shut down," Diane pointed out.

Hal held up a small plastic bag with something inside that looked like a splatter of mud. "Attach this on the bumper or other likely spot with some of our instant stickum and he'll never know. We can even change the color of the mud to match this location. Spray on a little glue, sprinkle it with dust from outside, and we have instant, authentic-looking mud."

"The only way we'd get caught is if the guy is a clean freak," Richie said. "Come to think of it, I notice the pickup looks freshly washed."

"The wash job came after some recent repairs he had done on the vehicle," Diane pointed out. "It was pretty dirty before he lost the windshield, right, Lee?"

"Yeah. We can use the bug, but we're going to have to wait until dark to place it. Glover isn't going to take his eyes off us for a while," he replied. Lee glanced at Diane. "Ready to go?"

She nodded. "Make yourself at home, guys. Food's in the fridge. But don't get complacent. Glover might just start throwing grenades or reveal some real firepower we don't know about. He's got to believe now that his life is on the line. And he's proactive, if you get my drift."

"We'll be ready." Jack nodded and turned toward the two men at the laptop. Richie gave her a thumbs-up, and Hal motioned toward the butt of the pistol extending a few inches out of his jacket pocket.

Lee put on his cap, gloves, and sunglasses, made sure his cell phone, pistol, and extra ammo were in his pockets or at his belt, then stepped outside, Diane just a few steps behind. They climbed into the SUV and drove down the street. One of the neighbors was on his front porch, cell phone in hand, looking up in the direction of their house, an anxious look on his face. His wife was staring out the window, a baby in her arms.

"Stop a second, Lee," Diane said. "We've got to warn these people to stay inside and out of sight."

Lee pulled to a stop as Diane rolled down her window. The man with the phone took a few steps toward them. "What's going on up there?" he shouted. "Looks like everyone's carrying a gun."

"It's Glover, causing trouble again. Please keep your family inside, or leave the area, sir. And if you know any of your neighbors, give them a call and warn them to stay away from our end of the street."

"Shouldn't we just call the sheriff?"

"How's that worked before, sir?" Diane asked.

"You're right. I'll warn the rest of the people around here. Glover deserves whatever he gets."

"He's crossed the line for the last time, sir. Just stay in the house or take a drive into the city—now. Okay?" Diane looked over at Lee, who nodded.

"Good luck. Glover's a dangerous bastard." The man waved, then motioned to the woman with the baby, who'd come to the door. He went inside and shut the door.

Two minutes later they were driving south down the highway, and a half hour later met with Officer Rodriguez, who was back on station near Sully's cabin, monitoring his activities. "Sully's still at home. Hasn't come out since I took over for Bill," Felix reported. "You want me to go in with you?"

"No, but thanks for getting us that loaner car. It'll help

bring Sully outside in a hurry. When we start leaning on him, he's going to get angry. At this point, we don't really know if he'll get violent or just try to run away," Lee said.

"Here are the keys." Rodriguez handed them to Diane, who'd already put on her Katie wig. Diane walked over to the yellow VW, the same model and color as the one driven by the underage hooker, and climbed inside. Lee returned to the SUV.

His cell phone vibrated. "I'm ready. Stay on the line," Diane said. Lee nodded to Felix. "Here we go."

"Good luck," Rodriguez offered.

Diane pulled up in the parking area beside Sully's mountain residence, noting the dusty Camry beside the screened-in front porch. She and Lee had worked this out already. Sully would see the car and at his distance would have no reason to believe it wasn't Katie. The sight of her coming to his house would certainly bring him outside. She wasn't even supposed to know where he lived.

Diane honked the horn, though she'd already noticed someone inside. Sully stepped out onto the top step. He couldn't have failed to hear the vehicle coming—it was so quiet out here, especially today.

She stuck out her arm and waved, honking again.

"What are you doing *here*?" Sully called out, hurrying around to her door. She'd parked with the passenger side facing the house so he couldn't get a better look.

"You're not . . ."

"Katie? No, Mr. Sully. But Katie sent me. I have a message for you about tonight." Diane got out of the car, watching for signs that Sully might want to run for it or get violent. He was anxious, looking around for Glover, maybe.

"Nobody's going to see us here, Mr. Sully. We need to talk.

Can we go inside?" Diane was dressed in clothes as close as she could find to what Katie had worn. Tight, revealing—actually similar to what she'd picked for her current identity. Something to get the wrong kind of attention.

Sully looked her over—checked out her breasts and hips, actually. "How did you find me? I didn't tell anyone where I lived."

From his tone and the step back he just took, the pervert was disappointed, seeing she looked thirty and wasn't built like a child. "Another client of Katie's told her where you lived, and Katie told me. Are you disappointed that I don't look like some schoolgirl?"

Lee was approaching from behind, doing his silent vampire thing, but he was still twenty feet away and Sully looked more worried than ever. He looked away from her toward the road again. All she needed was to hold Sully's attention a few more seconds. "I think I can get you a boy for your movie," she lied. "Not the one you've been counting on, but there won't be any risks, either."

His eyebrows went up and he was suddenly all ears, as well. "This have anything to do with Glover?"

"Yeah, in a way," Lee said, putting his hand on Sully's arm.

Sully jumped out of his skin, then tried to pull away, but Lee had him firmly. "Let me go. What's going on? Did Glover send you here to threaten me?"

"Not at all, Sully," Diane explained. "Calm down. We *all* know Glover is a rat bastard, we followed him a few days ago and found where he was hiding the Klein kid. When Glover left, we snatched the boy and dropped him off at home. We saw his parents split with him a while later. You wanna guess what the boy had to tell us about all this? He doesn't know who grabbed him. And that puts you at the top of the list."

Sully's faced blanched. "I didn't kidnap him. It *was* Glover."

Diane shrugged. "Think that's gonna hold up in court after you see what else Glover has on you now? It's time for show-and-tell. There's a movie Glover made of you and Katie the other night—while *you* were making your own little kinky movie. We've got control of it now, and if you don't want to see your face and Katie's on the Internet tonight, you'll cooperate."

Sully looked defeated, but he refused to make eye contact. "Blackmail—first that bastard, now you two. I'm going broke. How much money do *you* want?"

"We don't want *money*, Sully. We want Glover. If you help us, we'll help you," Lee said, urging Sully toward the porch, but not letting go of his arm.

Sully cleared his throat, no longer resisting, and walked up the steps with Lee. "You sure don't look like cops."

"Did we say we were cops?" Diane snapped.

"We just want Glover. It's personal," Lee added. "Maybe he told you about us. We happen to be his next-door neighbors. So far he's tried window peeping, intimidation, gunfire, and last night, a bomb. All this because we pissed him off. Glover's a walking dead man, and we just want to make sure he sees it coming," Lee said, hoping he didn't sound too Bruce Willis—or was it Dirty Harry?

"Glover is too smart to mess around with. If you want to kill him, better get yourself a gun, and some help," Sully replied. "I'd rather lose my money than my life."

"Did you know that Katie's only fifteen?" Diane said. "Glover has connections with the sheriff's department. If we hadn't liberated the CD of you and Katie, he'd have you by the balls major-league. You wanna live in fear at the state prison, trying to keep a couple thousand inmates from raping and shanking you, a suspected kidnapper and convicted child molester?"

They walked into Sully's living room. It had a homey-looking southwestern-theme decor with soft leather furniture, colorful Navajo rugs, and tasteful landscape photos of the Sandias and Manzanos. In the background, coming from the direction of the floor, was the faint hum of a motor, perhaps the generator.

"You're lying. There was no camera there except for my own, and Katie swore she was legal. I understand you wanting to get back at Glover, but I'd be stupid to help you."

"Wait a minute," Lee said slowly. "Of course! Glover must have something on you already, or you wouldn't be loaning him your Jeep, or groveling like you do."

"Yeah, we know about the Jeep. It's been across the street for a few days now, until last night when one of your station employees brought it back," Diane said. "You've got a DVD player, right?" She walked over to an antiqued wall cabinet with a tasteful Kachina-type figure on the door. She opened it up. Inside was a large disc player, VCR, and twenty-inch TV combo.

"Where's your generator?" Diane asked.

"It's on. Hear the motor?"

"If you say so." She reached over and found the remote. In a few seconds, she'd turned on the monitor and the disc player.

"Sit down, Sully," Lee suggested, "and I'll let go of your arm. Just don't try anything stupid, or you're going to be suffering an incredible amount of physical pain."

Sully nodded, his eyes on the image now appearing on the monitor. Diane turned up the volume. Sully's on-screen image and voice weren't high quality, but his identity was clear and his intentions obvious.

"Want me to fast-forward to the part that'll put you in jail?" Diane offered.

"No, just stop the damn thing. Okay, what do you want from me?"

Sully was on the phone, the cell phone he used to call Glover. Lee was sitting on one side of him, Diane on the other. She had brought out her pistol, to provide additional motivation, but Sully was eyeing the long commando dagger Lee was pretending to sharpen on a sandstone coaster removed from Sully's coffee table.

"Glover, I followed you the other night on that motorcycle and saw where you were keeping the kid. The old fallout shelter inside that fence, secret trapdoor entrance, and everything. I went back to check on him this morning, make sure he was still around, but Klein was gone. There was nothing inside but an empty cage, some canned food in a box, and those fifties survival posters on the walls. You trying to squeeze me? Listen, I paid you a shitload of money to find me a suitable young man for my films. If you don't make good by tonight, you're a dead man."

Lee nodded in approval, the dagger in his hand still now. The rehearsal had helped, at least so far. The emphasis had been on Sully standing up to the man.

Sully, looking more like a deer in headlights at the moment, looked down nervously at the script notes Diane and Lee had prepared for him. He had to make the key points. The rest of the BS Sully could improvise. They'd already made it clear that unless Sully cooperated, he was going to disappear like Glover—but only after everyone who'd ever known Sully, especially his mother in Salt Lake City, got a copy of Glover's film.

Sully started speaking again. "Me kill you, no. But I've still got enough money to get the job done, and I know just the guy

to do it. I had a customer stop by my station the other day. Big
Navajo man. Turns out he's Begay, a neighbor of yours, and is
just dying for an excuse to blow you away. A few buddies of his
are at his house now, I hear, just waiting for a thumbs-up or
thumbs-down on your immediate future. Hell, the only reason
you're not dead right now is because I'm paying them to hold
off a few more days. I need you to come across with a boy for
my movie. My customer base will pay top dollar for kiddie action, but I need youngsters for this market. Real, convincing
kids. You can buy adult porn anywhere."

Lee wished he could hear Glover's side of the call, but knew
the techs across the street from Glover were recording every
syllable. "Feeling the heat, huh? Glover, you prick," Sully responded to whatever was said.

Diane nodded to Lee. It was going well and Sully was convincing.

"You deliver the merchandise tonight, whatever it takes. After that, I'll trade my Jeep for your pickup, and you can drive on
to Mexico or wherever. Just disappear, if you value your life. I
think I can convince the Navajo and his girlfriend to take the
stuff in your house and call it even. But you'd have to be a real
dumb-ass to show yourself around here after tonight. And don't
try to run out on me before delivering what I've already paid
good money for. My arrangement with Begay and that Diane
chick is that I'll call them every hour. They're watching your
house, and each call is your lifesaver. I don't call, or you try and
leave without my permission, you're as good as dead."

Several seconds went by and Sully looked over at Lee and
shrugged. Lee held up his hand, instructing Sully to hold on.
Finally Glover said something to Sully.

"Okay," Sully responded at last. "We'll meet at the same
place as last night, eight P.M. sharp. You'll be watched, of
course, but they won't do anything as long as you keep your part

of the deal. After I pick up the boy and Katie, you're on your own. You'll have an hour, from my last call, to disappear before I set the dogs loose on you." Sully hung up before Glover could respond.

"Not bad, Sully. You've obviously learned a lot from watching television," Lee said. "Let's step into the kitchen while my ole lady makes a few calls of her own."

Sully led the way into the kitchen, a small, natural-wood-paneled area with a gas stove and refrigerator. A breakfast bar below a pass-through allowed them to see Diane in the other room. Sully sat on one of the bar stools and looked down at his hands.

Lee, still playing the ex-con role, opened the refrigerator. "Got any beer?"

"Just some lackluster California pinot noir, I'm afraid. I opened it last night, but couldn't even finish the glass."

"Wine? Gack. No Coors, not even a Bud Light?"

"Sorry. Life is tough."

Lee nodded, seeing a car pull up outside and recognizing the driver. "You have no idea."

"Felix is here, Lee," Diane yelled. She walked to the door and waved him in. "He's going to be looking out for you, Sully, until we get together again to plan tonight's meet with Glover. You're not to make or answer any calls before then, by the way."

Officer Rodriguez was out of uniform, in casual slacks and a Levi's jacket, carrying a nonregulation shotgun. He had a pistol stuck in his belt. "Can I shoot this pervo if he gives me any crap, Lee?" Felix said, winking at Diane.

"Just in the leg," Lee said. "We'll need him tonight if Glover really does show up."

"You sure you're not cops?" Sully whined.

"Do I *look* like a cop, dipstick?" Diane replied, giving Sully a sharp slap on the side of his head. "Cops would be doing all that reading-you-your-rights crap, then try to psych you out. And, just between the two of us, I would avoid mentioning the poe-leece in front of my boyfriend. He *hates* cops, prison guards, and lawyers."

"Add to that girlie men who don't have beer in the cooler," Lee said. "Wine? I'd rather be force-fed diet prune juice. Let's go, Diane."

Lee was driving, and waited until they were in the SUV, headed for the highway, before he spoke. "What did the techs back at the house get?"

"Glover powered up a computer even while on the phone to Sully," she answered, looking over at him. "We got his side of the phone conversation, of course, which included a couple of denials that he kidnapped anyone. Hal and Richie were recording Glover's keystrokes and he accessed his website. They've got two passwords, so it looks like we're going to be able to access and block the site. Once Glover logs off, he won't be able to get access to whatever he has stored on the Internet site."

"He could try to bail on us tonight, but he's got a big investment to hang onto. Without access to his website, he's going to have to get his hard copies if he wants to back up his blackmail operations with facts and photos. And his first stop should be the model home, where he thinks he's got more of the goods on Sully," Lee added. "I doubt he'll go near that fallout shelter. The details we provided for Sully tell Glover someone else *has* been there since the kidnapping. He doesn't know what happened to Timothy Klein or how he got out, either. Obviously the boy couldn't escape on his own, so it must have been Sully, us, or someone else who contacted Sully—like the cops. And if it was the authorities, Glover knows the place will be under surveillance."

Diane nodded, then reached for her phone, which was ringing. "Yeah, it's me. Hi, Andy." Diane listened for a moment, nodding in approval, then responded. "Good, just as we'd hoped. Just stay with Katie and don't let her make any calls. Glover is playing our game now. We'll keep you up to date.

"Glover called Katie, and she apparently did a good job, sticking with the script. Our neighbor sounded pretty tense, according to Andy, who was listening in. He promised her a big bonus if she can bring along a really young-looking guy for Sully. Then he warned Katie that if she didn't help him, he'd be extremely disappointed."

"How did Katie handle the threat? She's just a kid."

Diane shrugged. "Andy said she did really well, jerking him around a few moments, then finally saying she knew somebody who might work out. When we get back with Richie and Hal, they can play the conversation for us. I wish we would have had these resources from day one. Glover would have already been in custody, and we'd know which of the locals he's been contacting."

Lee shrugged. "But then Timothy Klein might still be sitting in that hole. Things have worked out, Diane, at least so far, and the link to the missing boy gave us the edge once that came up. Every agency wanted to get involved in the action. Now that Tim is safe, the pressure is off, in a way. They'll hang out with us for the next forty-eight hours, at least, hoping to nail Glover for the crime. After that, Logan might have to pull them—at least the techs and their gear. Unfortunately, not too many people can get this kind of hardware—outside the CIA and NSA, that is. Maybe DHS."

"I hope Hal and Richie will be able to gain access to Glover's website before tonight. Once we have that, we won't need to play Sully and the kiddie-porn angle. The whole idea makes me want to puke," Diane said.

"At least we'll be getting Sully off the streets. And, hopefully, we'll also get his list of potential customers. What do you want to bet, ninety percent of them are on the sex offender database already?"

"Once a pervert, always a pervert. Or damn close. What I want, Lee, are the names of those the public doesn't know about yet. We really need to take a look at Sully's customer base as soon as this is over."

"I hear you." Lee was driving north, just above the speed limit, and he looked down to check his watch. "Almost noon. Let's stop by and pick up some lunch for our house guests. They've certainly earned their keep today."

CHAPTER 19

Glover is a smart SOB," Hal said, turning around in his chair toward Lee and Diane, who were seated in the dining area going over their plans. "He has a series of passwords, apparently, and cycles through them. Until we learn them all, we won't be able to access any of his website."

"Isn't there a password-breaking program you can run?" Lee asked. "We're running out of time."

Richie shook his head. "There are various programs we could try, but Glover's provider is one used by a lot of hackers and computer pros. Every time a user logs on, he can try up to three different passwords. But if those fail, the site denies access to that computer for twenty-four hours. You'd need years, decades to get in unless you had hundreds of computers dedicated to the task, or a hell of a lot of time with one."

"But we've got a temporary block on his site, so he can't access it, either," Hal added. "The site owners are cooperating, which is something we couldn't legally force them to do."

"That's because of the child pornography and kidnapping connection. Unless we get something more conclusive on Glover, we won't be able to serve the provider with a warrant and force them to give us access to his site content. Even then, they might just claim it's impossible for them to spy on their customer's data," Diane said. "All they might be able to do is delete it, and that's something we can't afford right now."

"They might tell their clients that, but my guess is that's a crock. If you lean on them with a federal judge and keep it out of the press, they'll let you in—well, if you can convince the judge we've got a big enough bad guy here," Hal said, turning to check his computer monitor again.

"Which we can't do until we can pretty much prove corruption between Glover and a government official, deputy, judge, or whatever," Lee said. "Kidnapping is the offense we'd love to prove, but nothing at the old fallout shelter has been found linking him physically to the kidnapping. And Timothy Klein can't make a positive ID. Glover was careful with his disguises."

Diane stood and walked into the kitchen. "You guys keep doing what you can. At least we can still monitor Glover's cell phone. And once it gets dark enough, maybe Lee can place the GPS lump-of-mud tracking bug."

"Hey, you two do know we can track Glover's location pretty close just using his cell phone, right?" Richie said.

"The only problem is, it's mostly an approximation. Not as good as a dedicated GPS, not by half," Hal added.

"If Glover decides to take off early, before dark, we'll have to go with what we have," Lee said.

Gonzales, the trooper who'd been eating a quick dinner in a chair across from the coffee table in the living room area, stood. "I'm going to join Jack outside. Anything special I should pass along?"

"Glover is going to have to make a move soon. I'd recommend you guys keep him guessing and watch out for an ambush. When he takes off, unless he can pull a fast one and slip away, he'll know he's going to be followed and that job is going to fall on Diane and me," Lee replied. "You need to be ready to back us up, move in on his house, or protect yourselves if he gets hostile.

He's a good shot with a pistol, and my guess is that he's got a noise suppressor available, and a ballistic vest, as well."

It was getting dark, nearly seven o'clock, and Lee was still watching Glover's house, waiting for the opportunity to slip out and place the GPS bug.

But Glover was watching, too, mostly from the darkened living room, standing beside doorways that had no backlighting. He was moving around constantly, obviously concerned that his enemies would just be waiting for darkness before moving in. Lee had seen the barrel of some type of assault rifle behind a hassock in the middle of his room and the man had moved around some furniture to block access from windows and provide concealment. He was wary of a direct assault.

Richie, who was responsible for monitoring Glover's cell phone conversations, interrupted the relative silence of the room. "Glover's using his cell phone." He turned up the volume as Lee and Diane moved closer.

"It's me. I'm going to need your help later today. Stick close to my neighborhood, okay?"

"Okay."

There was a click. "That's it?" Diane asked. "Can you play it back? I didn't recognize the voice."

"Hang on a second. I'm trying to get a fix on the location of the other party," Richie said, shaking his head.

"Who was Glover talking to, Lee? It sounded like a man—not Sully."

"Sounds familiar. But one word . . . I can't say for sure."

Richie played the brief exchange back several times, but neither Lee nor Diane could identify the person being called. Finally Richie looked at the information on his map display. "It was a really short call, so I can't swear to it, but my guess is that the other party was moving, like in a car. It's northeast of here, along the highway."

"My guess it's one of the deputies we've encountered. The older guy, Harmon?" Lee suggested.

"Yeah, it could be him, and it makes sense. Quick call, hard to trace, and not much information for anyone snooping on the deputy. And no names," Diane pointed out.

"Everyone needs to watch their back if Deputy Harmon shows up." Lee quickly gave the four men helping them a description of the deputy.

Another half hour passed.

"Glover's trying to access his Web site," Hal announced. "He can't get in, but we've got another password now."

Another minute went by, then Hal spoke again. "He just got offline. Now he's exiting the operating system. Probably shutting down the laptop."

"He's messing with something in a big bag. Now he's out of sight," Lee said. He picked up his cell phone and punched Jack's number. "Glover may be up to something."

A few seconds later Glover came out his front door. "He's on the move," Lee said, loud enough for the three people around him to hear.

Glover strolled quickly toward the passenger side of his pickup Jeep, his eyes going back and forth between the two big trucks mostly concealing Jack and Gonzales, and Lee and Diane's windows. He had a pistol stuck into his belt, clearly visible, and Lee suspected the big barracks bag Glover was carrying held extra firepower and ammunition, plus his laptop and any cash or valuables he could carry. The man had on a bulky-looking jacket, probably with a flak jacket underneath.

Diane was watching from the other edge of the living room window, her pistol now out and down by her side. "Looks like he's taking off."

Glover slipped into the pickup cab from the passenger side, slid across the seat, and started the vehicle immediately. He reached down, out of sight for a second, then sat back up and looked back at Jack and Gonzales, who were moving farther apart from each other to present a more difficult target.

Then Glover backed the pickup out into the road, turned on the headlights, and drove off.

Lee and Diane were already at the door and followed Glover immediately in the SUV, keeping a distance of a few hundred yards. The entire neighborhood was dark, as if there'd been a power outage, but Lee noticed a few people peering out of their windows, watching them pass.

Diane was using the cell phone. "Glover's moving now, stand by," she said to Andrea Moore, who'd joined State Policeman Felix Rodriguez around 5:00. The two officers had taken Sully north and were now parked off the highway, hidden from view, about a mile north of the road leading to the FAC Hideaway Homes development. Andrea Moore was dressed and made up like Katie, including a wig, and according to Andy would easily pass for the young hooker at a distance. Katie herself was in protective custody somewhere in the Albuquerque metro area.

Diane had just put the phone down when it lit up and started vibrating again. She picked it up and listened for a moment. "You might want to consider moving to the south side of the house and staying away from the windows facing Glover's place," Diane said, then ended the call.

"Lee, Jack took a look through Glover's front window. There's something that looks like a motion sensor inside. Our perp might have activated a booby trap to take out any unscheduled visitors."

"So that's why you advised them to put a little distance between them and Glover's place."

"Yeah. We don't know if Glover plans on ever coming back

home, so he might have the place rigged to blow," Diane said. "Jack and Gonzales are standing by in case we need them, and the techs are still trying to hack into Glover's Web site. Richie thinks they're getting close."

Diane called Andrea again and advised her that Glover appeared to be keeping his appointment with Sully, despite having no human "merchandise" to sell, and that she and Officer Rodriguez needed to move over to the meeting site and get ready for Glover's arrival.

While Diane was on the phone, Lee continued to follow Glover's pickup north on the mountain highway. It was dark, but he'd have had no trouble even if Glover's taillights weren't clearly visible.

Lee's phone began to vibrate and he picked it up. "Grand Central Station."

"Lee, this is Hal. Glover just made a call. All he said was 'Clear my tail.' The other party, same one as last time, we think, said, 'Okay.' That's it."

Lee checked the rearview mirror and could see headlights. He'd noticed them earlier, but they'd been too far away for him to get a make and model of the car, though the vehicle was white—the basic color of the county's sheriff's department units.

"Glover called his backup. It might be the vehicle behind us, but be ready from any direction."

"I think we need to identify ourselves as cops, just in case the deputy *isn't* dirty," Diane said. "We can't afford to give Glover too much room. Andy and Felix are ready and know Glover is heavily armed, but the guy is a shark. We need to stack the deck heavily in our favor."

"Agreed. If the deputy acts up, we'll leave him in handcuffs for Jack and Gonzales to pick up later."

Lee glanced back again. "He's closing up the distance, and

it looks like Deputy Harmon. If he pulls a weapon, we'll have to neutralize him quickly."

"In the meantime, what about Glover?" Diane, having looked in the rearview mirror, was now looking forward again, trying to locate the taillights of the pickup.

"Once we get pulled over, he'll speed up. So let's settle this with Harmon right now."

Lee slowed quickly, signaling to pull over, even though Deputy Harmon still hadn't turned on his emergency lights or signaled them in any way.

"Just don't let him get around us, Lee."

"Don't worry." Lee watched Harmon's reaction. Surprised by their sudden drop in speed, his vehicle closed the gap so quickly for a moment Lee wondered if the deputy was going to ram them.

There was the sound of skidding tires, sudden bright lights from behind, then red and white flashes and a touch of siren.

"That's our cue," Diane said, placing her hand in her jacket pocket as Lee pulled onto the shoulder of the narrow highway and came to a stop.

Lee and Diane both got out, knowing it would send an honest cop's heart pumping—the danger of a quick, unexpected attack. But time trumped caution tonight.

Deputy Harmon hesitated, not expecting this kind of reaction. Then he opened his door and stepped half out using the door as a shield. "Get back in your vehicle—now!"

"We're law enforcement officers. Get back into *your* unit, Harmon, and don't interfere with our investigation," Diane yelled, holding up her gold shield as she walked toward the deputy's blue-striped unit.

Seeing Diane on one side, and Lee moving straight toward him also holding his badge up in the light, the deputy did the totally unexpected. He ducked.

CHAPTER 20

Lee looked over his shoulder. "Glover!" Lee yelled, hearing the pickup coming back toward them, headlights off. Sudden blasts erupted and flashes of gunfire appeared as Glover fired some sort of weapon with his left hand out the driver's side window.

The first few bullets whistled overhead, then Lee felt the impact on his back as rounds struck him. He dove between the vehicles as more hits struck window glass and thumped against metal.

Lee rolled off the narrow gravel shoulder into the ditch beyond, groping for his pistol and looking down the road for Diane. He saw movement in the tall grass, which meant she'd also reached cover. Glover continued shooting and there were two louder-than-usual pops.

Tires screeched. Then an engine began accelerating away and Diane returned fire. Lee scrambled over to the hood of the SUV, pistol out, and took aim at Glover's fleeing pickup. Headlights blocked his sight picture, and Lee held fire as a car came upon the scene from the north, passing by Glover. The driver, an old woman, saw Lee, his pistol aimed in her general direction, and quickly accelerated past them to the south.

Diane raced out into the road, stopped, then got two more

quick shots off. "Shit! I missed." Then she turned and looked toward him. "Lee? You okay?"

He walked out from behind the SUV into the glare of the headlights from the cop car. The flashing emergency lights gave an eerie, strobe effect to the scene, as they always did. "I took some hits to my vest. No AP rounds this time, though. He had a carbine of some kind."

Diane trotted over, then cursed again, looking at their SUV. "Crap, Glover shot out our tires." Lee turned for a look at the driver's side tires, then remembered the two strange pops he's heard.

"Deputy Harmon. Where'd he go?" Lee said, then brought his pistol up again, swinging it around toward the bullet-riddled open door of the county unit. He inched forward cautiously, seeing Diane coming back around to his left, providing cover as he moved in.

In addition to the bullet holes in the door, there were hits in the front fender and the driver's window had been shattered. As Lee inched around the door, he saw the deputy's head first. A bullet had struck him in the left temple and there was a growing pool of blood on the asphalt. Harmon had sagged backward onto the pavement. His eyes were open, but it was clear that whatever he was seeing now wasn't of this world.

Lee put his pistol away, then motioned to Diane. "He's very dead. Climb in. We're going to need this car to catch up to Glover. Even without kidnapping, we've got enough on him now to send him to jail for the rest of his life."

Lee brushed out most of the glass on the seat, then climbed in, reaching over to unlock the passenger door for Diane. As soon as she was in, he put the car in reverse, turning the wheel as he backed up to avoid running over the body. "Call—"

"Already on it," Diane said, punching out the number for Officer Moore. She paused. "Damn, Andy's talking to someone else. Pick up, woman."

Lee checked the mirror for oncoming traffic, then pulled out onto the road, hitting the gas. The department unit responded sluggishly and Lee looked down at the gauges. There was a red light on the dash. "Damn, Glover must have hit a fuel line or something."

"Go as long as we can, Lee. I'm still trying to get through to Andy."

"Try Felix instead."

She punched out another set of numbers. "Busy, too. They might be talking to each other. Come on, Felix. You've got call waiting!"

Diane looked over at Lee. "You smell gas?"

He nodded, backing off on the accelerator pedal. The deputy's unit had barely made thirty miles an hour and white smoke was starting to drift up from the engine compartment.

He touched the brakes. "We're in trouble."

There was a sudden whoosh, then the hood blew up with a bang, rattling loudly as it bounced over the top of the car. "Lee!" Diane yelled.

"Hang on." He held the car straight, allowing it to coast for a few seconds before he felt for the brakes again and managed to bring the cruiser to a stop. Black smoke was billowing now and orange flames leaped up from the engine. "Get out before it blows!"

Lee threw open the door, not worried if any cars were coming, and jumped out. "Hurry Diane. Get back!" He saw her still standing beside the open passenger door, looking for something.

"My cell phone, it's on the floor somewhere." She started coughing, choking from the billowing cloud of smoke inside the car and around the front end.

"We'll use mine. Get back!" He dove across the top of the car headfirst, ducked, and rolled to his feet, then whirled around, planning on pulling her out of the car, if necessary. But she was already moving on her own.

Shielding her face with her arm from the heat and glare, Diane yelled as they ran. "How far?"

"More!" He reached around her with his arm, scooping her up and carrying her faster than she could move on her own. They reached the shoulder of the road and he stumbled into the weeds. There was a flash and roar, and the wave of heated air struck them like a tornado from hell, throwing them down a split second before the shreds of flying metal flew past with a shriek. Lee pulled Diane against him, covering her as much as possible with his body.

Glass and debris rattled and clunked on the road, but only a few small pieces actually struck them, and the hot pieces were easy to brush off after the explosion subsided.

"Sorry if I was too rough," Lee said, rolling over and taking his weight off her.

"I forgive you—this time," she mumbled, pushing away some weeds that had gotten in her face.

Lee sat up and reached for his phone. "Damn!" Only the top half was intact. The bottom section, below the hinge, had a dime-size hole right through it. Half a circuit board was gone, along with the battery. "We're screwed. Glover killed my phone."

Diane stood, then looked up and down the road. "We've got to catch a ride. We need to cover Felix and Andrea. Screw Sully."

They both began to run in the direction Glover had gone.

"Move as quickly as you can, and once a ride comes, catch up to me. And be careful, in case Glover decides to come back this way again." Lee accelerated to a pace only a vampire could maintain, knowing that he could cover a mile in two minutes easy. The pavement was a good, hard surface, the night cool, and the darkness complete enough to hide his beyond-normal ability. Pistol secure in his belt, he concentrated, letting every muscle of his half-vampire body work with the strength, efficiency, and endurance the unique "affliction" gave him. He'd long ago cast aside wishing he were a full vampire and even faster. The extra vulnerability to sunlight wasn't worth the bonus in speed and strength. Too bad that turning into a bat thing was strictly fiction, though. He could use a little shape-shifter boost right now.

Remembering every twist and turn of the road, Lee knew that once he completed the next turn, there was a straight section of highway directly ahead. Then almost at the end of that stretch was the left-hand turn that led into the FAC housing development. Officers Moore and Rodriguez were supposed to be there—and Sully. The pervert was in a dead-even tie with Glover for achieving the lowest form of humanity, but Lee had assumed responsibility for Sully's safety. And the officers? No way Lee was going to let them go down. Hearing gunshots in the distance, his heart skipped a beat, then he really poured on the speed.

Lee sprinted down the highway, keeping to the left lane. He had his pistol out and ready, held tightly in his right hand. Glover's red pickup was visible ahead, parked right beside the yellow VW that Andy was using in Katie's stead. Sully's Camry was gone and Felix was supposed to be inside with him.

Lee noticed the thin mist of dust still settling across the road from the vehicles. The Camry had gone that way, obviously. But who was driving now?

Nobody was in sight. Lee glanced over his shoulder, detecting a noise behind him on the road. From the engine rattle, it was a diesel coming his direction, and at a good clip. Slowing down was necessary to hide his half-vampire speed, but people ahead might be wounded—or worse.

Or he might just get run over. He slowed to Olympic

sprinter's speed and moved across the highway to the softer gravel on the right shoulder. He was hoping to reach the vehicles before the approaching vehicle came into sight and it looked like he would. Perhaps the hillsides of the small canyon behind him had amplified the sound of the approaching car.

Pistol ready, Lee yelled as he jogged up to the VW. "Andrea, Felix?" He looked down and found a cell phone—at least what was left of it.

The door to the yellow car was open, but nobody was inside. Andrea's purse was on the passenger's seat cushion. Then he heard somebody groan. Lee hurried around to the other side of the VW. Sully was there, dead from a bullet in the forehead, but Felix Rodriguez was alive. He was bleeding from his arm and upper body, but the officer had managed to turn over onto his back and was conscious.

"We were doing our hooker-pimp act when Glover caught us off guard. He sucker punched Andy, then pulled out a forty-five and shot me and Sully," Felix managed. "I got a round off, but Glover must have been wearing a vest. He flinched, then shot me again. Tossed us out of the car. Heard him drive off."

"Where's Andy, Officer Moore?"

"She's not here?"

"No. Hopefully, Glover took her as a hostage." Lee checked Officer Rodriguez's injuries. He'd been shot in the upper arm and shoulder and had a bloody spot on the side of his head. Glover must have thought the wounds were fatal, or not cared, knowing Felix would be sidelined, incapacitated.

"You're going to make it, Felix."

Lee heard a vehicle's horn, then turned. It was one of the pickups from the house, flying up the straightaway. The big truck geared down with a mighty whine, then slid to a stop about fifty feet away. Diane jumped out first, followed by Gonzales and Jack Allen.

Lee stood. "Call the EMTs. Rodriguez is down. And bring a first-aid kit. We've got some bleeding to stop."

Diane ran up, saw Sully, then shook her head. Jack stopped and brought out a cell phone. Moving quickly, Gonzales stepped back over to the big pickup and climbed inside.

"Glover took Andrea, which means she's still alive," Lee told Diane, bending down to check out the wounded state policeman again.

Diane looked down at Felix, who tried to smile. Gonzales ran up with the first-aid kit just then. "I've got it, Lee."

Lee stood, then he and Diane walked toward Jack, who was still on the phone. "Pass any Camrys on the way?"

Jack shook his head. "Just some old woman speeding away. Diane said she passed through during the incident."

"My guess is that Glover hauled ass up that road." Lee pointed toward the FAC development. "Or spun around in the dirt and drove north."

"More backup units have the highway covered just this side of Tijeras," Jack said. "I'll tell them Glover may have a hostage and advise them of the Camry."

Diane nodded. "Do you suppose Glover knows Andy's a cop?"

"She wasn't wearing a vest—her call—and I don't think she had time to pull her weapon. It may still be in her purse in the VW. Hopefully, her ID is in there, too, and he never saw it. Felix said Glover walked right up and sucker punched her, then started shooting. Maybe he believes Sully already has the boy and was going to stiff him."

"Hopefully, Andy wasn't injured too badly and she's playing dumb. She's obviously got a brain. Wanna take the truck?" Diane suggested.

"Yeah. We'll take Jack and have Gonzales stick with Felix

until help arrives. You ready to roll?" Lee said to Jack, who'd just hung up.

"Just a sec. I called the techs at your house and they're going to be ready if Glover comes back home or tries to do a number on them. Let me tell Gonzales what's going on, then we're gone."

Lee and Diane ran over to the VW and got Officer Moore's purse. Inside was her ID and handgun, which suggested that Glover *hadn't* discovered that she was really a cop. With her youthful looks, attitude, and slender shape, Andy might have been able to pull off her cover as a civilian. Having worked vice might have kept her alive.

A call from the techs yielded some important information. They'd locked in on Glover's cell phone, which was turned on, and had traced his location. He was on the move, in an area west of the highway, but there weren't enough cell towers in the area to get anything more precise.

They crossed over into the development and drove to the model home first. Outside, security lights were on and a quick look through the garage window confirmed no white Camry inside. They moved on, quickly checking the driveways, and spotted another of the popular Camrys, but of a different color. They'd taken the back entrance to the development, planning on circling around back to the highway, when a call came in from Richie.

"Glover has moved south again and is not too far from his home?" Diane repeated aloud what she'd just heard, turning to Lee, her eyebrows raised in question.

"Don't tell me the bastard is out to hit our place again," Lee said. "The guys need to shift over to defense."

He looked over at Jack, who was listening closely. "Back to the house, best speed."

Jack nodded, took a left turn instead of the right he was halfway into, and everyone felt the pull of their seat belts as the truck slid, then gained traction again. They were only a half mile or so from the highway, but the road was bumpy.

"We're going back. Watch out for Glover. He's on the warpath," she told the person on the phone. "Why would he go back, Lee?" Diane asked, lowering the phone for a second.

"Take out the other guys, get something he left behind. Money, drugs, lipstick, and a plus-size dress? Who knows?"

Jack's eyebrows went up, but he kept his eyes on the road.

"There is no sign of the Camry, Lee, but they're getting a better fix on his cell phone," Diane reported. "It's within a mile, give or take."

"I've got a feeling he's going to ditch that car. But if he's on foot and Andy's still alive, and with him, she'll be slowing him down," Lee said. "Tell them to concentrate on a visual and less on their gear. And remember that Glover might just decide to set off some explosives."

"Cheerful thought." Diane repeated Lee's warning and then asked the men to keep the line open, not wanting to continue to distract if Glover was now within range.

Ten very anxious minutes went by before Jack reached the turnoff to Quail Run. Suddenly, Lee had a thought and told Jack to pull over by the mailboxes.

"I'll be going on foot from here, just outside the north fence, behind the row of houses on the right. Get back to the house as fast as you dare with the headlights off. And watch for an ambush," he told Diane and Jack.

"Diane," Lee added. "You ride shotgun. Jack's going to have to watch the road and his side. I'll take the cell phone and give you a call when I reach Glover's house—from the rear."

"Hey, don't we still have that bug in place by Glover's back gate?"

"I'd forgotten about that. You take the cell and call Richie and Hal. Have them check out the receiver. If Glover goes in through the back gate, they'll know."

"But we'll be back at the house long before you can hoof it up, Lee," Jack said. "Maybe you should take the cell."

"I'm pretty fast on my feet. Don't worry," Lee replied, not elaborating. "I better get going now. Watch for me coming in the back door if I don't run across Glover and his hostage."

Lee jumped out of the pickup and jogged away, heading northwest toward the first house on the right side of Quail Run. He suspected that Glover would park the car down the road and then take Andy through the back the rest of the way—unless she was dead already, of course.

Trying not to dwell on that possibility, Lee ran up along the fence, passing the first home on his left. Not worried about being heard, Lee looked around for the Camry. All he saw were a small motorboat, a pickup, a children's swing set, and a fifty-five-gallon drum used to burn trash and weeds. Farther ahead was the second house, still darkened inside and out, like all the others in view.

He only had time to check out one side of the neighborhood, but Lee figured that if Glover was coming here, he'd be heading to the end of the street via the most direct route—this one. Lee pressed on, wondering if Glover had noticed that nobody in the neighborhood seemed to be at home tonight.

At the third house, Lee saw a man and woman outside beneath their carport. It was the Sernas, according to the mailbox corresponding to that address. As he got closer, the Camry became visible, parked by the side of the house behind an SUV he'd seen days earlier. Jogging silently by, Lee noticed that Mrs. Serna was pointing at some spots on the driver's door and that Mr. Serna had a rifle in his hand.

Deciding the spots on the car were probably bullet holes,

from the moment Sully was killed, Lee picked up speed. Diane and Jack had probably already spotted the car on the way up. That meant they were ready for trouble, but it also meant they were in danger.

As Lee got within a hundred yards of the rear gate to Glover's house, he saw Jack and Diane's pickup parked in the middle of the street halfway between his and Glover's house. The outside lights at Glover's were on, but there were no lights inside either house and no sign of anyone, anywhere. The absence of bodies, broken glass, and obvious bullet holes in the pickup suggested that his people were laying low, watching for Glover.

Somewhere ahead he heard a thump. Pistol out, Lee hurried on. The gate to Glover's backyard was open, which meant that Diane already knew somebody had passed through, thanks to the motion sensor there. Lee stopped, bent down, and looked for footprints.

There were two sets, large boots that Lee had seen before—Glover's—and small, pointed ones that couldn't be more than a size six or seven. Those belonged to Officer Moore—Andrea. Keeping very low to the ground, Lee inched forward. Glover and his hostage were inside the house, apparently, because they weren't in the backyard. He stepped through the yard at a crouch, ignoring the surveillance camera and following the prints. They led to the large plastic trash container atop a concrete pad maybe three feet square. Lee looked all around the pad, but the footprints had disappeared.

Knowing that both of them couldn't fit inside the trash can without removing major body parts, Lee eyed the slab closely. He reached over to set the trash container aside, but it wouldn't budge. It was stuck on the bottom. Opening the lid, Lee discovered a plastic trash bag inside. It must have contained leaves or paper because it was light and rustled as he lifted it out. Below, at the bottom of the container, was a piece of plywood bolted to the bottom.

Checking the slab more closely now around the edges, Lee discovered it was actually a wooden door covered with a layer of masonry cement to make it look solid—like movie set concrete. Glover had a trapdoor leading underground, and that's where he'd gone with Andy. The thump he'd heard was the heavy door closing. He looked over at the big pile of dirt he'd noticed days earlier. Now he understood where it had come from. There was a hole or tunnel somewhere below.

If the boy had been hidden here instead, they might have had an easier time finding him. Unfortunately, Glover had been careful to keep some distance between himself and his captive, at least until tonight. The good news, and maybe the bad news, as well, was that Glover was desperate and making mistakes now.

Without a cell phone, Lee was forced to improvise. Looking around quickly, he spotted an eight-foot section of a pine tree trunk, trimmed of branches and destined to become firewood someday, no doubt. He picked it up and set it across the door. The log, about a foot in diameter, easily weighed two hundred pounds. There was no way Glover would be opening this door anytime soon, and, providing the sleazeball was in a position to watch, he'd know why.

Making sure the sensor was still in place, Lee ran to the back gate, closed it behind him, and hurried in a wide circle around to the rear of his and Diane's place. Whatever came next would require careful planning if Glover was to be taken without anyone else being killed.

CHAPTER 21

I t's Lee. Hold your fire," Lee said loud enough to be heard by Jack, who'd moved around to the pickup, the one left behind earlier, at the end of the street.

Jack jumped and turned, rifle in hand. "How'd you do that, Lee? Damn, you're sneaky."

"It's the Navajo thing," Lee said. "Glover is either inside his house or underground in a bunker in the backyard. There's an access door disguised as a concrete slab below the plastic trash container. And he has Officer Moore with him, judging from the second set of fresh footprints leading to the spot."

"You want to tell the others in the house?" Jack handed him a cell phone. "Keep it. Richie gave us each a spare after what happened earlier. They're all programmed with our numbers."

There was a loud noise overhead and Lee looked up. It was a large U.S. Forest Service helicopter with a big bucket dangling below on a cable, heading south. "That's not for us, right?"

"No. Hal picked up the radio chatter when it came by on an earlier pass. There was a lightning strike near Capilla Peak, farther down the Manzanos, and the forest service has a lookout tower close by. The copter's already made one water drop, and this must be another one. Think we could use it to help take down Glover?"

"Maybe. Something to keep in mind. Ask Hal if he can get them on the radio and have them stand by a few miles away after they make this run."

Jack nodded.

Lee, still watching Glover's house, called Diane. "I'm with Jack. Glover took Andy in through a hidden entrance in the back just below that plastic trash can. He's either in some underground bunker, or he's dug a tunnel connecting with the house. You see anything from where you are?" He paused, then nodded. "Where *are* you, anyway?"

"Outside, behind the green pickup, in the street opposite you, keeping out of sight. I'll wave."

Lee saw a hand come up for a second behind the front of the pickup. "I got you."

"What's the plan, Lee? Glover's not going down without a fight and he has a hostage now. We can wait him out, I suppose."

"That's usually the strategy with hostages, but he'll know that, too. My guess is he won't wait, knowing he'll have a better chance now than after sunrise when we can see every move he makes. As soon as he's ready again, he'll come out, probably using Andrea as a shield." Lee thought about it a second, then continued. "So we'll have to take the initiative. He can't cover every direction. We can pin him down, move in from two directions, and do what we can to get Andy back."

"We can put him away on what we have already. And once Glover is in custody his provider won't have any reason not to give up the site, and we can get the blackmail material. At least we don't have another murder yet to add to the charges. Felix is going to make it, I heard on the way."

"Good news. So screw the hard copies. We need to get Officer Moore back."

"Thought you'd say that, Lee. I'll be the tunnel rat and go in from the rear. You guys can hold his attention, right?"

"Diane, I should be the one going in through the tunnel."

"Why? With your physical abilities you shouldn't be limiting your movement potential. I'll put on two vests and load up with AP rounds, You know you excel at getting the bad guys' attention and keeping them really pissed off."

"I see your point. I'll have the guys advance from the front and west side, covering each other with shotgun fire but aiming high unless they have a sure target," Lee said reluctantly. "Meanwhile, I'll be everywhere else at once."

"Think we can use that forest service helicopter? Maybe make some noise and keep Glover looking up?"

"I'm thinking of another use right now."

"What?"

"You'll see. Meanwhile, you slip back inside our house, get armored up, and come over to where I'm at behind Glover's. Hurry before he makes his move. I can give you cover until you get in that hole. Besides, I need to move a tree for you."

"Huh? Never mind, I'll see, right?"


Less than five minutes later the assault began. Richie, having sneaked out of the house, turned on the engine of Lee and Diane's pickup, pulled around, and turned on the headlights, directed into Glover's living room window. Hal, now over by the green truck, fired a shotgun at the front door.

Jack, in position to view the surveillance camera and floodlights at the rear corner of the house, shot out the camera with his rifle, then one of the floodlights.

From the cover of the trees, Lee took out the other rear-facing light, then he and Diane moved forward into the yard, coming through the back gate. Lee watched the windows, covering Diane as she ran to the log resting upon the trapdoor. She then covered Lee as he came up beside her.

Without a word, he kicked the log away, then yanked up the trapdoor with one hand, pistol in the other. Simple wooden steps cut from two-by-fours led down into a tunnel about three feet high and wide braced with planks on the sides and top. Lee dropped down inside, forced to get on his hands and knees. The tunnel, which required crawling, led a straight path, twenty feet farther to the end. A supporting wooden framework surrounded a wooden ladder leading up.

"Hey," Diane whispered harshly. "That's my job."

Lee climbed back out. The blast of gunshots and the massive helicopter swooping over covered their noise quite well. "Wanted to see what you're getting into before you gave yourself away with a flashlight. Twenty feet farther is a ladder leading up. Watch for traps and trip wires."

Diane brought out her little flashlight, twisted the end to produce a strong, filtered red light, and then climbed down into the tunnel. "Just keep Glover busy. When I find Andrea, we're coming out any way we can. But close up behind me in case Glover looks out a window."

"Be careful. And come back," Lee said. "I need you around."

She gave him that crinkly nose grin. "Me, too."

He shut the trapdoor, then ran over to the side of the building. Returning fire came from the inside front of the house, and maybe the west side. Glover was fighting back, or at least doing what he could to ward off the assault and keep their heads down. Lee slipped underneath one of the bedroom windows, then cringed as the glass broke from bullets flying out overhead. Glover was now shooting in every direction, just in case, Lee realized.

The cell phone at his waist vibrated. "Can you hear me?" It was Diane, maybe less than ten feet away, down below beneath the house.

"Yeah."

"I got a quick peek and saw Glover moving around inside, firing and filling a gym bag with CDs and stuff taken from stash spaces in the wall panels. Andy's on the floor in the bedroom, tied up with duct tape. The trapdoor is in the hall closet. He put something on top and it shifted when I raised it about an inch. If I move it any more he might hear. Can you find a way to make a lot more noise to cover the sound? If you can, I'll force the trapdoor up, grab Andy, and pull her down into the tunnel. Then you can take Glover out."

"I've got an idea. How strong do you think his roof is? Never mind. Just hang on a moment while I make a quick call."

"Hurry, Lee. Glover is going to bail soon, and probably come in my direction, leading with Andrea."

"Understood. Call me back in one minute."

Lee jumped up onto the windowsill, then reached to grab the edge of the roof. Suddenly a bolt of pain pierced his right foot. Pulling himself onto the roof, Lee rolled up the slope while bullets punched holes in the shingles. Glover had seen or heard him and was firing blind into the ceiling.

Standing, knowing it presented the smallest target from inside, he looked up as the big helicopter came up the ridge line behind him. Lee remembered hearing stories about crewmen and soldiers in helicopters over Vietnam. They liked to sit on flak jackets and anything solid they could find to protect the family jewels. Right now, his own undercarriage was at risk. Too bad.

He called Hal and the tech was on the line instantly. "Hal, this is Lee."

"Yeah, I see you on the roof. What's the plan?"

"We need some awesome noise to cover a move Diane's going to make. Can you raise that helicopter directly?"

"Hell yeah. With our gear I can call the president. You want these boys to hover over Glover's house? Rattle the windows?"

Lee explained what he needed, at the same time noting that Glover had finally stopped shooting through the roof. From the way the pain was subsiding, Lee also knew that the wound in his foot was starting to heal.

Hal spoke again. "You sure about this, Lee? The helo crew is a little concerned."

"My responsibility. We need a fucking big diversion."

"I'll convince them," Hal promised.

Another fifteen seconds went by. Lee could hear the helicopter moving in. Now, barely a hundred feet above the tree line, he could see the flying crane and the big water bucket dangling down from the heavy cable. Water was sloshing over the edge, scooped from a swimming pool a few miles over the ridge at the FAC development instead of its earlier source.

"Here they come. Just get off the roof in time, okay?"

"Don't worry about me. Once they're directly overhead, I'm outta here."

Lee half hopped, half ran over to the rear of the house, leaned over the edge, and started shooting into the window, angling his rounds down to strike the floor.

Glover responded and fired back, his bullets flying through the roof where Lee had been a few seconds earlier. By then, Lee was standing fifteen feet away on the crown of the roof, waving up at the helicopter. A spotlight from the big machine swept across the roof, then found and transfixed him.

Hoping Diane was ready, Lee gave the helicopter a thumbs-up, then ran toward the edge as the copter slipped sideways. Already feeling drops of moisture, Lee jumped down into the backyard. He hit and rolled as hundreds of gallons of water struck Glover's roof. The ground shook, metal creaked, and wood snapped, but Lee didn't have time to stop and watch. In three fast steps he reached the hatch of Glover's tunnel and yanked it completely off the hinges. Hearing scuffling sounds, he thought about dropping inside, but instead he waited and watched Glover's windows. A shape appeared, and Lee shot high, not knowing for certain it was Glover. Whoever it was ducked.

"*Mumph*," someone muttered. Lee looked down and saw Andrea, duct tape on her face, at the base of the ladder. He grabbed her hand.

"Hang on." He pulled her up, hoping the force and angle wouldn't break her wrist, then took her other hand when it was offered. Swinging her around, he set her on the ground and reached back down, trying to find Diane.

Suddenly a loud explosion shook the tunnel—a gunshot. Either it was Diane firing cover fire or Glover was firing into the tunnel. Not knowing for sure and not having the time to look, Lee placed his trust in his partner's skill. It was time to invade Glover's personal space.

Standing, he looked around for the log. "Ah, my own battering ram."

He grabbed the section of tree trunk, cradling it in his arms, and ran to Glover's back door. As he reached the step, Lee shoved the log into the door just above the doorknob, using all the strength he could muster. The door flew open as the frame around the latch shattered.

Lee hugged the wall just outside the utility room, whipping out his pistol. Three quick bullets cut through the air where he would have been standing had he followed the log inside. Then he heard a faint click and a curse.

Recognizing the sound of a firing pin on an empty chamber, Lee slipped past the wreckage and ducked inside. Glover, trying to watch and reload by feel in the semidarkness, quickly ran out of the kitchen and into the dining area, ducking below the breakfast counter partition.

A blast came from the front of the house and someone inside

grunted, probably Glover. The next sound he heard was a squishy thud on the carpet. Lee jammed his pistol into its holster and took two steps, diving across the kitchen counter, under the pass-through, and into the living room.

Lee hit the floor and slid on his chest across the wet carpet. Bouncing off the wall, he managed to roll to his feet and turn toward Glover, who was still on his knees, groping around on the water-soaked floor for his carbine.

"You're a fucking panther, Indian. You've screwed up my life real good and now it's time for payback," Glover yelled, scrambling to his feet. His right hand was bleeding, but in his left hand was a marine combat knife. Glover was weaving it back and forth, just like in the movies. Illumination from flares the guys had tossed in the front yard provided long shadows and just enough light for Glover to see.

Lee reached down and pulled out his long commando dagger, a six-inch, double-edged Sykes-Fairbairn blade. The balanced weapon had always fit his hand perfectly.

Glover took a step back, his eyes getting bigger by the second. "What the hell are you? Military? Cop?"

"You're going down, Glover. Give it up and you'll die in prison instead of here—now. You've got enough sense left to know I'm not going to have a scratch on me when I walk out of this dump. You, on the other hand . . ."

"You'll never find the boy without me," Glover said, his voice harsh. "You need me alive."

"We pulled Tim from the cage in that fallout shelter last night, moron. Nobody needs you in any way other than dead. Give up and drop the knife before I get ugly."

"Fuck you!" Glover fled into the kitchen.

Lee followed, but Diane was standing just out the back door, blocking the way. Glover never broke stride, yelling instead and charging at her with the knife. She fired twice, then stepped back. Glover's forward momentum carried him into the utility space, where he struck the washing machine with a thud before bouncing back onto the floor.

Lee put away his knife, saw movement to his side, then waved to Jack, who'd stepped though the shattered front window into the living room while their attention had been diverted.

"I put some buckshot into his hand a minute ago and knocked the carbine away, but he wouldn't give up. Then I had to duck away to reload. Is he dead?" Jack asked, his shotgun out as he walked across the sodden carpet. Water was trickling down in a small stream from between shattered ceiling tiles.

Diane stepped back inside via the utility room entrance and looked down at Glover. "Can't tell for sure in the dark." She reached into her pocket and fumbled for her flashlight. Her hands were shaking.

Lee stepped over, his pistol out again, and looked down at Glover. His shirt had been torn by an earlier shotgun hit, but he had on a vest underneath, which had stopped the buckshot from penetrating. Diane had been using armor-piercing rounds, obviously, and there were two entry wounds in the center of his chest. Bending down, Lee felt at the man's wrist for a pulse. "He's gone."

"To hell—if there's a God in heaven," Jack declared. "Damn, I almost wish he'd have lived long enough to make it to trial. Some of the testimony would have been really interesting. Like that forest service water balloon. And the Nixon mask on the floor over there." He pointed. "What's that doing here?"

Diane walked across the small kitchen and aimed her flashlight up at the dining area ceiling, which was sagging in the center. Water was still dripping through several ever-widening gaps in the ceiling tiles and the carpet was pooled about an inch deep or more now.

Lee realized he hadn't paid much attention to the water, having been so intent on Glover. Turning around, he saw a gym bag in the hall, just in front of the opened closet. He walked over and picked up the bag. It was unzipped, and inside were CDs, a computer hard drive, bundles of cash, and the .45 pistol with the laser sight. He zipped up the bag and looked into the closet. The inside floor was hinged, tilted up, and he could see a handle on the bottom. The top rung of the ladder had been split by the impact of a bullet.

"Glover started to come down after you? I heard a shot."

Diane nodded. "Yeah, I'd managed to get Andy past me— good thing we're small—and cut the tape on her hands and feet so she could crawl. But I wanted to back out of the tunnel so I could watch and make sure Glover didn't poke his head down or try to follow. He stuck his carbine down to fire blind, I guess, and I drove him back with a shot. No way Glover was going to put a round in my ass."

"Yeah. I had similar thoughts while walking around on the roof," Lee replied.

"What's in the bag that was so important he had to risk coming back one more time? His blackmail material, money?" Jack asked. He waved at Richie, who'd come up to the back door with Officer Moore—Andy. The two had pistols.

Lee nodded to Jack, then glanced over at the others. "You guys okay?"

Andrea's face was bruised, her lip was cut, and there was a red streak across her cheeks where the tape had been. She looked down at Glover's body. "I am now."

"Hal's still over at your place, Lee, calling the cavalry. EMTs, Captain Terry, Agent Logan," Richie said. He was wearing a headset and pointed to it. "Any other requests?"

"We need to keep the local deputies and area residents away from this house until we've had a chance to locate and review all of Glover's blackmail material. There may be more than what I have in this gym bag. Lots of people will have secrets to protect and we don't want anything to disappear. Tell anyone who shows up that it's unsafe to come inside." Lee looked up at the ceiling. "Come to think of it . . ."

"I'll shut off the main power and gas," Richie offered, then stepped back outside. "Hey, remain on the street, please, sir, ma'am," they heard Richie yell. "Crime scene."

Diane looked over at Andrea Moore. "You wanna go over to my place and change your clothes? Anything you can find is okay."

"Yeah. I look like one of those girls in *Chainsaw Hookers*, don't I?" Andrea said, looking down at her short skirt, halter top, and leather boots. A pistol was still in her hand because she had no place to stow it.

"Hey, don't knock it. I *saw* that movie," Jack said, and they all laughed. Andy hurried out back to avoid having to cross the street directly in front of the house.

"We'd better get outside and set up a perimeter," Diane said to Jack. "Lee, you wanna stay in here and protect the evidence—and make sure Glover didn't leave any explosive surprises? Okay?"

She tossed him the flashlight—for cover purposes only. He was the only one of them who could safely check out the entire house at 2:00 in the morning with the lights out.

Diane led the way out, followed by Jack. Lee glanced at Glover, who was still dead, and decided to return to the living room for a rug or throw to cover the body. Through the open door and shattered front window, Lee saw Jack and Diane meeting eight or nine civilians, most in obviously thrown-on clothes. Three of the men, including Mr. Weiner, were carrying rifles, but they were holding them casually, not presenting a threat.

"Glover. Did you get him?" Mr. Weiner shouted to Jack.

Jack turned to Diane. "He's dead," she answered immediately.

"Good," Weiner said, nodding.

Mrs. Weiner started clapping and immediately the other neighbors joined in.

Lee, still carrying the gym bag, did a quick run through the house, looking for an obvious bomb, a booby-trapped weapon, or something equally dangerous. Ending up back at the kitchen, he saw Richie turning off the gas with a wrench and remembered thinking about covering Glover's body. He looked in the laundry basket and found a satin designer sheet in a deep cranberry color. That would do.

Two hours later, Diane and Lee were seated at the kitchen table with SAC Logan and Captain Terry, Lee's boss. Across the room, Hal and Richie were close to breaking into Glover's website. When successful, it would corroborate the blackmail material they were already screening on the big laptop Diane was operating.

The CD, one of several taken from the gym bag Lee had liberated, was paused on the image of a local judge and a young man not her husband. Glover had been thorough enough to provide names and a crude audio narrative of the action, using a altered computer-generated voice that mimicked a popular TV newscaster. At least he'd had a sense of humor, Lee thought.

"Well, with these images, copies of documents from the gym bag, and the recorded conversations of the payoffs, we'll have enough to begin the investigations of . . . how many is it now?" SAC Logan asked, looking over at the notes Captain Terry was taking.

"Harmon, the late deputy sheriff, two FAC developers, a county commissioner, the real-estate broker, the owner of that

Buffalo tavern, two other businessmen, and the gunsmith at that shop in Albuquerque. That's probably where he got the AP rounds and the bullet-resistant vest," Diane said.

She looked at Lee, realizing she'd given out too much information. The only time Glover had actually used those AP rounds was when he'd shot Lee a few days back with the .45 pistol. That incident wouldn't go into any of the reports, of course.

"Agent Lopez?" Hal called from across the room. "Excuse me, but there's an e-mail you're going to want to see."

Diane walked over, looked at the screen, then asked for a printout. She returned to the table immediately. "Good news. All we need is a warrant and the Web site owner will give us legal access to all of Glover's Internet files."

SAC Logan nodded. "I'll take care of this first thing in the morning. With what we have on these discs already, there's no sense in walking up a judge. Agreed?"

The others nodded.

"I'll be interested in reading the statements neighbors and other locals will be giving us," Lee said. "Once they realize that Glover won't be able to touch them now, I'll bet everyone and their brother will come forward with information."

"There's no doubt Glover was a master at finding people's weaknesses and exploiting them," Captain Terry said. "And those he couldn't blackmail he bullied. Locals would call the sheriff's department, but things would only get worse for them if Deputy Harmon showed up. The few times Glover was arrested, his judge or political contacts would make sure he got off. Glover had a network going here, and now we have enough information to take all of these people down, too, or at least neutralize them."

"Then there's Sully," Diane added. "Even dead, he can open new doors for us. We need officers to go over every piece of property he owned and check his computer for his supposed 'kiddie porn' customers. Both our agencies are working on that, right?"

Logan nodded. "And APD. Officer Moore's commander is putting her on the team the Albuquerque department is adding. The county sheriff wants in, too. Apparently, he'd already suspected that Deputy Harmon was on the take and dealing drugs on the side. One of Harmon's relatives owns the place where Glover was stashing his drugs, so there's another possibility that needs to be explored. The sheriff's embarrassed and angry that we were the ones who broke the case, so heads will be rolling."

The four officers sat there for a few more minutes, no one saying anything. Finally Logan stood. "People. I'm going to check on the crime scene work, then call it a night. I recommend you all do the same. We've got to follow up in the morning."

Captain Terry nodded. "I'd better run by the mess Hawk and Lopez made on the highway. The county is pressing to get a look at the two shooting scenes and the wreckage of their unit. If the wind had been up, that burning cruiser might have started a forest fire."

"I'm thinking of dropping by the hospital and looking in on Felix—Officer Rodriguez," Lee said. "He's out of surgery?"

Terry nodded. "In recovery. His wife and daughter are there now."

Diane moved over to Richie and Hal. "When you guys leave, lock up, okay? I'm going with Officer Hawk to the hospital."

Ten minutes later, Lee and Diane were alone in the SUV, driving down the winding highway north toward the interstate. They rode in silence for a while, then finally Diane spoke. "That forest service helicopter and the water, good idea, Lee. The ground shook so much it raised some dust in the tunnel. I thought maybe Glover had set off a bomb."

"Yeah? Guess it's a good thing the crew refused to do what I really wanted."

"What was that? Land on the roof?"

"Worse. I asked them to drop the water *and* the bucket. The water balloon from hell."

Diane nodded. "That it would have been."

Several more minutes went by and finally they reached the interstate. Taking the westbound ramp, they were soon driving toward the city. In the distance they could see the glow of Albuquerque and the Rio Grande Valley.

"Glad this is pretty much over?" Lee whispered.

"Very. I never thought I'd want to get into my conservative Bureau slacks and blouse again, but this slutty look and bimbo hair gets old in a hurry. But we did all right, Lee. Glover, Sully, and the others who've corrupted themselves are either gone now or are on their way out."

Lee nodded. "Think we've made a difference?"

"To this community, yes. Together, we make a great team."

"I like that word, lady."

"'Team'?"

"No, 'together.'" He reached over and grabbed her hand, not letting go until they reached the hospital.